The Author

Richard Denning was born in Ilkeston in Derbyshire and lives in Sutton Coldfield in the West Midlands, where he works as a General Practitioner.

He is married and has two children. He has always been fascinated by historical settings as well as horror and fantasy. Other than writing, his main interests are games of all types. He is the designer of a board game based on the Great Fire of London.

Author's website

www.richarddenning.co.uk

By the same author:

Hourglass Institute Series
(Science Fiction)
1.Tomorrow's Guardian
2. Yesterday's Treasures

Northern Crown Series
(Historical fiction)
The Amber Treasure

The Praesidium Series
(Historical Fantasy)
The Last Seal

For Jane, Helen and Matthew

The existence of this revised and expanded edition owes much to the encouragement of authors Helen Hollick and Jo Field. In Helen's case it was her support and words of wisdom that I value most highly. There is no one I know who so enthusiastically supports new authors. Jo, meanwhile, is quite simply a superb editor who really gets into the story to the extent that she knows the characters as well as the author. Many thanks to both of you. I would also like to thank Cathy Helms for her amazing cover design that really brings the book to life.

Finally I want to add my thanks to my family and in particular, John and Margaret (my parents) and Jane (my wife) without whom none of my books would have ever been written.

Tomorrow's Guardian

by

Richard Denning

Written by Richard Denning

© Copyright 2009 Richard Denning

Hardback version First Published 2010

This Paperback edition published 2011

ISBN: 978-0-9564835-6-0
Published by Mercia Books

A catalogue record for this book is available from the British Library

Book Jacket design and layout by Cathy Helms
www.avalongraphics.org
Copy-editing and proof reading by Jo Field.
jo.field3@btinternet.com

Author website:
www.richarddenning.co.uk
Publisher website:
www.merciabooks.co.uk

CHAPTER ONE - THE DREAM

*L*ieutenant Edward Dyson was fighting for his life amongst the cook fires and tents of the army's camp. A huge Zulu warrior screamed as he charged towards him, a spear held menacingly in his right hand. Edward sidestepped to dodge the attack and clipped the enemy on the back of the head with the butt of his revolver – the blow sent the warrior stumbling to the ground.

Edward shook his head in disbelief: how had it come to this? Not four hours before he had been one of an army of well over a thousand highly trained and well-armed soldiers. Now, almost all were dead.

Yesterday, the army had advanced this far from Rorke's Drift with little sight of the enemy. Last night they set up camp here on the plain beneath the conical shaped mountain of Isandlwana. His fellow officers had invited friends from the 2nd Battalion over for drinks to celebrate the rare event of two battalions from the same regiment serving overseas together. The last time that had happened, the 24th had almost been wiped out in a battle against the Sikhs in India. Someone had joked that they hoped it did not happen again this time.

Not that this was likely. Indeed, it was preposterous. Surely these Zulus facing the might of Queen Victoria's British Empire were nothing more than savages with spears and wicker shields. Rapid firing, breech loading Martini Henry rifles, artillery, rocket batteries and well-trained light cavalry would be more than a match for these barbarians.

Edward had thought so: but all that soon changed.

Late in the morning, a squadron of Natal cavalry attached to the British expedition had been scouting far out on the plain, perhaps half a mile or so from the camp. Cresting a rise, one of the patrols

1

suddenly came across thousands of Zulus hiding and resting in a valley. As one, the Zulus rose and hurtled up the slope toward the horsemen, who fell back in alarm and then started exchanging rifle fire with them. The enemy had few firearms and were poor shots while the British were superb marksmen, but the sheer number of Zulus forced the horsemen back towards the camp.

Soon, whole regiments of Zulus emerging all along the British front. The red-coated soldiers formed up into a firing line and began shooting at the natives. The brave enemy warriors fell in droves, but still they came on: as unstoppable as a tidal wave, as irresistible as a glacier. Only the devastating volleys from the British companies kept them back − for the moment.

By now, Edward was learning a new respect for this enemy. His men and those of the other companies were inflicting dozens of casualties with each shot, but the Zulus did not run away. Instead, he could hear them chanting their terrifying war cry: an angry buzzing noise that sounded rather like a swarm of infuriated wasps on a hot summer's day.

The order now came to fall back five-hundred yards to the camp. Some of the companies moved more quickly than others, creating wide gaps between them. Furthermore, Edward became aware that his men were running low on ammunition. They were sharing out the rounds they had and trying to continue shooting as they retreated. Overall, the result was a slackening of the fire upon the enemy.

Suddenly, with a great cry of "uSuthu!" almost twenty-thousand Zulus surged forward in a charge on all fronts. The British were quite unable to stop them and entire companies disappeared: swept away as if that tidal wave had finally come crashing down upon them.

So it was that Edward now found himself fighting in the chaos of his camp. He fired his revolver at a fierce looking brute who had just stabbed a redcoat, saw him fall and then looked about for his men. Three were fighting in a small triangle twenty yards away; one firing

2

whilst another reloaded and the third threatened a score of Zulus with his bayonet. A moment later, all three fell to the blades of the vengeful Zulus. To his right, a cook and his assistant were swinging cleavers wildly and shouting in terror that they were not soldiers – but it did not save them. The Zulus came upon them, stabbing with their short spears. As his compatriots died, Edward realised he was alone. He glanced around in horror: above him the sky had turned a dark, angry red.

Fifty enemy warriors closed in on him from all around. His mouth felt dry. Shaking with fear he fired his revolver, heard the hammer click on an empty chamber. He fumbled for his sword, knowing he had only moments to live...

"Tom, wake up lad; wake up now! Your friends will be here soon."

Tom Oakley opened his eyes, sat up in bed and stared wildly around his room, taking in the PC in the corner, a heap of abandoned clothes and trainers on the floor and the Nintendo DS on the bedside cabinet. Finally, he turned to where his father stood at the open door and gave him a bewildered stare.

His father's eyes narrowed and he came and sat on his son's bed. Reaching over, he swept Tom's hair to one side and touched his forehead to see if he felt hot.

"What is it lad? Did you have another of those nightmares?"

Tom nodded.

"One of those dreams when you think you're someone else?"

"They seem so ... real, Dad," Tom answered.

His father frowned at him, searching his face. "They're just dreams, boy; nothing more," he said at last, getting to his feet.

"Come on, get dressed." He paused at the door and turned to look back at Tom before adding, "Oh yes; happy birthday, son."

Tom rolled out of bed, walked over to his mirror and stared at his reflection. For a moment he was almost surprised to see the young lad with brown eyes and jet black hair staring back at him. Why surprised, though? Was he expecting another face? He rubbed his eyes, yawned and then moved away to get dressed.

It was a warm day in the early spring, so he held his birthday party in the garden. He and his friends played football and then cricket, until he slogged a six over the fence and lost the ball. That turned out to be the signal for tea. There was the usual party food, including cakes and ice cream along with his father's homemade burgers, cooked – and half burnt – on a barbecue. Then, of course, there was the cake.

It was baked in the shape of a dalek and as his mother walked out of the kitchen door carrying it, there were shouts of "Great" and "Wow" from his friends. The words 'Happy 11th Birthday Tom' were written in blue icing on the top.

His mother now started singing, "Happy Birthday to You," and all the boys joined in. His oldest friend, James, was singing along with the alternative words, "You Live in a Zoo," and Tom stuck his tongue out to blow a raspberry at him. James simply smiled and sang louder.

Tom bent forward, took a deep breath then blew all eleven candles out. His mother put down the cake and turned to take a knife to cut it into slices.

That was when it happened.

The world seemed to give a slight judder up and forwards and Tom felt as if he was being thrust backwards, like he was in a car that had suddenly accelerated, pushing him back against the seat. Feeling dizzy, he closed his eyes for a moment. When he opened them again, he blinked, because right there in front of him was the cake with all the candles still burning brightly. Around him the boys were singing, *"Happy Birthday to Thomas, Happy Birthday to You,"* and cheering. He was convinced they were all playing a trick on him. All the boys were in on it and his mother must have used those party trick candles that keep re-lighting themselves: that was the explanation, obviously. He leant forward and blew the candles out again and then went over to give James a friendly slap on the top of his head.

"Heh," James muttered, rubbing his crown. "Just for that I won't keep a look out for Rogers!"

Kyle Rogers was a bully and Tom's enemy. Only two months older, but about two feet taller and much wider too, or so it seemed to Tom, who had been only eight when he had ridden his bike round the corner of the street without looking and almost knocked Kyle over. The other boy just had time to jump out of the path, straight into the milk bottles outside Mrs Brown's house, smashing two and ending up sitting in the milk.

A charging bull would move less quickly: Kyle had exploded at Tom, kicking him off the bike and onto the road and then laying into him with bunched fists, before Mrs Brown came out of the door and chased them both away. Tom ran home with a bleeding nose and did not go out for a week. From that moment on, Kyle took every opportunity to corner Tom and make his life a misery. Fortunately, James was around him most of the time and Kyle did not bother to take them both on, but he still found other ways to get at Tom, like sniggering at him in class when he made mistakes. They were now in the last term at primary school and so Tom endured the jibes, thinking he did not have to put up with them much longer. The summer holidays were fast approaching and it seemed that Kyle was going to a different school in the autumn.

"I'm much cleverer than you, Oakley," he had chortled, "I'm off to King John's Grammar school in the autumn, not that smelly old comp down the road you two are going to."

For the next few weeks after the party, Tom and James enjoyed counting down the days until their time with Kyle Rogers would finally be over. Kyle said nothing and just smiled at them. He left it till the very last day at the old school to find Tom in the toilets then he walked up and thumped him on the arm.

"Ouch! What was that for, Rogers?" Tom asked, rubbing his shoulder.

"Just something to remember me by, Oakley − until next term, of course."

"What do you mean, 'next term'?"

"Oh, didn't I mention that I'm going to Parklands Comp as well?"

"What? You said you were going to King John's!" Tom said, feeling his heart sinking.

Kyle smirked, "Nah! Was having you on. I couldn't miss out on keeping you company for the next seven years," he added with another vicious punch, this time to Tom's belly. Tom collapsed onto the toilet floor and Kyle walked out laughing then turned to add a parting shot.

"Have a good summer, Oakley; I'll see you in September."

Tom dragged himself to his feet and groaned: Kyle, at the same school for the next seven years? Somehow, the summer holidays didn't seem long enough.

If the strangely real dreams and the event at the birthday party back in April were the only odd things to have occurred, Tom might have forgotten about them, but a few weeks later the peculiar feeling, like sudden acceleration, happened again. He was on holiday with his parents and his sister, Emma, in Spain. They were playing a game of cricket on the beach with some new friends who were also on holiday, watched by a group of puzzled Spanish kids. Tom was bowling as Mike – a boy from London who was staying at the same hotel – took strike with the bat. Tom ran up and bowled. Mike swung his bat and missed the ball, which clattered through the wicket sending the stumps flying. Emma cheered and clapped and their father, sitting on a towel nearby, shouted, "Well bowled!"

Then, again, Tom felt the judder and strange feeling of being thrust backwards. He blinked and opened his eyes and now saw that he was once more at the beginning of his run up, the ball still in his hand. Mike was standing bat at the ready waiting for him to bowl and behind him the stumps were still intact. Tom was about to shout to Mike that he was out and what was he doing still at the stumps when, abruptly, he felt dizzy and the world seemed to spin like a fairground ride. A moment later, he was lying on the sand with his father and all the kids around him. His father picked him up and carried him to one of their rented sun loungers.

"Are you all right, Tom?" said his father. Except that somehow it didn't sound like his dad. The world seemed very peculiar, though he could not exactly say in what way: it was just – odd.

As if from a long way off he heard his mum ask his dad if they should get him to hospital, when there was a click in his head as if something was fitting into place. Straight away, he felt fine again. He sat up, but his mother told him to lie back down and rest.

"It's ok, Mum, I feel ok," he said.

His dad leant over him and felt his forehead. "Um … he's a bit hot: probably too much sun. Best get him to bed."

Back at the hotel his parents called out a local Spanish doctor who prodded him a few times, looked at his throat and made him go "ah" before announcing that he could find nothing wrong with the boy. He then left after giving Tom's father a bill. His mum came over and sat down on the bed.

"Oh well, Tom," she said, "if it was the sun you should be ok tomorrow. We're flying home and granddad says it's raining in England!"

As Tom had feared, the summer holidays did not last long enough and it was soon September and time to go to his secondary school. Kyle was unfortunately in the same class as Tom, but if the move to the comprehensive was accompanied by an old enemy, it at least brought some new friends.

James and Tom met Andy in the first science lesson of the new school year. Andy introduced himself by pulling out a long ruler and raising it like a sword above his head and swinging it down towards Tom. Tom ducked down behind the desk … just at the moment that the teacher walked in.

"You can have detention, boy!" he boomed to Andy, who was caught wielding the ruler over Tom's head. That was Mr

Beaufin, a clever man who taught science well, but was a terror if you made him angry. So that was how Tom met Andy. The pair became great pals in and out of school. Andy lived close by and the two of them were often out getting into trouble for sneaking into 'haunted houses' or rather, in this case, just an old spooky house whose owner, Mr Henry, did not take kindly to the boy Ghostbusters stalking round his windows.

Whilst the boys were lurking under a tree near the house one day, Tom had imagined he had seen a ghost in the window of the house and – without thinking – had picked up a stone and thrown it at the window, breaking it. The police were called in and Tom's parents were, to say the least, furious when he was driven home in a squad car. That had meant no puddings, computers or TV for an entire week. However, the worst thing was he had to go and apologise to Mr Henry and offer to pay for the repairs out of half a year's pocket money. At first, Tom had refused to go, saying he did not want to: having to face "orrible old 'enry', as the kids called him, was not a pleasant thought.

Tom's dad insisted, however. "Sometimes, doing the right thing is not pleasant and nice. Indeed, sometimes it is horrible and painful. But, deep down you know in your heart that it's the right thing and you do it anyway: whatever the cost."

Well, that seemed rather pompous and Tom and Andy were not impressed, but off they went anyway. In the end, it wasn't all that bad. 'Orrible old 'enry had seemed fierce at first, but ended up giving them hot chocolate along with cookies and then he let the boys play with a train set he had in the attic.

The experience strengthened the friendship between Andy and Tom and the two of them gathered a gang round them that included James and two others – Mark and William. They called themselves the *Desperados,* which was a name used in western movies for bandits, so James had said. Tom thought that James would know: movies were an area he seemed to be an expert on. Andy had been impressed as well and one day he made them all swear an oath of loyalty to the gang and to promise to stand by each other whatever the future might bring. They toasted the oath with coke and then they all recited a solemn vow.

"Loyal desperados are we, whatever, whenever, whoever and however anything happens!"

"All for one and one for all," James had added, having watched an old film recently about the Three Musketeers.

A couple of months went by full of maths homework, French lessons and rugby matches and Tom began to forget the strange incident in Spain. Then, several things happened that convinced him he must be going mad. The first time was on the 5th of November – Guy Fawkes' night. His family had gone to a firework display held in a local park, getting there early to see the bonfire lit and then round the fun fair to go on the rides. An hour later there was an announcement that the fireworks were about to start. They all bought hot dogs and made their way down the slope to the display area.

Tom was about to bite into his hot dog, when he felt the same strange juddering feeling coming on again but this time, it was different. The sensation of movement did not thrust him backwards as had happened before, but forwards. The unexpected change of direction threw him off balance and he swayed to his left and his right. He reached out to hold on to his father, but his floundering hands grasped nothing more than thin air. Looking around him, he was surprised to find that it had suddenly got a lot darker. The crowd of many

10

hundreds that had gathered to watch the fireworks had apparently left and he was standing totally alone in the centre of the eerily dark playing fields.

The fairground rides should have been behind him, but there was no sound coming from that direction. Turning round, he could see there were no people there either, none of the rides was moving, the multicoloured lights had gone out and plastic sheets had been pulled over the top of most of them. Back the other way, the bonfire had burnt down completely and there was just a heap of glowing ash, where a moment before a raging blaze had been. Tom shivered, although it was at least as much from fear as from the chilly autumn night air.

He peered anxiously out into the gloom. "Help me!" He shouted, "Somebody, please help me!"

CHAPTER TWO - AULD LANG SYNE

T here was movement in the darkness on the far side of the embers and a moment later a torch light flashed in his face.

"Over here: we've found him!" shouted a voice and then, half a dozen people came running up out of the gloom.

One was a policeman. He peered at Tom, asked, "Are you hurt, son?"

"Er ... no, I don't think so," Tom answered.

"Where've you been, lad? You've given your family quite a worry," the officer said, "missing for hours you've been. They tried ringing your mobile, but you didn't answer."

"Look, Sarg," another policeman said, "he came back for a hot dog."

They all laughed at this and Tom looked down to see that he was, indeed, still holding his hot dog. The strange thing was, it was still warm in his hand.

He was about to ask to go home, when he felt another juddering motion; but this time it was as if he was being thrown backwards. Above him, the sky was suddenly shattered by a huge bang and a blinding flash of intense blue light.

Tom cried out and dropped his hot dog in surprise. The firework display had started, around him there were now hundreds of excited, smiling faces, all turned upwards to take in the spectacle. About fifty paces in front of them, the bonfire was blazing whilst behind them all the pounding music from the fairground throbbed through the night air.

The shock of the transition was too much for Tom. He felt a wave of dizziness and suddenly the ground came up to meet him and darkness took him as he passed out. He was not sure how long he was unconscious, but at last he felt that click in his head that made everything alright again and opened his eyes. Blinking, as he tried to focus on his surroundings, Tom was very hazy about what happened next. He was dimly aware of his parents leaning over him and heard them say something about epilepsy, then he was being taken home and put to bed, but beyond that he could not recall a thing.

As he lay in bed, Tom heard his dad saying to his mum that children bounce back easily from shocks and horrors. His mum had replied that it may be so, but you never knew if a childhood trauma will later emerge to influence the man or woman they became. Tom found himself agreeing with his mum. To adults, kids might seem quiet and self-absorbed and although most were probably only thinking about the latest toy or game, a few were suffering inside just like he was now. Usually happy and contented, on that Guy Fawkes Night Tom became miserable for pretty much the first time in his life. He had known children who had it tough, of course: William – one of the Desperados – lived with his grandparents because his parents had both died in a car crash. Helen, a girl in his class, spent week nights at her mother's and weekends at her father's. The only time they spoke to each other was to arrange the times to hand her over, like she was nothing more than a parcel being collected. Tom always reckoned he was lucky to live with both his parents and that they got on. He had become increasingly aware that fewer and fewer of his classmates were as fortunate as he; they all had reasons for being sad and he really didn't – until now.

Now, one thought kept coming to him. He was going mad. Yes: it was as simple as that and soon other people would see it in him too. Then, the doctors would come for him and they would take him and lock him up in some mental hospital: he was sure of it. The kids who lived in his street all reckoned one of the housewives was mad. Mrs Brown from number 39, Pinewood Road told everyone that in a previous life she had been a nurse in the Crimean War. She said she had been Florence Nightingale and that she had flashbacks and dreams in which she was working in the hospital with the wounded soldiers. The kids called her a loon and they would now call him one too.

In fact, his classmates were given some excuses to call him all sorts of names soon after bonfire night. He was fairly good at school, enjoyed science and history, but hated French. The morning that he first had trouble at school, his class was having a French lesson. They were learning how to conjugate the verb meaning 'to be'. Mrs Spencer, the French teacher, who Tom thought looked a little like a pterodactyl as she perched on a stool at the front of the class, asked Tom to recite the verb.

"*Je suis,*" he began, then, "*tu es , il est, elle est, nous suis...*"

"*Non! Non!* The correct phrase is *nous sommes,*" shrieked the pterodactyl. Start again!" In the row behind, Kyle Rogers laughed and whispered the word "Thickie" under his breath. At that moment Tom felt the forward judder and tried to ignore it. He closed his eyes and concentrated on speaking French and so, gritting his teeth, he continued. "*Je Suis, tu es, il est...*" He stopped, because the class were all laughing at him. He opened his eyes and then blinked because he now found himself not in Mrs Spencer's French classroom on the ground floor, but in Mr Morgan's history class on the second. Mr Morgan was standing

15

at the front of the class and looking a little like a firework that was about to explode. Tom thought he could almost see smoke coming out of the teacher's ears.

"I asked you to tell me the date of the Battle of Bosworth, boy; not babble on in a foreign language!" Mr Morgan erupted.

"What's wrong with you today, Oakley?" Kyle muttered at his back.

"Oh, push off and get a life!" Tom hissed at him, but not softly enough; he saw Mr Morgan jump to his feet and come stomping towards him.

"Maybe you should go to see the headmaster!" he yelled.

Tom thought quickly, closed his eyes to try to remember the date and stammered out, "1485, Mr Morgan."

There was an ominous silence and then laughter again. Oh no, thought Tom, not again! What was happening to him? He opened his eyes to see that he was back in Mrs Spencer's class and it was Mrs Spencer's turn to launch herself of her perch and lean over him. Tom noticed that her finger nails were long and sharp and he was reminded of claws, which only made the pterodactyl image stronger. One talon-like finger now pointed at the door.

"Stand outside until you can recover your senses!" she screeched. As he was evicted into the corridor, the last thing he saw was the smugly satisfied face of Kyle smirking at him, just before the door slammed shut.

After lunch there was Mr Morgan's history class. Tom tried hard to spot the moment that his mind would play its trick on him, but he failed and so had to live though the humiliation a second time, like he was stuck in a time warp. Struggling to fight back traitor tears, he ended up standing outside the second classroom that day and going home with two detentions to explain to his parents. As he dragged himself home with Andy keeping him company, some of their class mates cycled past them. Kyle hovered alongside for a while, before shouting out in a high pitched voice, "How do you say, 'We are' in French, Oakley? Is it '1485, Mr Morgan?'" before riding off with a couple of his mates, all of them howling with laughter. As they disappeared down the road, Tom caught Andy looking at him oddly, like he was not quite sure what to make of his best friend.

The school experience had been bad enough, but next came Christmas. On Christmas day, his grandparents joined them and they were all sitting in their living room opening presents. All year Tom had been asking for the newest video game console. It was the 'in' gadget that winter and all the Desperados were hoping for one.

Tom was sitting on a beanbag and had just opened a small present from his uncle, which turned out to contain *Kestrel's Flight*, a book by his favourite author. This was the latest book in the series and as the previous one had left the story on a cliffhanger he was both pleased by the present and keen to start reading it. He had to put it down though, because his parents were passing him a large box, which he grabbed from them and opened enthusiastically, tearing off the gold-coloured paper in a few seconds. Inside, he was thrilled to see the console containing the game system and taped to the outside, two new games for it. He was about to open the box and take the machine over to the TV and plug it in, when the judder happened again.

A heartbeat later he was still sitting on his beanbag holding his copy of *Kestrel's Flight*. His parents were handing him the console, still wrapped. That was it, he was fed up with all this and had just about had enough; he slammed the book down on his knees.

"Not today, please!" he moaned in a tired voice.

His mother looked at him, "Tom, what are you complaining about? I thought you wanted that book. You have been talking about it all month."

He was about to answer, when he felt the world spin around him. He felt confused and disorientated, dropped the book and put both hands over his head.

"Tom, what's up?" asked his mother, the concern showing in her voice.

"Nothing, Mum, I just feel a little dizzy," Tom answered. Then, he felt the click in his head and in an instant, the dizziness vanished and he felt fine again.

"There, I'm ok now," he told them.

"Probably too much Christmas cake," suggested his grandmother.

They all continued opening their presents. "Here you go, Tom," said his father, passing him the present in gold wrapping paper.

He tried to act surprised as he opened it and found the console inside, but he noticed his mother kept looking at him. He waited in anxiety to see if he would feel the juddering again, sighing with relief when the moment passed with no incident.

The final event to occur happened right at the end of the year: New Years Eve. Tom's grandparents were over again and he and Emma, who was now eight years old, were allowed to stay up late that night. Just before midnight, like always, their parents would turn on the TV and listen to Big Ben chime in twelve o'clock and then, the New Year would begin.

While they were waiting, Tom's father gave him a little cider for the first time, although his mother 'tutted' at that. The family played charades and then Tom challenged his grandfather to tennis on his new arcade game. He had easily beaten the old man, but despite the rising score line against him, his grandfather kept saying, "Remember the score, I'll catch up soon!"

"Right, switch off the game, Tom, it's almost midnight," his father ordered after a while.

When he had packed away the game and switched over the TV channel, the cameras were already pointing at Big Ben. The screen changed to pan across the excited crowd. A policeman was trying to look professional as two ladies with silly hats attempted to kiss him. Twenty Scotsmen were dancing in kilts in the road and Tom counted at least three gorilla suits. Then the TV showed the clock face again. The minute hand was almost at twelve. Suddenly, the bells began chiming.

Ding dong ding dong, ding dong ding dong, they rang musically and rather cheerfully. Then there was a brief pause and in the living room everyone gathered in a circle and they all seemed to hold their breath.

Then ...

Dong! Dong! Dong! Dong ... the great clock chimed as it summoned in the New Year. On the TV, everybody seemed to be kissing everybody else and the policeman had just vanished under a sea of ladies in silly hats, Scotsmen and gorillas!

"Happy New Year, Thomas!" his grandfather said, with a hard slap to his back. At that moment, Tom felt again that weird backwards movement and the briefest sensation of dizziness. As he recovered, he realised that he was sitting side by side with his grandfather again and they were playing tennis on the video game; his grandfather had just scored a point.

"Remember the score, I'll catch up soon!" the old man chortled.

Click – and that shift forward. He was now standing, arms crossed in front of him, holding his sister's hand on one side and his gran's on the other and they were all singing a song: *"Should auld acquaintance be forgot..."*

Overwhelmed by the sudden shifts and changes, Tom felt a wave of nausea wash over him. Then, without warning, he passed out.

For a while, he felt nothing apart from a sensation of floating in blackness then, with a rush, he woke up to find he was lying on the sofa with his mother sponging his forehead.

"I told you he was too young for that cider. Maybe I should call the doctor," his mother said in a worried voice.

"He never touched the cider. I think he was just excited and tired. Look: he's coming round. How are you, son?" his father asked. Tom blinked and suddenly everything was in focus and his head felt clear.

"I'm ok, Dad. I don't need a doctor. I just want to go to bed." His mum nodded, but Tom noticed the glance his parents exchanged and it was one full of anxiety.

As he changed into his pyjamas and then got into bed, he had to admit that he was worried too. What was happening to him? Was he going mad? Was he ill? He didn't *feel* ill. He yawned and realised that what he felt was very tired: too tired to figure it out tonight. He would just have to think about it tomorrow. In fact, that was his New Year's resolution – to find out what was happening to him. He switched off his light and tried to get to sleep.

As he grew drowsier, he felt himself sinking. The sensation was similar to the way he had felt more than once before, when he had re-lived the same experience twice over, as in Mr Morgan's history class. Before he was finally asleep, his last thought was, *'Can't you leave me alone even when I am in bed?'* Then everything was dark and for a moment, nothing more.

In the darkness, Tom was sure he could see something moving, but he could not make out what. After a moment, shapes began to appear: fuzzy at first and indistinct – rather like looking through an out of focus camera. But then the objects leapt into clear view with an abruptness that made him dizzy.

He was standing in the middle of a campsite with white conical tents all around him. Overhead, a burning sun shone down and beneath his feet there was grass, bleached almost white in the heat. Tom stared around him, confused by what he saw. But then, after a moment, he realised that he was not Tom. It seemed to him that he was someone else: someone from another time, another place. Edward: yes, that was it, his name was Edward. And, as he remembered the name, he became Lieutenant Edward Dyson and he was fighting for his life amongst the chaos of the army's camp at Isandlwana ...

"No! This is not right: I was not there," he shouted and suddenly, the images, sounds and feelings of Edward Dyson vanished and Tom woke in the darkness of his room. Breathing quickly, he tapped himself all over to make sure he was unhurt then he swung his feet off the bed and, finding his slippers, padded off to the bathroom. Turning on the light, he stared at himself in the mirror. The eyes looking back belonged to Tom, not Edward Dyson, whoever he was. It was just a dream: that was all. He remembered two weeks ago at school when Mr

Morgan had been standing at the front of the class talking to them. What was it he had said? Yes, that was it; it was coming back to him:

"... The Zulu war opened with a great defeat for Britain," said Mr Morgan. "On January 22nd 1879, a Zulu army of twenty-four thousand warriors surprised and overwhelmed a British force of about fourteen hundred men at Isandlwana. Thirteen hundred and twenty-nine British and allied soldiers died, as well as at least one thousand Zulus. Many more were injured and some of them crawled off into the long grass to die later. Not one man of the 1st Battalion of the 24th Regiment survived. It shook the Victorian world. The Queen herself later asked who the Zulus were and why her soldiers were fighting them ..."

It had been a good lesson, Tom recalled. Mr Morgan might be a stickler for discipline, but he made history come alive. He had brought in a British red coat and a Zulu assegai and shield to use as props. Tom and his mates had played a pretend battle at lunch time, in which Tom had been an English soldier attacked by the others. He must have been dreaming of that: just a dream, that's all it was. And yet it seemed to Tom that he had dreamt this dream before. Ah yes – on his birthday – and that was before he had gone up to his new school; before he had even met Mr Morgan. So what was happening to him? Was he going mad after all?

Suddenly, Tom thought about Mrs Brown, his neighbour, telling everyone in a first aid tent at the school summer fair that she remembered bandaging wounds after the battle of Alma in 1854 and that they were doing it all wrong. Was what he was experiencing similar to what Mrs Brown had gone through? Tom hoped not, because Mrs Brown was now being treated at a local psychiatric hospital. Tom sighed, plodded back to his room and switched the light off.

He had hardly settled back in his bed before he sat bolt upright again. Someone was moving about in his room. The light from the street lamp outside his bedroom window was now blocked by a tall, dark shape.

"Dad? Is that you?" Tom asked sleepily.

The figure moved closer but did not speak.

Tom yawned. "What's going on, Dad? What time is it?"

"Time?" came a man's deep voice, with an almost mocking tone.

Before Tom had registered that it was not his dad, the man leant over him.

"Time?" he repeated. "Why, Tom, it's any time *you* want it to be!"

CHAPTER THREE - SEPTIMUS MASON

T om snapped the light back on and saw a slender, fit looking man in his late twenties. He had a neatly trimmed beard and moustache and was wearing tightly cut jeans and a smart black shirt. He moved away from the bed over to Tom's bookshelf and, having perused the titles, was now examining a mobile model of the solar system. He gave the planets a spin on their axis.

"Interesting – just nine planets ..."

"Er ... who are you?" Tom squeaked, his heart thudding.

The stranger turned back and looked at him.

"I apologise: that's bad manners that is! My name is Mason; Septimus Mason."

Jumping out of bed Tom started backing away from the stranger and towards the door. He glanced across at the window. It was shut. He could see that the security locks his dad had fitted after the neighbours had been burgled were still intact. So how had the man got in? His own door was shut and in any case, the landing went straight past his parents' bedroom: they surely would have noticed someone creeping up the stairs? On second thoughts, obviously not!

"Don't be afraid, Tommy, I'm here to help you – not hurt you," promised Septimus in an oddly accented voice, which was at the same time formal and polite, yet warm and friendly. Was it Irish or Scottish? Perhaps it was Welsh. Yes, it was Welsh; but somehow a little different, as if belonging to a man who had travelled and picked up words and phrases that were not native to him.

"How do you know my name? Who are you? What are you doing here and what do you want from me?" Tom asked, still edging towards the door and reaching out to grasp the handle.

The man shrugged and then pointed at him. "To myself and those I work for you have become quite familiar of late, young sir. I'm here to help you, I assure you."

Septimus moved closer. Tom froze.

"Oh yes," said the Welshman, "I forgot to say, Happy New Year. Stayed up to listen to Big Ben did we? Quite an occasion, eh? Tell me, did you enjoy it better the first or the second time around?"

After he had said this, Septimus stared at Tom for a moment, his eyes scrutinising him, as if waiting to see how the boy would react. Suddenly, his face relaxed and he chuckled.

"Best New Year party I went to was in 1945. All that relief after the war was won made people celebrate – even if they were still on rations and had to scrounge to get a decent spread. Food was a bit basic but nice enough, although the beer was warm – yuk, I hate warm beer, what about you?"

"Erm ... I've never drunk any beer; but this is all rubbish, isn't it? You weren't alive in 1945 – you couldn't have been!" Tom shouted, but his voice betrayed some lack of conviction. This man seemed to know a lot about him and if so, perhaps it was foolish to dismiss him so easily.

"Thomas, go to sleep!" shouted his dad from down the corridor.

Tom glanced at Septimus and then carried on in a whisper. "Why should I trust you and not yell for my dad right now?"

26

"Come on, Tommy boy, I know what has been happening to you. I understand it: I can explain it to you. No one else can, at least, no one in your family. Not them, nor a doctor: not even a psychiatrist," he said, smiling as the boy gave a little gasp of surprise. "Yes, Tommy, I know you must have been thinking that you're going mad. Am I right?"

Tom nodded slowly, still suspicious, but wanting to know more.

"You are not. You are discovering your talents. And very rare and special they are too."

"What talents?" Tom asked, letting go of the door handle.

"Well, I'm not talking about playing the recorder here, boyo! No, your talents are extraordinary, I'm sure of that, but you will need to trust me. Come with me this night and I will show you what you want to know."

"Come with you? It's three in the morning on New Year's Day. My parents would not ..."

"And it still will be when we finish and your parents will never know what happened," Septimus interrupted.

Tom hesitated. When he was younger his parents always told him never to go off with strangers. Not that they had ever covered the variety that materialised in your bedroom at three a.m. and promised to tell you the secret of your existence. Tom was pretty sure he would have remembered *that* conversation! He thought of the strange events these last few months and how he was convinced he was going mad. It had to be worth any risk to get to the bottom of all that.

"Ok, I'm in. Let me get dressed."

"Nothing too heavy, mind: no jumpers," the man suggested.

"Mr Mason, can't you see that there's ice on my window?" Tom protested.

27

"Ah, but where we are going there won't be ice for a million years!"

Tom stared at the man for a moment, but in the light of all the other bizarre occurrences he decided to let that one pass. He walked over to his wardrobe. Five minutes later, he was dressed in jeans and a shirt but with a jumper tucked under his arm just in case.

Septimus had been reading Tom's book on the history of the world and giggling occasionally, but finally he replaced it on the shelf, looked Tom up and down and said, "Ready now?"

"I guess so," said Tom, wishing his voice would stop quavering.

"Then, let's go!"

It was like changing channels on the TV. One moment they stood in the dark bedroom of the terrace house. The next, they were standing on a sun-bathed hillside looking down upon a valley with a river meandering lazily through it. Ferns grew all about them and dotted here and there were bushes and trees.

Shocked by the abruptness of the change, Tom staggered backwards, tripped on a rotting tree trunk and fell with a cry onto his behind.

"Where am I?" he blurted out.

The strange man was smiling in amusement. "Yes, it fair takes the breath away the first time, doesn't it?" he observed with a laugh. "Don't worry – it did the same for me, also."

"But ... but what have you done, where am I? We were in my bedroom a moment ago!" Tom insisted. Suddenly, he heard a snort from behind and spinning round, he saw an odd creature standing there. It was about the size of a pig, green in colour and looking a little like a lizard as it waddled along on short stumpy legs. Seeing it, Tom gave another shout of

28

surprise. The creature snorted in alarm and scuttled away through the ferns.

"You know, Tommy, you are going to have to stop shouting, or you might alter history by giving some vital species a heart attack," Septimus commented. Then, crouching down beside the boy he patted him on the shoulder. "Don't worry. It's all just to show you the truth. You asked me what had happened to your bedroom, didn't you? Well, in a way we are still standing in it." He waved his arms across the vista, "In two hundred and forty million years, or so, this will be your city. Of course, it will spend most of that time at the bottom of the ocean, for this is Pangaea: all of Earth's land mass in one lump. This is where your house will be, America is only about two hundred miles that way; the continents have yet to split and the seas to form." He pointed, "That green creature was an early dinosaur, by the way."

Tom was not sure whether he believed Septimus or not, but that beast did look like a picture in his dinosaur book. So, in that case, was this all some kind of museum? James had been telling them all, just before the holidays, of a museum in America he had visited with his parents, which had amazing animated monsters that seemed almost lifelike. Maybe he was in one of those? But even if that were true, how had he been brought here, and so fast? Had he been drugged and while asleep, somehow put on a plane and flown to America? Was that any more likely than Septimus' statement that they had travelled back to the time of the dinosaurs? The other possibility, of course, was that he was again dreaming – and yet this time, ridiculous as the strange man's claim would have seemed a few months before, Tom was willing to at least entertain the idea that all this was real.

"Ok, say I believe you for now, what is the point of this?" he asked.

"Good question. Well, you need to know what talents you possess: what you can do and how. I brought you here, but I could not have done it without tapping into the power you have. You have more power than you can dream of, more than most of us certainly. That's why I came to you. You have been drawn to our attention."

"Who are you? Hang on − you said 'our attention'. Who else is with you?" Tom glanced nervously at the ferns in case one of Septimus' allies was there.

"All in good time, you're rushing ahead. Let me explain a little about the powers you have," Septimus said.

Tom shrugged and let the evasion pass for the moment. "Alright, go on then," he said and moved to sit on the log.

Septimus took a deep breath and started talking in a voice that sounded a little formal, as if he was lecturing a class. "I said earlier that you had many powers and talents. Most of the people on our planet don't possess them. They go about their lives, each living one day after the preceding day from birth to death. They are time-bound: immobile and restricted. They are happy enough for all that, I suppose. But we," and he indicated both himself, Tom and, with a general circular movement, unseen others, "are different. Over the centuries there have always been those who could see in some way outside the limited frame of their own time. Some were just good gamblers, able to predict the outcome of a race, or the roll of a dice. Others claimed to see the future and foresee disasters. Still more claimed to have lived previous lives in the past."

Tom nodded, thinking now of Mrs Brown and her tales of Florence Nightingale.

"I see I am striking a chord here," Septimus went on. "Well, those are all related talents. In some way they are manipulating time. They don't know it, of course. There are organisations that pick up and train those with the potential," he added.

"Ah, so you work for one of those?" said Tom. It all sounded phantasmagorical, but he was prepared to go along with it.

"Indeed," Septimus agreed with a quick nod then hesitated, "… more or less. So, you can perhaps begin to see that what you have been experiencing lately are all examples of these kinds of talents. In you they are at present, wild, uncontrolled and possibly dangerous. That can change. If you master them, given the raw power I can feel in you, you will be a force amongst the Walkers."

Tom frowned, "Walkers? Who are they?"

"Not so much who as what. Walkers is the name given to the most powerful Temporopaths or time manipulators: those who can move freely through time; those who can physically alter reality. I'm a Walker, but only a weak one. I tapped some of your power to bring us this far. You could do it alone."

"So, I'm some sort of god?" Tom felt dizzy. He had never seen himself as some all powerful being.

Septimus laughed and shook his head. "Don't get delusions of grandeur, boyo - you're still mortal. You can die and will do one day and that day might be soon if I don't start teaching you a little."

"Teaching me what?" Tom asked, wondering if he was having another of those lifelike dreams.

"It's time for your first lesson in Walking. Time travel for dummies, if you like," Septimus said. Then he stopped and looked searchingly at Tom's face, "That is, of course, unless you want me to take you home and you can just pretend it was all a dream."

Tom shook his head. "Not on your life! Not after what you have just shown me. I need to see more."

"Very well," Septimus placed one hand on Tom's shoulders. "Close your eyes and relax: try and clear your mind. I'm going to teach you how to Walk through time."

CHAPTER FOUR: LESSONS

Tom took a deep breath and waited for the next instruction. "Good, now what you must do next is imagine a clock in your mind. Any clock, but it helps if it's one you are familiar with."

Tom smiled. His grandparents had such a one: a tall grandfather clock, which stood in their hallway. It was made of polished mahogany. The clock face had elegant hands pointing at Roman numerals. Beneath that was a smaller circle with the phases of the moon and the date rotating. Finally, at the bottom, visible through a glass door that could be opened, a long pendulum of silver and brass swung majestically to and fro giving a deep and solemn *tick tock* with each passing second. He had been fascinated by it for as long as he could remember. His grandfather would let him open the little door and use a small key to wind it up.

It was this clock, standing in a hallway of a building which, if Septimus was speaking the truth, would not exist for millions of years that he called to mind.

"Excellent, I can feel you have a good sense of what you need. Now, as the clock moves, reach out and feel time moving."

Tom could not have said that he understood exactly what he was doing, nor could he have taught others, but he was suddenly aware of the passing seconds. The pendulum swung, the clock ticked and he felt time pass.

"Yes, that's it. Now, what we are going to do is reach out and move the hands of the clock in your mind. Move them faster than they normally move and at the same time, do not let go of that link to the passing of time around you."

Tom opened his eyes and frowned at Septimus; he was not sure what the stranger wanted him to do, but Septimus said no more, so he closed his eyes again, summoned the image of the clock and felt time moving once more. Then, in his mind, he saw his hands reach up to the clock face and move the hands clockwise an hour. Suddenly there was a juddering feeling and when he opened his eyes and looked around, Septimus was nowhere to be seen. Tom started to panic as he saw that he was quite alone in the prehistoric swamp. He was just about to call out when there was a soft popping sound and the Welshman materialised next to him on the log.

"Sorry about that, Tom. I didn't expect you to get that right so quickly: you took me by surprise. Well done, you have just travelled an hour into the future! Now, we will try and move backwards in time."

This was much harder for Tom. Septimus explained that humans were used to travelling forward in time, albeit only as fast as time itself moved, but backwards was not natural. On the other hand, Tom had done it by himself – without trying to – several times in the past few months and after concentrating, he finally felt a falling, spinning sensation and found himself standing alone in the swamp, but in the middle of the night.

Contrary to what he might have expected, Tom was almost overcome by a great feeling of relief. His fears of being shut up with Mrs Brown in a psychiatric hospital began to recede. What the stranger told him was true: he was a Walker and he wasn't going mad after all.

Septimus appeared after a moment, saw him and smiled. "Well done: you're doing well. You're a natural in fact. I reckon it's the computer games – they speed reactions and stimulate the abstract areas of the mind that you need in order to manipulate time. It was different in my day!"

Tom looked at him, quizzically. "Just when was 'your day'? Where are you from anyway? Where is your home?"

The Welshman looked startled. "What a lot of questions for a young lad. Well, let's just say that I have wandered though a lot of places and a lot of times. I have picked up what some folk call a pretty mixed up accent from the countries I have been to, doing my job."

"What job do you do, Septimus? Why are you teaching me all this anyway?" Tom asked.

The man stood up without answering and moved away. "That's enough work for now," he said abruptly. "I think you can go home and rest. You have a lot to think about, I'm sure." Septimus blinked and suddenly the prehistoric valley with is ferns and strange creatures was gone. The journey through time took only an instant and again they were standing in Tom's bedroom. As he looked at the digital clock beside the bed it flicked to 3:05. Tom could hardly believe it; they had been gone for just a few minutes – it had felt like hours.

"What happens now?" Tom sat on the side of the bed. Suddenly the idea of waking up on New Year's morning, or going back to school in a few days and seeing his friends all seemed ridiculous and unreal.

"You must grow a little, Tommy. You must use some time to think about what we have spoken of. There is more, much more ... and some of it less than pleasant. If you choose to use your powers you must be trained so you can use them wisely.

As for what you do with them then, well that's a long story." Septimus spoke in a very serious voice – quite different from his bubbling and joyful nature in the prehistoric world - but even so, he went over and playfully spun Tom's globe so it rotated gently whilst he looked at it.

"The skills you have open up to you a world you could never have imagined. But with that world comes danger." Moving away from the globe, Septimus came to sit next to Tom on the side of the bed.

"I came here tonight because you have started to show yourself to those of us who have the same powers. Whilst you were just an ordinary schoolboy you had nothing to fear, but now you are showing these powers, I'm afraid there are men and women out there who will try to use you to suit their aims and goals. You have made a potential target of yourself."

'And a spectacle too,' thought Tom, thinking of the events at school recently. He grimaced.

Septimus seemed to read his mind. "Perhaps your friends and family have noticed odd behaviour in you?"

Tom nodded.

"Right then, this is what you must do. You must NOT use your powers until we have trained you. Keep that clock in your mind. When you feel anything happening, hold tight to that clock and try to avoid random time travel. See if you can keep quiet and unobtrusive for a little while and one day I will come for you."

"You're saying I've got to keep my head down."

"Exactly."

"Ok," Tom nodded and then stifled a yawn.

Septimus slapped him on the back and in a blur he was gone.

For a moment, Tom wondered if he had imagined the entire event, if indeed it had all been a dream. In the corner of his room, though, he heard a noise that told him it was real after all: the soft squeaking of the globe, spinning gently to a halt.

When Tom woke up late the following morning his family were all already up. His dad and his sister were, from the sounds of it, playing on the video game. He heard the words, "You haven't got a chance" from his dad and, "You cheater!" from Emma. The smell of bacon and eggs was drifting up the stairs and he could hear the bubbling of the kettle as it reached the boil.

Struggling into his clothes he went to join them, wondering if everything might return to normal now. Would he be just another ordinary boy, leading an ordinary life?

To begin with, life did seem normal: the new term at school started and finished without any incident and the weeks drifted by. Soon the Easter break was over as well. In April, Tom's twelfth birthday came and went, this time without any magically relighting candles. Although, of course, he knew now that they hadn't been relighting candles at all.

Four months had now passed since the New Year. In all that time there had been no opportunity to practise what Septimus had told him. Four months of normality; no Septimus and no time travel. Not that Kyle Rogers failed to take up any opportunity to remind everyone about the 'Nutter' in the class. But that was, in itself, normal enough.

Then came June and Sports Day: Tom had been entered into the hurdle race for his team. He did not really expect to do that well because in the past he had usually tripped over one hurdle or another. Andy, who was racing for another team, usually won.

"Good luck, Andy," he said as they and two other boys lined up at the start.

"You too, mate!" Andy replied and winked at him.

Kyle Rogers, who was also running, was quick to get in his opinion. "You'll need more than luck, Oakley, with your bandy legs!" Tom just shrugged and turned away.

The signal gun fired and they were off. Tom started well and taking the first two hurdles in his stride found himself slightly ahead of his friend. Off in the crowds he heard his dad bellowing:

"Come on boy, run!"

He ran.

He felt the thrill of the race and the pounding of his heart pushing him on. Three hurdles to go: now two and then one more. He leapt high and he was over! He sprinted for the finish and cheered as he realised he was the first across the line. Andy, close behind, was smiling at him.

"Well done, mate, good race!" his friend said.

"That's my son!" yelled his dad to anyone who would listen. The clapping and cheering went on for a while. Tom had never won a race before − or any other sport for that matter - and loved the feeling. Even better to savour was the sickly look on the face of Kyle, who came in last, arriving just in time to witness the scenes of celebration.

Then, there was a click and a heave in Tom's mind. Suddenly, he found himself approaching that last hurdle again. Except, this time he had now lost his stride and timing. He tried to jump it, but with a sickening smack he hit the wooden board hard with his shin and went down in a heap. Andy leapt the hurdle next to him and ran on to win.

Tom hit the ground in frustration and shouted out: "No! NO – I won, I won!!"

Everyone was staring at him now, each face showing a different reaction: his teachers angry at his behaviour; Andy, hurt and upset that his mate had done this to him, while Kyle was hopping about in glee at having more evidence of his rival's mental instability. In the crowds, his father looked embarrassed and was certainly not telling anyone that Tom was his son, now. Tom's face flared red with embarrassment and he turned his head to look away from his father.

He was just trying to work out exactly what had happened when he spotted another face, one he did not recognise. Tom was pretty sure it was not a parent of anyone at the school. It wasn't just that he was a stranger, but there was something odd about him. In the sports ground was an old oak tree that provided shelter on the sunniest of summer days. Leaning against it, where Tom was certain no one had been a moment before, was a man. He was tall and thin, maybe about forty-five years old, with once blond hair that was now turning white in parts. He was smoking a cigarette and staring at Tom from under a rather old-fashioned hat like the sort spies wore in black and white movies.

There was something else odd too: the sun was beating down and Tom was sprawled on the ground panting whilst sweat trickled down his back. Yet only fifty yards away, the man was wearing a thick winter coat and showed no signs of discomfort whatsoever. A moment later, Tom's view of the man was blocked by the shoes and legs of someone he certainly did recognise and just as certainly did not want to meet right now.

"Just what was that all about, Oakley?" asked the shoes' owner, Mr Beaufin, from under his raised and rather bushy eyebrows.

Tom glanced up at him and then back at the tree, but the man and his rather out-of-place coat had vanished.

That night, after serving detention yet again, Tom had a dream - except, he was no longer Tom and did not know who Tom was anyway. Indeed, he was not a he: he was a she and her name was Mary.

"Mary!" The voice was urgent. Someone was banging at her door and shouting. It was late, maybe one in the morning or a little later. Confused and sleepy she opened her eyes and said, "What is it?"

"Mary, come quickly!" She now recognised the voice. It was Jack, the master's journeyman. She got up and threw a shawl around her shoulders. Opening the door she saw him hopping from foot to foot in front of her. She was about to send him away and go back to her bed, when she noticed smoke drifting up the stairs from the ground floor. Behind Jack huddled Mr Farriner, the baker, and his family.

"Jack, I can smell burning!" she said in alarm.

"Mary, you stupid wench, the whole place is ablaze. Come quickly, we have to get out!"

Mary lived over the bakery in Pudding Lane in London. It had been her turn to put out the oven fire the night before, but she had forgotten to do it. Around midnight, sparks from the fire must have flown out of it and landed on the pile of firewood that was always neatly stacked nearby, for soon after midnight the fire was raging. It had spread all along the ground floor and was already igniting the neighbouring houses. Farriner's apprentice, Jack, had been woken by the smoke and went to investigate, but was forced back upstairs. He had then roused the household – Mary being the last.

"What do we do?" asked Mrs Farriner. "We can't get out: we'll all be burnt!"

The children now started crying. Jack tried again to get down the stairs, but could not: the heat was intense and the very air was aflame. He suddenly snapped his fingers. "Out the back of my bedroom," he said and hurried them all into his room. He moved across to the window, which was already open to provide ventilation on this hot September night. "We can climb out onto that roof," he pointed.

Close behind Jack, Mary could now see that the roof of the adjacent house abutted the bakery beneath the window. She stood back while the baker's family climbed out and across the narrow gap onto the roof opposite. It sloped steeply and the children had to cling to their parents as they made the perilous crossing. Suddenly, from behind Mary there was a crack, a pop and a spitting noise. She spun round and gasped, for now she could see the flames had reached the upper passageway and were rippling towards her along the floorboards, which buckled, blackened and split as the fire advanced.

"Come on, Mary!" Jack urged from the window, as he reached out to her with one hand. She stepped toward the window but, looking down, she could see the ground far below. She felt dizzy and started to panic. Terrified of falling, she froze.

"Mary, you must come," Jack urged as he moved out onto the roof ahead of her.

The fire was scorching her now, but she was paralysed with fear and simply could not move. Suddenly, the fire swept down the wall of Jack's room and leapt across the window, blocking the only route of escape. She screamed.

"Mary!" Jack yelled in despair, "Mary!"

41

Tom woke up, sweating all over and screaming his head off. "Fire!" he yelled, "Fire!" Then, he got up and started running about on the landing. His dad was out of his bedroom in a flash. Grabbing Tom, he shouted at him.

"What is it, Tom, what's going on?"

"Fire! I think ... I mean ...," Tom stuttered and then opened his eye wide and looked about him. He was standing on his own landing and there was no fire to be seen anywhere.

He allowed his dad to take him back to bed.

"You ok, Tom?"

Snuggling under the covers, Tom nodded. By now, he was calming down and had no intention of telling his father the full details of the dream. "Yeah, Dad. Sorry about that. It was just a nightmare, I reckon."

His father nodded, but gave him a strange look as he left the room. Tom rolled over and pretended to go to sleep, but a few moments later, he got up and opened up a history book from his bookshelf and flipping through it, found a paragraph that began:

'Early on the morning of the 2nd September, 1666, began the Great Fire of London. The first victim was the Farriner's maid. She died when she refused to leave the bakery through a window in order to escape across the rooftops ...'

CHAPTER FIVE - THE INSTITUTE

T he following day, Tom's dad took him to see the family's doctor at Parklands Medical Centre. Their GP was a red-haired Cornishman who spoke with a strong West Country accent. Tom's father explained that he was worried about this business of Tom falling over at the race and then the disorientated behaviour he had shown during the night that followed. He also told the GP about the odd events of the previous summer, at Christmas and the New Year. The doctor asked Tom's dad a lot of questions, examined Tom and took a blood sample, but said he could find nothing wrong. He pointed out that the boy was almost a teenager and going through changes in his life, which night account for the fainting fits.

"But," he said, "there are other explanations we must consider. All these symptoms might be nerves and anxiety and I think it would be best to get a child psychologist to have a look at him."

The doctor turned to peer at Tom. "I must ask you, Tom; is there anything you are worried about right now, anything at all? School perhaps?"

There were plenty of things on Tom's mind but he was not about to tell the doctor! He just shook his head. The doctor gave him a look that suggested he was not fooled for one minute, but in the end he just nodded.

"You said there were other explanations, Doctor ..." Tom's dad prompted.

"Well, if there is nothing worrying the lad then we must consider that during these times you have seen Tom collapse, it is just possible he was having a fit. So I am going to suggest that we send him to see a neurologist. They can arrange a brain scan and an E.E.G. – that's a special test to check for epilepsy. May I go ahead with the referral, Mr Oakley?"

After thinking for a moment, Tom's dad said he would talk to his wife and get back to the doctor if they wanted to take it further. All this time, Tom sat there wondering if he was going to be sent away or locked up, just as he had feared through all of last year. On the one hand, he believed he was not going mad and all these strange events were due to him being one of those people Septimus Mason had called a 'Walker'. But he couldn't tell his parents, or the doctor for that matter, about that – could he? They would certainly think he was going crazy then. Mind you, Tom thought, on the other hand, if this was just an illness and that whole thing with Septimus was just a hallucination, maybe it would be curable with some tablets. That being so, in a way, he hoped Septimus was wrong after all; or that he had in fact dreamt up the strange Welshman and that entire trip back in time. 'And he woke up and it was all a dream,' had a nice ring to it, Tom thought to himself. Yes, if he had dreamt all that, then all that remained were these odd occurrences. They might, after all, be due to some illness which tablets could make better. Perhaps he would ask his mum and dad to take him to see the specialist the doctor suggested. Then, he could take his pills, be well again and get back to being ordinary Tom Oakley.

For the time being, Tom ignored the little voice that nagged at the back of his mind, 'But you didn't know much at all about the Great Fire of London, and you'd never even heard of Farriner and his

44

maid, Mary, the girl who died, and yet it actually happened. Ordinary? I don't think so!'

They left the room and went out to the car. Whilst his dad fumbled with the keys, Tom decided that he was going to ask to go and see a specialist, but he was definitely *not* going to tell his dad about Walking, Septimus, the dinosaurs, the dreams and all that. That would surely convince his father to go back into the doctor and ask him to refer Tom to the psychologist after all. He didn't want that – he didn't want word going round at school that he had a mental illness and had to see a 'shrink'. He opened his mouth to speak, but his father beat him to it and looking across the top of the car, spoke first.

"You know, Thomas, maybe you *are* suffering from stress. Maybe you *should* see a psychologist. It's nothing to be embarrassed about, you know. We can keep it quiet from your school."

Just then there was a snort behind Tom and he turned round, with a growing feeling of dread, to spot the one face that he least wanted to see at this precise moment: Kyle Rogers, climbing out of a car not ten feet away. He fixed Tom with an evil stare, his face wearing a look of triumphant discovery.

"Hi Tom," he said, followed by a horrible moment's pause and then, "See you in school tomorrow ... we will have lots to discuss with everyone, won't we ...?" Then, Rogers went into the surgery with his own father, leaving Tom standing red-faced on the pavement.

They got into the car and drove part way home, stopping at a supermarket. Tom stayed in the car while his dad, leaving the keys in the ignition, got out, said, "I won't be long, Thomas, just got to get something for dinner," and disappeared into the shop.

45

Alone now and thinking back to that embarrassing moment outside the medical centre, Tom screwed up his face and closed his eyes in horror, trying not to think that by this time tomorrow he would be well and truly labelled the 'Nutter' of Parklands comp. Suddenly, he became aware that he was not alone in the car. He opened his eyes and then jumped when he saw Septimus sitting in the driving seat. Tom felt his hopes begin to fade: unless he was hallucinating, the man was real after all. He looked real and - Tom put out a hand and grasped Septimus's arm, squeezing it hard - he felt real. So he was not mad then, but neither would a pill make everything normal again. With a nasty sinking feeling, Tom knew he would never be 'ordinary.'

Septimus laughed, "Hello again, boyo! Fancy going for a spin?"

Before Tom could answer, the Welshman reached down and turned on the ignition, reversed out of the parking bay and was heading towards the road.

"This is not a good time, Septimus! Besides, my dad's going to go ballistic if he comes back and the car's gone with me in it!"

The Welshman grinned and then gave a wink, and as he did, Tom felt that they had just 'Walked'. The supermarket car park was gone and they had appeared on another road and were travelling past tall, white, Victorian town houses that had wrought iron railings outside, all painted black. Septimus had just parked outside one of these, when a bright red double-decker bus went past them, followed by a black taxi cab. So then, they were in London, somewhere.

Septimus got out of the car. He then went round and opened Tom's door.

"Septimus – the car ..." Tom began.

"...will be returned to the supermarket just after the moment we left, you know that ..."

Tom nodded slowly, remembering the New Year trip to the past that had seemed to take almost no time at all.

"So, what are we doing here, then?" He looked up at the building they were parked outside. It was just an ordinary house with three stories. A tall, panelled wooden door painted green stood at the top of a flight of pristine white stone steps. A large brass knocker hung in the centre of the door. To the right of the door was a brass plate. Tom squinted at it. On it he could read the polished letters:

Head Office of the Hourglass Institute
Professor Neoptolemas (Secretary)

Underneath were written words Tom did not understand:

Custos crastinos

He was about to ask what it meant, but before he could, Septimus stepped up to the door and used the knocker with a rattattat. A few moments later, a young man dressed in a smart suit opened the door a short way and peered out. Then, seeing Tom's companion, he flung the door wide open.

"Ah, Mr Mason, come in immediately."

"Thank you, Matthews," muttered Septimus.

The young man led them down a passageway, passing several closed doors on either side. The walls were covered from floor to ceiling with hundreds of antique maps. Tom saw one entitled *A True Mappe of the Ancient Countye of Kente*. That

47

title seemed to have far too many e's, Tom thought. Further along, there were paintings and prints of scenes from battles. One showed men with red jackets on horses charging past cannons. The caption read, *The Royal Scots Greys charge the French guns at Waterloo.* Interspersed amongst all these were technical drawings. Some depicted flying machines; others, submarines or clocks; whilst still more showed circles, arcs and spirals labelled with confusing scientific symbols, which reminded Tom of algebra. Finally, they came to a heavy oak door at the end of the corridor.

Just in front of the door was a desk, which showed evidence of a fastidious mind. It was well-ordered and kept perhaps a little too tidy with neat piles of papers in trays marked 'IN' and 'OUT'. A man in his fifties, wearing a rather old-fashioned, long-tailed jacket and a high stiff collar, sat at the desk with an open diary in front of him. As they approached he looked at them rather suspiciously.

"Name and purpose?" he demanded.

The Welshman grinned and said, "It's me."

The man looked at Septimus and in a slightly over-exaggerated way consulted his diary.

"I'm afraid," he said, in a supercilious voice, "that we do not have a Mr 'It's Me' down as having an appointment. Perhaps you would like to arrange one on another day?"

Septimus sighed. "Come on, Phelps, it's me, Septimus. We spoke only an hour ago. I have Tommy here with me, to see the Prof."

"Rules exist for a reason, Mr Mason. Now state your name and purpose."

"Oh, very well! Septimus Mason here to see Professor Neoptolemas and accompanied by Thomas Oakley," the Welshman said in a resigned voice.

Mr Phelps looked down again and reaching for a fountain pen on his desk ticked off an appointment in the diary. With a brief glance at Tom, he said, "You can go in, immediately."

Matthews knocked on the heavy wooden door and from behind it, loud and clear, a voice called them into the room. Gesturing to the visitors to enter, Matthews opened the door and stood back whilst Septimus, followed by Tom, stepped into the room beyond. It was furnished as a study: shelved books lined three walls; hundreds of them on many subjects, but Tom noticed there was a heavy emphasis on history and he also saw a number of old atlases. A large section, near the door, appeared to consist of physics text books. There was an open fireplace, although with the hot summer weather outside no fire burned in the grate. The wall opposite the door contained a set of French windows through which Tom could see a walled garden complete with a sundial mounted on a low pillar, and beyond this an iron gate that led out through a high brick wall to what looked like an alleyway at the rear.

In the middle of the room stood a desk; behind it sat an old man. He was mostly bald, except for small dashes of shock white hair over his ears. Startling blue eyes behind a pair of steel-rimmed spectacles studied Tom as he walked in. The old man looked quite fit for his age, which must, Tom estimated, be a little over seventy. He did not look surprised to see them.

"Thomas Oakley, I assume. I've been expecting you! Come over and please sit down."

In front of the desk were two antique chairs and Tom went over and sat down carefully. He felt strangely nervous in front of this man; it was a bit like being called in to a meeting with his head teacher.

The old man's eyes turned now to Septimus. "Thank you for your services, Mr Mason. You are as efficient as ever."

"There's proud, I am," responded the Welshman, "and pleased I'll be too, when you pay me."

The Professor's expression changed and he looked slightly disappointed. After a moment, he sighed. Then he reached into his desk, took out an envelope and tapped it on his other hand. "I see it is money first, as always, Mr Mason. You're a talented man: the Institute could use you ..." said the Professor, pausing to look over his spectacles at Septimus, "... should you ever want to join in the struggle."

Septimus smiled wryly and reached out to take the envelope. Then he gave a chuckle, not unkind, but gently mocking. "You fight your good fight, Prof. I'm happy to help where there is payment involved, but I'm not the heroic type. Good day to you. Oh, Tom, I'll be outside when you and the Prof have talked," said Septimus, strolling to the door and closing it as he left.

For a moment, the Professor stared after him. The room was silent, save for the ticking of a brass carriage clock on the mantelpiece.

"Sir ... er, why am I here?" Tom asked, breaking the silence.

The Professor glanced down at him and then smiled. "Thomas Oakley, you are a rare individual. There are not many of us who have powers to transcend the normal boundaries that time puts round us. Such powers can be dangerous, but if used well can help to protect our world from those who would change it for their own gain. There is also a need to police their use in case individuals with an eye on opportunities for wealth go too far," he added, looking again towards the door through which Septimus had disappeared.

"Sir, I don't understand. What are these 'powers' as you call them? How can I travel through time? I mean I've seen it in the movies, but you don't really get time travel in real life, do you?"

"Yet your experience runs contrary to your statement, does it not?" said the Professor, whilst peering over the top of his glasses.

"Yes, I suppose it does," Tom nodded thoughtfully.

"So then, if we accept for the moment the premise that time travel is possible, then the rest of your question is – as I understand it – *how* is it possible? Am I correct?"

Tom frowned for a moment as he tried to catch up then nodded. The Professor spoke formally and sometimes he found it hard to understand. It reminded him of the time he had been taken to see a Shakespeare play: to begin with the language had been hard to follow even though it had been adapted for children, but after a while he kind of got into it.

"Well, that is complicated," the Professor went on. "There have been many theories about how an actual time machine might be made. Einstein, in his theories of relativity, showed that if you go really fast, time will travel more slowly for you than it does for others. So, get in a rocket and accelerate to almost the speed of light and a small time for you can be a long time for those left behind. You would come back to earth years later to find they had aged, while you had not – or not a lot."

Tom thought about the old movie, *Planet of the Apes,* in which just that kind of thing had happened. The character played by Charlton Heston had come back to a world overrun by apes, which had evolved speech and had humans as slaves.

Moments for him had been millennia for the rest of the world. Tom grunted. "Ok I get that, but ..."

"But we don't have a rocket, you were going to say. Also that method would take you forward in time, but not back. Well, other physicists have taken Einstein further. They now know that energy, such as a laser beam, moving round and round in a spiral can also affect the flow of time."

The Professor patted several magazines on his desk. Tom now saw that they were actually papers from academic journals with titles like *Foundations of Physics*. He caught a glimpse of a heading, *The Gravitational Field of a Rotating Light Beam*. The Professor picked that one up and flicked through it. Tom saw strange symbols and equations that made no sense to him.

"We study these and other works to try to understand what happens to us. In these, you can read of work being done in America to build a time machine using lasers. But again, there is a problem," he shrugged.

"Er... that we don't seem to be trapped in the middle of a cylinder of laser beams?" Tom suggested.

The Professor looked nonplussed for a moment, but recovered quickly. He tossed the journal back onto the table. "Very well then, there are *two* problems. As you say, we don't seem to be trapped in the middle of a cylinder of lasers. That is the first problem. The next is that if you build such a machine, you can use it to travel back in time only as far as when you turned it on. It creates a loop of time between the future and when you switch it on, you see."

Tom was not sure that he did, but he nodded anyway.

"So, Thomas, how is it that we - by which I mean *you* - seem to be able to travel without a visible machine and without any obvious limit to how far back we can go? Why also are only some people able to do this and not others?"

Not sure what he was expected to say, Tom shook his head: he had no idea.

The Professor took off his glasses and polished them on a handkerchief, which he then folded neatly back into his pocket. Then, putting the glasses back on his nose, he focused on Tom.

"Well, we believe that it is to do with biology as much as physics. Darwin. Evolution. Do you understand what genes are?"

Tempted to make the obvious joke about denims, Tom saw from the Professor's expression that he was waiting for just such a comment, had heard it all before and would not find it amusing. So he nodded and mentioned they had done it in biology. "It's what we all have inside us that tell us how tall to be and what colour our eyes are," he answered.

"Indeed," the Professor nodded, "that – and far more besides. In fact genes are blueprints for our bodies. So, something happened in history. Some genes got altered. Biologists don't really know what most of the genome..." he paused, seeing Tom's mystified expression. "That's the collective name for the complete set of our genes, yes?"

"Yes, if you say so."

"Well, we don't know what most of the genome actually does, but what we think is that some of it controls, in some individuals, the production of a certain type of energy - some as yet undiscovered force: a time energy or 'temporal' energy, to use the correct term. These individuals can manipulate this energy and then, just as the cylinder of lasers creates a time loop with laser energy, they can create a loop or tunnel back and forth in time. They gain the powers to create time loops or fold space by themselves, without any machinery."

Frowning in concentration, Tom said nothing for a moment then he smiled, "Wow. That's erm ... that's quite a jump from rotating lasers, Professor, if you don't mind me saying! Can bodies really produce energy?"

"Oh, definitely; bodies actually do emit an electromagnetic field. Electro−cardio−grams or E.C.G.s as we call them, which are used to do a heart tracing, actually measure the currents inside the heart. E.E.Gs: Electro−encephalograms do the same with brain waves. Your whole body is basically a battery.

"Oh, I see... " mumbled Tom, not certain that he did.

"So then, we think that this 'temporal' energy source is emitted by us 'Walkers' and if so, it can be used to manipulate space and time. This is the key to the power that we all have." He now pointed at Tom, "Indeed, which you have."

This neatly brought the conversation round to the important part − from Tom's point of view at least. So, something built into his genes − his blueprint in fact - was behind all that had been going on. That was a bit frightening really. Once he had realised that he was not going mad, or was ill, Tom had assumed that what had been happening was outside him: some external force that maybe he could find a way to block out. Now, however, it transpired that it was all a part of him. If so, what could he do about that? Maybe, there was nothing he could do. Maybe there was no escape. Feeling a sense of gloom and desperation, he asked another question.

"I'm not certain I want these powers," he said quietly. "Is there nothing I can do to be rid of them?"

CHAPTER SIX: REDFELD

T he Professor nodded. "They have caused you much grief, have they not? Confusion and ridicule too, perhaps?"

Tom grunted an assent.

"Well, indeed, I can understand that. Many of us have wished we had not been born with these powers, or have been given reason to have them removed," said the Professor.

"Is that possible?" asked Tom, feeling a glimmer of hope. What was the old man saying?

"Indeed it is. We have a way of removing the power forever: an injection that switches off the gene that you use to control Walking. But it is not a choice to be taken lightly as once gone they can never be returned. That is why I had you brought here today: to give you that choice. It is a decision you must think about for a few days, but not forever. We have found that in a boy the choice must be made before their thirteenth birthday. After that − or around that time - the powers become permanent. So you do not have long, Thomas, just until next April, I believe?"

Tom nodded and got to his feet. "Is that all, sir?" he asked.

"Yes, unless you have anything to ask me about?"

With a shake of his head Tom turned to leave, then remembering the strange words on the door plate, he asked what they meant.

"*Custos crastinos*? Loosely translated, it means, 'Guardian of tomorrow'."

That did not mean anything to Tom and his face must have shown his ignorance, for the old man gave him a kindly smile and explained: "It's our motto, Master Oakley."

"But what does it mean exactly?"

"It's hard to explain, young man. Let me just say it is a neat summary of what we do here. Now, is there anything else you wish to ask?"

Tom thought about the dreams he was having and wondered whether to tell the Professor, who was studying him, head tilted to one side in expectation, but Tom shook his head, muttered, "No sir, thank you," and left the room, closing the big door quietly behind him. Matthews was waiting to escort him to where Septimus was leaning against his dad's car.

"Fancy a milkshake?" the Welshman asked. Tom, suddenly aware of being thirsty, agreed.

At the end of the road was a café. They sat at a table outside on the pavement and drank in silence for a while. Tom thought about what the Professor had said and after a time he asked his companion what he thought should be his choice.

"Well, if it were me, I would keep the power and use it. With some discipline and training you'll be able to control it well," Septimus answered promptly.

"Use it for what, though? The Professor spoke of protecting the world and also of ... erm..." Tom stopped, his face going a little pink.

"Of controlling the likes of me, eh?" the Welshman responded with a chuckle. "Ah, the Prof's not so bad, but he's a bit of an old stick-in-the-mud. If you take my advice, you will use your powers for yourself: for your bread and butter. Pop back to ancient Greece and pick up a nice piece of pottery that are two a penny and then sell it today at an antique market or at an auction, for thousands of quid. What's wrong with that?"

"So that's what you do, is it?"

Septimus grinned, "That and many other things. In your case I was hired to locate you and bring you to the Professor. But I liked the look of you, so I threw in some extra advice and teaching for free. My point is, you can do more than Professor goody-goody suggests and earn a bit of cash along the way. Where's the harm in that, I ask you?" Septimus said, with a shrug of his shoulders.

Tom was about to answer, when he was interrupted by a voice coming from behind them. "So, the boy has the choice of being a freelance peddler, who makes his way trading up and down the time line, or a policeman regulating others' use of time travel," the voice said, speaking with crisp, precise and slightly accented words.

Septimus and Tom turned and saw another man sitting at a nearby table. He was smoking a thin cigarette, despite the laws on smoking. Neither the waiter taking an order from another customer inside the cafe, nor any other customer seemed to have noticed. The man had a long nose beneath which grew a thin, well-trimmed moustache, which like his short, neatly cut hair was jet black. His eyes were a deep green colour. He wore a smart but rather dated looking suit, which struck Tom as more fitting of characters in black and white movies from years before, than from the twenty-first century. Somehow, the man seemed familiar and although it took a moment to place him, the long overcoat, which was hung over a chair, and the old-fashioned brimmed hat that sat on the table, confirmed to Tom that this was the man he had seen briefly under the tree at his school the previous day. The man took a sip from a steaming china cup, which he replaced on a saucer next to the hat.

Tom and Septimus exchanged glances and shrugged.

"Permit me to introduce myself. I am Joseph Redfeld. I am a – how do you put it – Walker, too."

"Oh, enjoy a bit of rambling do you, boyo," Septimus asked. "Have you tried the Pennine Way? Or how about Wales; I hear Snowdon is nice this time of year."

Redfeld glared at him. "Don't take me for a fool. You know what I am talking about."

Tom sensed a slight change in the feeling of time flowing, almost like the lurch he had felt when he once went to France on holiday and the ferry had pulled out to sea and gone over the first big wave.

Without warning, Redfeld deliberately knocked his cup to the floor, where it smashed into dozens of pieces. A waiter came rushing out with a cloth. Then, Redfeld gave a wave of his hand and Tom felt a slight judder again and suddenly the waiter was running backwards into the café. The cup reassembled itself and spun back up onto the table, followed by the coffee, which poured itself neatly into the cup. A moment later, the coffee cup was intact and gently steaming, and the waiter was back inside taking an order from another customer just as before.

Redfeld took another sip from his coffee and then glanced over at Tom. "See how we can use our power to destroy and to rebuild? I am not just talking of coffee cups, you comprehend. I am talking of nations and empires. The opportunities we have are massive and he," Redfeld indicated Septimus, "talks of selling Greek vases, whilst that old man down the street has no vision or courage! *Custos crastinos*? Pah!"

The man pointed his finger at Tom. "I offer you a third choice. Come with me and you could be immortal. The power you have is truly great. I could make you a god! Very, very few are granted these powers. Even fewer can master them. But those who can have the potential to change their world: for good, for evil, for gain and for duty ... forever, in fact. Would you turn your back on the chance of that?"

Still keeping Tom under an unflinching gaze Redfeld continued in a softer tone, "There is much that can be achieved which that old man does not understand, Tom. I can make it happen for you. I ask you to give the matter your deepest consideration." At last he looked away, drank his coffee in one tilt of his head and stood up. On went his hat and coat.

Suddenly, behind him, a bright point of light appeared and this expanded until it was hanging in the air in what Tom could only describe as a hole, blocking his view of the cafe behind. Through the hole, Tom caught a glimpse of part of a room. There was a table, a book shelf and next to it a bank of computers. A moment later, Redfeld seemed to step into the hole, which hung there for a moment longer and then collapsed behind him. With that, he had vanished. About them, the cafe customers carried on with their lunches, apparently oblivious to all this.

Tom looked at Septimus who winked at him. "And there he was – gone!" he spoke, in a broad Welsh accent, before adding, "Well now, you do have a lot to think about. Come on, boyo – I need to get you home sixty minutes ago!"

"Who was that, Septimus?" asked Tom breathlessly trying to keep up with his companion as they ran back the car.

"I'm not quite sure, sounded a bit foreign to me, boyo!"

And that was all he would say. If Septimus did know who Redfeld was, he was keeping it quiet and did not give Tom another opportunity to ask. Reaching the car, Septimus got in and waited for Tom to do likewise.

"Sorry, Tommy, but it's the Professor's orders. He wants me to teach you a little more. I guess he hopes you will work for him. In any event, I'm going to have to ask you to do it."

"Do what?"

"You must take us where we need to go."

"What! How?" Tom panicked. "I can't drive!" He had images of his dad's car nose down in a river somewhere.

"Don't worry, I'm not asking you to. I want you to move us back through space, like you did through time.

"Septimus, don't be daft. I'm not even sure I want this talent, so there is no point teaching me more," Tom said.

Looking irritated, Septimus said with a sigh, "Look, Tom, I can't make you do this, but until you decide to be done with it all, you are in danger. You *must* learn how to control these talents better."

"What if I say 'no'?" Tom said, crossing his arms and jutting his chin out.

"Fine, that's ok then. I'll just get out and walk away and leave you alone."

"But Septimus, what about my dad's car? He'll go nuts if we don't get it back. How would I explain it being here in London and how will I get home, I haven't got any money!" Tom felt his palms going sweaty and his heart pounding within him.

"You're a clever boy. I'm sure you will think of something," Septimus said with a wink and then reached out to place his hand on the door handle.

"This is not fair – you're blackmailing me!"

"Yup, boyo . Not done it often before, but I could get used to it," Septimus replied, grinning.

Tom gave in. "Oh, very well, have it your way, what must I do?"

"Close your eyes. I'll guide you as well as I can. In your mind, imagine that clock face again. This time though, make each minute equal an actual minute as you slowly wind back time. We don't have to worry about exact accuracy so don't bother too much about the second hand. Start rotating the minute hand backwards, slowly. As you do, feel the time about you, me and the car. You must take the car with you: make it move."

Tom concentrated on the image of the grandfather clock in the hallway of his grandparents' house. Then, with a jump, he felt them begin to move backwards and downwards. The strain of moving the car as well brought sweat to his forehead and he felt rather dizzy.

"Wow, slow up, Tommy, you're going a bit fast. Coast a bit. We need to sort out the geography," Septimus said.

Tom eased off a bit on spinning the hands of the clock backwards and felt the speed with which the time was passing slowing down. "So, how do we decide where to appear?" he asked, his eyes still tightly shut.

"Much the same as moving through time: you must think of a map or a globe in your mind. Find where you are, where you want to go and then imagine your finger moving towards it. Your talents will do the rest," Septimus explained.

Tom thought about maps. His parents owned a print of an old map of the world called the *Mappa Mundi*. It had been drawn in black ink, highlighted with red and gold leaf and using blue or green for rivers and seas. It was the work of monks from the thirteenth century, although his parents' version was a well made imitation produced by art students and sold door to door. His dad had liked the look of it and so bought one. However, the detail was not high and it certainly did not have the modern housing estates nor the supermarket marked on it. No ... he needed another map. Then he remembered that his father kept a road atlas in the car. Tom had used it once when his dad took him to Scout camp last summer. They had got lost a few times in the Peak District, so he had become rather familiar with navigating.

He concentrated on the map and in his mind he visualised moving his finger across it. He could feel that he and Septimus were physically moving, as well as spinning backwards through time. The two sensations together made him feel confused and not a little nauseous at first. He found it difficult to concentrate on precision in controlling their journey; it was hard to hold the images of both the clock and the map in his mind's eye. Eventually, however, he started to get the hang of it.

"Well done, boyo!" his companion said.

Tom opened his eyes just as the supermarket car park popped into view around them.

"Well done indeed," Septimus added, patting Tom on the shoulder. "Oops, here comes your dad – speak soon." Then, with a wink and a slight popping sound, he was gone, leaving Tom staring at the empty space he had occupied.

A moment later, the door opened and Tom's dad climbed in, grumbling. "Sorry I took a while. Hell of a queue in there!" his father said, starting the car. "You know, I could have sworn we were parked in the next row – took me a few minutes to find you."

"Hah – fancy that!" Tom forced a laugh.

That night, Tom found it hard to get to sleep. The strange world he had been shown, which existed in the shadows of the time-bound world, at once excited and frightened him. He thought of what Professor Neoptolemas had said, then about Septimus' comments and finally about that stranger, Redfeld, who had interrupted them. They were all right: he had a choice to make. He could take Neoptolemas up on his offer and allow his powers to be removed and live an ordinary life. Or, he could keep them and do ... what? Win the lottery? But no, the Professor wouldn't allow that, it probably came under 'opportunity for wealth.'

He gradually dropped off to sleep thinking of choices and options. He started to dream that he was in the school hall doing multiple choice questions in an exam. He looked at the paper. It read:

a) Forego your powers and become normal again.

b) Use your powers to serve mankind.

c) Use your powers to take what you want and get rich quick.

In the dream, Tom chewed on the rubber end of a pencil and then tapped it on the desk while trying to decide on the answer. Then, the dream changed and he changed with it. Yet again, as twice before, Tom was gone and forgotten. This time he was Charles. No, that wasn't what he was called. It was his proper name, certainly, but his mates called him Charlie ... *Charlie Hawker.*

CHAPTER SEVEN - CHARLIE

"You'd better come up!" Lieutenant Monrose shouted down the ladder from the conning tower.

Able Seaman Charlie Hawker was standing, waist deep in water and almost completely naked, in the control room of a German U-boat. The water was coming in quickly now and the level rising fast. He started to panic: they weren't going to make it.

Charlie was a crewman of HMS Paladin, a P-class Fleet destroyer. Earlier in the year the ship had left Scapa Flow and had sailed the long way round Africa and up through the Suez Canal, to join the Twelfth Destroyer Flotilla based in Alexandria. During the long journey, the Paladin's Captain and his First Officer, Clayworth, had drilled the crew for the task of capturing enemy torpedo boats and U-boats.

On September 23rd 1942 the flotilla had received word that a U-boat was in the vicinity and they were ordered to find and sink her. The following day they located the U-boat using their ASDIC sonar equipment and closed to attack. Next there followed half a day of cat and mouse action as the destroyers picked up the U-boat on their sonars, dropped depth charges and waited to see if there was any result. Scores of depth charges were dropped by the flotilla but, so far, without any result.

Finally, quite late at night, a searchlight illuminated the rising image of the stricken U-boat which, having blown its tanks, was surfacing. With pom-pom guns and a Lewis gun the Paladin opened fire on the crew as they emerged on deck. It ceased fire soon though, because the enemy were clearly abandoning ship.

Hawker was on deck at this point helping to man the Lewis gun. As the U-boat surfaced, he heard the Captain order Lt. Clayworth to take a boarding party across. Clayworth ordered a boat to be prepared, but did not wait for it. He stripped off and dived overboard. Impetuous, careless of his own safety and quite overtaken by the adventure, Hawker pulled off his uniform and followed the officer into the sea.

The two men swam across the gap to the U-boat and pulled themselves up the side and then up the conning tower, all the while watched by bemused Germans floating in the waves around the submarine. Climbing down into the control room they found it already a few inches deep in water and Clayworth immediately ordered a search for log books, orders, papers, documents and any signalling equipment. Charlie helped to pass heaps of papers to Lt. Monrose who, accompanied by several other seamen, had now arrived with a boat from the Paladin.

Clayworth and Charlie went back into the control room to look for anything else that might be useful to Intelligence, at which point Charlie noticed the water level was now much higher. It was already up to his chest and rising quickly. Above them, Charlie heard Lt. Monrose order the other sailors to go back to their boat.

"You'd better come up!" Monrose yelled down the conning tower a second time, before he turned away to jump into the sea. Charlie moved towards the ladder. As he did so, the U-boat gave a violent lurch and started tilting backwards.

"Come on, sir, we must go!" he urged Clayworth, who was dragging some machinery and struggling against both the surging waters and the slope of the U-boat deck. A moment later, Clayworth gave a shout of alarm as he was swept off his feet. He hurtled through the door leading towards the engine room and vanished. With a crack and a fizz, the U-boat's lights went out, plunging the control room into darkness. Terrified, Charlie was now alone, with water up to his

neck and he was starting to panic. Desperately, he turned towards the ladder, put his hands on the lower rungs and tried to pull himself up. He never made it.

It happened in an instant: water came rushing down from the conning tower and the U-boat sank ...

Tom woke up choking and feeling that he could not breathe. He stared around the room, half expecting water to come surging in through the windows or the door. However, he was in his bedroom, which was dry and warm and certainly not beneath the waves.

A few hours later, after breakfast and a fruitless search for Charlie Hawker on the internet – there were thousands, but none that had drowned at sea in 1942 - Tom decided he needed to talk to the Professor about his dreams. It seemed obvious to him that they were not just flights of fancy. He had *lived* those moments; they were much too vivid to be just his imagination – and besides, there had been Mary; she at least had actually existed. *'The Professor will know what they mean,'* Tom thought.

His mother had gone to do the Saturday morning shop; Emma was at a sleepover at a friend's house and his father was dozing in front of the football on telly. Tom had not 'Walked' on his own before and he was a bit nervous, but knew he had to try. As before, he reached out in his mind and imagined that map again. He zoomed in on his house and then panned out until he could see London in his mind. Then, he allowed himself to follow his thoughts and in a moment, he felt that he was leaving his bedroom and the terrace house and moving towards the capital. Around him there was only the darkness of the void between places, the nothingness between one instant in time and the next. There were shapes in that darkness, hints of the places he was pacing through, indistinct impressions only, but his motion past them told him that he was on his way. In his mind, he zoomed in until he could see the street in London which he and Septimus had visited the day before. A moment later he was walking in the middle of a road in the centre of London.

A huge honking blared out behind him. Spinning round, he saw a sports car screeching to a halt barely inches from his knees. He gulped and leapt out of the way. The driver gave Tom a scowl and yelled at him, "Blasted kid, jumping in front of my car!" and, with a vroom and a squeal of rubber, the car was off again.

Tom stood panting for a while and then, having recovered his breath, jogged across to the door next to the brass plate. He knocked and was admitted.

He came to a halt in front of Mr Phelps' desk. "I need to see the Prof straight away – it's urgent."

Mr Phelps regarded him disapprovingly and Tom thought he was about to ask if he had an appointment, but Tom's expression must have been distressed enough to convince the man, or maybe the Professor had told him that if Tom returned he should be seen right away. In any event, he just tipped his head towards the door and sat back down to his papers.

Entering Neoptolemas' study, Tom hurried over to the desk and blurted out breathlessly: "Sir, I need to tell you about my dreams."

Across the table, the old man raised an eyebrow and then nodded his head toward the empty chair opposite. Tom sat down and without pausing for breath started talking. He spoke about the battle with the Zulus, the fire in the bakery and the sinking U-boat and of the three people he had briefly become.

Half an hour later, he and the Professor were drinking tea. There had been silence for a long while after Tom had finished telling the old man about his dreams. The Professor had sent for Mr Phelps, along with several assistants and much activity had followed. There was a lot of scribbling of notes and checking of reference books, studying of maps and discussions with words like *Euclidean geometry, invariant distances in space time, rotation of coordinates* and *Lorentz transformation,* which Tom did not understand, but for the last few minutes everyone had left except for the Professor, who was silent, as if thinking. Then, at last, he opened his mouth.

"I am glad you came to me with this, Thomas."

Tom was about to respond, when there was a knock on the door. A young and very anxious looking man entered with a sheet of paper in his hand. He handed it to the Professor and then glanced at Tom appraisingly, as if trying to confirm something.

"Well, what is it?" The older man asked sharply, drawing the younger's attention again.

"I have had a reader check the details the young man has given. We believe we have located three potentials, sir."

"When?"

"1666, 1879 and 1942," was the response. "Currently the traces are strong. Within days or a few weeks they will start to fade, for the present cycle."

The older man nodded and smiled at Tom. Then, he leant back in his armchair, closed his eyes and murmured, "We will have to move quickly."

"We have no Walkers strong enough at present," the young man said.

Neoptolemas did not open his eyes, but just nodded his head and answered, "Then, we must find one quickly! Is Mr Mason still staying at the Imperial?"

"Yes, sir – although I believe he has gone to the café down the street."

"Well, go and fetch him, Crosby," ordered the Professor. Then, turning back to Tom, he continued talking.

"As I said before, I am glad you came to see me about these dreams. I imagine you had to think hard about doing so. You perhaps felt that they were only dreams after all, and why make a fuss? Or maybe you felt, I would think, that you were going mad?"

Tom nodded. After he had woken following this third dream he had spent a long time thinking things through. In the end he had decided the worst that could happen was that the Professor would dismiss the experiences as insignificant, just dreams. He told the old man this and saw him nod.

"Well, that was sensible. But they were not just dreams, Thomas, and I believe you suspected as much. Some of us can not only walk in time and space but can also experience directly the lives that have gone before. We all know stories of folk claiming they had a past life. Chances are that most of these are Walkers but do not know it. In your dreams you picked up on the powerful feelings and experiences of folk who once actually lived." He paused for a moment before asking a question. "So, do you feel you might be able to help me with a task?"

"What sort of a task?" Tom asked, looking up at the old man suspiciously.

"There are indications that you could be one of the most powerful Walkers I have ever met – at least for a long time –

and Thomas, I need use of those powers. It's urgent or I would not ask one as young as you. I need you to help rescue three individuals from the past," Professor Neoptolemas said.

"Why? Who are they?"

"I think you know them: Edward, Mary and Charles? They too were Walkers: individuals with potential to manipulate time. These, though, never knew of it, until a moment of extreme trauma magnified their potential to the extent that we can sense it across the years, as you have done. That sometimes happens when a Walker is in mortal danger. But these three could not have helped themselves, any more than you could until Septimus told you how. The thing is, Thomas, we need all the help we can get and these three are in great danger and may die; if that happens they will be lost to us. If we can rescue them, they can help our cause. Most especially we need to prevent them from falling into enemy hands."

Tom wondered who the enemy were and what was the cause the Professor cared so much about, but there was an even more burning question he had to ask. "I don't understand. You say these people are in the past. If so, aren't they already dead? How can they be in 'mortal danger'? They can't die twice! So how can we help them?" Tom was already feeling utterly lost in this strange new world.

The old man reached for a hard-bound notebook that Crosby had left on the desk. He flicked through several pages then looked up at Tom.

"History says you are right. Edward Dyson was a Lieutenant in the British army that invaded Zululand in the 1870s. According to the regimental records, he died at the battle of Isandlwana, but his body was never identified. Charles Hawker was in the Navy in the Second World War. The records say he went down with a U-boat he was raiding at the time. Finally, there is Mary Brown. She was the first victim of the Great Fire of London. Her body was never found amongst the ashes of Pudding Lane."

"So, how can they be rescued? Tom's mouth dropped as the implications of what Professor Neoptolemas was saying began to register. "But ... if ... I mean ... won't you be changing history?"

"Possibly, but I don't think so. Remember, these are not ordinary people; and furthermore, their apparent demise is of the type of ideal situation we look for."

"I'm not sure I know what you mean."

The Professor linked his fingers in front of his chin and looked at Tom for a moment as though considering how best to explain. "There were no bodies, Thomas. Where no one found the bodies, no one will be surprised by their absence. You see? The trick is being able to snatch them out at the last moment before death.

Tom nodded slowly, but before he could ask another question, the Professor took his breath away.

"And that, Thomas, is where you come in. You are quick, learn fast and possess great power. You can save them and bring them back here.

Tom stared at the old man, unsure what to say and how to respond.

The Professor seemed to sense his confusion. "You are thinking perhaps, that you would rather return to normal life and lose this power for good. To be, once more, just the schoolboy called Thomas Oakley: reliable and dependable, but only an ordinary guy. Well, that is an option we can grant you. The other choice is to join us. There are adventures waiting for

72

you: challenges and a chance to protect your world. A chance to be a hero in fact: not everyone gets that chance."

Tom gulped. It didn't sound like him. So here it was: 'The Choice'. Despite what Professor Neoptolemas said there were in fact three choices, all of which he had tried to work through last night. To recap: he could lose his powers and become again plain Tom, as he had been before he was eleven. He could take his powers and use them as and when he wanted to and become a mercenary, like Septimus - or whatever it was that Redfeld had in mind. Or, he could fill the role that the Professor envisaged.

Part of him longed to be released from the troubles this power had caused him over the last year: embarrassment, confusion and even a strain to his friendship with James. There was also the worry for his parents and nights of lying awake, convinced he was mad. That had been his lot these many months and now he was offered the chance to leave it all behind and rebuild his life. It was tempting, and yet … and yet, there were those words of Redfeld's:

"Very, very few are granted these powers. Even fewer can master them: but those who can have the potential to change their world. For good, for evil, for gain and for duty ... forever. Would you turn your back on the chance of that?"

I don't know, thought Tom. I can't decide, but then he recalled the people in his dreams. I've *been* these three people. I've lived their despair. They are not just ink on paper: names from long ago that no one cares about. I've experienced their fear and know how it felt when they knew they had only moments to live. How can I abandon them, knowing all that?

Tom sighed. "How do I start?" he asked.

CHAPTER EIGHT - RESCUE

There was not time, Neoptolemas told Tom, to train him properly. The need to rescue the three before their deaths was pressing and he, Tom, must go soon.

That puzzled Tom. He thought he was able to travel in time. Surely he could spend five years training and still be able to appear at any moment he chose.

"Ah, well, you would think so wouldn't you, but it's not the case," the Professor explained. "There are cycles to time and as a result we cannot always go to a specific point. There are moments when it is easy to visit a given date and then a few days later it becomes impossible. We are fortunate, given the time that has elapsed since you first dreamt about Edward Dyson, that we can still trace him. Suffice it to say that these three events are resonating strongly across the years and it is simple to pick up that signal and move back along it, but leave it a few days or weeks and it will be too late. It could then be years before the opportunity arises again, if ever."

"So... then, I only get one shot at this?" Tom frowned as he thought it through, "I mean, if I mess up, I suppose I can't ..."

The old man finished the question, "Just try again? No, certainly not. Firstly this is not a video game. You can't load a saved game or whatever the correct terminology is. Secondly, you can't begin to imagine the complications of actually meeting yourself. Other than it being extremely embarrassing, that is. I mean who else knows all the bad things about you, except you!" The Professor smiled then grew serious again,

"But aside from this, it breaks a fundamental rule of the Universe and while we may manipulate time to a limited degree believe me, my boy, when I say we do not break such rules. Thirdly, you just can't. It's been tried. You cannot, having visited a time, revisit those same moments. It's as if somehow time keeps a record and blocks those years from you forever."

Tom began to wonder what he was expected to do. He could not fight off an army of Zulus, he was not a fireman and he knew nothing about submarines. What could he really do? He asked the old man these questions. Neoptolemas smiled and opened a drawer. He pulled out a chain made of cast iron and soldered onto a thick glass globe the size of an orange, inside of which was a liquid.

"This is an anchor," began the Professor, "but not in a nautical sense. This helps bind you or will pull you to a certain time."

Tom did not understand the explanation and frowned. Neoptolemas saw his confusion and tried a different tack. "Do you believe in ghosts, Tom?" he asked.

"Not really, well I don't know, perhaps I do ..." Tom trailed off, realising he had given three separate answers.

"Well, ghosts do exist. Perhaps not the troubled souls of the dead like you see in films, but an image of the troubled souls of the past. It has long been believed that bodies of water and metals like iron can store impressions of events that have occurred nearby. I am not talking about someone making the tea or a mundane activity such as that. No, I mean that a violent event – something terrible – produces so much energy whilst it occurs that some of that force soaks into the surrounding structure. Old rock, iron, water – it can all store such impressions and then, one day, an individual visits who is open to such images. They feel or even see something they cannot explain and call it a ghost."

The Professor fingered the glass globe, "This chain and ball: they are made up of iron and water, among other things. Some of my agents are talented in forcing the image of a place and time into them. If Walkers carries such a device, it can help them find the way home – the way back here – however far they have gone. You will carry it with you. Persuade those you must rescue to hold or touch it and then with your help they will arrive back here. That's all. No heroics, Tom. And above all *do not* attempt to change history. London burned in 1666, the British got massacred at Isandlwana and that submarine did sink. You aren't there to alter that. Just get the three of them out!"

Tom took the ball. The chain clinked slightly against the glass as he held it up to peer at the water inside. "How does it work?" he asked. "Do I have to push a button?"

"No – as I said, you simply persuade them to hold it. You touch them and try and Walk back here. The anchor will make it easier and you might feel a pulling towards us. Just allow it to bring you back."

Tom started to think of what he had to do. Suddenly, he felt a wave of panic wash over him and his hands started to shake. "Sir, I … don't think I can do this alone," he said quietly. The Professor opened his mouth to speak, but just then a voice rang out.

"But, you won't be going alone, boyo. I'll be coming with you," said Septimus, from the doorway.

Another room: a boardroom high up on the top floor of an office block. Ten men in grey suits sit around a table. At the head of the table is another man, who is somehow familiar to Tom, although he has certainly never met him. Then, as before, he is no longer Tom; he has become the man at the head of the table: an older man with silvery grey hair and he feels a burden upon him, for he has a duty and that duty is more important than anything else. On the table top in front of him is a long, shallow, open topped wooden box, full of silver and copper sands: a sand table, in fact, but not smooth, neat and static – this sand is moving; its surface shifting this way and that. There are forms and patterns metamorphosing within it. In some places there is order, a duplication of shapes that suggest some plan or purpose behind it. Large areas of the sand box are like this: predictable and repetitive, but oddly reassuring to look at. The old man regards these areas with calm and pleasure. Then there are, of course, the two opposing lines of struggle.

Parallel to each other, running the length of the table along the edges, two ripples run, starting at his end and moving away from him. Even they have some symmetry. Sometimes they come together and join before breaking apart again and deviating from each other. If one veers this way, the other mirrors the move the opposite way. Yes, they are disturbances, but they are usually predictable and therefore acceptable to his ordered mind.

Then, suddenly, as if someone has dropped a stone into a puddle, a disharmony rises up and where there has been order, all around are chaotic swirling shapes in the sand. The old man frowns, and leaning forward, squints for a moment before turning to the man on his right.

"Find him. Find him now!" he orders. He stares back at the table. The ripples caused by the disturbance threaten to change everything. What would be there afterwards? He sniffs at the thought. That is irrelevant. It is now that matters. His musings are disturbed as someone shakes him by the shoulder.

"Tom!" a far away voice calls. But who is Tom? For a moment the man's mind looks inward at himself and is surprised to find he is not alone. Then, he recognises the boy.

"You! Tom...?"

"Tom!" shouted Septimus.

Blinking, Tom stared all around him, confused for a moment. Then he recognised Septimus and glancing down saw that the suit was gone and he was Tom again. He had been daydreaming. He looked up and nodded at his companion.

"You ok, boyo? You were absent for a moment then. I mean, the lights were on, but no one was at home."

Tom shook his head to clear the last images of that strange vision in the boardroom. Best not to mention it for the moment, at least until it made more sense. "I'm ... ok, Yes, I'm ok. Let's get on with it."

The heat of the mid-afternoon sun was beating down upon the plateau in front of an oddly formed mountain. It was cone shaped and reared up suddenly from the plain. All about there were whitewashed cairns and here and there tombs and burial plots. It was the battleground of Isandlwana. Tom and Septimus had arrived and stood for a moment looking around them.

"The British came here, confident in their ability and the might of their arms, but they were swept away by a vast force of Zulus. Still, for either side, it was a terrible day. Almost three thousand men died here," Septimus observed.

Tom looked around. "These stones ...?" he asked.

"Placed over the bodies of the dead," his companion replied and looked thoughtful for a moment. Then, seemingly focusing on the present problem again, he continued. "The British were arranged in a line across the plateau facing north, where most of the Zulus were. The problem is in knowing where Dyson was. It seems his company was somewhere in the middle of the line. The Professor lent me a book, which I have here," he pulled it out of his small rucksack. There is an account by a member of a rocket troop who survived the battle, which mentions Dyson: a certain Gunner Joseph Garrant."

Septimus flipped through the book and found the page. With a glance up at Tom to check he was listening, he started relating how the artilleryman had passed Dyson's company on horseback as he tried to escape the Zulus who had overrun his position earlier.

"Garrant left us a good account of where his rocket troop had been placed. It was initially away from the camp out on the plain. They were attempting to fire on the Zulu's left horn – that's the name they gave to the wings of the army – when the battery was overrun. The gunners tried to pack up their equipment and escape. They panicked and most were killed. In the confusion, Garrant became separated from his crew and headed directly towards the mountain. The camp lay in his path and so he found himself passing Lieutenant Dyson's company, just in front of the tents. He witnessed Dyson's men, with the Lieutenant himself following along behind, running back into the camp. There, amongst the cooking fires, was where he last saw him before carrying on his own flight toward the mountain. Once there he was able to find an escape route across the pass and get away to the British territory of Natal."

Septimus stopped talking for a moment, because he had found a small note from the Professor stuck into Garrant's book, like a bookmark. He read it and laughed.

80

Tom gave him a quizzical look. "What is it? What's so funny?"

Septimus hummed to himself and then whispered some words that sounded as though they came from a hymn. *"Crown him the Lord of years, the potentate of time. Creator of the rolling spheres, ineffably sublime ..."*

"Eh?" Tom said.

Septimus looked smug. "Would you believe that at the precise moment the British positions in the camp were being overrun and our rocketeer was riding past our soldier, just then, at that very moment – there was a solar eclipse!"

"Cool! I was watching a programme on telly about eclipses. Did you know that astronomers know when they have happened – even down to the actual minute? That means ..." his voice trailed off as he realised Septimus was grinning at him, one eyebrow raised.

"Yes, Tom, precisely: it means we have our time fixed. The Prof says it was about 2.15 p.m. that the eclipse began, but it reached its height at 2.30 p.m. The Professor also gave me a map. It shows the positions of Garrant's battery, the camp, the cooking fires and the mountain, along with the positions of the various infantry companies at certain time intervals. I think that we can estimate Dyson's location at about 2.30 p.m. that day to within a hundred yards. That is the best we can expect. We can appear just before 2.30 p.m. where we think he will be." Septimus finished and took a deep breath. Then, with a shrug, he went on. "After that, it's down to luck."

Tom took the map and turning it so the mountain lay at the opposite side of the page, orientated himself. Using the landmarks that Septimus had mentioned, he tried to picture in his mind where the camp had been. He thought back to that confused, terrifying dream. Had there been there an eclipse? Yes, now he thought about it the sky had been a dark red colour. So then, where had the camp been? Where indeed had Edward been?

They walked forward, across the scorched grass and through the sweltering heat, towards the camp. Mount Isandlwana loomed above them. They moved about for a while, estimating the position they were looking for from the map and the landmarks. After a while they agreed on the most likely spot to try. Septimus put the book and map away. He reached into the rucksack, pulled out another book and flipped through a few pages. Tom could see it was full of black and white photos.

"Right then, here we are," Septimus said, passing the book to Tom with one hand and tapping on a photo with the other, "front row, second from the left."

Tom looked at the picture indicated. It was an old black and white photo of eight officers standing or kneeling around some flags. They were all in the same uniform. He looked at the second from the left. He was a young man in his twenties, cleanly shaven, tall and looking very proud. Tom wondered if any of his fellow officers in the photo had survived the fateful battle.

"That's the guy we are looking for?" Tom asked. Septimus nodded, putting the book away and fastening his rucksack.

"When we arrive, it will be chaos. The Zulus won't stop to notice that we're oddly dressed. We are white faces: they will kill us if they see us. We keep out of sight and locate Dyson. We have no idea how long he lived after Garrant left him, so we can't waste time. Furthermore, we cannot alter anything else that occurred. Focus on the task at hand and remember that photo. And make sure you've got your ball and chain ready. Let's go!"

Tom nodded took a deep breath and put his hand on Septimus' shoulder.

The jump was not a long one. They did not move at all in terms of position on the surface of the planet, although Tom had learned that his talent for Walking somehow took account of the movement of the earth, its solar system and even the rotation of the galaxy. All he had to do was manage the move back through some one hundred and thirty odd years.

They juddered to a stop and found they were standing between rows of conical white tents. Above them the sky was darkening to a deep blood red. Tom could see the disk of the moon already cutting across the sun, dimming the light as it did so. It was his first eclipse and it was a frightening sight. All around them was noise. Somewhere nearby, a man screamed. Elsewhere there was a crackle of rifle fire and the shouting of orders. And behind it all, like the noise of a swarm of bees, the terrifying buzzing war cry of the Zulu warrior. He had heard it before: in his dream. Tom was rooted to the spot.

"This way, boyo," shouted Septimus above the din. He dragged Tom along and pushed him between two tents. They emerged onto a scene of chaos. They were indeed near the cooking area: a dozen fires heated bubbling cauldrons of stew that would never be eaten. The cooks huddled together and tried to keep the Zulu warriors away.

Zulu warriors! Now Tom could see them in the flesh, they were terrifying. Naked, except for loin cloths, head and arm bands made from animal skins, they were armed with short spears - just like the assegai his teacher had brought into class - and wooden clubs, using both effectively as they ran, stabbing

83

and smashing at the enemy. A few did have firearms, but the vast majority seemed to favour surging at the British in great groups and overwhelming them by sheer weight of numbers. Fortunately for Tom, he and Septimus had emerged from the tents behind the huddled groups of red-coated British riflemen, who still kept shooting down scores of their foe. For the moment, the Zulus were being kept away from the Walkers. Tom looked about, then his eyes widened. A hundred yards away − near the cooks − he spotted Dyson.

"There he is!" he shouted and started forward.

Septimus came after him, yelling at Tom to be careful, but Tom hardly heard him. He was closing in on Dyson, fumbling at the ball and chain fastened to his belt when, with a roar, a dozen Zulus burst through the thin line of red coats and ran into the camp. One came towards Tom, screaming at him. Tom stopped dead in his tracks, terrified and pinned to the spot with fear. He saw the warrior draw back his spear.

"Look out, Tom!" yelled Septimus and the voice freed Tom from his paralysis. At once he knew what to do. He charged towards the Zulu, then, just before the spear point reached his body, he Walked through the void, shifting himself a few steps forward. To the Zulu it must have seemed as if Tom had vanished and then reappeared behind him.

Confused, the warrior spun round and as a result, he did not see Septimus approaching until the Welshman's fist was crashing into his face. The time traveller leapt over the Zulu, who had collapsed like a sack of potatoes, and sprinted on after Tom.

Tom could see Dyson, but was still yards away when a score of Zulus closed in on the Lieutenant. Their spears went back ready to strike him down. Tom shifted himself ten yards forward in an instant. Reappearing in front of the startled officer, he grabbed the man's jacket and shifted them both another dozen yards into a nearby tent. A split second before he Walked them both, Tom felt a hot pain in his side as a spear point ripped into his flesh. Then they were gone, reappearing inside the tent. He and Dyson collapsed onto the ground. Shaking with fear, the Lieutenant was on his feet in moments and with trembling fingers was trying to push a bullet into the empty chamber of his revolver, when Septimus burst through the tent flaps.

"Damn, but you're good, kid! I've never seen anyone move so fast. I er ..." Septimus stammered as he saw the blood trickling down Tom's side.

Wincing, Tom looked up at Dyson. The English officer's face was pale and he was panting hard as he stared at the two of them, his eyes wild and confused.

"Who the blazes are you?" Dyson demanded. He pointed his revolver first at Septimus then at Tom, swayed and collapsed in a dead faint, toppling to the ground.

Septimus leaned over Tom and pulled him to his feet. "You're wounded, boyo. We must get out of here!"

Outside there were growls, roars, screams and yells as the battle raged on. Then, they heard raised voices in a language Tom did not understand, coming closer. He tried to reach out to the Flow of Time, but he was now weak and exhausted and could feel nothing there. He began to panic. "I c- can't," he whispered.

"Tom, we must go now!" Septimus said urgently, his face etched with anxiety as he flicked his gaze to the tent flap. Tom tried again, conjuring the clock face in his mind, but he could

85

still not feel the stream of time he needed in order to Walk the three of them back to Neoptolemas' office.

"Sorry, Septimus, I can't do it," was all he could manage to say before gasping in pain. The assegai wound must have been deeper than he first thought, because the pain was getting worse. Reaching down, he felt the blood trickling out of him and it seemed as if his strength was dripping away with it. The world was starting to go dim and distant. Yet, somehow, he knew that he must get them away from here. In his mind he saw the cone shaped mountain of Isandlwana and with his hands, he reached out for the unconscious body of the British officer.

Septimus had picked up the officer's revolver and stepped back to stand between Tom and the door. The tent flap was suddenly yanked to one side and two huge Zulu warriors entered: their bright spear points at the ready. Then, there was the sharp crack of a gunshot and one Zulu reeled back, grasping his shoulder. His fellow roared and advanced on Septimus, who pulled the trigger again. But, this time, there was only the click of an empty revolver. Septimus looked at the useless weapon and then back at the Zulu and shrugged.

The fierce warrior grinned in triumph and swung back his arm ready to throw the assegai.

CHAPTER NINE - IMAGINE THE POSSIBILITIES

As the assegai came forward Tom reached out and grasped Septimus by the shoulder and, with a desperate effort, he Walked all three of them away from the tent. A moment later they appeared on a rocky hillside, the skies still dark and blood red above them. For a few seconds Tom stood on his feet feeling dizzy and nauseous as he looked around at the barren landscape, then he felt himself falling backwards as if into an abyss and he passed out.

When he came to, he was still lying on the rocky slope hidden behind boulders, high up on Isandlwana hill. Slowly, because his head was still spinning, he sat up and looked about him. Down the slope a few yards away he saw the British officer, still unconscious and slumped with his back against a rock, his head lolling on his chest. Now that Tom had a moment to look at him he realised the young man was also wounded. Someone, presumably Septimus, had ministered to him as he had a bandage wrapped round his belly.

Tom tried to stand, but felt a sudden pain in his right side just under his ribs. Glancing down, he saw that he also had bandages around him. He slid back onto the ground, then manoeuvred himself until he could peer through a gap in the boulders at the British camp far below him. Just visible in the growing dusk, scattered points of light revealed where the camp fires were burning themselves out. In their glow he could make out the Zulus moving about. He caught the slight sound of a footstep. Septimus emerged from behind a mound of scrub growing lower on the slope.

"Glad you're back with us, boyo!" he said softly, climbing towards Tom. "I've just been observing the Zulus. How do you feel?"

Tom considered this. His side was painful, but his head was clear and he felt stronger than he had before. "Not bad. Where'd you get the bandages?"

Septimus patted the rucksack, "Emergency supplies; I always carry them. I've daubed you with anaesthetic salve."

"Well thanks, it seems to be working."

"Good, because we must leave soon; it's all over down there," he pointed down at the camp.

Tom could see scores of Zulus milling around, but no British soldiers alive. The ground was littered with their sprawled bodies. History had repeated itself. The Battle of Isandlwana was over. Tom nodded, feeling sad and disturbed by the killing he had seen. It was time to get away from this terrible place. "Well, we have what we came for: we completed our mission!" he said, nodding to where Lieutenant Dyson lay. "Is he going to be ok?"

Before Septimus could answer they heard a shout of laughter.

Startled, Tom turned his head to locate where it was coming from then, disbelievingly, he recognised the voice as Redfeld's.

"Yes," he was saying, "but consider how much more you could have done!" The man stood a little way up the hill behind them, partially concealed by a rock. He appeared to be reading a newspaper.

"What are you doing here?" Septimus hissed.

"Oh, I'm just an observer, this time," Redfeld remarked, folding the newspaper neatly, "I, how do you say it, 'hitched a lift' with you when you Walked back here."

He stared at Tom for a moment then folded up the newspaper, crossing his arms over it in such a way that Tom could see the front page. It was *The Times* and it featured a picture of a ruined city with tanks parked in the street outside a large, domed building; the roof had a big hole in it. The headlines read: WAR IN EUROPE ENDS! Tom's class had learnt about the ending of Second World War in Europe when Germany was defeated. Something struck him as odd about the picture, but he could not quite place it. He glanced back at Redfeld and saw that the man was fixing him with the same intense stare as he had before, in the cafe.

"History, Thomas, it's a fascinating subject don't you think? It teaches us what has gone before. By learning about the past, we can hope to avoid the same mistakes in the future. Indeed, we can build a better future." With these words and a sweep of his arm, he indicated the world at large, "At least, that is what they believe in their world; their *time-bound* world." Redfeld paused and regarded Tom for a moment, then smiled. "But what you need to realise is that for people like us, it is quite different. There exists the possibility for us to change the past to make a better present."

Tom shook his head, "The Professor told me we should not alter the past. What is gone is gone and should not be changed. The Professor ..."

"Thomas, you need to open your mind!" Redfeld shouted.

"Shut up, Redfield, you'll bring the Zulus down on us like a ton of bricks!" said Septimus, looking anxiously around the hillside.

Redfeld shrugged then continued as if the Welshman had not spoken. "The possibilities are endless. The Professor is an old man; he is scared of what we might achieve – people like you and me, Tom. Come, let me show you."

Flinging his arms wide, Redfeld leaned towards Septimus and Tom as if waiting for the unlikely possibility that one of them would offer to hug him. He was not, it transpired waiting for a sign of affection, for a moment later Tom felt himself and the others moving through time. The feeling, however, was odd somehow. He had Walked now a number of times and Septimus had Walked them both, and the sensation had been similar on all those occasions. Now, however, there was something different. It felt awkward; like driving an English car in France - it never quite felt right to be on the right-hand side of the road.

Then, with a jerk, they were back at Isandlwana, still perched high up on the same rocky mountain; still looking down at the same camp. Yet, from the position of the sun and from the calm and order in the camp below them, it was apparently earlier in the day.

Redfeld beckoned the two over to him with a wave. They went and stood on either side of him and he pointed to the plain below. "Remember what happened on this day? The cavalry patrol located the Zulu army over in a long valley that way," the man pointed at the haze, where even now a body of horsemen was moving away from the camp. He then took a pocket watch out of his breast pocket and examined it.

"It won't be long. Now, in your history, the Zulu army effectively surprises the British army here and because the commander does not fortify the camp but elects to fight the Zulus far out on the plain, he is overwhelmed … yes?"

"You are not showing us anything we do not know, Redfeld," Septimus muttered irritably.

"Patience, my good sir; I will show you something quite new. Look over there," he ordered, pointing to the south-east of the camp. A lone horseman in a red coat was galloping toward the tents.

"That is an … associate of mine disguised as an officer from Lord Chelmsford's staff – the general who commands this invasion. His camp is a few miles that way. The general left the camp with half the army earlier today and actually knows nothing, as yet, of the Zulu attack. But my man will pretend to be an officer from Chelmsford: watch now; see what happens."

Down in the camp, the impostor reigned in his horse and saluted an officer standing there. "That is Pulleine – the commander here," Redfeld explained.

Redfeld's man was pointing towards where the Zulus would attack and then at the wagons in the camp. Major Pulleine was now shouting orders to his officers and moments later, Tom could clearly hear the bugles calling and abruptly the camp became a flurry of activity. Wagons were being dragged into a ring and chained together into a *laager*: a wall of wagons that made the vulnerable camp into a fortress. Some soldiers were digging trenches in front of the wagons. Soon the army was assembling together within the confines of the makeshift fortress. Guns and rockets were being pushed into gaps between the companies. Ten minutes after the bugles had sounded Pulleine's army was dug in behind very well protected barricades.

Tom looked at all this in amazement. They watched as, soon afterwards, the Zulus emerged far out on the plain pursuing the retreating cavalry and surging on towards the British camp.

They were met by the lethal volley fire of the superbly trained British riflemen and fell, as before, in their hundreds. But this time, the army was well protected in their fortress. The guns supported the infantry. Everyone had immediately available ammunition. There was no slackening of fire, no collapse of unsupported lines of infantry. Secure in the enclosure, the British slaughtered the Zulus and hardly suffered any losses. It would be recorded as one of the great victories of the British Empire.

Suddenly, Tom realised the enormity of what had just occurred. One message at the right moment had altered history dramatically and enormously. He felt his heart pounding: maybe Redfeld was right. The power was his to use as he could. There really were no limits to what was possible. He glanced round looking for Dyson expecting him to have vanished. The Lieutenant was still there, slumped unconscious against the rock as before. Tom was still trying to work out how that could be, when Septimus swore.

"There's going to be trouble when Professor Neoptolemas finds out about this, for sure," the Welshman said. Tom could see that Septimus was looking, not at the battle below or at Redfeld, but at Tom himself − as if he perhaps suspected the thoughts running through Tom's mind.

"Why should we care?" Redfeld protested. "Look what we just did. Who is he to tell us what to do or how to act? Men such as us!"

Septimus was shaking his head. "Redfeld, look down there. You've just changed history. Who knows what effect saving those fifteen hundred will have?"

"Is that so bad? I have saved lives!" Redfeld pointed out.

"But, you have taken them as well," Septimus responded pointing down at the heaps of black bodies littering the ground. "How many thousands of Zulus died here that did not originally die? What impact does that have on history, on their families, their children?"

Tom had been feeling the thrill of the power Redfeld had demonstrated, but, like a punch to the gut, Septimus' point stunned him. Even from here the stench of blood reached them, mingled with the acrid smell of smoke. Suddenly this was not an example from history, but real. Tom felt suddenly ashamed: he had been dreaming of the power he could have used whilst men had been dying below.

"That's enough, Redfeld. Septimus, let's go home," he said quietly.

Redfeld looked astounded and then a little angry. "What? No! I have shown you what you can achieve. If only you will use your power, this – or something like this – could be accomplished. Why should men like us not rule the worlds, Thomas?"

"Worlds? What worlds?" Tom asked.

"I meant, world," Redfeld replied quickly, but not convincingly. He was hiding something, but before Tom could ask what, Septimus interrupted.

"Hang on, you said, 'could be accomplished'. Do you mean this has not actually occurred?"

"No," Redfeld shook his head, "this was just an example of what could have been. It is not real. I can use my talents to create a hypothetical alternative to reality. It is a useful tool and the knowledge gained can be used in the real timeline."

"So, you have not actually altered anything then?" asked Tom anxiously, wanting to be sure he understood.

Redfeld looked disappointed, but again he shook his head. "No, but we could ... you could if you wanted to," he said and then blinked.

Tom felt the same strange upside down or wrong way up sensation. Then he realised they were back above their version of the battle, with its shattered British camp and triumphant Zulus.

"Have you ... I mean is history...?" Tom stammered.

His lip curling in disgust, Redfeld nodded in answer. "History is safe, the way it occurred before. You and your Professor need not worry." He turned to walk away up the hill then stopped and added quietly, "All I ask, Tom, is that you consider what might have been ..."

Redfeld had barely finished speaking when, just as before in the cafe, a door seemed to open behind him bringing with it a glimpse of the room beyond and then, in a moment, both he and the room had vanished.

Tom raised his eyebrow in query at Septimus, about to ask a question, when he heard a shout of alarm behind him.

Swinging round, he saw five Zulus coming towards them, screaming in anger and gesticulating with their spears as they ran up the hillside. They were about fifty yards away and closing fast.

"Time to leave, I think," Septimus observed and Tom nodded.

Gathering his concentration, one hand cupping the glass ball, he Walked himself and his companions away from Zululand to where, half a world and over a century away, the Professor's study was waiting.

CHAPTER TEN - A VICTORIAN OFFICER

A few moments later, Tom, Septimus and Edward Dyson materialised in a heap on the rug in front of the Professor's desk. Neoptolemas was sipping a cup of tea and in surprise he coughed violently as most of it went down the wrong way. After spluttering for a few moments, he finally recovered and pulling out a handkerchief patted himself dry. Then, he smiled at them from over the top of his glasses and gave a nod of satisfaction.

"Well done, Thomas ...," he began, but then noticed the bloodstained bandage around Tom's waist. His eyes widened in alarm, "But you are hurt – I must have the doctor examine you at once. I see our young officer is hurt as well," he observed as he reached over and rang a bell on his desk. Mr Phelps came in wearing his usual haughty expression, which fell away completely when he saw the injuries. Instantly, he took charge and a few moments later Tom found himself whisked away from the office and upstairs. Here, there were offices filled with files and books and further up still, on a second floor, bedrooms. In one of them, a somewhat overweight man in his fifties, with a florid complexion and red hair, introduced himself as Doctor Makepeace and then promptly ordered Tom to strip and get into bed.

"But, my family, my school – I have a French test. I must get home. Septimus!" he objected to his companion who was standing in the doorway, having helped the Professor's secretary carry the still unconscious Lieutenant Dyson upstairs.

"That wound will need three days before you go anywhere my lad!" the doctor pointed out.

"Besides which, you know how it works, boyo. Once you are well we will whisk you back home earlier today. No one will know you have gone anywhere," Septimus said and helped Tom swing his legs round and then pulled up the sheets.

"The doc here will sort you out and then you must sleep. If you need anything, that phone there will reach Phelps," Septimus instructed, nodding at a rather old fashioned telephone on the bedside table.

Tom gave in and allowed the doctor to clean his wounds then inject him with some local anaesthetic. He then needed half a dozen stitches and a sterile dressing. Soon, the pain was settling and he did feel a little better. The doctor left him and moved on to the other bed where Lieutenant Dyson was lying.

At first, Tom was still wound up and on edge with images of the battlefield rolling around in his head. As the horrors at Isandlwana replayed themselves across his mind he feared he would get no sleep for days. However, he was truly exhausted after the day's activities and only ten minutes later he was fast asleep.

When he awoke, bright sunshine was blazing in through the windows, so he reckoned he must have slept through the night and it was now the following morning. He sat up slowly, wary that he might pull on his wound and pop open the stitches, but he was surprised to find that he had little pain at all. He glanced over at the other bed and jumped in shock as he saw that Edward Dyson was also sitting up in bed staring at him.

"Where am I? And who the blazes are you?" the officer demanded.

"Er ... I think I'd better get the Professor," Tom stammered.

"Professor? Where's my regiment? Is this an army hospital?" Edward glanced around then got out of bed, wincing slightly as his feet found the floor. "I was injured, wasn't I? I remember now. I was fighting in the camp. The Zulus charged. I thought to myself, 'The game's up old chap,' then ..." His face screwed up as if he was trying to focus his mind on the memory. Suddenly his gaze snapped back onto Tom. "You were there; you appeared out of nowhere. Then we were in a tent. After that ... I don't remember anything else."

Dyson slumped back on the bed. Tom picked up the phone and found that it started dialling automatically. A moment later the Professor's secretary answered. "Yes?"

"Erm, is the Professor there?" Tom started to say, but he did not get any further, because there was a loud crash from the other end of the room. Edward had leapt out of bed and come charging towards him, knocking the bedside table flying. He grabbed the phone from Tom and stared at it suspiciously.

"What is this? Is this some kind of weapon? Where am I? Am I a prisoner? You certainly are not the Zulus. Are you French or Prussian, maybe? Are you helping the Zulus? Are you trying to build your own empire inside ours? Bloody cheek!" he shook Tom by the shoulder, "Answer me, boy!" The officer shouted, getting angrier by the moment.

"It's difficult to explain, Mr Dyson ... I think ... the Professor ..." Tom stammered, both terrified by the wild look in the other's eyes and amazed by Dyson's apparent recovery as though his wound had miraculously healed overnight.

"Who is this Professor? Tell me now: I want answers!" He shook Tom again, rattling his teeth.

"I am the Professor," said a voice from the doorway, "and if you will release Master Oakley, I will give you answers. I am afraid to say, though, that you will find them hard to accept." Something in the Professor's voice gave him authority.

Edward glared at the old man for a moment and then relaxed. "Very well, sir. That is all I ask." His tone was respectful and releasing Tom, he almost stood to attention. Tom recalled learning at school how the Victorians had been raised to respect their elders. *'How times have changed,'* Mr Morgan had remarked wryly at the time. Clearly, Edward Dyson was what Mr Morgan would have described as a 'good' Victorian.

"Good man. This way to my office then ..." Neoptolemas said, pointing the way and, after one more glance at Tom, the Lieutenant followed the Professor out of the room and on down the corridor.

After they had gone, Tom slept most of the rest of the day. The doctor visited him a number of times and changed the dressings. As the day wore on, he became aware that the pain in his side was becoming much easier and that although he felt stiff he could get out of bed and walk as far as the bathroom, along the corridor.

The next morning he woke early and found that all the pain had gone and he was famished. After he had demolished a big breakfast of kippers followed by bacon and eggs, brought to him on a tray, the doctor visited and Tom expressed his surprise at how quickly he was getting better.

Doctor Makepeace nodded, removed the dressing and smiled with satisfaction. Looking down, Tom saw that there was only a tiny scar where a little more than twenty-four hours before there had been a huge gash. "How... when ... wow... I mean, cool!" was all he could manage to say.

"I have certain powers to manipulate time the same as you do – but in my case, I have found a way to accelerate the healing process considerably. Umm ... yes. I think you can go home today: you have done well," the doctor declared.

"Thanks, Doc!" Tom said, then he leapt out of bed gave a whoop of delight and, after getting dressed, went downstairs. He made his way to the Professor's office and found Neoptolemas reading a book. Without looking up, the old man pointed at the seat in front of him.

Tom sat. He turned his head sideways to read the title on the book's spine. It was entitled *Artefacts from History and Legend*. The old man certainly reads a lot, he thought to himself.

After a minute, the Professor scribbled a word in a notepad on the desk, carefully marked his place in the book with a folded envelope and finally smiled up at Tom.

"How are you, Thomas?" he asked.

"Fine, I'm fine. The doc says I can go home today. That is good: thought I would have to stay longer."

"Yes, that is good indeed. But in fact, you will be going home two days ago. Today is Monday and you are already at school. Or you will be once you return to Saturday."

Tom nodded. As crazy as it sounded he was actually starting to understand all of this. "Professor, how is Lieutenant Dyson?"

The old man took his glasses from where they were perched on his nose and gave them a polish on a handkerchief before answering. "The Lieutenant is recovering well from his ordeal at Isandlwana and is resting in the lounge. His body is fine, but I am concerned about his mind. For him the battle was only the day before yesterday, not more than a century ago.

"For me the battle was only the day before yesterday too, Professor," Tom observed.

"Perhaps, but we have wrenched this man out of his world. All that he knew is gone. One moment he was fighting in his regiment alongside his men and fellow officers and the next he is in another century, in an England very different from that which he left when he got on the boat to go to Africa. He might take a while to adjust. It is quite possible he will never adjust."

Something in the old man's voice and the distant look in his eyes made Tom ask a question which popped unbidden into his mind. "This has happened before, hasn't it?"

The Professor gave him a sharp look, as if reappraising him, and then nodded. "What you must realise, Tom, is that what we do is dangerous. More than that: it is, in a way, unnatural. Time flows at a set rate. Always has and always will. Men are born for the time they are in. Not everyone adapts to moving outside their years as well as you and your companion Septimus have done. Sometimes the experience is not a good one. Sometimes they have gone mad ..."

Tom thought about that for a moment. He imagined suddenly waking up to an alien world; all the people he had known and loved gone to dust. His surroundings full of weird and wonderful contraptions – frightening until you knew what they were. Yes, he could begin to imagine the horror. He became aware that Septimus was standing next to him, looking down at him with that half smile as if he knew what Tom was thinking.

"Time for you to go home for a few days, boyo."

With a nod Tom got to his feet and with a brief wave at the Professor, he followed Septimus out into the corridor.

They Walked back the forty-eight hours or so and the short hop home to Tom's house and bedroom, timing the arrival to be a few minutes after he had first gone to see the Professor.

His mother was still out shopping; his father still ensconced in front of the TV. To Tom this state of affairs was beginning to feel quite normal.

Septimus patted Tom on the shoulder. "Nice work, Tom. I'm sure you were scared; indeed you would be dumb not to be with fifteen thousand Zulus after your blood. But you did not let it stop you. You got the job done and done well. See you soon." Then, with a wave of his hand, he was gone.

Tom stood for a few moments, taking it all in. He was in his bedroom only moments after he had first left it to travel to talk to the Professor. It seemed difficult to believe that he had been to London, gone back over a century and been involved in a famous battle. He could well understand that men might go mad tampering with time. What he did know was that, despite a day and a half's sleep, he was still knackered. He collapsed on his bed and slept most of that day and the following day – a Sunday – surfacing only to eat food. At one point he overheard his dad saying to his mum with a chuckle, "Well, he's a practically a teenager now, dear; I've heard they sleep all day. He's just getting in some practice!"

On Monday morning, Tom staggered out of bed and into his uniform and so to school. He looked at his timetable. First period – double French. Now, that rang a bell. What was it? Was he supposed to remember something?

Later that same day, Tom was aware that his French teacher was hovering in front of his desk, waving a piece of paper at him. The entire class was looking on as well, prepared for whatever entertainment might follow. Kyle seemed to be taking particular notice and was leaning back in his chair, his hand behind his head and a broad smile on his face. He loved it whenever Tom fell foul of the teachers – which did seem to be happening a lot lately.

"Two out of twenty! Thomas Oakley, did you actually study *any* of this?"

"Erm ... I did, I mean I forgot ... sorry ..." Tom stammered. Now he knew what had been niggling him: he had a French test and was supposed to have studied for it that weekend - the weekend he had spent in Zululand or recovering at the Hourglass Institute and then later at home. His teacher was glaring at him and the glare seemed to go on forever. It was interrupted by a knock at the door; then the door was opened by the school secretary.

"Well?" snapped Mrs Spencer, "What is it now, Mrs Brown?"

"Message for Thomas Oakley: a family friend is here. Can he come to reception?"

Mrs Spencer looked about to say no, but after a moment she nodded curtly towards the door. "Go on then, Oakley. But next Monday I will test you again and you had better know the vocabulary by then, or I'll have your hide: that is not an idle threat!"

"Yes, Mrs Spencer ..." Tom replied and hurried towards the door before the French teacher changed her mind.

"Going for your counselling, are you, Oakley?" Rogers whispered after him, but loud enough for most of the class to hear and snigger at.

His ears burning, he followed the secretary along the main corridor and then across a courtyard to the school offices. As they entered, Tom stopped suddenly. There, sitting on a chair looking at an old school book with the title, *History of Empire 1850 to 1950* and shaking his head slightly, was Lieutenant

Edward Dyson. He was wearing his bright scarlet jacket and army trousers and looked here and now, not so much a Victorian officer, as a historical re-enactor preparing to refight a battle.

Tom stepped forward, aware that Mrs Brown was glaring at them both, her face wearing an expression that seemed to ask if he was related to the weirdo in the uniform. Tom stared at her, forcing her to look away. With that, she walked out of the office and left them alone.

As soon as he was sure she was not listening at the door Tom went over to Edward and whispered under his breath. "What are you doing here?"

"Right now, I am reading about what happened after we left the battle," Edward said, not looking up but pointing at the history book. "It says here that no one from my battalion survived. Poor old Colville and Melville tried to save the flag, but were caught and killed in the Buffalo River. In fact, we all died there."

Now he did look up at Tom, his face white and strained. "I *should* have died there, instead of being whisked away by some hocus pocus. Why did you do it?"

Tom was not sure how to answer that. He had not thought much about what Edward would say, but he supposed he had expected some degree of gratitude. "Did you want to die? Septimus and I saved you. How can that be wrong?"

The history book snapped shut. "It was my place and my time to die. I should be safely hidden away in this kind of book – my body a thousand miles away, covered in stones and soil," he said with tension in his voice. "Instead, I find myself in a place I don't know and in a strange land!"

"It's England!" Tom said.

103

"Is it? It's not much like my England!" Edward replied.

Tom put his hand on Edward's shoulder to try and calm him down. "Come along, Mr Dyson. Let me show you something. I think it will make you feel better."

They walked out of the school and along the path towards the playing fields. They passed first a football and then a rugby pitch. Then they came across a class of boys playing cricket. For a local comprehensive school, Tom's was very traditional in some ways and the boys wore whites. Edward stopped and looked, for once, more relaxed. Beside the cricket pitch was an old oak tree and under it a bench. The two of them sat down and watched the game for a while.

Edward turned his head to take in the surroundings. The cricket pitch stuck out between a wood and a park, so there was not much of the modern city in view. Tom realised there was nothing here to show you were in the twenty-first century, save the distant noises of traffic.

"It could almost be England ..." Edward muttered, under his breath.

"It is England, Mr Dyson ..." Tom replied, but was interrupted by the man holding up a hand.

"Please, Tom, call me Edward. After all that we have been through, I think we can dispense with formalities." Tom was surprised, but smiled at that. Perhaps he was starting to get through, at last.

"Right then ... Edward. As I was saying, it is England. We still play cricket, football and rugby. Do you know we won the Ashes last summer ...?"

"What are the Ashes?" Edward asked looking puzzled. Tom thought for a moment and squinted to recall a date mentioned in a TV report. His eyes widened slightly.

"My God – it must have been after your time. But, have I got a treat for you! It's almost the end of the day. My parents won't be in for a couple of hours and my sister is at Brownies. Come on: let's go home. My dad has got the entire series on DVD ..."

"What is DVD?" asked Edward.

"Come on, I'll show you. By the way, how on earth did you find me?" Tom asked as he led the man behind the oak tree and then, with a pop, they were gone.

Several hours later, at the Professor's office, Tom was sitting drinking coke and explaining what had gone on that day at his school.

"Well, I don't know what you did or what you showed him, but our Mr Dyson does seem calmer," the Professor said.

"It was not me really, sir. Edward seems in his head, so to speak, to have already got used to the reason we rescued him. He knows now that he is a Walker, it's just that he has difficulty accepting it ... in his – well, I suppose you would say, in his heart."

"And you say he used his powers without training to locate you and then to travel to you?"

"Yes, that's right. He said he could sense where I was. Says he knew just where to find me. He's a bit vague on what happened next, but he said he thought about coming to see me and the next minute he was outside my school. Don't you think that this is amazing, sir? He says he just thought about it and he Walked to where I was!"

"Most extraordinary! This means we were right to rescue him. He is clearly one of us. Somehow he can sense other Walkers. That is a very useful talent he has, Tom: very useful indeed."

"Like a dog following a scent?" Tom suggested.

The Professor nodded. "I suppose so, yes," he looked thoughtful as if considering how he might use this new found skill. A few moments later he picked up a fob watch from the desk, looked at the time and gave the winder a few twists before placing it back down again. Then he looked up at Tom.

"Well, if you feel sufficiently recovered," he said, "I think we should rescue Mary Brown from the Great Fire. What do you say to that?" the Professor asked.

Tom thought about the trip to Isandlwana. He had been injured there and he might have been killed. The horror of the battle still haunted him. Adventures sounded fine in theory, but when a dozen Zulu warriors were charging you with razor sharp assegais, the reality was much less pleasant. He had been terrified and if he was honest with himself he had hoped that the single trip would be all that was needed. But, he simply could not leave Mary to burn in the heat of that fire. He had felt that heat. He had been Mary; had known her terror. No, he must go and fetch her.

"I'm ready, Professor," he said quietly.

CHAPTER ELEVEN - LONDON'S BURNING

Stars sparkled in the ink-coloured sky, whilst in the houses around them few candle lights were visible and all was in shadow. Late on that warm night, Septimus and Tom stood in Pudding Lane opposite the front of the bakery, surrounded by half-timbered buildings that rose up all around them: buildings made of wood, twig and thatch, ready for the spark that would kindle disaster. Smoke was already climbing out of a downstairs window and the glow from the beginnings of an inferno cast an orange light into the street: the inferno that would destroy the heart of the medieval city of London and leave it in ashes.

"The family slept upstairs. Their maid was Mary Brown. She probably had her own room, but we have no record of where that is," Septimus was explaining.

"Only Mary died, right?" Tom said.

"Indeed," replied Septimus.

"So the others escaped, right?"

"Yes," answered Septimus, "they could not come down the stairs, so they went out via a high window to the rooftops behind. For some reason, Mary did not. Nothing survived the inferno so they found no body. And stop saying right all the time, it's annoying."

"Right ... I mean sorry! The point is that they escaped from the top floor. So, we need to get up there," Tom suggested.

"Yes, but not before the fire is spotted by the occupants; we don't want to run into them. We might bungle it and the whole family die. We could wipe out hundreds of descendants in one step."

Tom thought of the idea of his own family being swept into oblivion by something changing history so that they never existed. He shivered. The idea was worse, somehow, than living but then being killed. At least that way someone would remember you. "Seems anything we do could mess things up big time," he commented.

Septimus appeared to ponder this for a moment whilst nodding his head. Then he shrugged. "Not anything. Time is unpredictable. Say we went back in time and prevented Edison being born ..."

Tom knew about him. He was an American who invented the light bulb. They had read about him in a school project; "The light bulb guy?"

"That's the man. Well, if he had not existed, any of a dozen men around the world would have developed the same device or something very similar within a decade. The times were right and science had advanced to the point that it was inevitable."

"Well, from what you are saying then, none of us is important. So it would not matter if we did accidentally wipe out this family and all their descendants," said Tom, pointing out a flaw in Septimus' thinking.

"No, that is not what I am saying. What I meant was that history is like a great river surging along. Its force and power is irresistible. Mankind would always have invented fire, learned to write, made machines and explored his world. Nothing could have prevented those things. But even so, sometimes everything hinges on what one person, man or woman, does ..."

Their conversation was interrupted by a shout of alarm from the building they were watching. The baker's apprentice had spotted the fire and was rushing upstairs to raise the family.

"But right now, everything hinges on what you and I do in the next few moments," Septimus observed.

Tom nodded and started forward, gathering his energy for moving them about fifteen feet up and across. Just as he was about to do so, Septimus grasped his shoulder and pointed to a window at one end of the top floor. The frightened face of a young woman had appeared at it. For a brief moment, she looked into Tom's eyes and then turned away and disappeared into the building. Did he hear a male voice calling her name: calling "Mary"? Fleetingly Tom recalled the dream: now was the moment.

"Got it, mate, right let's go!" Tom grasped Septimus' hand and Walked them both upwards and forwards. In his mind, he passed through the raging flames that engulfed the ground floor and up to the first floor. There, he and Septimus appeared at the end of the landing. Tom heard voices and turned to see a family group standing facing away from him at the far end. He spun round looking for a hiding place, but then jerked backwards as his companion tugged him by his collar into a room at the front of the house.

"Hush, we must not be found," Septimus whispered, holding his finger to his lips, "at least, not yet."

Tom looked about him; they were apparently in the baker's bedroom. There was a large low bed in the room with a cot at its foot, but otherwise it was pretty bare and Spartan; not even a rug on the bare floorboards. He thought back to his own room full of books, games, clothes and junk and was amazed at how little these folk had.

They heard a clattering on the wooden landing as the family came towards them, then halted at the top of the stairs leading down to the ground floor.

"What do we do?" A woman's voice; frightened. "We can't get out. We will all be burned!"

There was the sound of children crying. They were terrified. No wonder, thought Tom – he was too. Then, a young man's voice shouted out.

"Quick, out the back of my room!" and there were more running footsteps as the family moved away, searching for an escape route.

"Right, come on!" Septimus ordered. They opened the door and went back out onto the landing. At the top of the stairs in the rear wall was a door leading into another room. From it, they could hear the voices of the family. Moving quickly to the door and peeking round it, they could see the children being passed up to a young man who was outside the window, balancing on the roof of the next house in the row. Only then did Tom recall that in his dream Mary had called the young man Jack. The baker and his wife moved past Jack and up onto the roof. As soon as they were safe, he came back to the window and was now encouraging Mary to join him. She stepped forward, but then appeared to lose her nerve and backed away from the window.

At that moment, fire surged up the stairs towards the two Walkers. Septimus cried out, then stumbled and fell hard onto the wooden floor, pulling Tom with him. Weakened by the fire from below, the wooden landing collapsed and they both fell through the hole.

Tom managed to catch hold of a ceiling beam as he fell, leaving him dangling down into the room below. Septimus landed with a crash on top of the baker's table in the middle of the room on the ground floor. Despite the inferno all around it the table was as yet intact. It was, however, smouldering.

"Septimus!" Tom yelled, but his friend did not respond and appeared to be out cold on the table below. The flames advanced on them both from all sides. Tom tried to Walk, but could not concentrate enough to focus on the Flow of Time. With a growing sense of despair, he felt the heat rise. His hair crackled and his shoes started to smoulder. Below him, one leg of the baker's table caught fire. The table creaked then, with a snap, the leg gave way and the whole thing collapsed, throwing Septimus' limp form onto the floor.

There was another roar and from the ends of the room two huge waves of fire swept towards them; at any moment it would surround them. This was it, Tom thought. Who would have reckoned he would die in the Great Fire of London? He braced himself, the muscles in his arm screaming at him to let go of the beam.

"STOP!" yelled a female voice from beside him.

What happened next, Tom would not have believed possible, had he not been hanging there waiting to be incinerated. It was as if someone had pressed the pause on a DVD: the banks of flame just froze. From the roaring further back, it seemed this effect was very local but, for a moment at least, they had a reprieve. What, Tom asked himself, had stopped the flames in that extraordinary way? He looked round and saw that right next to him, kneeling on the landing and peering down through the gap, was Mary Brown. Her face wore an expression of intense concentration. Still gritting her teeth, she slowly turned her head and looked into his eyes.

"Cannot hold it ... much longer," she finally said, sweat running down her face.

Tom nodded. Explanations could wait until later. So, hanging on with one hand he reached down and pulled the long iron chain out of his belt and threw the end of it to Mary, who caught it and then stared down at him.

Tom yelled, "Hold this a mo!" and letting go of the beam he dropped down into the room below. The chain had enough slack so Mary could hold one end; the other end with its globe of water was still tucked in Tom's belt. He felt the searing heat from the wall of flame, halted in its tracks, but beginning to waver. Bending down he grabbed Septimus by the lapel then reached out to the Flow of Time, relieved to feel its presence once again. Just then, Mary, overcome by fumes, gave a grunt and fainted to the floor, the chain still clutched in her hands. At the same moment, the fire surged forward once more, reaching the table, which now erupted into flame.

As Tom pulled all three of them away, the landing above them collapsed and showered the ground with burning rubble. In the nick of time they had gone from the seventeenth century, forward three hundred and fifty years, away from the Great Fire and into the present day.

Tom materialised, smoking and coughing and with his clothes smouldering, onto the floor of Neoptolemas' office. The old man was as usual sitting behind his desk writing notes on a sheet of paper and was, yet again, taken by surprise. He dropped his pen.

"Good grief, you almost gave me a heart attack!" he said in a faint voice, whilst patting his chest, "... again!"

"Sorry sir!" Tom managed, before slumping down into the chair opposite the Professor. It took him a moment to catch his breath and before he did, the old man was speaking again. "Not to worry: no harm done – I think," he said, still patting his chest. "I will have to work out the best spot for you to return to, so you don't give an old man kittens every time!"

The Professor stood and walked around the desk. "Well now, I see we have our second guest," he observed, looking down at Septimus and Mary, who were both unconscious on the floor. Mary still held the other end of the chain. The Professor reached forward on his desk and picked up the small bell, which he rang. A moment later, Mr Phelps appeared and immediately set about having the pair moved to rooms above and the doctor called.

By the time they had gone, Tom was beginning to recover and at the Professor's insistence, was sipping some sweet tea that Phelps had brought in. "So, how is Edward?" Tom asked when the cup was empty.

"More settled, although also more thoughtful. Once he has time to get used to the idea a little, I think he will adapt to our world and who and what he is. For now, he is spending a lot of time in our library. It transpired that he read history at Oxford before joining the army. I think the idea of studying his own time and the years since as if it was a history lesson is helping him cope with the transition. Victorians were, in many ways, rational and open to progress and ideas beyond their experience. It was the age of the Industrial Revolution; they had vision far beyond that of their ancestors ..."

He was interrupted by Mr Phelps, who came to say that Septimus was conscious and insisting he did not need a doctor.

A moment later, Septimus himself walked in. He crossed to Tom and patted him on the shoulder.

"Well done, boyo – you saved my bacon. So then, are you beginning to like this life, eh?"

Tom grimaced at that. "Actually, it was Mary who saved both our bacon.

"It was?" Septimus' eyebrows shot up to his hair line, "How?"

"I'll tell you later. Look, Septimus, I'm only doing this to rescue these three people, because I know what they felt in those final moments and no one deserves that kind of fear. But all this is dangerous and what is more, my mates think I'm mad. My teachers are giving me bad reports and my parents keep taking me to doctors. Right now, I think I would like to be done with it all. I will wait until I have finished the job and then we'll see."

Septimus and Neoptolemas exchanged a meaningful, but silent glance and Septimus cleared his throat.

"Right then, no time like the present: fancy a trip to the 1940s, Tom?"

CHAPTER TWELVE - *EMPRESS OF INDIA*

|| "This time it's going to be rather difficult," the Professor
said.

Septimus, Tom and the old man were still sitting in the
Professor's study. A pot of tea and a stand of cream cakes were
on the desk, next to a map of the eastern Mediterranean.

Bending over and peering at the map, Tom could see Italy,
Greece and its islands, Turkey and Cyprus, along with the
coasts of Egypt and the Holy Land. On the map, the Professor
had drawn a blue pencilled line leading out of a port marked
Alexandria on the coast of Egypt and ending in an X on the
map. A second line in red emerged from Taranto – an Italian
port - and zigzagged around a number of Greek islands before
ending up at the same point.

On the table were two books. He knew that they were the
logbooks of HMS *Paladin* – a British destroyer from the Second
World War - and U-356, a German submarine or U-boat. The
books had been scooped up by the boarding party that had
tried to capture the U-boat, before it sank. There were also a
number of papers and faded documents from the war years.

The Professor pointed at the log books. "These give us a
good account of the stalking and locating of the U-boat and its
eventual destruction. The co-ordinates we have are accurate
enough as is the precise time of the boarding operation.
However," he emphasised the point by tapping the Royal Navy
book twice, "the coordinates only enable us to be accurate to
within a few hundred yards or so. That's potentially quite a

distance at sea. I trust you two boys don't want to be dumped down in the water!"

Septimus winked at Tom and then grinned. The Professor sighed at the younger man and went on. "Furthermore, the U-boat log becomes very confused after the British started attacking her with depth charges and the account from *HMS Paladin* is equally vague, so we really don't know precisely where U-356 was in relation to it. That's going to make Walking on board her extremely difficult for you two."

Tom nodded. At Isandlwana he had a precise location to work from in the present day. That made Walking back to the battle and keeping his bearings quite easy. Likewise, with the Great Fire, maps existed of old London; Pudding Lane was a recognisable landmark, as was the bakery. There was even a monument in modern day London to mark the spot where the fire started. Had there been some error, it would have been easy to adjust when they arrived. But, with this last rescue, it was not so easy. They would appear in the middle of the sea if they had no fixed point to work from.

"How about a boat or a plane?" Septimus asked the old man. "We take a boat with us or Walk a plane back. Then we can locate the U-boat and board her ..."

"While the Royal Navy are boarding her? Without any intervention on their part or the Germans'?" the Professor pointed out.

"Ah; you're right, I guess, besides, pulling a plane or boat through time would take a lot of strength. Even Tommy boy might struggle," Septimus allowed.

"How about another submarine?" Tom suggested. The two men looked at him.

"Our agency might have some assets and influence, but they don't include access to a submarine," replied Neoptolemas after a moment. Tom sighed and slumped back in his chair. Then, he noticed a small pile of red-coloured glass beads on the table. Reaching forward, he picked one up: it was quite heavy. Curious, he held it up.

"Sir, what is this?" he asked.

The old man looked at the bead. "It's a tracker," explained the Professor.

"What's that?"

"It gives off a strong temporal signal that we can trace, using a kind of radar we have downstairs in the basement. We even have a portable version - about the size of a mobile phone - with shorter range. Each signal can be used to assist Walking to a precise location and a given time because the signal decays at a certain rate. That knowledge can be used to calculate the time co-ordinates. It's like a GPS transponder, except it works across time."

"Clever stuff your boffins come up with, boyo. But I can't see how that helps us now − given that we don't have one of them there trinkets on the U-356," Septimus observed, and the Professor had to agree.

The three of them were silent for a while. Tom studied the map of the Mediterranean. The old man was flipping through the *Paladin's* log. Septimus picked up a few other papers and photos amongst the pile on the Professor's desk. Idly he glanced though them. After a few minutes he suddenly sat up straight and stared at the map, then back at the sheet in his hand then slowly glanced up at his companions, smiling.

"Maybe we can't stretch to a submarine, but it gives me an idea. Tommy, how good a sailor are you?"

The boy looked confused. "What are you getting at?" he asked.

Septimus pointed at the line on the map showing the route of the German U-boat. Then, picking up a pen, he added another line. The end of it coincided with the point where the U-boat was sunk and where the *Paladin* found her. The other end of the line emerged from a small island south of Scilly – almost a dot in the sea. Tom leant forward to read the name: Malta.

"This paper is a log from the *Empress of India*. That was a merchant vessel that plied the lanes between Malta and Alexandria. It brought food and supplies into the Island of Malta during the years from 1940 to 1943, when that island was under siege by the German and Italian air forces."

"A heroic battle," mused Professor Neoptolemas. "The entire population of Malta was awarded the George Cross collectively for their bravery you know. Indeed there was a story..."

Septimus interrupted him, "Yes, yes, very interesting I'm sure, but we are getting away from the point."

"Just what is the point, Septimus?" Tom asked in a tired voice. He had a headache and wanted a rest.

"The point is that we have been looking at this from the perspective of the *Paladin* or the U-boat, but there was a third vessel present during all of this," Septimus observed, throwing a black and white photograph across the table towards the old man. The Professor picked it up and looked at it.

"The *Empress of India*?" the Professor suggested.

"Indeed, what do you think the U-boat was stalking when it was detected by the *Paladin* and its flotilla? The destroyers were sailing east for Alexandria. The *Empress* had left Valletta three days earlier. U-356 spotted it and closed in for the kill. It was about to torpedo the merchant vessel when the *Paladin* arrived and launched an attack on the sub. According to this log, the *Empress* was advised to stay with the flotilla in case there were other U-boats around, so it was only a few hundred yards away at the time the U-boat went down."

"How does that help us? We don't know any better the coordinates of that location," Tom pointed out.

"We don't need to, Tommy boy, if we can get on board the *Empress* before she leaves port – and I have here the departure time and date – well, then we know it will take us to the fateful encounter. Look, I even have a photo." The Welshman reached over, taking the photo back from the old man and then holding it up to show the boy: a faded and damaged image of a large ship with two funnels.

"If we can get on board at the right moment and locate a safe point on the ship, we can leave one of the Professor's trackers there. We can then Walk back and forth from here to there until the time comes to take action. All we then need is swimming equipment and breathing apparatus in case we are underwater during the rescue. Which reminds me, boyo, can you swim?"

Tom nodded and explained how he had picked up some experience with scuba equipment when the family were on a package holiday in Kenya a couple of years before. His father had approached the new hobby with enthusiasm, taking advantage of the lessons offered as part of the package by their hotel. Tom and his dad had dived off the Kenyan coast and visited the coral reef, whilst his mum and sister had chosen to explore the sea in the more sedate, if rather touristy option of a glass-bottomed boat.

"Excellent!" Septimus beamed.

The Professor's agency might not run to a submarine, but it appeared that it could stretch to scuba diving equipment. A few hours later, as Tom put on his wetsuit and examined the breathing equipment to remind himself how to use it, he thought of that holiday and of his family. Life had seemed so normal then, with no hint of danger. The most adventure they'd had was avoiding a jellyfish and sunburn. He wondered again about returning to that life of normality, of having Professor Neoptolemas remove these strange talents in his genes. Tom had promised to help rescue the three Walkers. Now there was just one left and then the job was done. What would he decide to do? He tugged on his wetsuit, a thoughtful look on his face.

Using the Professor's map to focus in on a small part of the world, Tom reached out and felt the now familiar link with the Flow of Time. For a few moments he let its power and strength flood through him. The world had become a confusing and changeable place lately. Something about the eternal nature of the time stream made him feel comfortable. Whatever happened to him, to any of these other Walkers, indeed to his world, time was still there. But, he now needed to concentrate on the job at hand.

Tom reached out a rubber-coated arm to his companion and with an ease that came from a certain degree of practice, he Walked them both away from London in the early twenty-first century, across Europe and back through time to the dark years of the Second World War. There, in the waters of the Mediterranean, he focused in on a spot on a map: a dot which represented the rocky, but beautiful island of Malta. They emerged into a warm autumnal day to find they were several feet above the waters of Valetta harbour.

Plunging into the sea when, moments before, he had been standing on the floor of the office in London, disoriented Tom and it took him a few moments to surface and locate his companion. He found him floating on his back a few yards away. As he swam up to him, Septimus opened his eyes and softly sang, "*Oh, I do like to be beside the seaside ...*"

Tom frowned at him. "Don't you ever take anything seriously?"

"Not if there's any other way!" the Welshman replied with a wink. Then, he swung himself round, so he was treading water like Tom and asked, "Can you see any sign of the *Empress*?"

Tom paddled round in a complete circle scanning the harbour. At first he could see nothing, but on a second scan across the waves he made out a dirty smudge in the distance. As he peered in that direction, a wave took him upwards for a few seconds and now he caught a glimpse of sunlight reflecting off metal. It was a warship and next to it, huddled like a chick near a hen, was the smaller form of a merchantman. It certainly looked like the picture in the Professor's study.

"I think so," he pointed.

Septimus gazed that way and squinted, "Maybe half a mile, perhaps more. It will take a while to swim it. Let's get on with it."

Pulling up his mouthpiece, Tom got it comfortable in his mouth and tried a few breaths to test it. He then pulled the mask down to shield his eyes. The two of them submerged and swam in the direction of the *Empress of India,* wondering what would happen if they were spotted. Two young men in frog suits swimming around Valetta harbour in the middle of a war would certainly be thrown in jail, thought Tom - if they weren't shot first!

They approached the ship on the side facing the harbour, furthest from the quay, and saw that the merchantman had rope netting hanging over side. It dangled almost into the sea and Tom and Septimus, cautiously surfacing and expecting to hear shouts at any moment, clambered up it until they could peer over the side. A dozen burly deckhands were heaving crates about on the deck and tying them down. None was looking in the Walkers' direction. After a while, the crew went forward to fetch more crates from the quay.

"Now," hissed Septimus, rolling over the side and stealthily approaching one of the crates. Using the knife at his waist, he prized open the lid and looked inside. Smiling, he beckoned Tom forward.

Tom peered inside, puzzled to find it was empty. "Why are they loading empty crates?"

"Malta is being blockaded – effectively it is under siege. It needs food and supplies and above all, fuel and ammunition. It has little to send in exchange. Crates come here full and go back empty, to be refilled," Septimus explained.

Tom nodded.

"Right then, in we go," Septimus said. Stripping off his gas cylinder he lowered it into the crate then climbed in after it, squeezing himself into a corner. Tom followed suit, pulling the lid in to place behind him.

"Ok, here we are then. I'll just drop the tracker," Septimus said and Tom heard a slight tinkle as the bead hit the bottom of the crate, "Right that's it. Let's go."

Tom felt a sense of relief as he Walked them both forward to Neoptolemas' office. When they arrived, Septimus held onto Tom and told him not to move. He then had Mr Phelps measure a square within which they were sitting. Only then was Tom allowed to move. He watched as Mr Phelps, using a marker pen, drew the square onto a tablecloth.

"So, when we go back, we sit within the confines of that square and we know that we will be inside that crate," Septimus explained.

"So, what do we do now?" asked Tom.

Septimus looked at his watch and then pulled out a device similar to a GPS handheld unit. Tom could see a time counter on it and various coordinates and numbers he did not understand. Septimus studied it and looked thoughtful for a moment. Then he glanced at Tom and the Professor. "As we are using a tracker and we need a precise fix in terms of location time, the safest way is to let time pass here and in the past. We know from the log book that it was about three days after the *Empress* left port that the U-boat was attacked in the vicinity of the merchant ship when *HMS Paladin* arrived. We have the precise time in fact, programmed into this gizmo," he waved the electronic device around. "So, I think we should meet again here a little time prior to that event. Say you come here after school on Thursday, Tommy – is that ok?"

Tom nodded. That was easy enough given that his parents were not in till after six and his sister often went to see friends after school.

"In that case, we will call it a day..." the Professor started to say, but was interrupted by a gut-wrenching scream from upstairs. There was a crashing of furniture and then a loud bang followed by the sound of something made of glass smashing. The screaming continued.

The Professor, Septimus and Tom ran out of the door and up the stairs.

Suddenly, the screaming got closer: it was coming towards them; it was coming down the stairs!

CHAPTER THIRTEEN - MARY

"Witches and warlocks, you'll go to the Devil, you will. I'm a good, God-fearing girl: let me go, you demons!" screeched a girl's voice. There was another crash, then a thud of something blunt hitting something hard. Tom, who was bringing up the rear of the three, was startled to find Septimus tumbling back towards him, blood trickling down his face.

Then, like a blur, the girl from the fire — the housemaid Mary Brown — was past him and hurtling on, down the stairs. Tom spun round and tried to grab her, but she was already going too fast and his arms closed on air. He staggered after her. When he reached the hall, he saw Mary running out of the front door, still screaming about witches and the Devil. He followed her, but by the time he had got to the door and gone out onto the pavement, the girl had vanished from sight. He looked both ways along the road, but she was nowhere to be seen.

"Damn it!" he cursed and stamped the pavement in frustration. Septimus and the Professor now arrived at his side, the Welshman holding a hand to his face. They looked at Tom expectantly. He shook his head, "Sorry, Prof, but she's gone!"

"A young lady from the seventeenth century, as yet untrained and with no idea what world she has come to, is loose in London?" the Professor said grimly.

"Yup, it's what you might call a cock-up!" Septimus said, dabbing a handkerchief with an hourglass symbol on the corner to his wound in an attempt to stem the flow of blood.

"You think?" observed Tom, wryly.

"How do we find her?" Septimus asked.

"I can help with that, if you will let me assist."

Turning round they saw Edward Dyson, looking somewhat less out of place dressed as he now was in normal, twenty-first century clothes, rather than his regimental red coat.

"How can you?" asked Septimus, but Tom knew how.

"Because, he can sense her: he can sense Walkers, can't you Edward? That's how you found me at my school."

Edward seemed to consider this for a moment before slowly nodding. "Back before I left England ... my England that is: before I joined the army in fact, I realised that I was different from my friends. It started with games of hide and seek. I was not very good at hiding, but I was a natural at the seeking part. Or at least, seeking one particular friend and one of my sisters ..." He paused for a minute and then realised they were all staring at him.

"I'm sorry, but I was just thinking that I last saw my sister and friend at their wedding. I was the best man, you know. That was the summer of '78 just before I sailed to South Africa. The memory is quite fresh. Yet it happened more than a century ago. It's still taking a little getting used to," he explained in a sad voice.

"Your sister and your friend," the Professor prompted, "you are saying that back in 1878 you used to find them easily when playing hide and seek?"

Edward blinked and nodded. "Yes indeed, always them and always very quickly. Made Dotty ... erm ... Dorothy, quite mad ... oddly though, not anyone else," he smiled, his eyes distant. "But it carried on later at school, at Oxford and then in the army. Once or twice I'd spot an ambush because I could sense someone was hiding nearby."

"I think, young man, that those people you were able to spot might have been Walkers – temporopaths – too; or at least they had some hint of talent," the Professor suggested.

Septimus coughed and said, "Which is fascinating stuff really. But don't you think we should try and find the girl?"

The Professor nodded and they all turned back to Edward, who closed his eyes for a moment and then suddenly spun round to point through the house and southwards in the direction of the park.

"She is that way. Not far – just a few hundred yards – but she is running, I think. Quickly now, follow me," he instructed and then took off, sprinting along the street towards the next junction. Tom and Septimus followed. Tom glanced back to see the Professor walking more slowly in their wake.

Rounding the corner, he saw that Edward was now some fifty yards ahead of him and just managed to catch a glimpse of Mary Brown as she turned left at the end of the street, a few hundred yards away; her long hair streaming untidily behind her. He risked Walking a couple of hundred yards at a time to catch up. When he stepped out of the second hop, expecting to be on the pavement just short of the junction, he found he had misjudged it and was standing now in Bayswater Road with a very large, bright red London bus speeding toward him, horn blaring. Then, with a blur, Septimus was besides him and had seized his jacket and pulled him sideways, into the island in the middle of the road.

The bus driver opened his window, swore at them both and muttered something about crazy pedestrians appearing in front of his bus.

"You ok, boyo?" asked Septimus in a concerned voice.

Still in shock and unable to speak, Tom nodded. He stood for a moment, catching his breath.

"You really ought to be more careful where you pull that kind of trick, Tommy. Personally, there are a lot of risks I'd take before standing in the way of a London bus when your life depends on its brakes working!"

Tom nodded again and finally managed to respond. "Yes, sorry about that. Was rushing I guess. Thanks mate."

"Come on then, let's be going."

By now, Mary had vanished in the direction of Marble Arch, which they could see in the distance. Edward was running that way – once again leading the pursuit. Septimus and Tom re-crossed the road and carried on after him. Weaving through the crowds, they reached Marble Arch and found Edward standing at the entrance to the underground station. He pointed down the steps.

"She ran into this building," he said. "I came here the other day to have a look; amazing how they've changed since my day – travelling under the ground was all quite new then, you know," he said breathlessly as they gathered around him.

They all hurtled down the stairs, narrowly avoiding knocking a group of Japanese tourists over. The tourists each took a photo of them as they ran on past yelling apologies over their shoulders.

As they reached the platform, Tom realised that a tube train was just pulling out. They ran to catch up, but it was gone. He braced himself to Walk after it, but Septimus put a hand on the boy's shoulder to hold him back.

"No, Tom: it's too dangerous!"

"Damn it, Septimus – she's on that train!" Tom yelled, ducking out from under his friend's restraining hand.

"Gentlemen, you are wrong," Edward said from behind them.

They turned. Edward was pointing to the other end of the station. Mary was standing on the edge of the platform, staring down onto the track. There was a look of horror on her face. As the three of them walked closer, Mary looked up at them in terror.

"It's the Devil's work: beasts of steel moving without horses; evil sorcery and witchcraft. You will burn for this, all of you!" she shouted, backing away. Around them the Londoners were ignoring them and carried on reading papers and listening to their iPods as if nothing was going on. Tom knew he would be the same: it was the first instinct of a commuter to ignore the lunatic in case they were on drugs or had a knife or, even worse, wanted to speak to you!

Septimus moved towards Mary, his arms open wide to show he meant no harm. "It's alright, Mary. Everything is alright. We are people just like you and not evil, believe me," he said, taking another step forward. Mary backed away, towards the edge of the platform.

"Mary, be careful you'll fall!" shouted Tom. But it was already too late as, with a shriek, the young woman fell over the edge and down onto the rails. She gave a shout of pain as her leg hit the rail nearest the platform and she rolled over. Her right hand was only inches from the live central rail through which thousands of volts of electricity ran: enough to kill her in an instant.

Tom and his companions ran to the edge of the platform. Just then, a bright light from the tunnel, a gush of warm, musty air and an insistent clankety-clank noise, warned of the approach of the next train. It was coming fast and would be here in moments. Without thinking, Tom leapt into the path of the train and pulled Mary up by her hand. A look of sheer terror again rode her features as she stared at the oncoming train.

On the platform, the Londoners were finally looking: even they could not ignore what was going on. Fifty mouths were open and fifty pairs of eyes stared at him and Mary from all along the platform: iPods and newspapers, for the moment, hanging limply by the commuters' sides.

"Tom: the train, look out!" yelled Edward and Septimus, together.

Tom spun round and saw the tube mere feet away. Instinctively, he reached out to the Flow of Time and Walked for an instant. It was enough: he and Mary collapsed onto the floor of the tube train's first compartment whilst the nearest passengers screamed at their sudden appearance. The tube slowed to a halt and the doors hissed open. Edward and Septimus jumped in, their faces etched with concern that now changed to relief as they saw Mary and Tom were unhurt. The passengers jostled past them out of the carriage, some panicking at what they had seen, others not sure what they had seen, but it seemed that most, swept into the crush of exiting commuters, had not even noticed.

The four staggered off the tube and as the platform emptied, Tom and his companions collapsed panting onto the station seating. It took Tom a few moments to catch his breath. Then, his heart still pounding, he turned to Mary and saw that she was gazing at him, tears running down her grime-streaked face.

"Mary, I ..."

"You saved my life," she said, her voice still tense but less shrill. "Twice now: here and in the fire."

Tom was taken aback at that and just shrugged. Could it be she was unaware of what she had done, freezing the flames? Mary glanced over at Edward and Septimus and then back to Tom. "Who are you people? If thee be not devils and witches, what then are you?"

"Just people, Miss Brown," Septimus said softly, "just people."

"People who can appear in a fire and lead me through it like angels: folk to whom solid walls are no hindrance?"

"Yes, people who can do that. We are people who can do things others cannot do. Like command a fire to stop and it stops. People like you," Tom answered.

Mary's eyes widened at that and she opened her mouth to say something, but in the end just nodded. Tom could feel her shaking.

"You are not a witch, Mary," he said. "You are one of us. That is why we came for you, why we rescued you from the fire. All this," he swung his arm wide, "is hard to grasp, I know, but it is not that we are devils nor is it magic. You have been brought out of your time into ours and in those three hundred years the world has moved on. Do not be afraid," he smiled, "we are not going to hurt you; we are still just people, but with unique talents."

The young woman studied Tom's face for a good minute, as if to see if he was lying or even worse perhaps tricking her into admitting to something. But, suddenly, she seemed to relax and slumped back on the seat. "They would have hanged me for a witch had they known what I can do," she muttered. Then she leaned forward covering her face with her hands. Tom heard a sob. Edward placed a hand on her back.

"It is alright, Miss Brown. Even if you were a witch - which you are not - they do not hang them now; the last one was hanged in Exeter in 1684. You are quite safe here."

Mary looked up at them all now, wiping her eyes on her cuff. "I have been so afraid: so alone. I thought ... I was sure one day I would be found out. But now ... it has all happened so quickly. Everything is so strange. I must have time to think."

She stood up and walked off around the station, staring in wide-eyed fascination and confusion at the lights, the signs for the next train, the posters of rock groups and the rails themselves. The station was beginning to fill up again, people filing along the platform to wait for the next train. Tom reflected that Mary didn't look at all out of place in her seventeenth century garb: her long skirt and tight bodice could be taken for just another fad of fashion – if anyone noticed at all.

"What is this place?" she asked as he and Septimus caught up with her.

"It's called an underground station. It's for getting on and off trains going under the ground," he explained. "It is faster than trying to travel through all the traffic above ground."

"What, pray tell, is a train?" Mary now asked, looking even more puzzled.

"Your beasts of steel," Tom grinned, "they are just-"

Septimus cut across him, "Sorry to interrupt Tom, but let's just get away from here before the Professor thinks we have all got lost, eh? Questions and answers can come later."

132

"I'm sorry I hurt thee, Master," Mary said, looking at the huge bruise on the Welshman's face, which was no longer bleeding.

He smiled, "It's nothing. Come on now, let's be going."

"In my day, they had just started building tunnels for trains under London," said Edward leading the way towards the stairs. "The District Line was already running then. I read about it in the papers but I only visited London once on the way to Africa, so I never tried them myself. I always thought these underground railway networks were a bit dangerous. Do these people travel like this every day?" Edward asked.

Septimus grinned, following him, with Mary and Tom bringing up the rear. "Yup; some folk do this twice a day every day for forty years!"

"Really? I'm surprised they live that long," Edward muttered.

CHAPTER FOURTEEN - 'FOR THOSE IN PERIL ON THE SEA'

The Office again. High up in a tower block somewhere, sometime; there is a meeting going on. Where is this place? Tom wonders briefly, before he again becomes one of the men in the room: the old man with the grey hair and a well-fitted charcoal grey suit. The man in the suit is irritated. The sand table in front of him shows random patterns; one in 1666, another in 1879 and finally a third developing in the 1940s. Such things offend him. To him, order and predictability are all important. The time lines he was created to preserve should flow naturally, but these random variations make that difficult. It is the boy, of course. The man can sense him out there somewhere in one of the realities. He interferes and creates chaos and he must be stopped.

But that is where the trouble starts, for the boy is difficult to locate. Something is shielding him and protecting him from the old man. Perhaps it is the very nature of his randomness that makes it difficult for the old man's ordered mind to locate him. Or maybe there is something more than that. Still, he now has the possibility of ending the problem. He studies the other two present at the meeting. One is an officer, dressed in a military uniform, sitting bolt upright, almost at attention. The other is looking out of the office window, his face turned away from the old man. The sunlight coming in silhouettes him and makes it hard to pick out his features.

"So, do we have an understanding, sir?" the officer says in a brisk voice.

"Indeed we do. The boy is a threat to the stability of time. You bring him to me and I will deal with him," the old man replies.

"What will you do with him? Will he be harmed?" asks the third figure still standing at the window."

"He need not be. He must lose his powers, though. In return he will be safe, I guarantee it," the old man promises.

"I have your word on that, do I?" asks the man at the window and as he does so he turns towards the room...

Tom squinted to make out his face, but, by then, he was the old man no more: he was Tom again and he was confused. These dreams were different to those involving Mary, Edward and Charlie. The dreams about those three had shown times when they were in mortal peril. But the two dreams in the Office did not seem to relate to mortal peril, did they? And they seemed not in the past, but the present. Who were the three men? One seemed to have been Redfeld. But he had no idea who the old man or the man at the window were.

"Ah there, you see? it's flashing now, I think it's about time we were going," Septimus said, coming in through the door. Tom blinked and realised he was sitting in the Professor's office and had been day dreaming. It was a couple of days after he, Edward and Septimus had chased Mary across London and finally found her in Marble Arch tube station. Tom had spent two ordinary days at school — if any of his life at present could be considered ordinary — and then arrived back at the Institute. He was now able to control the random movements in time or in space that caused such embarrassment to him and such hilarity in others. He was still forgetting homework, however, and seemed as a result to find himself in detention more often than not. However, Thursday evening had finally arrived and he had Walked to London where Septimus was waiting for him.

On the floor in front of them was the table cloth with the square drawn on it, representing the confines of the packing case on the *Empress of India*. As soon as they had again changed into wetsuits and diving apparatus he and Septimus sat in it.

"Good luck, gentlemen," said the Professor. With a nod at the old man, Septimus turned to Tom.

"You must this time add in another element to your Walking, boyo. It's no good just aiming for the sea around where we think the ship should be. The tracer I left in that crate is giving out a signal. It's sending out waves of temporal disturbance. You know the date and you know the rough area. As we Walk you must locate the signal and use it to guide us to the crate on the *Empress*."

"How do I do that?" Tom asked.

"You ever used a mobile phone?"

"Yes, of course. Mum and Dad bought me one for my birthday!"

"Well, you know that sometimes the signal is poor? You only get one bar or even none on the signal strength indicator?" he asked and seeing Tom nod went on. "So what do you do then?"

"Well, if you can't get a signal you might try ... you might try moving about a bit. Sometimes just the other side of the room has a better signal."

"And if you are talking at the time and get a fuzz or buzz on the line you can try the same thing?" suggested Septimus. Tom nodded.

"Right, boyo, so what you do is similar; reach out for the Flow and as we walk back you will feel something like a buzz or fuzz in it. Try and follow that buzz and it will lead us back."

Tom felt a bit apprehensive but then he nodded, "Ok."

"Now, Tommy, when we get to the *Empress* again it should be a few minutes before the U-boat surfaces. We will need to locate her and then try to get on board and find young Charlie *after* the British boarding party have left, but before she sinks. If it all goes wrong we pull out and get away fast – understand?"

Tom nodded again, although he had no intention of leaving Charlie behind. He had been Charlie during that dream and knew the fear he had felt. All the same, he was very frightened once again. In the last two weeks he had been stabbed by Zulus and almost burnt to death in the Great Fire of London. Was he about to drown? It seemed a dangerous thing, this time travelling.

"Right then, Tom, time to go," Septimus said and Tom, checking that the ball and chain was secured tightly round his waist, took his companion's outstretched hand and reached out for the Flow of Time.

Feeling its now familiar presence, he Walked them both back along the Flow and towards the Mediterranean. At first, he could not feel any signal or disturbance until, all of a sudden and with an almost violent jolt, he felt it. It wasn't much like the buzz Septimus had described, but now he knew what to look for it was very easy to lock on to the tracer signal and he followed it until, a moment later, they were sitting in the packing crate. There was hardly enough light to see, but Tom felt the motion of the ship rising and falling and also it was tilting gently from side to side: they were definitely at sea.

There was a rustling sound followed by a click and suddenly Tom was blinded by a bright light shining right into his eyes. He squinted and saw Septimus had switched on a torch.

"Oops! Sorry about that, boyo. Just need to find the tracer. Ah, here it is," and he scooped up the tracer from the crate and then clicked off the torch. Right then, I'm going to lift up the crate lid now. Quiet!"

Septimus gently pushed up the lid and they both peeped over the top. Outside, it was night-time, the sky illuminated by stars as well as a sliver of moonlight. For a moment, they could see little. Then, with a bang, there was a burst of light high up in the sky and the sea was revealed for a few moments. Over the side of the boat they became aware that there were two, three, no ... four ships visible. One close by the *Empress*, the others further away. The light faded and the *Empress* was alone in her own world again.

"That's the *Paladin's* flotilla," Septimus said, "looks like they are still searching for the U-boat. I ... oh my word ...!"

Whatever else he was going to say was cut off by a loud pop and another star shell soared up high. This time, Tom saw the nearest destroyer pass close to the *Empress* and suddenly several barrel-like objects were flung high and far from the rear of the destroyer. They arched up and then plummeted into the sea. There was a moment's pause and then a deep boom under the water, followed by the surface of the sea erupting upwards.

"Depth charges, Tom. The destroyers are closing in on the U-boat. I think ... quick! Down!" Septimus said and they sank back down into the crate, hastily replacing the lid. Tom heard several thumping footsteps, as a number of sailors ran past the crates.

They waited a few moments and then dared another peek. The crew seemed to have moved off to another part of the ship. Now that his eyes were adjusting to the gloom, Tom could see

139

the destroyers out at sea were circling around a small patch of water. Then, more depth charges were fired.

Suddenly, only two hundred yards away, a sleek grey shape burst into view: it was the U-boat! It shot out from the sea bow first, almost like a dolphin jumping for fish at the aquarium. It lay silent for a moment and then Tom saw men emerging from inside and coming out on deck. On top of the U-boat was a single large gun and Tom thought the crew were rushing to man it and fire at the merchant vessel. The British destroyers must have thought the same because they turned towards the German submarine and began firing at it. There was the boom of a large gun on the nearest destroyer and soon afterwards a rapid *pom-pom* of smaller pieces and the *ratatat* of machine guns. Some shots hit the side of the U-boat low down and along the conning tower. Then, the shooting stopped, because the German crew were obviously abandoning ship and jumping overboard.

"Not long now, boyo: better get out," Septimus ordered.

They clambered out on deck then moved to the rail deep in shadow at the side of the ship. A few moments later they saw a lifeboat being lowered from the nearest destroyer, which had to be the *Paladin*. As they watched, two sailors started stripping off uniforms. Tom saw them dive overboard. They swam across the gap to the U-boat, passing the groups of floating German sailors and hauling themselves up the side. "There's our man," whispered Septimus. The lifeboat now crossed the gap and came alongside the U-boat. Several sailors got out and followed the other two sailors up the conning tower.

By now, the U-boat was starting to sink: it was already low in the water and little of the deck remained above the sea level.

"When do we go, Septimus?" Tom cast his mind back to the dream, imagining Charlie in the U-boat searching for documents and machinery.

"Soon, Tom ..." Septimus began, but then he froze.

"Tom, I think someone is poking a revolver into my back," he hissed.

Tom turned his head: saw a crewman standing right behind them, holding a gun to Septimus' spine.

"Don't move or I'll shoot!" He was about six foot six, with a wild black beard and looked about as wide in the shoulders as he was tall.

"Now turn round; slowly. I've caught me two German spies by the looks of things. German spies who just escaped from their U-boat, eh? Well, you picked the wrong boat to land on."

"We aren't German spies, boyo," Septimus protested, raising his hands.

The sailor gave a humourless laugh. "That supposed to be a Welsh accent? It's pathetic. Don't train you Nazis very well, do they?" His gaze rested on Tom, "Start 'em young, too."

Tom shivered. He could hear the frantic cries of drowning Germans in the inky black water. Further out to sea came the intermittent thud of shellfire. Nearer at hand men were shouting as the rescue operation continued. He risked a quick glance at the sub. The water was now creeping up the conning tower.

"Look, we are running out of time and really need to go," Septimus said urgently out of the corner of his mouth.

Tom nodded. The sailor snorted, waving the revolver from Septimus to Tom and back again. "I said don't move. You are not going anywhere!" he growled, his attention suddenly caught by the ball and chain glinting at Tom's waist. "What the hell is that?"

"Um, er, a m-m-marker buoy," Tom stuttered; it was all he could think of.

"More likely some kind of grenade; planning to blow us up, were you? Give it here. You two are going into the hold until I've got more time to deal with you." The sailor ground the revolver into Septimus's chest, at the same time reaching out a large hand to grasp the chain.

"I really mean it. We need to be going right *now!*" Septimus rolled his eyes and jerked his head, "If someone would just provide a *distraction*, Tom ...," he hissed in desperation.

Somewhere inside Tom's head, the penny dropped and gathering himself, he Walked. Only a couple of feet, but, from the sailor's point of view, just as he was reaching for the chain, the boy disappeared and reappeared right behind him.

Stretching out his hand, Tom tapped the *Empress* crewman on the shoulder.

"What the heck...?" began the sailor, spinning round.

Septimus moved fast. Throwing the torch to Tom, he punched the sailor full in the face. The big brute whimpered slightly and collapsed.

"Well done, Septimus!"

"Yes ... but for a moment I did not think you were going to move. Bit slow on the uptake, Tommy, eh?" said Septimus, blowing on his bruised knuckles.

Tom nodded apologetically, "Sorry, I ..."

"Never mind. Right then: we Walk straight from here across to the U-boat. We will need to appear five feet beyond the side of the sub, towards the rear − in the engine room. Should be empty of Germans and probably no Brits will be there either. Think you can manage that?"

Tom nodded and got ready to Walk.

"Oi you!" shouted a voice from the darkness near the stern of the *Empress of India*. Then suddenly a shot rang out. It ricocheted off the railing in front of Tom and punched a hole in the crate the two of them had been hiding in earlier.

"They are shooting at us, boyo. Let's go."

Without a word, the pair Walked off the deck of the ship and traversed the short hop to the U-boat.

They appeared in the submarine's engine room, which was already four feet deep in water with more gushing in through the door leading to the conning room, where Charlie would be about now. Tom suddenly lost his footing; he slipped in the oily water and fell under the surface. He came up, gasping for breath and coughing, as strong hands pulled him onto his feet.

"You ok, Tom?" asked Septimus. Tom coughed up some more filthy water and then nodded weakly, one hand still clutching the torch.

"This way then, son," Septimus ordered and led—him towards the door. The sub's lights were flickering and water was surging through now so that the two Walkers were forced to struggle against the current. It was hard work and they had to pull themselves along by the expediency of grabbing pipes and pieces of equipment on the walls. The next compartment was a bunk room where the crew slept and rested when off duty and here they found that blankets, items of clothing and even books were floating past them.

Finally, they made it to the door at the end of the bunk room, beyond which lay the control room. They attempted to step through – or rather swim through, because now the water was up to their necks and they were kicking with their legs whilst still hauling along the walls. Suddenly, they heard a scream ahead and saw a man shoot past them, carried along by the current. Tom glanced at his face. It was not Charlie, but the *Paladin's* Lieutenant. He seemed to have hit his head on the door and he was unconscious as he floated off towards the engine room. Tom reached out to try and catch him, but Septimus pulled his arm away.

Tom glared at him angrily, but Septimus just looked back sadly and shook his head.

"No boy, we cannot help him. He is not the Walker: he could not travel with us."

"Damn it, Septimus, we must help him."

"No! Do as I say and oof ..." Septimus' reply was cut off because Charlie Hawker had just come hurtling through the door pushed by a surge of water and had knocked Septimus under the surface. The U-boat moved suddenly over on its side and all three of them were dashed against the side wall. Charlie was knocked out, Septimus was nowhere to be seen and Tom was left floundering. He pulled his mask down and manoeuvred the mouthpiece of the diving equipment into place. Just then, the water reached the U-boat's lights and with several pops they went out, leaving Tom in pitch blackness with the sub now full of water.

Tom, trapped in a pitch black submarine, which was now sinking fast towards the bottom of the sea, had never been more terrified. He had to tell himself to calm down and try to think. Charlie was the priority: he had no breathing equipment and was now underwater. Tom clicked on the torch and shone it around. Sheets of paper billowed about and a tin can floated past. Then he saw Charlie a few feet away, sinking and still out cold. He reached across and grabbed him by the hand. Then he quickly looked about for Septimus, but his companion was nowhere to be seen. The water was dark with oil, making it impossible to see down through it more than a foot or so. Next to him, Charlie was fighting to breathe: Tom could wait no longer. There was nothing he could do about Septimus, Charlie was drowning. He closed the young man's fingers around the glass ball and held them there, then reached out for the Flow of Time.

Moments later, Tom and Charlie lay collapsed on the floor of the Professor's room, drenching his nice Persian rug. Charlie gasped in a breath of air, vomited up a stomach full of water, opened his eyes a brief moment and then slumped back, unconscious, on the floor.

"Thomas, where is Septimus?" asked the Professor.

Tom, noticing that on this occasion the Professor had not been surprised by his sudden appearance, lifted his head up and looked sadly back at the old man.

"Gone, sir, I think he's dead."

CHAPTER FIFTEEN - REDFELD'S OFFER

Dead? Mr Mason is *dead*? Are you sure, what happened?" the Professor asked.

"I just told you, Prof – he's dead. It's not fair, I tried but ... but I couldn't find him!" Tom replied and started pacing around the room.

"Thomas ..."

"It was dark ... I could not see him ... the water was black ..."

"Thomas, please ..."

"Charlie was drowning ..." Tom's voice was now high-pitched in agitation.

"Master Oakley!" Neoptolemas shouted, slapping his palm on the desk top. Tom jumped in shock and stared at him.

"That's better. I'm sorry, Thomas, I can see you are upset, but please just take a deep breath and explain it all to me slowly."

Tom's shoulders dropped and he sighed before sitting down heavily on a chair across the desk from the Professor. He then took the deep breath as instructed and started speaking as slowly and as calmly as he could.

"We were in the U-boat and it was flooding. Charlie and I were underwater and I could not see Septimus. The lights went out and it was very dark. I had to bring Charlie back before he drowned. So I did: I left Septimus behind."

"You did the right thing," the Professor said.

"But I can go back now?" Tom suggested.

The old man shook his head. "I've told you about this. You know you cannot go back to the same time."

"But sir!" Tom sobbed and then, realising he did not have the energy to Walk again in any event, he slumped down in the chair and rested his chin on his hands, his shoulders heaving.

"Besides which, I think it would be a waste of time!" the Professor said smiling, staring towards the door.

"Eh?" Tom asked.

"The Prof's right, boyo!" Septimus said. Tom spun round and saw Septimus standing there dripping with water, looking exhausted, but otherwise quite well.

"Septimus, you're alive!" shouted Tom jumping to his feet.

"Sure as eggs are eggs, boyo."

"What happened? Did you put your mask on and Walk back here?"

"Eventually, yes; after I got tossed to the side of the boat I managed to struggle the mask on. The U-boat hit the seabed and I was knocked unconscious for a moment. When I came round I looked for you and Charlie first and then got away.

"Well done. Well done indeed, both of you," the old man said, ringing the bell for Mr Phelps.

The Professor now had Charlie carried upstairs, whilst Septimus and Tom went off to change their clothes. They met back downstairs in the hallway.

"Fancy a milkshake, Tom?" Septimus asked.

Tom nodded and they left and walked down the road to the cafe on the corner and both ordered strawberry milkshakes. A few minutes after they had sat down, they heard a familiar voice.

"Hello, gentlemen, a very good day to you."

It was Redfeld. "Did you enjoy your trip on a U-boat, young sir?" he asked Tom.

"What do you want, Captain?"

"Rescued young Charlie, did we?" Redfeld asked as if Tom had not spoken.

Tom nodded.

"What about the Lieutenant? Retrieve him as well, did you?"

"Leave it alone, Redfeld!" warned Septimus. "We couldn't rescue him: he wasn't a Walker."

"You sure of that, are you?"

"What are you saying?" Tom asked, his eyes narrowing.

"I am simply asking what if he was a Walker? Or what if you are wrong and you could actually take non-Walkers with you as well?"

"Well, we can't say what would happen," Septimus said.

"Oh, but we can, can't we ...?" Redfeld said, with a nasty grin.

"Redfeld, don't even think about it ..."

But it was already too late. Redfeld whisked them away from the cafe and in an instant they were back in the U-boat. The U-boat was sinking and was filling with water fast. But, although they were standing knee deep in it, Tom's legs were not wet, nor could he feel any current as the water sped past them. He glanced at Redfeld. "We are not really here are we!" Tom exclaimed, remembering the images Redfeld had conjured at Isandlwana.

"No. This is an image; a construction, a 'virtual' U-boat if you like. You gentlemen are about to enter the act," the Captain explained and pointed at the far door leading to the engine room.

The next moment Tom saw himself and Septimus come wading through the door just as they had done not many minutes before. It was weird: like watching himself on film. The other Septimus and Tom did not seem to know they were there. The water level was rising quickly and Tom saw himself and Septimus struggling to keep their heads above the surface. They finally made it to the door into the control room. Then, the instant they were trying to move through the door, just like before there was a scream and the *Paladin's* Lieutenant came hurtling out of the room and shot past the other Tom and Septimus. Tom saw himself reaching out to grab the officer and as before, miss the target. This time, though, the other Septimus reached out and managed to grasp the unconscious officer by his wrist and pull him back. Then Charlie, carried on a wave of seawater, came spinning through the door. As before, the collision knocked them all down and they went under the water.

The water level now came above the real Tom's head and he started to panic that he would not be able to breathe. Then he realised that Redfeld, Septimus and himself were still standing on the U-boat floor and were still not wet; could breathe quite easily, in fact. The whole thing was an illusion created by Redfeld: none of them was actually there. So where were they then: in some dream? Were they all asleep at the cafe in London or maybe in some sort of trance?

Tom watched his alternative self rescue Charlie and then vanish with him, but this time, Septimus held the Lieutenant and Walked him away from the scene. When they had gone, leaving Tom, Septimus and Redfeld alone on the virtual U-boat, the scene began to fade.

"So," said Redfeld, "you now observe that had you acted differently you might have saved that man."

"You are assuming he was a Walker. If he was not, your idea is poppycock," Septimus objected. His eyes narrowed, "And you do not show us what happened to the young Lieutenant next, do you. He would most likely have died."

"I'll allow that is a possibility." Redfeld directed a curt nod of his head at Septimus then, turning to Tom, he said, "But that's not the point. Just consider what I am saying. Your Professor confines himself - and you - to saving a few individuals. If you dare to take action you could do far more. Just think of the disasters you could avert. The thousands who could live that died before."

Yet again, as at Isandlwana, Tom found Redfeld's words strangely seductive. Why? Was it power he wanted or was it simply the thought of what he could make happen: just to imagine the possibilities made him dizzy. Tom could see himself changing the world - for good, of course. He would just change the past to make things better. Where several thousand had died in an earthquake a few weeks before, he could save them all. Predict the disaster and warn the authorities and have the city evacuated. Or ... what about wars? Maybe he could stop them. Then again, why stop there? Was it not reasonable that one with such powers should rule others? It was obvious that they should. They had the abilities to alter events and stave off disaster. Maybe he would be Prime Minister one day! It was heady stuff and Tom could not help the thrill that coursed through him.

He thought back to the battlefield in Africa, memories coming back to him of that horrible alternative Isandlwana Redfeld had created, and he shook the thoughts of glory and the image of himself as a hero from his mind. His history teacher had quoted something at them the other day: *'All power corrupts and absolute power corrupts absolutely...'* Tom could see how that might be true. Even a glimpse of power and there he was imagining himself as Prime Minister! What next: a god? Changing history might make the world better for some, but could make it far worse for others. He could not rescue *everybody!* He made his choice. He would not meddle just to be the hero. If the consequences of taking action were to alter lives and wreck futures across the millennia then the changes he could make came at too high a price.

Examining his conscience, Tom was relieved he felt this way. If he was honest he had been tempted and for a while he had teetered on the brink of choosing an action that would have changed him. But he had turned away from that. Redfeld had made him see the possibilities, but in the end it was Tom who could see the dangers.

"No, Redfeld, I want none of this. I want my normal life again and to leave others in the past, present and future alone to live theirs."

"Don't be a fool, boy: you must use your power. What kind of coward are you? Power is everything. If you have it you must use it. I insist!"

"No, Redfeld!" Tom snapped angrily. "Enough of this. You don't get to command me. Who do you think you are – Napoleon, Alexander the Great ...or maybe Hitler?"

Redfeld recoiled at this and his eyes grew wide and furious.

Tom turned and walked back to where Septimus was standing a few yards away.

"Take me home, Septimus, please," he asked quietly. His companion nodded and placed a warm hand on his shoulder.

Tom looked back at Redfeld, who was now marching towards them. "Walk away from me, boy, and you'll regret it, I promise. Do you hear me, boy?" Clearly, Redfeld was boiling mad at this mere youth who had the temerity to say no to him. "Don't you leave ... don't you dare go....this is your last chance ... " but, a moment later, Redfeld and the U-boat vanished.

Tom and Septimus moved erratically through the void they occupied whilst Walking. Tom was confused by the fact that they were trying to navigate away from an illusion to the real world. He had no idea how Redfeld had created it, where or when it was and so no idea how to find home. His companion did not seem quite as confused as he was and directed them, slightly unsteadily, but always onwards. When they appeared, however, it was not at Tom's house, as he had asked, but in London right back in the cafe. Tom's milkshake was still on the table in front of him. He looked at Septimus. The Welshman was panting and his eyes were out of focus. Tom himself felt agitated and angry still, and also completely disorientated. After a moment, Septimus turned to him.

"Phew – that was hard. I have come across such a thing before but not for many years. I wasn't sure I could get us back. Now, I need to go and make sure you will be safe. I ... I don't trust Redfeld, so I think we should get away from here quickly. But before I take you home, I want to see what's at your house and make sure it's safe. Why don't you stroll down to Hyde Park and wait at Speaker's Corner. I will find you there!" he said. A moment later and with the usual pop of in-rushing air, he was gone.

Tom thought about going in to see the Professor after what had just occurred with Redfeld, but was not sure he was ready to admit how he had felt during the trip: how tempted he had been at Redfeld's suggestions. So, he obeyed Septimus and walked down to the park.

The Institute was on a road branching off one of the side roads of Bayswater Road, which ended opposite Hyde Park. Tom walked that way and sat down on a bench at Speaker's Corner, only then realising just how exhausted he was. More than exhausted, he felt drained – like a battery in a torch that had been left on too long and whose light was fading. The day was warm and he felt his eyes become heavy.

There is a place that is no place and a time that is no time. It exists between realties and in the gaps between moments. In the brief instant of choice that split two realities from each other it was created. There are inhabitants of a sort. Created to balance the disharmony between the realities, they exist for one purpose: order and equilibrium. From the energy of the nothingness about them they weave a world and mould it as they see fit. Driven by a desire to achieve order and conformity, they take from the realities concepts of authority and stability and make their own reality in that image. An office exists in a tower block amidst the void. In the office is a table with raised edges around a surface covered in sand. The sand moves in ripples and lines. The inhabitants regard it with satisfaction when all is in balance: if the realities cancel each other out and any variations in the course of time in one reality are countered in another. They are the Directorate. In this office they look like typical bank managers or lawyers – except that they seem to have taken conformity too far and all wear identical grey suits. This Tom knows, for the dreamer who is Tom, is Tom no more but an old man – the same old man with silver-grey hair. The man in the suit: the Custodian.

Now another man appears before them. He does not wear grey but black and silver. He salutes the Directorate who remain motionless.

Their leader silently indicates a chair and the visitor sits. The Custodian knows the man as Captain Redfeld.

"I have a proposal of interest to both you and me," the Captain begins.

"Indeed?" the old man replies.

"It concerns a boy. A boy you wanted to eliminate."

"I had thought we had already dealt with that. Did you and I not make an arrangement with the other gentleman? Was he not to deliver the boy to me here?"

"I have to report our associate has proven most unreliable. We must make alternative plans. I will get the job done, but you must grant me and my guards presence in Der Andere Weld *to achieve it. We must be able to interact."*

The Custodian snorts. "It seems you have failed on your part. We know that the boy has survived somehow. He is protected, for the moment, by the Hourglass Institute in his reality, but that will not last long. I think we had best dispense with your services. The Directorate can deal with him. We do not need to involve you."

"I'm not so sure. He is different, this lad, and more powerful than you think. We felt it, even in my reality," Redfeld points out.

"Indeed, that is why he must be dealt with. He disturbs the balance between his reality and yours, Captain, and threatens both. This is Directorate business: our only business."

"And that's what my proposal is about. Let's talk business. About his parents ..."

The old man leans back in his chair to regard the officer.

"Very well; go on, I'm listening ..."

Tom woke with a start, not sure where he was. On a soap box opposite, an elderly man with medals on his jacket front was telling anyone who would listen why they should give money for the British Legion and the Poppy Appeal. Tom relaxed when he could see that he was still in Hyde Park. He had been dreaming again.

That dream in the Office – what was that about? What was it Redfeld said about him? That he was different – powerful - he had been talking about his Walking and his talents. But there was more. Redfeld had spoken of being aware of Tom in his reality. *His* reality? What did he mean by that? Should he mention this to the Professor or Septimus? But, wait a moment, what did he really know? It was a dream and nothing more. Just day-dreaming on a hot day in the park, like any of the scores of office workers Tom could see, enjoying an hour of summer weather after work. He yawned and then stretched.

The speaker's voice droned on: "You should all be glad that because of those who fought for your freedom you never have to see a battlefield or experience a war," he said, rattling his collection can at passersby, who mainly ignored him. Tom watched him for a moment whilst images from both the battles of Isandlwana he had experienced floated past his eyes, along with the horrors on the U-boat. Then, reaching into a pocket, he pulled out a pound coin and walked over to put it in the tin.

"Thank you, young sir," the elderly man said, beaming.

Septimus arrived as Tom turned to go back to his bench. "Right then, everything is ok at your house, boyo," the Welshman said quickly. "If you're ready, let's go!"

Before Tom could ask any questions they were away, Walking the short distance home to his house. He was hungry, looking forward to tea and not paying attention, so what happened next took him completely by surprise.

Tom was expecting to find himself standing on the floor of his bedroom. Instead and with a jolt, they appeared some ten feet above the ground, in a gaping hole where that floor should have been. With a shout of alarm, they tumbled down towards the ground below and landed with a thud.

"Oh blast! I hate it when that happens!" Septimus said. Moaning and getting onto his feet he stood, brushing leaves and dirt off his clothes with his hands.

"What do you mean?" Tom asked. He had landed in a bush and was disentangling himself from the branches, "and where on earth is my bedroom?" He finally got to his feet.

They were standing in the ruin of a house. Bushes and creepers had started to grow over and through it. Septimus turned to Tom.

"Don't worry, boyo, this ain't your house. We are just off course. Just let me get my bearings ..." he said. Abruptly he stopped talking and stared down at something in the rubble at the corner of the house. He then bent over and picked it up.

"No worries, Septimus ... it's been a busy day for us all and you did hit your head on the U-boat. I expect ..." Tom stopped, having just seen the expression on Septimus' face; he looked grim. "What is it? What's up?"

Septimus looked back at Tom and walking over placed a hand on his shoulder.

"I'm sorry, kid, but I was wrong. I hate to say this but ... this is your house, after all. I don't know what's happened: but it's gone!"

Tom stared at him.

"I'm sorry, boyo." Septimus said again.

"For what? You just brought us back to the wrong house, that's all."

The other man shook his head, "No, Tommy, I didn't ... the house is just not here. It's burnt down: it's gone! Recognise this?"

He held up an object. It was scorched and the glass front shattered but, without a doubt, it was the brass wind up alarm clock that belonged on Tom's desk!

CHAPTER SIXTEEN - NEVER BORN

Tom walked a few paces away from Septimus and stared in horror around the burnt out husk that was once his home. Could a fire have destroyed it whilst he was away? If so, where were the fire engines or the police and why were there no crowds? What was going on?

In the distance he heard church bells ringing; the bell ringers practised at the local church every week on Thursday nights. So it was now mid-evening on the same Thursday night he had left his house and gone off to rescue Charlie. All that adventure and the encounter with Redfeld, even his doze in the park had taken just four hours.

It all seemed frankly ridiculous, like some nightmare. Yet, he was becoming aware how easy it was to change history. Feeling panic rising, he spun back to face his companion.

"It's not possible! It can't be the right day. We must have gone to a different day in the future or something," Tom said, his voice quavering.

"Dad! Mum!" he shouted into the ruin, but there was no reply. Under his feet he felt the crunch of broken glass.

Septimus moved towards him and again placed his hands on Tom's shoulders. It was obviously an attempt to comfort him and perhaps calm him down. Unfortunately, Tom was not in a receptive mood and he glared at Septimus and felt himself shaking, although whether through rage or fear he was not sure.

159

"Well, what's going on? Did you do this? I trusted you. Was this all a trick to get me away from here so your friends could do this?" Tom demanded.

The Welshman shook his head. "I promise I didn't do anything of the sort," he said, but Tom thought he had a guilty look on his face.

"Well who did? Who burnt the house down? Can you tell me anything, Septimus? Can you tell me if my parents are alright?"

Letting go of Tom, Septimus reached into his trouser pocket. He brought out a small device that looked a little like an iPod. There was the sound of beeping as he pressed a few buttons. He then held the item up at arm's length and swept it around in a half circle. After pressing his buttons again he looked up at Tom, but said nothing.

"Well? What's that?" Tom asked, knowing he sounded rude, but not caring.

"We call it a Time Sniffer. Probably got a more technical name but I don't know it. It can detect deviations from the time line."

"Eh?"

"If someone does something to alter history this tells me it has happened," the man explained.

"Alter history: you mean this might have happened in the past?" asked Tom, thinking it would explain why the house was cold as if the fire had happened long ago. He swallowed, tried and failed to keep the anxiety out of his voice, "Well, has anyone?"

Septimus nodded, "I'm sorry, but yes. I am confused though. This thing is giving me mixed messages. Something more complex has gone on than a simple change. This device detects two types of change. It feels the change in a location. Someone has changed history relating to this spot. But also it detects change relating to people." He suddenly stared down at the boy. "Of course, that's it! It feels it on you. Some change to do with you. It's a strong signal and I think ..." He stopped speaking and dropped the device.

"Oh my God! It can't be, can it?" he said, staring at the device as it lay on the ground and then leaning over and picking it up again. He grimaced as he took in the symbols on the screen, then looking up he stared at Tom.

"What? Septimus, what is it?" Tom thought the Welshman seemed a little afraid of him and it scared him.

"Something very bad has happened here. This thing says the fire occurred twelve or so years ago and that your parents died in it. You are a paradox, my boy: you don't exist. You were never born!"

Tom stared back, dumbfounded. Septimus *seemed* to be in earnest, but now he was speaking nonsense. "That's rubbish. I was only here this afternoon. Obviously that device is wrong."

"Tom, you know better than most that history can change. There are various powers in this universe with vested interests in the course of time. They seek to change it, to preserve it, to observe it or some just to profit from it. "

"Yes, I know – we have been through all this already, and we know which sort you are, don't we?" Tom retorted sharply. His companion looked just a little ashamed, but kept on talking.

"I'm trying to explain that someone is interested in you," Septimus went on patiently. "The fire was started to destroy you."

"Me? It's my family that has disappeared."

"Maybe, but it's an old trick," the stranger said, then seeing the puzzled expression on Tom's face, explained. "Say that I killed your father and mother thirteen years ago. How could you have been born?"

Tom felt the colour drain from his face, but he answered anyway, "Well I couldn't have been, of course."

"Quite. This little device," he waved the small box, "can see what happened. By the look of things, in the year before you were born there was a fire here. Your parents were trapped and killed. You and your sister were never born. Someone went back and tried to make it that you never existed, because of the powers you have. To prevent what you perhaps have already done or maybe one day will do."

"Redfeld! It's that Redfeld. He said I would regret it!"

Septimus narrowed his eyes, a thoughtful look crossing his face. "But the clock – what is that doing here? Your room never existed so how is the clock here?"

Tom looked at the clock lying scorched and tarnished in the rubble. Crumpled as it was, it had the appearance of a shiny sweet wrapper that someone had screwed up and thrown away. Even so, or perhaps because of this, Tom felt a lump come to his throat and tears found his eyes.

"My father," he said, quietly wiping the tears away.

"What was that?"

"It was a family heirloom. My father gave it to me when I was ten."

"And so it would have been here in this house before you were born?"

Tom's hands were shaking and he felt cold. His head was spinning. He nodded in answer.

"But, if what you say is true. If they are ... gone," he gulped and felt his eyes moisten again. "If that is so, what am I still doing here?" he asked wearily.

An hour had passed and they were sitting in Professor Neoptolemas's study. Septimus had insisted that they both return at once. The Professor was sitting at his desk looking sadly at Tom in a chair opposite, whilst Septimus was pacing around the room.

On returning, Tom had been distraught and kept asking the Professor to help bring his family back. "Professor Neoptolemas. What about my family? Can anything be done to bring them back?" he said, his voice quavering. "Can't we just go back to the night my parents died and stop the fire from burning down the house?"

"We must proceed carefully, Thomas. We must plan this. If we go back and get it wrong, we cannot try again."

"Yes, but ..."

"But nothing! We cannot revisit a point in space-time that we have already visited."

"Why?" Tom persisted. "Why can't we?"

"Because it's rather like taking two magnets and then tying to push both north poles together: the two poles repel each other."

"But I have been here when I have also been at home − like after Isandlwana when I stayed two days healing up, haven't I?"

"That's something to do with distance. You can still put the two magnets on a table and that's fine, it's only when they are close − within each other's magnetic field − that they repel each other. We believe that we all have a kind of temporal field

163

around us and that is what prevents us meeting ourselves. Does that make sense?"

Tom shrugged, "A little, perhaps. So there is no way to help my parents – is that what you're saying?" Tom could feel the tears welling and tried to swallow them back.

"No, I think we can help, *but* we will have to think of a plan.

"When can we start?" With a burst of hope, Tom sat forward in his chair, his gaze fixed on the old man's face.

"Straight away: but first we must go over everything that has occurred to you. Everything real and everything you have dreamt about. Somewhere amongst all this there is something I don't understand. There is some other factor we are overlooking; can you think what it might be?"

Tom stared at the old man and then began talking. He told the Professor about Redfeld and their previous meetings. Then he told him of the visit to the alternative Isandlwana and to the U-boat and of the final argument. Then, painfully, he spoke of going home and finding the awful truth that his parents were gone.

The old man had, at first, looked anxious and then had lapsed into silent thought for a long time afterwards. Tom was still stunned and shocked by what had gone on with his parents and had not minded the long time of quiet.

"So, you have met Captain Redfeld? What does he want from you?" the Professor had finally said, softly, almost as if to himself.

"Redfeld!" said Tom, jumping to his feet in alarm. "Do you know him?"

"Thomas, be assured that I am not in league with Captain Redfeld. Don't worry; he and others like him are the enemy of this Institute as well as enemies of yours. Please sit down and let's think about what might have occurred."

"But how do you know Redfeld?" insisted Tom, still alarmed at this revelation.

"It's a long story, but please believe me when I say I am as worried about the Captain's intentions and plans as you are. But we must stay focused on the matter at hand. Why, for example, are you still here if your parents were killed, you asked me, yes?"

Tom sat down and nodded. Behind him, he heard Septimus stop walking and then start tapping his fingers on the back of Tom's chair. Finally, he coughed.

"Ah, well that would be my fault. I took you out of time for a while. We went back to Malta in World War Two ... or maybe it was whilst we were in Redfeld's version of history," Septimus said. Something did not sound quite right about that, but Tom could not place it.

"I don't get it. How was I here to travel with you if my parents died some twelve years ago?"

"Astute question, Mr Oakley", said the Professor. "That's one of the strange realities of time travel," he said, his hand moving across to a pile of books which, as ever, occupied much of the desk.

"It's something to do with the fact that if someone leaves a point in time and travels back to alter that point in time, only those present at that point in time can be altered."

"Eh?" Tom said.

"Learning curve a bit steep today, eh, Tommy?" said Septimus with a kind laugh. "Don't worry I don't get it either. But then I am not a scientist. The bottom line here is that

165

because we were not *here* you still *are*. Ahem ... that's even more confusing – sorry!"

"You can say that again ... what's up?" said Tom, noticing a thoughtful expression dawn on the other man's face. "Septimus? Hello?" Tom said again, waving his hand in front of the strange little Welshman's face. Septimus blinked and looked at him.

"Sorry, Tommy, I was still trying to figure out when he did this. It seems unlikely that he would have ordered it before I, we – I mean you – declined his offer and I left you on the way to the park. But if not then – when?"

"Thomas, was it possible you Walked after you returned from Captain Redfeld's last encounter? I mean before you Walked home just now?" Neoptolemas asked.

Tom thought about the strangest of the dreams he had experienced: the ones occurring in the Office; those with the old man in the grey suit – the Custodian – and the rest of the Directorate. Those dreams did not make sense. He had thought they were meaningless, now he was not so sure. Who was this Custodian and how was he involved?

"Well, sir, there was a dream. Yes a dream. I was in Hyde Park and I dozed off."

"You had one of those dreams when you seemed to be somewhere else, and someone else? Is that what happened?"

"Yes, there was a man in a grey suit who looked a bit like you, Professor. He was in an office and there was this weird table with sand on it ... and Redfeld came and ..." Tom went over the last dream. Then he reported the earlier dreams of the same place.

At the end the Professor looked thoughtful. "Thomas, there is a lot going on here I do not understand and the part played by many in this is unclear," the old man said, looking first at Septimus then at Tom. "Give me a few hours to think this over and we will talk again."

"But my parents….." Tom said.

"You have my word that we will find them if it is possible. We will bring them back. But I need some time to think about it."

"I must go chaps," Septimus said suddenly and Tom realised that he had been very quiet for a long time.

"What? Where are you going, Septimus?" Tom said.

"Indeed, I would like to know that, Mr Mason," the Professor asked, leaning forward to peer over his spectacles, now looking rather like Mrs Rogerson, the English teacher at school, Tom thought darkly. Although, was it really still his school if he had never been born?

"You do your thinking, Prof. Tom, you rest and I will go and see what I can find out," said Septimus. His shoulders slumped down and with a sigh he added, "I'll make everything ok again, Tom – I promise!"

Then, before either of the others could protest, he swept out of the room. A few seconds afterwards, they heard the front door slamming shut, leaving Tom staring at the Professor who, like Tom, seemed to be wondering exactly why Septimus was so upset.

CHAPTER SEVENTEEN - BREAKFAST

||"Thomas Oakley, you are a brave lad. Many would consider you heroic considering what you have gone through these last few weeks," the Professor said after Septimus had left.

"That's rubbish, Prof. I'm no hero. I've spent most of the last few weeks terrified or running away. Heroes are brave and fear nothing."

"Where then is the heroism?"

"Eh? What do you mean?" Tom frowned.

"A man who fears nothing and stands in danger's path is not heroic. He might be considered perhaps foolish, or maybe lucky not to be afraid, but why heroic? More heroic is the man who is afraid and still faces the danger: because he chooses to for others' sake - like you did, despite your misgivings about your talents, and despite the fact that you really just want to be normal, Thomas Oakley."

"I see what you mean, sir. But I ... I mean, well I couldn't leave those three to die. It wouldn't be right," Tom said.

"Maybe that is so, but there are many who would. Yes, you are brave. You will need all that courage in the time to come. Before this business with Redfeld is finished, before we try and rescue your family, you will also need to believe that what I – what we – must do will come right in the end. Belief is very important, Thomas. It's all to do with acorns really."

Tom blinked. Acorns? Had he heard the Professor right? "I'm sorry?"

Neoptolemas smiled. "Let me tell you a short story, Thomas." He glanced over towards the fireplace. Tom followed his gaze to where, above the mantelpiece, was mounted a photo of an old building made of stone, but with a wooden roof. "That is my college at Oxford. Very old it is and possesses a great hall, used in my day and I think even now, for formal meals. The hall has a striking vaulted ceiling supported by timber archways all made from aged oak – black and woodwormed with age.

"Five hundred years ago, the then Master of the college ordered the Head Groundsman to plant acorns in readiness for the day when the roof would need replacing. Three hundred years later the then Master of the day looked up at the then rotten and derelict roof and announced that the college must have a new roof. 'But' – said the Bursar of the college – 'where will we get the wood, for we have not enough money?' At which point the Head Groundsman of the day popped up and said something like, 'It's funny you should say that but...' for of course, by then the oak trees were mature and ready for cutting."

Tom nodded still not sure what the Professor was getting at.

"The point is this, Thomas: when the original Master and Groundsman planted their acorns they were making a leap of faith and had tremendous trust that one day it would all make sense and their actions would be worthwhile. They knew it would be long after their time, but they were content to play their part in a bigger plan. Hold on to that idea Tom in the days ahead. If it all seems too big and beyond you, then trust that it will all come good in the end: remember that from little acorns great oaks do grow," the old man finished with a smile and then added, "go; rest a while. If you like it, we have a telly in the lounge or there are books in the library. I'll tell you when Septimus is back or when I have thought things over."

Tom had been so engrossed in the Professor's story that he had momentarily forgotten that he had no home to go to. The thought kicked in with a sickening lurch. He realised he still had many questions.

"Redfeld," he asked, "who is he and where is he from? What does he want from me? Won't he attack here, once he finds out where I am? Who is that man in the grey suit; the Custodian and the Office, where is that?"

The old man raised his hands to stop the flow of questions. "Relax, Thomas. I know all about our Captain Redfeld. Don't worry; neither he nor anyone else can just Walk into here for all it looks like an ordinary house. There are ways of blocking access to the Flow of Time and creating barriers to access. But you must rest and eat," Neoptolemas insisted. "Tomorrow, I will answer all your questions."

That was that. The old man rang his bell and Mr Phelps entered and led Tom out to the dining room. He was given some soup, but his stomach was still twisted up and he found he could not eat. He stumbled out and was shown to a bedroom. A pair of pyjamas his size were folded neatly on the pillow. He had assumed he would not be able sleep, but despite that doze on the park bench earlier, all the excitement and anxiety had exhausted him. He collapsed on to the bed and slept for hours.

The next morning he sat down to a plate of bacon and eggs. Still maudlin and thinking about his family he thought he was not hungry, yet his body needed food and after one bite he realised he was ravenous and stuffed the rest down. While he was eating, he heard a door shut and, looking out of the open dining room door, he could just see down the corridor to the Professor's room. Charlie Hawker, Edward Dyson and Mary Brown were walking towards him, having just been in with the Professor. They came and sat down, opposite him.

It was the first time Tom had seen Charlie since the rescue. He was glad to see that the young man now wore jeans and a shirt, rather than still being almost naked. He was half expecting Charlie to react violently to what had occurred, as Edward and Mary had done, but he sat calmly in his chair. Perhaps it was because he was younger than the others, Tom reflected; and, of course, he had not travelled so far in time as had the other two. The world would still seem strange, but not *that* strange.

"Thomas Oakley, is it?" Charlie asked. Tom nodded.

"I have just been speaking to the Professor. I think it was a similar conversation that Edward and Mary must have had with him." The others nodded.

"Charlie has had the same thing happen to him as us," Edward said. "We have all been wrenched away from our time against our will and deposited here in this strange world. At first the shock is unbelievable and almost unbearable."

Tom gaped; he had risked his life to save them and all three were angry at him. "Well the thing is ..." he started, but Charlie stopped him.

"Let us finish, Thomas, please. I was going to say that the shock is indeed horrible. But then we listened to the Professor. He explained who and what we all are ...Walkers is it? More than that, he explained that it was that part of us that made us show ourselves to you so you could feel us dying, all these years later. You could have ignored it, you know. You told the Professor you wanted rid of these strange abilities you had.

172

You could have left us dead and gone on with your life, but you did not," Charlie continued. "You came and rescued us at great personal danger. Not for thought of gain or reward and probably thinking it would be the end of the matter, is that not so?"

Relieved that he had mistaken their anger, Tom, feeling faintly embarrassed, just shrugged and nodded.

"So, whatever the shock we are going through, we all agree we owe you our gratitude. On balance we feel it is better to be alive now than to have died back then. Maybe it is also better to have a chance to understand who – or what - we are."

"And you don't mind that we brought you away from your world and your time?"

Charlie shook his head. "No, at least I don't. I can't speak for the others. I said it was a shock and it is, but you see I had no one in my time to worry about. I had no family left alive. My world was going mad trying to kill itself and we were losing the war. Know what I thought when I realised that I would die on that stinking boat? I thought that soon everyone would be dead and we would lose the war. I had a pretty carefree attitude to my own life because I did not think it would last long anyway. I had decided just to have fun and a few adventures along the way."

He suddenly laughed. "It's probably why I jumped into the sea practically naked and swam across to the U-boat. Seemed like a good idea at the time," he went on. "My only regret was not knowing for certain who was going to win. Well ... now I know. The war is over; the world is safe and an amazing place to be. I don't want to go back and I want to thank you and the rest for rescuing me. But what I also want is some bacon and eggs!" With that he got up and helped himself to a plate of food.

Edward glared at Charlie and then said with a certain emphasis, "*We* came to see how Tom was, *not* to have breakfast!" In response, Charlie just winked at him.

"Tom," Edward said, "the Professor gave us each a choice; three options as it were. If we really objected to being here we could go back. Return to a few moments after we left and take our chances.

"But if you did go back to Isandlwana or Mary to the bakery and Charlie to the U-boat," Tom said, "then ..."

"Yes. It would be certain death for all of us, but the Professor said there was no other way. If we lived on in our time the effects on the future would be unpredictable. So, the other choice is to stay here and try to become normal people. He would find us a place in the world and jobs and we would live out our lives in this time."

"Or? You said three options."

"Or we join the Institute and use our talents to protect the world and serve the aims of the Professor. He has given us some time to think it over."

Tom looked at Mary. Last time he had seen her she had been almost delirious and convinced they were all demons. "How ... er ... how do you feel, Mary?" he asked tentatively. He braced himself for a tirade about them all going to Hell.

"Quite well, Master Thomas," she said shyly, "I beg your forgiveness Master in that I called you a devil and demon."

"Er, thanks, no problem. You were confused. But I meant what do you feel about the choice you have?"

"Well, like Charlie, I was bewildered by this place, 'tis true. But when Professor Neoptolemas explained to me what I am ...

what we all are, it was as if a veil dropped from mine eyes. It was clear as day that he spoke the truth. All my life I thought myself a witch for that which I could do, and believed I would hang one day and burn in Hell. When the fire came and then I found myself here, I imagined that I *was* in Hell and had been done to death. For the Bible it sayeth that 'you shall not suffer a witch to live'."

"Mary, you are not in Hell."

The girl nodded her head. "I know that to be true, Master Thomas, and I know I am not a witch, nor are you demons. So, if I am still on earth it must be for a reason. I believe the Lord has given me the powers of angels and granted the same to thee. There is a purpose for all that has happened. I was meant to help you as were these kind sirs. The Lord may have brought me to a strange place out of my time, but it matters not. I will serve Him wherever I can. For the Lord's purpose will be done!"

Tom blinked. He was not sure if Mary was any better off. Beforehand she was certain they were demons. Now she believed that they were all part of some divine plan.

"Mary, you need to know God did not send me. I had these dreams of the three of you dying and – well I had to help. It is true that we all have talents and powers, but I don't want you thinking God sent me to bring you all here to serve His plan, even if I knew what it was. The truth is the Professor wanted me to save you so you could help him protect the World. As for me, I just wanted to save you and then go back to my normal life ... my normal life," he repeated in a whisper as thoughts of his family came to him. He had no normal life to go back to. Not anymore.

Mary patted him gently on the arm. "Don't alarm yourself, Master. I do not think these things because you have tricked me into believing them. I see the truth in what has happened even if you do not. That the Lord chose you to do His work might seem strange to you, but I am sure of it."

Tom shook his head and glanced at Edward. The Victorian officer wore a modern suit and now looked quite at ease with his surroundings and all that had transpired. As if reading a question in Tom's mind, Edward spoke now.

"As for me, I'm a rational man, born of an age when reason and science were driving back the superstitions of old times. I accept what has happened and seek to understand it. While that is going on, I am tempted to work for the Professor and help him in his aims to use these talents we have to protect our world and our time."

"Our world; our time? What about all that you said about your time being over and that you should be dead? I thought you in particular might take the Professor's first choice."

"It's my world and my time now, Tom. Isandlwana was part of my life, but I realise that it is a bit foolish to wish to have died just to make my conscience better because I lived when all my friends and fellow soldiers died. I still feel duty and loyalty ... I have not changed. I just need to find the right cause to vow that duty to."

Tom now turned to the third figure at the table. Charlie was still munching on a sausage. "What about you, Charlie. What do you want to do?"

"I have not got that far. My plan till now was to have some fun," he said in a muffled voice while piling in some black pudding, "but I reckon I will take a look at the world, hang about a bit and see what happens."

Something about the image of Charlie eating his breakfast with such relish reminded Tom of his dad, who had loved a 'full English'. The memory stirred his emotions yet again and he felt his eyes moisten.

Mary reached out and put her hand on Tom's, which startled him, but then it felt comforting and he sighed.

"Thou feelest the loss most deeply: thy parents, thy sister. Dost thou not, Master Thomas?"

Charlie looked up, a sausage still held in the prongs of a fork.

Tom felt a gnawing in his middle and suddenly did not feel like any more food. He nodded. "Yes – I do. I still can't believe they are gone! I was never born. But I am here. It doesn't make sense."

Suddenly he felt angry and needed to be alone. "None of this makes sense. What am I doing eating breakfast? What am I do talking to you lot? I should be somewhere else trying to sort this mess out!"

Pushing back his chair, Tom leapt abruptly to his feet and ran out of the room, his face burning, red with anger and frustration.

CHAPTER EIGHTEEN - THE TWISTED REALITY

As he left the dining room, Tom heard Charlie tell Mary to, "Give the lad a few minutes alone." But Tom had no intention of being alone: he wanted answers and was going to see the man who could give them to him.

He strode up to the Professor's door and hammered on it. The eternally agitated Mr Phelps glanced up irritated from his desk, took in Tom with an imperious glance that swept down onto the diary open on his desk and 'tutted'.

"The Professor has you down for 10 a.m., Master Oakely. It is only 9.28."

Taking a deep breath Tom was about to explode with just about every swear word he knew, when the door opened and the Professor was standing there.

"It is quite alright, Mr Phelps, I am free now."

Mr Phelps looked slightly affronted, but merely ticked off the appointment and turned back to his other work.

"Did you sleep and eat well?" The Professor asked ushering Tom into his study and closing the door behind him.

"Yes, thank you. But where is Septimus?"

"Sorry, Thomas – he has not returned."

Tom scowled. "What is he up to, do you think?"

"I really don't know. Once I find out anything, you will be the first to know."

"Thank you, Tom nodded, barely pausing for breath, his words tumbling out like water from a burst dam. "Yesterday you said you would answer my questions. Just what is going on? Who is Captain Redfeld? What is that Office place and what will you do about my parents?"

The old man said nothing, but turned to look out at the garden where the bright morning light blazed through the French windows. The clock on the mantelpiece chimed the half hour and he took out a fob watch from his waistcoat and flipped it open to check the time before giving the winder a few turns. Finally, he shut the watch with a loud snap and then looked back at Tom.

"I will tell you what you want to know, but it is a long story."

"That's fine. Right now, I don't belong anywhere, so I'm in no hurry," Tom said, tersely.

"The first thing you must know is that Captain Redfeld is not from our world. He is from a parallel world − a world where history played out in a different way."

Tom stared at the Professor in disbelief. Before that dream in Hyde Park he would have dismissed the statement as plainly ridiculous. But, after what Redfeld and the Custodian had said about Redfeld's reality being different from Tom's own, he was not so sure.

"Are you are telling me that Redfeld is not human?"

"Oh, he is human alright: as human as you and I."

"Sorry, Professor, but you're going to have to explain it to me."

"Well then. To begin with, what do you know of Quantum Theory?" the old man asked. Tom blinked.

"Only what you get from Star Trek. I am only twelve, you know."

"Quite, quite. Well: you need to know a little. There is a concept called the Quantum Theory of multiple worlds. The idea is that there are an infinite number of alternative Earths, indeed an infinite number of alternative universes. Effectively, for every choice made in the universe a new universe is created. Say you are in a restaurant and you order hamburger and French fries in our universe. However, there is a universe where you ordered bangers and mash and another where you had pasta and so on. The number of possible alternative universes is literally infinite. But all that does not really affect us because there is no way of getting to those universes and no way of them affecting ours."

His eyes widening at the image of hundreds of replicas of himself each eating a different plate of food, Tom frowned, "Then if that is so, how did Captain Redfeld get here?"

"Because when his reality split from our reality it was not the same way that it usually happens. Something different occurred. We call it 'The Event'. His reality and our reality did not simply diverge because of a decision being different here to there. If that had happened then each reality would be distinct and separate. But that is not true. Both realities occupy the same place or, if you like, the same quantum address. They struggle against each other to be the survivor and in so doing overlap, with occasionally bits of his reality merging with parts of ours and vice versa."

"Why don't we see parts of his world then?" Tom objected.

"Well, because most of us would reject them as unbelievable and deny it even if we did see it. That subconscious denial creates powerful barriers to any crossing-over between there and here. The realties mostly touch and show themselves when our defences are low and we can't easily deny it: in our dreams or when we are ill. It may be that near death, when people talk of out-of-body experiences, they are in fact experiencing something of that other reality," the Professor answered and stopped speaking, staring into space for a while pondering all this.

Tom was silent, trying to grasp the concept; it was staggeringly complex and yet at the same time so simple an explanation that he wondered why he had not thought of it before.

"Indeed," the Professor went on as if he had not stopped speaking, "not so much dreams, as nightmares. For Redfeld's reality is a nightmare. Our world might look bad, but in that place the worst of what happened here occurred there too, and then even more terrible events. We call it *The Twisted Reality*." With a sigh the Professor walked slowly to the desk and sat down.

"You see, Tom, in his reality the Second World War panned out in quite a different way to here. Britain lost the Battle of Britain and surrendered. With no war in the West to distract him, the Hitler of that reality was able to throw all his weight into the invasion of Russia. Moscow fell in the winter of '41 and the rest of Russia surrendered when the German tanks reached the Urals in 1942. With Europe at his feet, Germany helped Japan defeat America before the United States could develop the atom bomb."

"How do you know all this?" Tom asked.

"Oh, we have captured some Walkers from Redfeld's world in the past and questioned them. What is more, I have seen it myself. I have been to Redfeld's world and seen its horrors. As for 'The Event' – the moment when the realities split? Well let's just say it's something of a specialist subject of mine. I am a Professor, after all, Thomas!"

182

For the first time that morning, Tom almost smiled at the old man's wry humour. "Next question," he said. "What is the Office and who is the Custodian?"

"The Office dates back to the Event, as does the Custodian and the rest of the Directorate. To put it simply, they try to balance our reality with the Twisted Reality. They take it very seriously because if they ever failed to keep that balance, the worlds could simply obliterate each other."

"Ouch."

"Indeed, ouch!"

Tom wanted to know more about the Office and the Event but he also wanted to know about Redfeld. "What does he want me for? He knew me. It seems he was searching for me."

"I think he wanted you, Thomas, because he knows, as I do, that you are one of the most powerful Walkers ever. You might be able to do many amazing things with time. You may be able to help Redfeld and his master – his 'Führer ' – achieve their objective," the old man replied. "I only wish I knew what that was."

"Well, if he wanted my help, he's rather blown it now. I mean he took my family away and I could have been wiped from existence! In the first place that hardly makes me likely to want to help him and in the second place it's only by chance that I still exist. So, is it just that he has a bad temper or is the man incompetent?" Tom asked then noticed the old man's frown. "What is it?"

"It just occurred to me that the degree of interference between realities exercised by Redfeld in destroying your family would not usually be permitted by the Directorate. That is why Redfeld had to go and see the Custodian and try to persuade him to allow it. The Custodian was already anxious about you and your potential to disturb his precious balance so it was probably easy enough for Redfeld to win that argument."

Deep in thought, the Professor absent-mindedly removed his spectacles and polished them on his handkerchief before replacing them on his nose. Tom waited for him to continue.

"It might have suited the Custodian to obliterate you, Thomas, but I am sure Redfeld has something far bigger in mind than protecting his world from you; something that he may not have divulged to the Head of the Directorate. He seems to be nurturing you, preparing you for using your talents in some way. But for what? If we could find out more about their agreement, it would help. Let us think a moment about the dream in the Office when the Custodian and the others seemed to agree a deal concerning you. That third man at the window: could that have been ..."

Tom had been wondering about that too. He had been thinking about how oddly Septimus had acted when the Office was discussed; how he had left without explanation and how he was still to return. "Septimus! It must be Septimus."

The Professor nodded, "Then it is to Septimus we must speak. If he is the third man, if he has done some deal with Redfeld and this 'man in the suit' then he knows a lot about all that is going on."

Suddenly the old man stood up. "There is also another way to find out about the agreement and I am sorry, but I can only do this alone. I am starting to fear that the dangers are far greater than I at first suspected. I must go at once."

Tom stared at him. "What? Are you leaving me, too?"

"Sorry, Thomas, but I really must go for a short while."

"What? Hang on a minute: that's not fair. All we've done is talk for two days. You still have not said what you are going to do about my parents?"

"I must ask you to trust me, Thomas," the Professor said simply.

"Why should I?" Tom felt his anger return.

"I don't have time to explain – a lot might be at stake beyond just your family."

"*Just* my family!"

"Tom you are overreacting!"

"Overreacting ... aaaaghh!" Tom screamed and waved his hands about.

The Professor rang the bell on his desk. Mr Phelps emerged and before he had a chance to speak further, Tom found himself outside the Professor's rooms and pushed into the hall. He turned back to talk to Neoptolemas again, but found the door shut and Mr Phelps wearing an expression that reminded Tom of his science teacher, Mr Beaufin, in an angry mood, so he backed off a few steps.

Fuming, he stomped off down the hallway. He almost opened the dining room door, but then he heard Charlie laugh and Mary giggle and feeling that he could not face them all right now, he went through to the library and drifted about the room, scanning the spines of books vaguely, while he tried to think.

The Professor had a large collection of books on more or less every subject, yet here, just like in his office, the emphasis was on history, maps and politics. It appeared the Institute needed its Walkers to have access to as much accurate information as possible on all the times and places they might have to visit. Idly, Tom wondered what happened if history was changed.

Would the contents of the books change? He supposed they must do; unless a Walker was carrying the book back in time whilst the effect of changing time occurred. That is what had happened to Tom, of course. What had Septimus called him? An anomaly, a paradox? Something that could not exist and yet did. Septimus had explained that time travel had funny peculiarities, that when a Walker travels from one moment to another, the two moments become linked in some way.

Thinking about that, Tom realised it meant that whoever killed his parents must have travelled from the present day back in time in order to do it. Someone had gone back from the present and started the fire that killed his parents before he was born. But whoever it was had miscalculated, not realising that Tom was off with Septimus in that alternate Isandlwana that Redfeld had created, and so he continued to exist. Tom frowned, or had it happened when he was dreaming about the Office? Redfeld had started to talk to the man in the suit about Tom's parents. Had that been it then? Maybe he did not just dream, but actually Walked whilst he was sleeping. Tom almost laughed at that: it gave a whole new meaning to 'sleep walking'.

So then, Tom thought, one way or another he must have been absent from the world of his present reality at the moment in time when his parents' murderers travelled back, and so he was protected from the effect of his parents being killed before he was born and thus he continued to exist: an anomaly.

If that was so, could Tom travel back to the same day that he and Septimus had arrived at the burned out house and follow whoever the murderer was back to the moment the fire was set? Or maybe, he could even stop the murderer going back in

186

the first place. If only he knew who it was it would be a lot simpler.

Then, another thought occurred to Tom. What if he did go back to the day of the fire and either stopped the fire occurring or managed to get his parents out of the way, somehow? What might happen? The Professor had told him to be careful, but the Professor had disappeared. He should really wait and tell either the Professor or Septimus when they returned. But damn it, where were they both?

Now he started to think about when he had spoken of the dream in the Office and how Septimus had become very nervous. The Welshman had got out of the Professor's room as fast as he could. As for the Professor, he had calmly listened to all Tom had to say and then suddenly, without explanation or any indication of when he would be back, he had gone too.

The more Tom thought about it, the more convinced he became that it all hinged on his dreams of the Office. He reminded himself again how little he knew about both Septimus and the Professor. Who knows what they might be up to? They just told him to wait and expected him to obey. Tom balled his fists, his anger threatening to explode. They didn't seem to care about what he was going through. They were probably laughing at him right now.

So then, why wait? Why not just go back now and save his parents? Yes – go back now. But he could not tell anyone, for they would try to stop him. Tom was in no mood to be stopped and he had decided that he had done enough for this agency. He had rescued these Walkers and in the process lost his family. Let the Professor sort out Redfeld, whoever or whatever he was. Let Septimus play whatever games he was up to.

Tom was leaving!

CHAPTER NINETEEN - FAMILY HISTORY

Tom Walked back to his home and stood outside it. The fire had happened before he was born – so at least twelve years before – and yet it appeared that no attempt to knock the ruins down or rebuild a house there had been made. That was certainly puzzling.

But this was the odd thing about changing history. From his point of view, none of that had ever occurred: the fire never happened. His parents had lived on in the house and one day he and then his sister were brought home from the hospital where they had been born. But apparently no longer was this the case.

He continued to stare at the ruins: his mind struggling to accept it all. Perhaps it was a trick and maybe his parents still lived, but somewhere else instead. Maybe his sister was, at this very moment, at school. Tom strained to remember what class his sister had on – what day was it, a Friday? Let's see; he often bumped into her in the main corridor on the way into his chemistry lesson. Ah, that was it – she had General Science with Mr Beaufin. Right then, thought Tom, that's it then: I'm going to find Emma in Boffin's class.

The school was about a mile down the road and as Tom ran most of the way he was soon standing outside the tall gates, which were thrown open. He had only gone thirty yards when he heard a familiar terrifying voice shouting out at him.

"You boy: stop where you are and come here!" It was the Headmaster, Mr Patel, walking towards Tom across the school playing fields from where he had been watching a Rugby match. Tom hesitated, then, bolted towards the front door into the school.

"Hey you – stop. You boy, stop at once!" screamed the Headmaster.

Ignoring him, Tom clattered through the doors and turned right along the main corridor. As he did, he collided with a group of lads, knocking one of them to the ground who was then helped back onto his feet by his friends.

"Watch it, mate," the boy said. Tom stared at the familiar face of his best pal.

"Sorry, Andy!" Tom apologised, "Patel is after me and he'll kill me if he catches up."

"How do you know my name?" Andy asked. Tom felt his heart sink: so Andy did not recognise him.

"Andy it's me – Tom. It's Tom!"

"Who the heck is this guy?" Andy asked looking at the boys standing by him. They all shrugged, apart from James who peered at him and then replied.

"Apparently, his name is Tom."

"James, Andy, all of you: surely you remember me?"

"Look man, all I remember is you knocking me over. Oh, that and the fact that Patel is about to 'ave you!" Andy said with a nasty grin whilst pointing over Tom's shoulder towards the doors. There, the Headmaster was now emerging, searching up and down the corridor: his face so red with fury that it reminded Tom of a beetroot.

As Tom staggered away, he could hear Mr Patel thundering after him along with the echoing sounds of Andy and his friends laughing.

Tom ran on to the end of the corridor. There, next to the fire exit, was the Boffin's classroom. He looked through the window in the door and saw Emma's best friend Lucy, along with the rest of her class: but of Emma, there was no sign.

"Can I help you?" said a stern voice from behind. Tom spun round and saw that Beaufin was there, dressed in the black scholars' robes from Oxford University that he always wore. He scowled at Tom from under bristling eyebrows.

"Erm ... sorry, sir. I mean yes, you can help me – I'm looking for my sister, Emma Oakley. Can you tell her I'm here?" Tom said.

"I am afraid you are mistaken, young sir. I have no such girl in my class...," the teacher replied, but just then Mr Patel arrived.

"Ah, Mr Beaufin, I see you have apprehended our intruder. I want a word with him," Mr Patel said with a touch of menace in his voice.

"Intruder? I think you had better come along with us, boy, to the Headmaster's office," Beaufin said.

"I am not an intruder. It's me, Tom Oakley," Tom said, desperately.

"I don't know you, boy, but why are you not at school? I think we had better call the truancy officer. Which school do you go to?" Mr Patel asked.

"This one, sir – don't you remember me, Mr Patel? Mr Beaufin: you gave me detention three weeks ago for kicking a stone and smashing the biology class window," Tom insisted.

Mr Beaufin seemed to pause at that and think about it. "The window ... I remember it was broken and it was a pupil who did it," the teacher said and peered intently at Tom, as if seeing him for the first time. Then, he shook his head.

"Don't lie to me boy – I remember every pupil I ever had at this school – and certainly those I gave detention to," he said and reached out to grab hold of Tom's arm. Tom kicked him hard in the shin and leapt back. Spinning round, he pushed the nearby fire exit bar down hard and as the door swung open, jumped through and slammed it behind him. He then took off as if he was a fox with all the hounds in England chasing him.

Tom ran for as long as he could. His sides hurt and his throat burned, like it had once when he drank hot chocolate too quickly, but he did not stop running until he had left his school and the pursuers far behind.

So it was true. The school had never heard of him or his sister. The fire had killed his parents before he was born and so neither he nor his sister existed. He had to find out the date of the fire and try to stop it: but how?

His father had been a keen genealogist – or family historian: he had traced his family line back to the seventeenth century and found out that they were descended from Welsh coal miners. Tom used to snigger about how his gran had been convinced they had descended from nobility or royalty and been disappointed to learn the truth. Not that it bothered his dad. He was as proud of the coal mining great-grandfathers as he might have been finding Henry the Eighth was an ancestor.

Tom recalled being taken along to the Central Library and Records Office in the city centre. He concentrated, reached out for the Flow of Time and Walked the few miles there.

It was now after lunch time. Tom had been flicking through the newspaper archives for what seemed like hours and was getting tired. Perhaps it was time to give up and ask for help. Then, suddenly, he saw it. There was a picture of a burnt out

192

house on the front page above an article with the headline: **YOUNG COUPLE DIE IN MYSTERY FIRE** and a subheading: **Fire brigade baffled as to the cause**. Seeing it all there in print was a shock and Tom let out an involuntary gasp. An elderly lady on the next table frowned at the noise and pointed sternly at a sign that read *Silence Please*. Tom nodded, mouthed the word 'Sorry' to her and looked back at the picture on the page.

The article reported that Robert and Laura Oakley were non-smokers and that their house had been rewired only the previous year. He looked again at the photo: it was his house, no doubt about it. Even blackened and with no roof the shape was familiar. He glanced at the top of the page, where he could read the date: the 22nd August, 1997. That, then, was the date of the fire. The article stated that it had started at about 2.00 a.m. that day. So, now he knew, what should he now do? Go back and warn his parents? Yes, that was his plan. He had a date and a time, which he scribbled down on a notepad and leaving the library, walked home the normal way, using his feet and legs rather than his powers. He wanted to preserve those for later: he needed them to save his mum and dad.

As he turned into his own road he almost walked into Andy, who was coming out of the street, walking his bike. Andy jumped to the side to avoid the collision, dropped his bike and, tripping over a low stone wall, ended up in a flowerbed.

"Sorry, Andy, I didn't see you."

Andy stared up at him, a look of indignation on his face. "You again! You seem to be making a habit of walking into me! Who are you, anyway?"

"I already told you who I am – your best mate, Tom Oakley."

Andy picked himself up and swept the dirt of his trousers. "I'm sorry, but you are loopy, man. I never knew a Tom Oakley."

"But we founded the *Desperados* together, Andy. We swore to be together whatever came along."

Again, as with Mr Beaufin that afternoon at school, Andy leaned forward and stared at Tom as if trying to recall some long lost memory. Then he shook his head. "Loopy!" he muttered, getting on his bike and riding away. At the corner of the street he stopped and glanced back for a few moments: his head wrinkling into a frown. Then he was gone.

Tom grimaced. It seemed that if really pressed, some people did remember him, albeit very briefly. Or was that just wishful thinking? In any event they soon forgot. At best he was an echo – a whisper of a memory. Feeling dejected, Tom turned and walked up the street. He then stopped dead in his tracks as he saw Kyle Rogers and his gang cross the road and walk towards him. Great – he thought – this is all I need.

Kyle stopped in front of him. "Heh, you a new kid?" he asked.

"Kyle, don't bother me," Tom said.

"I'm only going to ask you to join my gang. Hang on how you know my name?"

"I er....." Tom stammered.

"Ah, everyone knows you Kyle – you're da man round here," said one of the gang in a toadying voice. Tom nodded.

Kyle beamed at that then stopped and squinted at Tom. "You sure you're new? Could 'ave sworn I knew you."

Tom shook his head.

"Anyway," Kyle continued, "You look the right sort to join my gang. I'm the boss and we are called the *Bandidos*. Our

194

sworn blood enemies are the *Desperados*. We are following that Andy guy. If we catch him, we are going to teach him a lesson. Haven't seen him have you?"

Tom shrugged noncommittally.

"Let's try the park. You coming along, new kid?"

"Later, Kyle. Got something I have to do," Tom replied.

As Kyle and his gang moved off down the road, Tom let out a long breath that ended in a whistle. Then he walked across the road.

Again he stood outside the ruined house and again wondered why it had not been rebuilt in the more than a decade since the fire. His mother worked - had worked when she had been alive, Tom added sadly to himself - in an estate agents and he remembered her telling his dad only last week that any land fit to build houses on rarely stood vacant for long. Yet this house still stood here as if nothing had happened in fifteen odd years. There was not even a 'For Sale' sign or anything.

Tom dismissed his musings; he had a job to do. August 22nd 1997 at 2.00 a.m. was the date. He recalled the image of his grandparents' grandfather clock. Then he paused and wondered if they still lived in the same house. How had they coped with their daughter's death? They were only four streets away. Maybe he could go there and tell them he was still alive. Then he realised they would have no idea who he was. He had never been born.

It was a moment of utter desolation for Tom: nobody knew he existed, not even the people he loved.

'Focus, Tom, get a grip. Mind on the job man!' the voice inside his head screamed.

Again, he reached out for the clock and he saw it as plain as day in his mind. He sent the hands spiralling backwards, but kept a firm grip on *this* spot, *this* place. Off he went. He Walked backwards to the day his parents died. All seemed normal until, abruptly, he felt the sensation change. It felt oddly different from what he usually felt when Walking and he could not quite place why, although the sensation was vaguely familiar as if he had experienced it before.

Then he was there.

He actually appeared a little before 2.00 a.m. and in the deepest part of the night. There was no moon, but a streetlight fifty feet away illuminated the front of the building in its yellow glow. The house was there: intact and unharmed and looking almost identical to how it appeared in the present day, although Tom noticed that the windows were different. Then he remembered that his parents had them replaced by double glazing when he was six. There were no lights on or any sign of life at this hour, but they would be fast asleep and not ready for the horror to come.

'Ok', Tom thought, 'what now?'

He stood for a few minutes pondering his options, then he shrugged and walked up to the door and grabbing the knocker, started hammering on it and yelling at the top of his voice.

"Fire! Fire! Get up, get up!" he shouted over and over again. All along the street, lights started coming on in upstairs rooms. Tom heard a noise behind him, spun round. The front door of the house opposite opened and an elderly lady peeked out and stared at Tom severely whilst clutching her dressing gown around her. Distracted, Tom heard the door of his own house open.

"What the hell is going on, boy!"

Tom turned and stood open-mouthed. There, in front of him, was his father. But, he looked so young. What age would he be, twenty-three or twenty-four? What struck him most was how thin he was. The father he knew, who was thirty-six, had just joined a gym to try to lose a few stone. "Dad, it's me," he whispered uselessly.

"Well, what are you shouting about, lad?" This question was not from his father but from one of two policemen who had just arrived and were standing beside him.

"I ... I" Tom stammered. The policemen glared at him.

"My mum and dad, I need to tell them something," Tom said at last.

"Is this your house?" the policeman asked. Tom nodded at just the same moment as his father shook his head.

"This boy is nothing to do with us. Maybe you should find his parents, Officer."

The policeman turned back to Tom, "I think, perhaps, you should come with us – oi stop!!"

By now, however, Tom had already made off down the street. The policemen set off after him, but they were much slower and Tom was able to lose them as he turned the corner, leapt into an alleyway and finally hid behind some wheelie bins. He heard pounding footsteps as the policemen came round the corner. The sound came closer and closer and Tom was certain they knew where he was hiding. Panicking, he started to rise from his hiding place, tensing himself to flee again. He saw the police hurtle straight past the end of the alley: and then they were gone, running on down the street.

Tom looked about him and decided the alley was a good place to hide. No streetlight penetrated the gloom here and the wheelie bins were in the darkest part. Crouching back down, he let the world about him go back to sleep and the policemen carry on with their beat. He waited well over two hours in the alley, his eyelids pricking as he fought against sleep. For a while a scrawny black cat came to keep him company, rubbing its arched back against his leg. It was strangely comforting and Tom was sorry to see it slink away.

Slowly the sun rose and daylight came early on this summer's morning. Looking along the alleyway that ran behind the row of houses, Tom could see his own house now. As far as he could make out, there was no sign of fire. Hardly daring to breathe lest someone hear, Tom emerged stiffly from the alley and tiptoed back past the front of his house. It was now almost 5.00 a.m. and the building looked safe; no flames nor any smoke were visible. Puzzled, he checked his link to the Flow of Time and made certain that he was here on the right day. He was.

Ah well, he thought. Everything seems quiet. Maybe, just by being here, enough had been done to stop the fire. Perhaps, the distraction he caused had prevented someone dropping a match or pouring petrol through the letterbox. Whatever the explanation, it was time to go home. Walking forward in time, he again felt that odd sensation as he moved through the years. Something different to the normal sensation of Walking – yet he could not be sure what it was, nor could he pin down the vague feeling that it had happened before.

Tom materialised outside his house in the present day. Eagerly, he looked up at his home and then, in an instant, his heart sank when he saw the burnt-out house in front of him. The disappointment felt like a punch to his stomach and he stood open-mouthed, staring at the charred ruins. How could this be? He had returned to that fateful night over twelve years before and had seen that the fire had not happened. Yet he could not deny the evidence of his own eyes. Here was the scorched skeleton of his house. Had he got the date wrong or was there some other explanation? What on earth was going on?

He walked through the wreckage and went into the back garden, past the weeds and bracken that had overgrown the interior of the building. There, he felt the gloom come down upon him like black clouds gathering in a stormy sky. He had failed. He could never revisit that same night, so he wouldn't be able to save his family and he and his sister would never be born. He would be left as a schoolboy who never existed. Tom felt despair well up inside him and he slumped down on the scorched remains of a wall. His eyes moistened and – having no idea what to do – he put his head into his hands and started to cry.

CHAPTER TWENTY - FLIGHT

"Here he is!" A voice shouted from within the ruins of the house. Startled, Tom glanced round, saw Edward standing there along with Septimus, and behind them both was Mary. All three were looking at him with relieved expressions on their faces.

"Boyo, you had us quite concerned for a while. We thought Redfeld had got to you. Thanks to Edward here we were able to track you down," Septimus said and then, seeing Tom's red eyes, put a hand on his back. "I'm sorry, Tommy! I should have known you would be here. Have a moment alone, if you need it."

"A moment alone? Where the hell have you been?" Tom snarled.

"Round and about – but I came back by all accounts only an hour or so after you had left the Professor's office. We got worried when we couldn't find you. We can talk later, so have a few moments rest and we will get away from here."

Tom was hardly satisfied with that explanation, but now Septimus turned to Edward and the two had a whispered conversation. Alone with his despair, Tom sat in silence. Then, he noticed that Mary had come forward and was looking at the burnt out wreck of his house.

"Mary, what are you doing here?" he asked.

"When Mr Mason said that they were coming to seek for you at the house of your parents, I asked to be allowed to come as well. You see, my home was destroyed by fire ..." she trailed off, looking around at the blackened walls and scorched timbers, "... I do not know what happened to any of my family in the fire. So, I understand a little of how you feel and I wanted to come and say how sorry I am for you."

Tom looked at Mary's face and noticed that she too had been weeping; her eyes were all red and her face marked by tears. Then he remembered that for her, the Great Fire of London was only a few days in the past and her grief was still almost as new as his own. Something recorded in dusty old school books was for her more than just history. It occurred to him that he could help her answer some of her questions. Tom wiped his eyes and took a deep breath.

"Maybe in the library at the Hourglass Institute there might be some information about your people," he suggested.

Mary shook her head. "I don't have my letters – I was never taught to read - but Lieutenant Dyson has already helped me look. Everywhere around Pudding Lane was destroyed by fire it seems but, praise God, my master and his family did get away. My mam and pa rented a house a few streets towards the river, but about them we could find nothing. My family were not rich and owned no land, so were not important enough for anyone to write about."

"Everyone is important, Mary, most particularly if they're your family or friends," Tom said and then felt the despair come back again. The two of them stared at his home, sharing their grief in silence for a moment.

Septimus and Edward had finished their conversation and Tom saw Edward nodding; a moment later he disappeared. The Lieutenant seemed to be getting good at Walking now, thought Tom, wondering what they had been talking about.

When Edward had gone, Septimus strolled over to join Tom and Mary. He had almost reached them when suddenly he gasped and stepped forward to seize Tom's arm.

"Ow!" Tom squealed. "That hurts; stop pinching me!"

"Sorry, but a very important thought just occurred to me about your parents and ...."

He never completed the sentence. His eyes widening in fear Septimus dropped to the ground yelling, "Get down!" and dragged Tom and Mary down next to him. Nearby, there was a loud bang and the brickwork behind where Tom's head had been only moments before, exploded. A shower of bricks and rubble rained down on them.

Mary screamed and cowered down even lower. Peering through the cloud of dust, Tom could see two pairs of boots standing about where his front door would have been. They started moving towards him through the bracken.

Before Tom could react, Septimus shouted, "Got to go!" He grabbed the pair of them and, with a sudden lurch, the burnt out house was gone and the trio where lying in a heap on the stone paving slabs of a huge cathedral. Mary looked shocked and stared about her. Tom thought she might scream and start on about devils and demons again, but she just gulped and took a few deep breaths. Tom got up.

"Who were they?" he asked.

Septimus had his little box out and beeps and squeaks were coming from it. "Don't know, not sure. But it seems that they want us – or at least you – dead," he grabbed Tom again and pushed Mary along and they all started running down the aisle. As they came out into the nave at the back, they collided with and knocked over a figure in a hooded cowl.

"*Mon dieu!*" came a curse from under the hood as the monk fell over onto his back. The three Walkers did not stop to apologise and seconds later they burst out through the cathedral's main doors. They emerged on a large town square crowded with a bustling market. The population wore tunics and britches or, in the case of the women, long dresses. Two of them spotted Tom, Mary and Septimus and stared open mouthed at them and their clothing. Septimus was dressed, as he usually was, in dark blue jeans and a leather jacket, whilst Tom had on a t-shirt and tracksuit trousers. Mary wore a plain linen dress, but together they must have looked very strange to the townsfolk. Septimus did not wait to talk, but rushed on with Tom and Mary in tow, along the front of the cathedral and down a side alley, before shifting them both out of that time.

An instant later, they were now standing in a formal garden near a fountain. In the distance was a large stately home. It was dusk and the garden was empty. Septimus crouched down and pulled the boy down as well. Mary joined them. They were all breathing fast and hard after the last few minutes' exertions.

"Ok, Septimus. What just happened? Where are we now?" Tom was the first to recover his breath. It took a moment for Septimus to answer.

"As I explained when we first met, there is more than one power at work in this universe. I don't know who they are. They might be Redfeld's men or someone else, but in any event, your death seems to be part of their objective. I needed to get us away from there, so I took a detour through fourteenth century Rouen before coming here. This is near Paris in the eighteenth century. Best not to linger here though: they will be after us and, besides, this is not a safe time. The French Revolution is just around the corner."

Septimus slumped back against a low stone wall and puffed out his cheeks. "Phew, but I'm getting exhausted. I can't really Walk more than just me, normally, so I'm tapping your talents to let me do a lot of this. I'm not as powerful as you, Tommy boy, and it seems it's beginning to tell. I need a rest," he said, yawning. Tom too felt very tired, confused and bewildered. He also wanted to ask Septimus about his family, but felt too weary to ask right now. He just nodded.

"Yes, indeed, we all need a rest," Septimus said, "so, we must find somewhere to hide. I know just the place and just the time. Whoever they are, they won't find us there."

He stood up but then slumped back down, looking pale and weak.

"You can't manage anything, Septimus," Tom said. "Let me Walk us all. Where are we going?"

"Rome ... let's say, AD 25. It's a busy city at the heart of a mighty empire: very easy to hide and hard for anyone to follow us there.

Tom nodded and tried to move them back to ancient Rome. He found it difficult to concentrate on the task, however. He was still depressed over his failure to save his family, as well as scared about being chased by these men armed with guns. So it transpired that, distracted by these feelings, they found themselves appearing not in the bustle of ancient Rome, but in a field. Tom stared around, realising that he had no idea of where they were or, indeed, what year it was.

There was a shout from nearby. As they turned at the noise, they saw a dozen men advancing on them from twenty yards away: men wearing tunics and sandals, helmets of bronze, and carrying large round shields, brightly painted with different symbols, and long, very sharp spears. Mary gave a gasp of terror and Tom felt his heart pounding, half with fear and half with excitement. These were Greek warriors: he recognised them from the movie *Troy*, which had been about the hero Achilles.

"Well, that could have gone better!" Septimus observed, as they were surrounded.

"Sorry!" Tom said weakly. He tried Walking again, but the journey they had undertaken, along with those earlier on in the day, not to mention that he had hardly slept the night before, had drained him.

One of the warriors said something, presumably in ancient Greek. To Tom's surprise, Septimus answered in the same language.

The warrior scowled and snarled a reply to the Welshman. Septimus' face blanched and he whispered a few words to Tom and Mary.

"Sorry to say, but we're in deep trouble. They think we are spies from their enemies and they want to execute us!"

The warriors now levelled their spears and advanced upon them.

CHAPTER TWENTY-ONE - ALEXANDER THE GREAT

T he warriors gestured with their spears to a group of tents some distance away, indicating that the three of them should move in that direction. They started walking that way and as they drew closer Tom could see thousands more tents stretching far into the distance. He realised the ones he and his fellow Walkers were being herded towards were just part of a vast camp. It had been sited beside a river and was surrounded by a huge flat plain that vanished into the haze all around.

It was hot – very hot. Tom was glad he was lightly dressed, as for an English summer, but even so he began to sweat. He had been to Spain once or twice with his parents on holiday, and on one occasion to Florida, but the heat here was far worse. Mary looked very weak and was visibly wilting. The temperature was much higher than any she would have experienced before in her lifetime. The Greeks, however, seemed not to notice the heat and moved lightly across the ground.

As they were marched towards the camp it became gradually more distinct and, as the haze diminished, Tom was able to make out the details of the tents and their inhabitants, which he could now see moving about. They entered along a sort of avenue running right through the rows of tents, passing hundreds of men - some in armour and others taking their ease in lighter garments. Many were gathered around cook fires, roasting cuts of lamb or carcasses of birds suspended upon spits over the flames, or else baking bread laid out upon hot stones around the firesides. A squad of soldiers marching past in the opposite direction - perhaps taking their turn out on patrol - stared at the three Walkers with avid curiosity. One or two pointed at Septimus' jeans and laughed, only to be reprimanded by their officer.

Tom heard a sudden whinnying noise and turning his head saw half a dozen horses being led towards the river. One of them was fractious and kept kicking up dust as it gambolled along at the rear. A flash of sunlight beyond the horses drew Tom's gaze and he now saw a line of chariots parked up awaiting the attention of a carpenter, who was repairing a broken axle.

"Where are we, Septimus?" whispered Tom. The Welshman gazed around and took a few minutes to answer.

"It's not really my specialist region or period, but I gather this is Persia and it's about three hundred years or so BC. That camp is full of Greek soldiers – thousands of them – and they are going to conquer all these lands."

Puzzled, Tom did not respond. Where exactly was Persia? He raised an eyebrow at Septimus, who clearly thought he had said something significant, for he tutted and rolled his eyes.

"Tommy, you need to read more history books. We are actually in what we now know as Iran, but it used to be Persia. Unless I'm very much mistaken, this army is commanded by Alexander the Great. They are embarked on the greatest campaign in history and won't stop till they reach India. Which is all very fascinating and romantic or perhaps bloodthirsty, depending on your point of view, but does not alter the fact that we're in dreadful danger. I'm drained, as are you. We need to get away and take Mary as well. So, there is a need to play for time to get our energy back."

They had reached the centre of the camp now. They were marched past groups of Greeks sitting in the shade of their tents avoiding the midday sun. Some were eating a little bread and olives or drinking wine. A few were playing games with dice. Most stopped and stared at Tom, Mary and Septimus and their modern clothes. The trio were marched into the heart of the camp and then made to stand in front of a large tent. One of the guards went in and a few minutes later a young man came out and asked them questions. Tom did not understand the words, but Septimus replied. The young man grew agitated and drew his sword, pointing it at Septimus' throat. The Welshman's eyes widened a little, but he kept on talking calmly and after a long pause, the young man thrust the sword back into the leather scabbard at his hip. Turning to the guards he muttered a few words and went back into the tent. Tom and his friends were then pushed into another tent and thrown to the ground. The guards glared at them for a moment then, after a few guttural comments and sniggered laughter, they left the tent.

The three Walkers lay for a few moments, gathering their breath, before Tom asked, "What just happened: I thought you said they were going to kill us?"

"Not today. I told them we were not spies but escaped slaves of their enemy, the Persians. I said we had worked in their capital and knew lots about their secrets and their army. I told them if they brought us writing material, I would draw them some maps of where the Persian armies were. He grew angry at that, as he did not believe a slave would be able to write, but I said we were merchants from the north - I thought that might account for our outlandish clothes – and that we had been captured by the Persians and forced to work for them."

209

"So, we are safe?" Tom asked.

"Not entirely. We have until sunrise tomorrow to prepare our maps, or we die."

"What do you know about the Persian army and their secrets?"

"No more than you, I was bluffing!" Septimus said with a helpless shrug.

"Oh great! What happens when tomorrow he realises this?"

"We must hope that you or I are strong enough to Walk us out of here to another time, or we're dead."

"Septimus, I would just like to say that my life was pretty good before I met you. Now my parents are dead, my house is a ruin and I am going to be killed as a spy from a land I have never heard of two thousand years before I was not born!"

"Yeah ... bit tedious isn't it?"

Tom was about to reply when a guard came in and threw down an armful of parchment, pens – at least, Tom assumed they were pens; they appeared to be made from hollow reeds sharpened to a point - and a flask of ink, and then left.

"Septimus – where did you go to when you left the Professor's office?" Tom asked the question that had been niggling since yesterday, but Septimus did not answer.

"Not right now, Tommy, we're in trouble. Your job is to rest and get back your strength. Even the ability to shift us a few hours might help. Lie down and go to sleep while I look busy and concoct some report for Alexander."

"Alexander! You mean that man was Alexander the Great?" Tom said, jerking up off the floor. Septimus smiled.

"That's right. See all the interesting places and famous people I take you to and all you do is complain! Now rest,

Tommy boy," Septimus ordered. "You too, Mary," he added to the young woman.

Tom and Mary tried to get comfortable on the hard ground. Tom closed his eyes, but before he could sleep, Mary asked a question.

"Master Thomas ..."

Tom opened his eyes and held up a hand. "Tom, it's Tom, Mary. You don't have to call me Master."

"Very well ... Master Tom, Mr Mason mentioned a name: 'Redfeld' was it? Who is he and why was he trying to kill you?"

Tom rolled over and leant on one elbow to look at Mary. "It's a long story, but I will give you short version ..." He took a deep breath and tried to explain. It was hard at times and Mary was confused by much of it. Phrases like 'alternative reality', 'planes of existence' or 'universes' were so far out of her world that Tom ground to a halt. Then, Septimus tried a different track.

"Mary, have you ever seen any plays by William Shakespeare?" he asked, looking up from the parchment, the pen dripping blobs of ink onto the map he was attempting to draw.

Mary thought for a moment then nodded. "Yes indeed, my Lord. My master paid for us all to go for a treat one year. It was '*Midsummer Night's Dream*', so it was."

"Splendid. So, you remember the fairies and enchanted creatures from fairyland?"

"Oh yes!" Mary's face lit up with a smile.

"Well then, where is fairyland?" Septimus asked.

Mary looked puzzled at that and took a long time to answer. "I suppose you would say all about us," she finally responded, "save not here. It's in dark corners and hidden in the woods and hills."

"So, it's another world really – don't you agree – alongside our world with strange enchanted creatures in it?"

Tom bit his lip and hoped that she would see where his friend was going with this. Mary's face contorted, revealing a mental struggle with ideas that were very new to her, but she nodded her head in the end.

"I think I start to understand what you are saying. This Twisted Reality is like fairyland?"

"You get it now," Septimus grinned. "And are these creatures in fairyland all good?"

"Some are – but many are not. Many are evil and mischievous," Mary this time responded quickly.

"So think of this Twisted Reality like that and the inhabitants like elves and sprites – cunning and plotting and up to no good," Septimus said.

Mary looked thoughtful. "So Redfeld is some type of monster from another world?"

"No," Tom butted in, shaking his head. "No, he is just a human, like you and me, and like us he has powers."

"It seems to me," said Mary with a shrug, "that you can be a monster, even if you are just a man."

Septimus looked up at that and nodded his head. "You are not wrong, lass, not wrong at all. Now, both of you try to sleep."

Settling back down, Tom found it was not hard to rest, he was exhausted and soon fell asleep. He was woken some time later by Septimus. A guard had returned and stood with a sword drawn at the tent flap. Tom gathered it was time to go and report to Alexander. Septimus was collecting the parchments on which he had drawn what looked like various landmarks. Some he had marked with maps, on others he had written lists. Tom wondered how much was fabricated and how much genuine.

"How do you feel?" Septimus asked.

"Less tired, certainly," Tom answered.

"Do you think you can Walk us out of here?"

Tom tried imaging the clock as usual, but he still did not feel any link to time flowing around them.

"Well?" the Welshman asked.

"I'm not sure, at least ..." Tom stammered. Inside he began to panic, wondering if Redfeld had somehow managed to destroy his power. Or was it because he had left the ball and chain in the Professor's office and no longer had a link to his own time?

Septimus' face was pale, "You mean, you can't do it?"

"Can you?" Tom asked in return. Septimus closed his eyes for a moment.

"No," he said after a pause, "I need to sleep to get my energy back and I stayed up working on these," he said, lifting up the parchments.

"What do we do?" Tom asked.

"I will stall for time, you keep trying. Focus on that clock. Ignore all that happens about you in here," Septimus ordered, pointing at the large tent they were being pushed into. Inside, half a dozen Greek lords stood around a map of Persia with Alexander at their centre. As they entered, the King addressed Septimus, who walked forward.

Tom and Mary hung back. Mary was shivering in fear, despite the oppressive heat, but Tom studied the young King with renewed interest, surprised to note that he was quite short and whilst undeniably handsome, his face was actually quite girly looking and his build, though muscular, was slight. He did not look like he would become the greatest conqueror the world has ever known, thought Tom.

Bowing, Septimus presented his reports and maps to Alexander, who looked over them. The minutes ticked by as he studied them, but then he let out a gasp of annoyance and screwed them together into a ball. For a moment he stood contemplating Tom and his companions then suddenly lost his temper and threw the parchments into Septimus' face. The King snapped at the guards who leapt forward and seized the three of them.

It was obvious that Septimus' ruse had failed utterly and Tom was afraid they were about to be killed. He tried to put that out of his mind and concentrate on the job of getting a connection with the Flow of Time, frantically visualising his grandfather's clock.

They were dragged out of Alexander's tent and marched roughly out onto a large open area in the centre of the camp. It was clearly a gathering point and could be used as a parade ground or for games and exercises. It could also be used as a place of execution. They were stood against some wooden posts and their hands tied with rope behind their backs. Then, a dozen archers marched out and forming a line facing the trio of suspected spies, notched arrows onto their bow strings and holding their weapons down by their sides, waited for orders.

'We're going to be used for target practice!' Tom thought, his stomach turning to water.

A guard officer bellowed an instruction and the archers raised their bows and pulled back the strings as they took aim.

Tom desperately tried to find the Flow of Time, but he felt numb with terror and could not locate it.

"Tom?" asked Septimus, his voice tense with anxiety.

Tom shook his head and muttered a quick apology.

The guard officer shouted a word that could only have been "Fire" and the archers released their arrows.

Just then, Mary shouted out one word. "Wall!" she screamed at the top of her voice. The arrows flew through the air towards them, but only ten feet away they seemed to rebound off an invisible barrier. Some shattered into fragments, others deviated wildly and went hurtling away to plunge into the ground. There was silence for a moment as the archers stared in open-mouthed disbelief as the fragments of splintered wood and feathers drifted to earth. Then several of them dropped their bows and stepped backwards, utter terror now etched upon their faces. The officer rushed over and struck three of the men with the back of his sword and then pointed at the abandoned bows. Reluctantly, and with their terrified gaze fixed upon Tom and his companions, the archers reloaded and waited for the order to fire again.

Sweat was pouring from Mary's brow and she muttered, "I cannot hold up the wall for more than a few moments, Master."

Somehow, Mary had made a wall: a wall of frozen time. Beyond the wall, as on their side of it, time seemed to be moving normally, but within the barrier, time was frozen and nothing, it seemed, could penetrate.

"*Apolyo!*" shouted the guard officer. Twelve more arrows leapt towards them and just as suddenly recoiled from the invisible barrier. This time the archers did not need to be ordered. They reloaded and were ready in a moment. Mary

215

gave an exhausted groan and slumped down and Tom realised she could not hold the wall up for much longer.

If the barrier fell, they were all dead!

CHAPTER TWENTY-TWO - BACK IN LONDON

As if he had been energised by the moment of extreme trauma, Tom suddenly sensed the link with time return to him. He stretched out with both legs so that his toes were touching Mary on his left and Septimus on his right. Then, with a jerk, he hurled them forward hundreds of years in a single leap. The exertion made him dizzy and when the Walk was over he collapsed onto his knees, his head still spinning.

When he could focus on the surroundings he realised that they had moved in time, but not in geographical location. The plain was much more arid and in places had turned almost into desert, whilst the river had narrowed and changed its course away from where the camp had once stood. Nevertheless, it was obviously the same place. The contours of the land were unmistakeable and yet, of Alexander's great camp and army, the executioners and of Alexander himself, there was no sign. Tom whistled softly. "It's like they were never here," he observed.

"*Time, like an ever-rolling stream, bears all its sons away; they fly forgotten as a dream dies at the opening day,*" Septimus mumbled to himself.

"What?" asked Tom.

"Oh, it's from an old hymn. It can take some getting used to how the great and powerful can vanish in the blink of an eye as though they had never been, the Welshman answered. "By the way, thanks to both of you for saving my life."

Still exhausted, Mary could only tilt her head in acknowledgement, while Tom just nodded and asked, "Well, what do we do now?"

"I suggest you have a bit of a rest and then see if you can Walk us back to London," Septimus said. "I might be able to do it myself, given a couple of hours' shuteye."

Some while later they appeared in the Professor's office. However, the old man was not there. Mr Phelps did not know where he was or when he would be back. It was irritating and Tom was getting impatient for answers. There was one man present who might give him some, so he turned to Septimus. But Septimus asked him a question of his own first.

"Boyo, I'm parched: fancy a cuppa. What about you, Mary?"

"Not for the moment, Master, I need to ..." she trailed off looking faintly embarrassed and turned towards the door.

"Right, just you and me then, Tom," said Septimus.

Tom nodded and they shuffled out of the Professor's room. They wandered into the kitchen where a cook and his assistants were making dinner for the Institute. The cook was a fat man with a red face. Never trust a thin man's cooking was what his dad used to say when he was cooking a chilli or a curry. His dad liked his food and Tom sighed as he thought about him. The pain of his loss was like a physical ache in the pit of his stomach.

"Hungry, lad?" The cook asked.

Tom shook his head. "No; just thirsty."

"Nice cup of tea for me, if that's ok?" Septimus said.

The cook poured Tom some apple juice from the fridge and put a kettle on to boil then went back to his work. Steam wafted over from the stove and with it a sweet, faintly spiced aroma.

218

Curry for supper then, thought Tom, reminded of his dad again. Feeling nauseous as he wandered over to a table he sat down, sipped his apple juice and looked across at his companion. Having waited for his tea, Septimus was carrying it over to join him. Tom noted that the Welshman was studying him closely, a look of determination on his face, then he nodded to himself as though he had just reached a decision.

"Tommy, we need to talk," he said, placing his tea on the table and sitting opposite Tom.

"Yes, we most certainly do!" Tom retorted.

"Well, I-"

Just then, the door flew open and Mary and Edward came hurtling in. Mary's face was taut with worry; Edward's expression was similar.

"What is it?" Tom got to his feet in alarm.

"It's Charlie. He hasn't returned here yet. He's been gone ages," Edward said breathlessly.

"What! Where did he go?" Septimus asked.

"He said he fancied a look around London."

"When was this?" asked Tom.

Mary and Edward exchanged glances and the girl took up the story. "This morning before we went to look for you. Charlie said we might as well give you an hour or two to come to terms with your loss and that meantime he fancied a look around the city. Then he went off and a bit later on when he hadn't come back, we went to your house and found you."

"This morning?" Tom muttered. "I should be getting used to it by now, but this Walking confuses me. We were away overnight, but we came back just the same day!"

"Actually, the time you were away was about ten hours and the same time passed here," Septimus said. "It was just that we

219

arrived in Alexander's camp in the afternoon and so we spent the night there. You left here about ten this morning and it's about eight o'clock now."

Tom tried to get his head round it; he was just thinking that he didn't remember it being night time in the desert when Mary piped up.

"Nevertheless; Charlie has been gone almost all day since breakfast. Supposing ..." Mary's voice trailed off.

"Supposing Redfeld has found him and plans to use him to get at me. That's what you're saying, isn't it?" Tom asked.

"From what you told me in the tent, that Redfeld sounds like a wicked man. We must trust that he will get his punishment in Hell one day," Mary said.

"Perhaps he might, but it's what he gets up to first that bothers me," Septimus murmured.

"Indeed, I have not met him either," said Edward, "but from what little Mary told me just now, he does seem a villain. Not sure what his game is, but it does not sound as if he would play fair. If that puts Charlie in possible danger, we need to act. Do you think we should inform the Professor?"

"I would love to, but he's not back yet," Septimus said. Then, groaning slightly, he dragged himself to his feet. "Right then, it seems there is no rest for the wicked. I think we should mount a rescue mission, don't you, Tommy?"

With a nod, Tom turned to the Lieutenant. "Can you sense him?"

Edward closed his eyes and frowned in concentration. After a moment he opened them again. "I think so... yes. Trafalgar Square: I'm fairly sure that's where he is."

"Right then, we'd better go, Lieutenant ... Tommy," Septimus said.

"Do not overlook me!" Mary insisted.

"Mary, it could be dangerous," Edward pointed out.

"So was being taken back to Ancient Greece. At least this time I have a choice."

Tom had to admit that Mary's skills had proven useful on that trip. He glanced across at Septimus, who shrugged his agreement, so Tom reached out and placed a hand on both Mary's and Septimus' shoulders and Walked them over the mile or so to Trafalgar Square, leaving Edward to transport himself.

They appeared in front of some American tourists who gawped at them, exclaimed, "Golly! How did you do that?" Then, thinking that Tom and his companions were some form of street theatre, a bit like the gold-painted statues dotted around the place that unnervingly came alive when you least expected it, they insisted on taking photos of the four of them. As a result, it was some minutes before they could escape from the attention of the Americans and get across to the centre of Trafalgar Square.

The square was busy with tourists lingering in the city and with locals out for the night. It took time to locate Charlie and Tom was getting anxious that he had already been found by Redfeld and that they were too late. Thus, it was with a sense of relief that he spotted the young sailor leaning back against one of the lions, enjoying the sun on this warm summer's evening.

They bustled over to Charlie, who gave a lazy wave.

"You ok, Charlie? We were all worried about you," Tom said, feeling faintly irritated when the young man laughed.

"Thomas Oakley, we are in the centre of London. What danger could I possibly be in?"

"You have been gone for most of the day, Charlie, so we were just wondering where you were."

"Ah well, you're probably right. I have been out a long time. Sorry, but it's just that it's all so marvellous," said Charlie. "Look about you."

Forced to smile at Charlie's cheerful enthusiasm, Tom, his irritation forgotten, did look. There was Nelson's Column, with the Admiral high above them, one arm missing and a pigeon perched on his head; the four lions, huge and unmoving, staring out eternally at the passersby. Some Japanese tourists standing under one of the statues were having a photo taken of them, whilst nearby half a dozen teenagers were doing tricks on skateboards or imitating a mime artist who was dressed as a harlequin. Pretty ordinary, he thought. He said as much.

"Yes indeed – pretty ordinary. But when I was last here, it was very different. There were piles of sandbags to help soak up bomb blasts. Half and more of the men were in uniform and many women as well. At night the sky was lit up, not by the bright lamps of a great city, but by searchlights scanning the heavens for German bombers. The sound of sirens rings in my ears even now, along with the crack and bang of 'Archie' – that's anti-aircraft fire to you – and the boom of bombs. That was the night before I left to join the *Paladin* and sail to the Med. It was all a bit grim really and there were certainly no tourists. To be able to sit here now and enjoy the evening without danger is wonderful."

Tom thought to himself that there were new dangers, but he could understand Charlie's feelings having seen something of war during his travels, and so he let Charlie enjoy the moment. The five of them sat and stared at the scene.

"It's all changed a bit since my day," said Edward. "The column was here then, of course, but a lot of these buildings are new."

"It is all new since, as you call it, 'my day'." Mary said, staring in awe at the lions, the pillar and the huge stone buildings. "Who is that man on the top," she asked, peering up at Nelson, pouting a little when they all laughed.

"It's a long story," said Septimus, drawing breath to launch into a description of the Battle of Trafalgar.

Mary forestalled him, "How about you, Mr Mason? When was your day?"

Septimus frowned, but before he could reply, Tom, who was listening with interest having wondered that same question, felt a sudden wrench in his mind. He was now learning, this meant that something was happening to time. Then, he felt a chill pass down his spine, as he noticed something odd. A few feet away, in the crowd of tourists, there stood five men in identical suits that looked new, as if they had just been bought. Indeed, now he studied them, he could see a price label still attached to one cuff. He first thought that these were the Directorate from the Office. Then, he caught a glance from one of them and was startled as the man smiled back at him. The men from the Office never seemed to smile, at least not in the dreams that Tom had.

The man came nearer and Tom saw that above the top of his trousers, the butt of a pistol was visible. Then he stepped forward: it was Redfeld.

"Mr Mason and Master Oakley, I am delighted to see you both again. Ah and I see you are accompanied by Miss Brown, I believe, fresh from the inferno of 1666 along with other vagabonds from the past. You three should choose your rescuers more carefully for these two are dangerous to be around," Redfeld said. Then he was quiet for a moment, peering at Tom. He seemed to be scrutinizing him extremely closely.

"I'm relieved you still exist, Master Oakley. Although I knew I could manage to arrange that," he said. Tom was going to ask what he meant, but Septimus spoke first.

"Captain, what you are doing here? I thought you understood that I wanted no part in your plan. Leave the boy alone," he said angrily.

"Changing the bargain is unacceptable. Most inefficient! Most unlike you," Redfeld replied coldly.

Tom's eyes narrowed; he thought quickly: so it appeared that it *had* been Septimus in the Office doing a deal with Redfeld and the Custodian. If so, could he trust him now? They had been through so much together, and yet ...

"Septimus," he said, "I don't understand? What's going on?"

"Confused are we?" Redfeld sneered. "I warned you not to turn your back on me, boy. As for now, if you wish to live, you will do exactly what I say!" The Captain's face wore a merciless expression as he moved towards Tom. Then, the expression changed to anger as Septimus stepped between them, blocking Redfeld's path.

"I told you the deal was off!" Septimus said; his tone steely and determined.

Redfeld merely laughed and shook his head. "I am afraid you have become an irrelevance, Mr Mason. The truth is we don't need you any longer because our plans have changed. I will take the boy now." He paused, added, "In fact, I will take

224

you all." He waved his men forward and they advanced on Tom and his friends.

"Who are these guys?" Charlie asked. The sailor was still sitting on his lion, peering down at Redfeld and his men and looking very confused.

"I will explain later," Tom said urgently. "For now we must get away. Everyone reach over and touch me," he ordered. "Now, Charlie!" Tom added as the sailor looked doubtfully across at him. "I need to get us out of here the same way I got you off the U-boat."

Charlie shrugged and reached out to take Tom's outstretched hand. Redfeld's men noticed the movement and moved closer.

"Now!" shouted Tom and searched for the Flow of Time. Something was wrong, though. He could sense it out there, but could not reach it: some force was blocking him and preventing him using it.

"Mary, I think they have made a wall. Can you sense it?"

Mary concentrated and then nodded. "I can't bring it down though, Master. But I do know it's one of them," she nodded at the approaching men.

His voice dripping with false sincerity, Redfeld said, "I'm afraid that you cannot escape that way. I took the opportunity to have one of my guards erect a wall around us here: a barrier between us and the Time Stream," he laughed. "No one can Walk in or out. We would not want to be interrupted now, would we?"

Redfeld had said 'guards' and now Tom looked at them they did look more like soldiers than mere hired guns. It was something about the way they walked, how they carried themselves that left him in no doubt: these were warriors.

The guards were coming closer and now, in an attempt to reach Tom, they pushed Septimus roughly to one side. Tom retreated a few more steps, but then it was if he had backed into a wall. Behind him he could see only clear air and a few feet away, the American tourists who had now wandered over to the lions. They were mere yards away, yet seemed to have noticed nothing untoward; it might as well have been a mile, for there was an invisible barrier as strong as steel preventing Tom from retreating any further. He stepped to one side to avoid one of Redfeld's guards who lunged at him, but that placed him right in the path of another one, who seized his arm and dragged him towards Redfeld. Tom shook free of the man's grip, but did not run away. Instead, he stepped right up to Redfeld and stabbed a finger towards him.

"So, are you going to kill me now, like you killed my parents?"

Redfeld shook his head. "My dear boy, why would I kill you? I went to so much trouble to ensure you survived and your parents did not."

Tom could barely contain the anger rising inside him and for the first time in his life he understood what people meant by 'seeing red'.

"I knew you killed them! I'll get you, Redfeld – I mean it!" Tom shouted but realised it sounded foolish, given the situation. Nevertheless he spat towards the Captain: a futile gesture perhaps, but it made him feel better. "You murdered my parents: tell me why? Was it really just to get your own back?"

"Oh, in part, it was a bit of revenge – sweet as that can be. But because of it, I have already gained more power in this world – in this reality – than I had before. Soon it will give me even more."

Tom didn't understand. "How did murdering my parents give you power?"

"Let's just say it gives me certain leverage over you. Serve me and I can help you get your parents back."

Stunned, Tom gazed at him. Did Redfeld mean it? Was there a way to bring his family back?

Septimus moved back to stand beside Tom "Hang on, if you wanted the boy alive and took great pains to make sure he survived, why then send one of your men to shoot at him in the ruins of his house earlier today?"

"I wasn't trying to kill the boy. I ordered my men to capture him and to kill anyone with him. The bullet was aimed at you, Mr Mason. I really don't like gentlemen who betray me."

"That's a bit harsh, don't you think, boyo?" Septimus asked.

Redfeld looked about to answer when Tom asked another question, but directed at Septimus this time. "I don't understand, Septimus. What have you to do with Redfeld and these men? Who are they really and what do they want with me? What was this 'deal' you made? I thought you were my friend."

Septimus opened his mouth to respond, but seemed unable to think of how to reply. Redfeld gave a sneering laugh. "Don't waste your time with such as him, Thomas. Mason is a mercenary, no more and no less. He agreed to hand you over to me for payment." Redfeld glanced at Septimus and then back to Tom.

"As to what we want? Well, I will tell you. Time, my boy, we want Time, and you are going to give it to us!"

CHAPTER TWENTY-THREE - TRAFALGAR SQUARE

Tom glared at Septimus. It was true then: the Welshman had betrayed him; had planned to sell him to Redfeld for money, for profit, just as if he was one of those Greek vases he had once spoken about. Tom's temper finally erupted. "Septimus, you lied to me!" Tom shouted. "You strung me along and pretended to be saving me when all the time you meant to betray me!"

Septimus at least had the grace to look embarrassed and one of the guards sniggered at his obvious discomfort. This appeared to make him angry because his face flushed a dull red, his eyes widened and he looked about to say something to the guard, but Tom would not let him be distracted.

"I trusted you – but you tricked me. All along you were working with people who planned to destroy my family!"

"Tom ... I ... I'm sorry ... I," Septimus started to say, but Redfeld cut across him.

"I told you not to waste your breath on him, Thomas."

"Shut up!" Tom spun round to glare at the Captain, his face a mask of fury. Unable to find any words to express what he was feeling, he glanced at his other companions.

Charlie and Edward were looking on in confused silence, unsure what was going on. Meanwhile, Mary had perhaps worked out a little more than the others, because she was staring at Redfeld with a terrified expression on her face, as if convinced she had found the evil monster she had feared him to be.

Turning back to Septimus, Tom's anger continued to mount like a raging torrent. "I trusted you and all the while you were working for these ... these people," he pointed a finger at Redfeld, who seemed to find Tom's tirade amusing. Both he and his men had stopped moving towards the Walkers and appeared to be enjoying the performance.

Tom finally stopped shouting and tried to control his breathing. As he did this, he looked at Redfeld and his guards more closely. He still found it hard to believe they were not from the same planet. "So, is it true, Redfeld? You really *are* from another world?

"*Deutschland* is our home, young man. But, the correct one," the Captain answered. "Germany did not lose the war like in your feeble version of history. In my world, The Glorious Third Reich rules from the Urals to the Atlantic and from the Arctic to the Sahara. Your world should not exist: it is an error to be eradicated, deleted and corrected. The true version of history will reign supreme and ... you will make it happen!" Redfeld's eyes now shone with an almost holy zeal.

Tom's face blanched. So that was what this was all about. "And how do you plan to do that?" He spat out the words in contempt.

Redfeld seemed not to notice, "A door: I need to open a door. You will be the key. That door will give me the present as well as the past and the future!"

"What's this nonsense about?" Charlie Hawker asked from his perch on one of the lions, "I don't understand what he is saying, but I don't like the sound of it one bit. The man's a damn Nazi! How'd you get involved with scum like him?"

"Look, Charlie," Tom gazed up at him, "all I can say for now is that these guys attacked Mary and me before and that they want to harm us!" Tom paused then added, "Me particularly!"

"Yeah? Well, that's good enough for me," Charlie stated. He jumped down in front of the lion and walked towards the guards.

"Charlie, what are you doing? They're armed!" Septimus yelled a warning.

Seeing Charlie approach, the guards stopped and one of them pulled out a pistol and levelled it at him. The young seaman froze. Then all hell broke loose.

One of the American tourists spotted the gun, shouted, "Terrorist!" and screaming, the crowds started to scatter like startled pigeons. A shot rang out followed by a ricochet as the bullet rebounded off the lion, chipping a piece off its nose. This time it was the pigeons that scattered in terror; with a whoosh of wings they took to the sky, creating a swirling cloud of grey and black.

This was when Charlie chose to act.

Tom was looking right at him at the time, so he saw him move like a blur through the terrified pigeons. Unlike when Tom himself Walked, such as when he was dodging the Zulu spears by hopping short distances, Charlie never totally vanished. What he seemed to do was make a series of multiple tiny jumps, each just a little further than a man could run in that instant. Nothing staggering as such, perhaps, but put all the minute Walks or jumps together and the effect was rather like watching a dancer at a disco when the strobe light is on. It was fast – blisteringly fast. One moment Charlie was just behind Tom and the next he had swung round and attacked Redfeld's guards from the side.

Like a rugby forward, the young seaman used his shoulders and his momentum to great effect, knocking two of Redfeld's guards down in short order and upon reaching the third, slapped the pistol from his hand. Two more guards finally reacted and turned to face this new threat. That left an opening and now Edward jumped forward and charged towards these two from their rear.

At that same moment, Tom saw Septimus swing a fist round into the final guard's face. With a crunch, it connected and the man let out a groan and collapsed onto the pavement.

The next few moments passed in a blur. Tom was vaguely aware of a lot of shouting from all sides, the barking of orders, the sight of yet another guard on the ground, spitting out blood, and Mary screaming as she was knocked over by one of Redfeld's thugs. Finally, there was the deafening bang of a pistol shot and Septimus let out a cry of agony.

Then, suddenly, as Redfeld reached out to seize him, Tom came to his senses and everything came back into focus. He kicked the man hard in the shins and Redfeld fell back grasping his bleeding leg. Tom scampered forward and jumped over him to land next to Septimus, who lay bleeding in a heap on the ground. Mary was beside him and as Tom came closer, she raised her hand like an evangelist preacher and shouted out the words, "Wall be gone!"

Around them there was a shimmering in the air followed by a cry of outrage from Redfeld who cried out, "My wall!"

Abruptly, Tom could feel the Flow of Time and he reached over and laid a hand on Septimus and Mary.

"Charlie! Edward! Come here now: we can leave," he yelled.

Charlie moved like a bolt of lightning towards them, followed more sedately, by the Victorian officer.

"Not so fast, my brave young men!" shouted Redfeld, climbing to his feet. From his pocket he pulled out a box, which looked rather like a TV remote control. He turned to point it away from Tom towards the far side of the square and pressed a button.

"He's putting his wall up again!" Tom gasped.

Mary shook her head, "This is no wall, Master Tom. It is more like ... more like a door. Look!"

Close behind Redfeld, Tom saw a pinpoint of infinite brightness appear and expand rapidly with a load crack. In the Square around them the remaining onlookers started shouting about a bomb going off and were scattering further away, whilst from the distance police sirens could be heard approaching.

Meanwhile, the bright point had now spread out to an ugly gash in the air five feet wide and ten high. On either side of the gash, the buildings on the edge of the Square were clearly visible, whilst through it Tom could make out the room that he had seen twice before: a room full of work benches and pieces of scientific equipment with gauges and wires showing. On one wall was a bank of computers, their screens depicting furious activity as rows of numbers and lines of code scrolled downwards. In front of the benches a couple of dozen soldiers were standing: all in grey uniforms with steel helmets and armed with rifles.

In the midst of the soldiers, there was some kind of machine. Tom squinted to make it out, but it was hard because of the beam of light that shone from it almost like a torch, directly towards the gash. No, not a torch – Tom could now perceive a few more details and saw that the device was more like a projector in a movie theatre. It was almost as if the guards were in a cinema watching the fight in Trafalgar Square.

Was this the door Redfeld spoke of? Tom doubted it. After all, Redfeld had done this himself. As he watched, six guards reached forward and touched the projecting device then vanished from sight. In the next instant they reappeared in the Square, standing to attention next to Redfeld.

"Get them!" Redfeld ordered, pointing at Edward and Charlie who, just as shocked as Tom, had frozen in their tracks and stood gawping at the scene. In a moment, the six guards swarmed towards them and, outnumbered, the Walkers were soon overpowered and forced to the ground. Tom saw Charlie take a clout to the back of his head from a rifle butt and then slump, lifeless, into the arms of two of the guards. Edward was still struggling, but to no avail. Before Tom could react, his new friends were dragged, with Edward kicking and screaming, back through the strange doorway into the room. With an ear-piercing clap, the gash slammed shut and the Square looked normal again: normal that was, apart from Redfeld and his original six guards, the wounded Septimus and the panicking tourists still screaming about 'terrorists!'

"Charlie! Edward!" Tom yelled, searching the empty sky.

"Well, that was easier than I expected," Redfeld chortled, "and now, Thomas, it's your turn!" he said. He stepped forward whilst cocking his pistol, levelled the weapon and pointed it at Tom.

Tom though, was already on the move. He Walked Septimus, Mary and himself away from the Square. At the last instant he heard a loud crack as Redfeld discharged his pistol. An agonising pain shot through his head: and everything went black.

All Tom knew of the next moments was a series of confused, fractured images in his brain: Mary and Redfeld sitting cross-legged like nursery children, building walls with toy bricks. Mary knocking over Redfeld's bricks and him running away crying and saying he wanted his mummy. Next, Tom saw Alexander the Great playing cricket. He was actually rather good at it and hit several sixes with his sword before having the umpires executed after they had given him out. A moment later, Tom was in an office building standing next to a man in a suit. The man was looking down at the table in front on him. The table was covered with sand. Images and patterns swirled across it. Then, all was calm. The man smiled, sat back down and crossed his arms.

Following this, Tom's dream changed to scenes from old black and white war movies: British soldiers driving trucks across the desert to fight distant battles. However, the men they fought were not the Germans that Tom remembered from all those Sunday afternoon movies. These had different uniforms and marched under a strange banner with a lightning bolt symbol on it. Tom saw the face of the figure carrying the banner and recoiled in shock as he realised that it was himself. Then he heard the voice of Captain Redfeld calling out to him in triumph.

"Did I not I tell you that you would give us Time?"

Then the dream changed again and Tom knew, as he always did, that this was no longer a dream: he was Walking again. But where was he now?

The Office again. And, just as before, Tom becomes the man in the suit. What is his name? Does he have one? If he ever did, it has no meaning or importance now. All that is important is preserving the two realities in eternal balance. That has been his job since – well, since he came to exist: since the 'Event'. He does not recall any life nor any purpose before this life and this purpose.

He is the Custodian.

The Custodian looks at the table. He notices that the lines representing that dangerous boy's family come to an abrupt end. Redfeld has done his job. He has travelled back and eliminated the boy's parents and thus the boy also. He permits himself the faintest of smiles. Then, the smile fades. He has just noticed the swirling confusion of lines twelve years after that intervention. Another line emerges from the present day, moves back through the sand a dozen years, before returning to the present once more. Then, with blinding alacrity, it hurtles back and forward across the centuries. What is going on? Finally, the line returns to the twenty-first century once more.

As he puzzles over this, he becomes aware that another figure is in the Office. He looks up and it is almost as if he is gazing into a mirror. For, another old man in a suit stares back at him.

"So, you have finally come to see me," the Custodian says and then adds the man's title, "Professor."

"I have come about a boy you would have dead," Neoptolemas replies, "... brother."

With a start, Tom sat up and stared, unseeing, all around. His heart was pounding and his palms were sweating. *Brother.* Had the Professor really called the man in the suit 'brother'? Tom was now used to these dreams and could tell which ones were real. Somewhere in the strange world between worlds where the Office was found, the Professor had met the Custodian. But if, along with Redfeld, the man in the suit was connected with the death of Tom's parents, what was Neoptolemas' part in all

236

this? Tom blinked and focused on his surroundings. Where was he? Not Trafalgar Square, certainly.

He was sitting on a park bench. Septimus was next to him and was still unconscious. Mary was lying on the ground in front of the bench, but there was no sign of Charlie or Edward. The three of them were in the middle of a park near a long lake with boats on it. A woman walking by pushing a shopping basket gave them a strange look: half curious, half afraid. Tom examined her clothes: she wore a modern, dark grey dress; so it seemed they were still in his own time. He realised she was staring at Septimus, who was bleeding from a wound on the side of his chest. When the woman saw Tom staring back she looked away and scuttled off. He felt moisture trickling on his scalp and probed at it with his finger tips. When he examined them, his fingers were covered in blood. The bullet had grazed his scalp and he had the worst headache that he could remember, but the blood seemed to be drying now so it appeared that the damage was slight and that he had been lucky. It also meant he had been here for some while; how long?

Septimus looked to be in much a worse state. The bullet had hit him in the chest and he was losing a lot of blood, his face was the colour of dirty chalk. The man needed help, but Tom could not carry him even if Mary could help. Though his scalp wound was slight, Tom felt weak and he knew he could not just Walk them to a hospital. For a moment, his anger returned as he remembered that he still had an unfinished conversation with the traitor Welshman. Then again, Septimus had fought against Redfeld and it appeared that whatever the deal he had once struck with the enemy, he had changed his mind and had tried to protect Tom. As a result Septimus now lay there, badly

237

injured. The conversation could wait. Tom had to try to wake him and get him to a doctor. Leaning over, he shook the Welshman by the shoulders.

"Septimus, wake up!" he shouted. The man groaned and opened his eyes. Slowly he turned his head to take in the scene.

"Where are we?"

"London; Hyde Park, I think. As for the date it's …" Tom squinted as he quickly checked his link with the Clock and the Flow of Time. "Gosh, it's July 2nd … why, it's still *today!*"

Septimus smiled weakly but then started coughing. He put his hand to his mouth and when it came away Tom could see flecks of blood on it.

"I must get you to a hospital," he suggested.

"No!" Septimus shook his head and winced. "They will be watching them." Pulling himself to his feet he stood swaying and pointed through the trees to the tall Regency buildings beyond. "The Institute is that way. It's not far, but we must move quickly. If we can get inside, the Professor's barriers will protect us." He started coughing again, his breath coming in hoarse gasps of pain.

Tom was far from convinced. He wanted to tell Septimus about his dream and his fears that the Neoptolemas was not what he seemed, but the Welshman was clearly badly wounded and needed help fast. He would have to risk it and hope the Professor was not there. Get Septimus patched up and … then what? Tom really had no idea.

He nudged Mary with his foot. "Mary, wake up!" he ordered. For a moment he was afraid she was still unconscious, but then her eyes opened and she stared up at him blearily without recognition for a moment, before sitting up and looking around fearfully.

238

Tom spared her what he hoped was a sympathetic smile. "It's alright. Redfeld isn't here, Mary, but we must get away. We will have to walk; I haven't got the energy to Walk." At any other time he might have found that statement funny, as it was, he grimaced.

Septimus gave a groan and collapsed back onto the bench. Pulling him to his feet, Tom let the Welshman lean on his shoulder. Mary scrambled up and moved to support him on the other side and together they moved off towards the gate. At one point, they saw a policemen peering at them from the corner of the park and could see him speak into a radio set on his jacket. They hurried out of the park and tried to cross the Bayswater Road. As they did, a police car hurtled past them. The driver craned his head round to look at them and a moment later the car's brake lights came on. Tom urged Septimus and Mary along and like some bizarre six-legged zombie, they staggered across the road. Tom suggested to Septimus that maybe they should get the police to help, but he shook his head.

"It would not be safe ... for them, I mean," the Welshman gasped, gritting his teeth. "When Redfeld turns up, he will show them no mercy."

They were now across the road. Marble Arch could be seen in the distance and Tom recognised the side road leading to the avenue where the Institute stood. They turned into it and Tom risked a glance behind. The policemen had left their car and, joining up with the officer from the park, were crossing the road. They were now just thirty paces away.

"Oh no!" Tom heard Mary cry out.

Glancing ahead again, his heart sank, for Captain Redfeld and two of his guards had just stepped out of thin air and were

239

only twenty feet away. For a moment, they were all looking north, away from Tom, Mary and Septimus. In desperation, Tom searched about for an escape route, hoping to get out of sight before Redfeld spotted them.

He was too late.

At that moment, one of the policemen following up behind yelled out.

"Sir, stop please; we just want to talk to you!"

Hearing this, Redfeld turned and saw his quarry. He smiled and reached for his pistol as his guards levelled their rifles.

Tom swallowed hard and waited for them to open fire.

CHAPTER TWENTY-FOUR - ABSENT NEOPTOLEMAS

Before Redfeld could pull the trigger, Septimus, with a superhuman effort, summoned what energy he had left and dragged both Tom and Mary hard left into an alleyway running down the back of the buildings on the Institute's road. Three steps into the alleyway, Septimus collapsed and Tom tumbled down next to him.

"That gate," the Welshman managed to gasp before he slumped back, unconscious. Tom looked down the alleyway and saw a wrought iron gate: recognised it as the gate he had seen at the end of the garden outside the Professor's study. Looking back towards the road, Tom could see that one of the policemen was armed and was pointing his gun at Redfeld.

"Armed police, put the gun down!" came the order. Focusing on each other's weapons, for the moment neither Redfeld's men nor the police were looking up the alley.

"Come on Mary," Tom urged the girl, "help me drag him in there."

Together, they pulled Septimus along, pushed open the gate and fell forward onto the lawn. Septimus started coughing violently and soon spots of blood speckled the grass. Mary turned and closed the gate behind them. Just then, they heard a brisk crackle of a half dozen gun shots in the road: Redfeld and the police were exchanging fire. Hearing the sound, Septimus stirred weakly and opened his eyes. He managed to drag himself to his feet and they stumbled on up the garden. In front of them were French windows, which were shut. Mary ran up and hammered on the glass. Tom was surprised when the windows opened almost at once. With relief, he saw that the man who opened them was Mr Phelps and not the Professor.

Mr Phelps helped Septimus to the Professor's high-backed chair, then picked up a phone on the desk and called for Doctor Makepeace. After he had replaced the hand set, Tom asked, "Is the Professor here?"

"I'm sorry, Mr Phelps shook his head, "he has not yet returned."

"Well then, do you have any idea where he is?"

"Afraid not, but where are Lieutenant Dyson and Able Seaman Hawker?"

Tom did not answer. Could he trust Mr Phelps? After all, he worked for the Professor, didn't he? There was no way of knowing who he could trust any more. He glanced back at the windows, half expecting to see Redfield and his bully boys, but there was no sign of them. Did the Institute's barrier work effectively as Septimus had suggested it did? Tom fervently hoped so.

Just then, Septimus groaned.

"Please, sir ... he needs help," Tom pleaded, turning back to Mr Phelps, who sniffed haughtily, but nodded and reaching out, rang a bell on the desk.

A moment later a young man appeared at the doorway with a "Yes, sir?" It was Matthews, the doorman who had let Tom in on his first visit. Phelps indicated Septimus and soon the wounded Welshman was helped out of the room. Mary, who had various cuts and bruises, followed.

"We will have the doctor look at you and your companions, Master Oakley," Mr Phelps said, peering at Tom's scalp and adding cheerfully, "nasty wound you have there. You'll probably need stitches."

"Gee, thanks," Tom replied and stumbled upstairs after Mary.

Busy with treating Septimus, it was over an hour before the doctor administered to him, but in fact Tom did not need stitches, just some painkillers and things the doctor called Steristrips, which his mother would have called 'butterfly stitches'. His mother... Tom smothered a sob. He was twelve years old; too grown up to be crying for his mother, he told himself. Free to come back downstairs he went to sit alone in the dining room.

As the terrifying excitement of the last half hour faded along with his headache, Tom's thoughts slowed down and he began to think constructively again. In a way this was worse because a feeling of despair and futility washed over him. The situation was hopeless. His parents were gone. There were only two men who seemed to think they could get Tom's family back. One of them, the Professor, had vanished and could be dealing with the Custodian right now – *brother*, Neoptolemas had called him – and he certainly appeared to have it in for Tom. The other man was Redfeld, who hardly had Tom's best interests at heart. What price would Redfeld ask to bring back his mum and dad? *'What price would I be willing to pay?'* Tom wondered.

Redfeld, of course, had captured Tom's new allies: Charlie and Edward and taken them heaven knew where. As for Septimus, he had certainly been up to no good, feathering his own pockets at Tom's expense. Tom felt doubly betrayed because he had begun to really like the little Welshman, but could he be trusted again, despite his efforts at Trafalgar

Square? After all, Septimus would have expected no mercy from Redfeld, so he may just have been protecting himself.

So, thought Tom, that left himself and Mary. As for Mary, what use would she really be? On the other hand, she had again demonstrated her unique talent in Trafalgar Square – not that it did much good.

At that moment the door swung open and as if on cue, Mary came in and sat down opposite him. "What wilt thou do now, Master Tom?"

Tom shook his head. He did not know where to start. "I have no idea, Mary. It seems hopeless. How can we go on with our friends gone and with no help from the Professor or Septimus?"

Mary looked up sharply at that. "There is help from Mr Mason. The physician told me that he had taken a bullet out of your friend's lung and that he will be well again, if he rests. I think the physician be a wizard for I do not think such an injury can be cured by normal means.

Too weary to speak, Tom nodded; he had thought that too. Doctor Makepeace had healing powers that went beyond the norm.

"Anyway," Mary went on, "he gave you permission to go up and see Mr Mason and I think you should. I think he is the most important person for you to talk to at this moment. But you must find it in your heart to forgive him."

Tom said nothing for a moment. A wave of stubbornness came over him. Why should he be forgiving?

Mary studied him for a while before speaking again. "I think you need to give Septimus another chance," she said with an edge of steel in her voice that Tom had not heard before. Even so, he was still not convinced.

"Why? He betrayed me and almost handed me over to Redfeld."

Mary put her hand on Tom's arm for a moment and said softly, "Almost is not the same as did. What he did was fail to abandon us in Alexander's camp. What he did was defy Redfeld and refuse to hand you over. Finally, he risked his own life and was shot to protect you. That is what he actually *did*. He might lack good intentions at times, Master Tom, but his actions speak for themselves. He does not wish thee ill, I am certain of it and I think he can help thee."

Tom felt his anger beginning to rise again, "If it wasn't for him, I wouldn't need help," he muttered, but Mary just sat there looking at him, her eyes shining with gentle determination. It was obvious that she knew she was right. Tom sighed. Then he nodded. Yes, she probably *was* right. He felt the fury subside a little: not go completely, of course, but the anger no longer controlled him. Instead it became a resolve to carry on. "You really think he can help me?"

"I am sure of it," she smiled.

He heaved himself to his feet and headed for the stairs, realising as he did so that the gloom was not quite so oppressive. There was hope: not much maybe, but a little and it was Mary who had made him see it. He turned and looked back into the dining room. He caught Mary looking at him and smiled at her before carrying on up the stairs. He had been very wrong: she had been a big help, in the end.

Septimus was sitting up in bed, his right arm in a sling and a bandage wrapped round his chest. He was staring out of the windows with a distant expression on his face. As Tom went in he turned and looked at him. Tom stood next to the bed.

245

Neither of them said a word for several minutes, but it was Tom who finally broke the silence.

"I need you to promise me that you were not involved with my parents' murder."

Slowly, Septimus shook his head. "I swear that I was not. I admit that I struck a deal with Redfeld whereby you would lose your powers and remain safe in exchange for payment. But, after all, you said yourself that you did not want these powers, so I figured there would be no issue. I thought that was all he wanted."

"But you did not hand me over to him."

"Not when I began to see what he was after. I may be a mercenary, boyo, but I'm not going to let the likes of him take over, am I? The guy's a monster."

Tom nodded. Maybe Mary was right about that too.

"Besides which, can you imagine the effect his regime would have on business: be murder to do my job," Septimus added with a wink.

Tom laughed at that and Septimus smiled back at him. Then Tom remembered the dream of the Professor in the Office.

He sat down on the corner of the bed and related his dream. Septimus nodded as he listened. It did not seem to surprise him that the Custodian had called the Professor 'brother'.

"You see, Tom, the Custodian is indeed the spitting image of the Professor. I saw that when I went to the Office."

"Exactly how did you come to meet him?" Tom asked.

"Ah well, that was Redfeld," Septimus replied.

"I think you had better tell me the whole story," Tom suggested.

Septimus nodded and pushed himself up the bed so that he was propped up against the head rest. He was silent for a

246

while, looking out of the window and across the rooftops and chimneys. Following his gaze Tom watched a bird take flight off a chimney pot and wondered if Septimus was wishing he had that same freedom, so he could fly away and avoid an awkward conversation. Eventually, the Welshman took a deep breath.

"Ok then, I'll tell you. It was shortly after you and I first met back at New Year that Redfeld contacted me. At the time he just said he was interested in meeting you. I didn't know who or what he was then. It was just business at that time. A small payment for an introduction and so I arranged to be in that café, with you. Later, he started talking about wanting me to help with kidnapping you and then taking you to see the Custodian. I had heard of the Custodian from the Professor once – a kind of pan-dimensional policeman who keeps the realities on track and not deviating from time lines. I thought Redfeld was his man, to be honest. They seemed bothered about your powers and wanted to take them away from you. I saw no harm in that at the time because you had said you did not want them. I was not keen on the kidnapping part, but they assured me that you would come to no harm."

"Make a habit of trusting Nazis, do you?" Tom asked, harshly. Septimus winced.

"No, it wasn't like that, honestly, Tommy. I didn't know that Redfeld was from the Twisted Reality or what type of man he was. But, when I found out, I refused to help him further."

"I see," said Tom. "So then he was forced to come up with some other plan to coerce my cooperation: something involving a deal with the Custodian and the death of my parents. He then promised to let me have them back if I did what he asked. Does that mean that the Professor is wrong about us not being able

247

to Walk back to the same point in time twice? Or maybe Redfeld knows a way to do it that he will tell me if I do what he wants?"

For a moment Septimus did not answer, tapping his fingers on the bedside table. Then he asked Tom a question. "If that was the case, would you agree to help him?"

Tom blinked. "I'd be lying if I said I was not tempted, but no, I'm not planning to help him. I don't trust him and we still don't really know what he wanted me to do, anyway. What is he *really* after?"

Septimus clicked his fingers and murmured beneath his breath, "*And Alexander wept, for there were no more worlds to conquer....*"

"What?" Tom frowned.

"Ambition, Tommy!" Septimus leaned forward, "It's a powerful motive. For many it is a driving force that gets us where we want to be: doctor, teacher, astronaut, soldier – whatever our dream is. But for a few, it is a curse. Napoleon, once the conqueror of a continent, ended his life in miserable exile haunted by past glories and the shadowy dreams of what might have been. Julius Caesar once burst into tears because he felt he hadn't achieved as much as Alexander. Ah ... and as for Alexander himself: in military terms at least, he achieved more than anyone before or since. He conquered Egypt; Asia Minor; the Persian Empire and even reached India, but his soldiers voted to end the campaigns and go home. At that point he wept and died within a year."

"I don't quite see," Tom said feeling confused.

"My point is this: some men are driven on by destructive ambition. Look at Redfeld's master. His 'father' or Führer - their 'Hitler' if you like - conquered Europe and defeated both the US and Russia. As the Captain told us, their Führer has gone even further and swept through Africa, Asia and into South America. All is at his feet. But that's not enough for him. He looks hungrily at us across the gaps between realities. He wants our world too. Not just our world, but our history. Remember when Redfeld said our history was the error to be eradicated?"

"Yes, I remember that."

"With your help, Redfeld can change our history and mould it to his desire. Our past can be erased and made to conform to his world: Britain could lose the battle of Britain, Russia could fall. The Americans could lose at Midway. Any of a hundred events that occurred in our past could be altered and he could change it so the Germans won the war in *our* reality. Except, Redfeld would go further and he or his master would rule our world as well as his own. With an eternal Reich across two realities on offer, I don't see them needing to weep like Alexander, do you?"

"He's mad!" Tom whispered.

"Oh yes, undoubtedly he's mad; a megalomaniac."

They sat in silence for a moment as they took in the full implications.

'Imagine the possibilities', Redfeld had said. The man's ambitions knew no bounds, or so it seemed. Eventually Tom broke the silence.

"Right then: next question. Why would the Professor call the Custodian, 'brother'?"

"That I don't know. One thing is certain; the two of them look almost identical. Perhaps the Professor is a little greyer, but that's about it. I think you will have to ask the Prof if you want to find out more."

"If he ever comes back, you mean. So then, where is the Office and how do I get there?"

"Quantum physics is not my specialty, boyo, but as far as I can gather, at the moment of the Event, the Office was created as a kind of neutral ground in the void between the two realities. At that moment, the Custodian and his minions came to exist and it seems they are very keen that the two realities remain somehow in balance."

"Ok, I know that bit – I have been the Custodian - but I can't get there except in a dream and then I am not myself; that's when I become the Custodian," Tom said impatiently. "How do I get there now: how do I get there as *myself*?"

"Sorry, Tom, but I can't help you get there either. You see, Redfeld took me the first time and at the end of that meeting the Custodian gave me a recall stone that was keyed to the Office in case I needed to return. It was like that ball and chain malarkey the Professor gave us to rescue Mary and the others: only this one was made of marble, like a paperweight; the stuff you get in posh offices. I guess, just as the iron and water helps to bring us back here, the marble would help you Walk to the Office. Unfortunately, I gave that stone back to the Custodian the second time and I don't have it now. I'm sorry, Tommy," Septimus apologised.

Tom covered his head with his hands and gave a loud bellow of frustration. "Damn it all! What's going on? What has the Professor to do with the Custodian? I need to find Neoptolemas NOW! If he is in league with the Custodian then he might also be working with Redfeld. Has that occurred to you?"

Septimus went a whiter shade of pale. "I really wish you hadn't suggested that. It's pretty damn terrifying, boyo!"

"Do you think it's possible?" Tom asked.

"I hope not. Think about it for a moment: Redfeld, the Custodian and the Professor; one man from each reality: our World, the Twisted Reality and the Office between the realities. Each man with a great deal of knowledge and power: that really is uncomfortable to think about."

"And each of them able to change history; yes, that is horrible, Septimus!"

They were silent for a while then Septimus shook his head. "No, I don't believe it – I can't believe it; not of the Professor in any event, can you?"

Tom was upset and confused and when he was in that mood all sorts of strange thoughts started going through his mind. He stood up and began to pace back and forth across the room. "I don't want to believe it, but I just can't be sure. We need to talk to the Prof. So, how do I find where Neoptolemas has gone to?"

Septimus shrugged, Tom stopped pacing and without speaking, they both looked out of the window and watched the birds for a moment. Then suddenly, Septimus snapped his fingers.

"Edward Dyson! He's the answer. He will be able to trace where the Professor is and lead us to him."

"Yeah, great, but Edward is missing with Charlie and we have no idea how to find him either!"

"Oh, yes, I'd forgotten about that...." Dejected, the Welshman's voice trailed away.

There was a knock at the door and Mary came in looking distracted. Tom glanced at her, blinked and looked again. After he had left her in the dining room she had obviously been persuaded to change her clothes. Gone was the full-skirted dress that fell to her ankles. She now wore a cotton blouse and a pair of jeans. Her long hair had been tied back and on her feet were a pair of trainers. She looked just like any other ordinary girl from the twenty-first century.

"Wow Mary!" Septimus commented, "Quite a transformation - but why the change?"

Mary blushed and looked down at her clothes. "It feels strange, I confess, but it was necessary. My own clothes do not seem to fit so well in this world: or leastways are not so practical."

"Practical?" Tom asked. "What do you mean by that?"

She grinned, "Well for one thing, I can run faster in this boys' garb."

"Ah," Tom smiled.

Mary's grin faded and she again wore a distracted expression, as if she had something other than clothes on her mind.

"What is it, Mary?" Tom asked.

"Master ..."

"Thomas, Mary!" he cut across her. "It's Thomas, Tommy or Tom. *Not* 'Master'," he shouted in frustration.

"Sorry, yes, Thomas, I keep forgetting ..."

"Ok, what were you going to tell me?"

"It's the magic door. I remembered something about it."

Mystified, Tom glanced at Septimus who looked back at him, equally puzzled.

"What magic door, lass?" the Welshman prompted.

"Captain Redfeld - his magic door. The one he magicked up with his sorcery at that 'Trafigalca' place."

"Trafalgar! You mean Trafalgar. Redfeld's portal to that projection room: to the Twisted Reality. What about it?" Tom asked.

Mary looked thoughtful again before answering. "Well, you see, I think I can help. With the... err, portal, I mean. I could still see it – *feel* it maybe says it better. I mean, after it was gone. The portal was closed and invisible, but I could still feel it. It was dim and faint, but it was there. And I think, I think ..."

Tom nodded, "Yes, what? You think what?"

Mary hesitated. The loud clonk of a clock pendulum on the landing was the only sound to be heard. Finally, Mary spoke.

"Well ... well, that is, I think I could open it again."

CHAPTER TWENTY-FIVE - THE PORTAL

"Mary, that's awesome," Tom grinned. She blushed and smiled shyly at him. Outside, the birds on the rooftop, spooked by some hidden threat, suddenly took off and scattered into the skies.

"We have to do it," Tom said, after a moment's pause.

"No!" Septimus exclaimed. "Just think about it, boyo. We haven't any idea what is through that portal. All we know – all we believe – is that it leads to a room in Redfeld's world: some kind of laboratory; a 'projection room'. That sort of place belonging to the military would certainly be guarded in our world. I can't see it being any less the case there, can you?"

"I know. I know it's a risk and it scares me, but we can't leave Edward and Charlie in *his* hands," Tom insisted. "We might as well not have rescued them in the first place!"

Mary nodded, fervently agreeing with Tom. "I am frightened too, Mr Mason," she said, "But they are our friends."

"I know all that. I agree, it's just ..."

"What?" Tom and Mary chorused.

Septimus shook his head and said nothing. Instead he pulled back the sheet, swung his legs out of the bed and stood up. Or rather, he tried to stand up. As soon as his feet hit the floor he groaned in pain and slumped back to sit on the bed, holding his side and wincing.

"Just what do you think you're doing?" said an angry voice behind them. Doctor Makepeace had come into the room.

255

"I'm just popping out for a moment, Doc – won't be long," Septimus said breathlessly, grimacing with pain.

The Doctor's face went red. He shook his head and pointed at the bed. "In! Now! You're going nowhere for at least a day."

"But ..."

"No buts, ifs or maybes around here. You had a bullet in your lung. I was able to Walk that out and start the lung healing, but if you move too much you'll bleed to death. Into bed for twenty-four hours' rest: no debate."

He turned to face Tom and Mary. "You two, get out now! I will tell you when it is safe to visit." They were shooed to the door and stumbled downstairs.

"Now what?" Tom asked.

"We still must go, Master ... Tom, I mean."

"Just us two?" Tom thought about that for a moment then he nodded.

"Yes you're right. It must be us and it must be now. We don't know if Edward and Charlie will still be alive this time tomorrow." He took hold of Mary's hand and sought the Flow of Time.

Emerging onto a pavement in Trafalgar Square was like stepping into a whirlwind. The place was surrounded by crowds, kept away by a line of policemen and women and riot barriers. Journalists prowled around like predators on the hunt, snapping away with their cameras at anything remotely interesting. Beyond the barriers, Tom and Mary could see an inner line of yellow tapes marked POLICE – NO ENTRY surrounding the area where he and the others had fought Redfeld's gang. Forensic scientists were collecting spent cartridges and even samples of blood.

"Blimey. We've walked into a crime scene!"

"The portal is still there, Master," Mary said.

Tom frowned, but let the 'Master' go by this time. Mary didn't notice and carried on talking.

"Truly I am certain I can open it, just as with a real door, but I think I need to be near to it; no more than a few feet away."

Tom looked back at the taped off area, the scientists and the police – many of whom were armed with sub-machine guns and dressed in flak jackets. He winced, "That could be a problem. How long do you think it will take?"

"It may take some moments."

"Can you create a wall around us, whilst you do it?"

"I ... I don't think so, Master. I think I will be too busy."

Tom nodded, resigned to being 'Master'; clearly it was too ingrained a habit for the young woman to change. He had no idea how Mary did what she did; she could not Walk as he and the others did, but her powers were unique and he just had to accept what she was saying.

"Ok then," he said, "this will be hard. We will Walk to just in front of the portal. I will distract the police whilst you get it open. We get through and we close it. You *can* close it, can't you?"

"Yes, I believe so, Master."

Exasperated, he tried one more time, "Mary – don't call me 'Master'; it's Tom."

Mary nodded but she was looking distracted, her mind on the task ahead.

"Ok; ready?"

Again, she nodded and held out her hand. Tom took it and Walked the short distance across Trafalgar Square.

257

"Bill, pass me the next bag will you ... oh my God!" were the words that greeted them as they materialised in front of one of the scientists. He was crouching down over the dried pool of blood that had once belonged to Septimus. He stared open-mouthed at the two youths who had just appeared out of thin air, right in front of him. Glancing behind, Tom saw another scientist, looking equally gobsmacked, standing next to some equipment cases on a table. Half a dozen armed police stood only a few feet away and these, attracted by the noise, had turned around and were also staring at them.

"Mary!"

"Shush, I am busy!"

She was. In front of them a pinpoint of light had appeared and was already getting larger.

"Armed police! Put your hands on your head and don't move!" barked one of the officers.

The portal expanded. It was now a foot wide and three feet high.

"I said hands on head: now! This will be your last warning!" the voice grew more agitated. The scientists had scuttled off to the side and the police were closing in on him and Mary.

Outside the riot barriers and yellow tape, the crowds had noticed the confrontation and fallen silent. Tom glanced around again: the portal was just a few feet away and was now large enough to jump through. Most of the police were gaping at it; one yelled, "Get Down!" Those nearest flung themselves to the ground as if expecting an explosion. There were cries of renewed terror from the crowd.

Right, thought Tom, they had no time to dawdle. He held on to Mary and reached out in his mind for the World Map. The link was there alright, but he was alarmed to find he could not move them through the portal. The map in his head simply did not extend through it. Of course it didn't, Tom muttered, kicking himself. It was another world. There would be another map.

"Hasten Master! We must flee," said Mary, sounding very seventeenth century, and very scared.

Tom nodded: time to worry about maps later, perhaps. He jumped through the portal, dragging Mary along with him. On the other side they crashed into two chairs, which they knocked flying, and their momentum carried them on under a bench. There, they lay for a moment, panting for breath. The portal was still open and three astounded police stood cautiously gaping through it.

"Close," muttered Mary, pointing her finger at the portal. With a resounding crack, it closed and the scene in Trafalgar Square vanished.

"Phew," Tom said. "Well done Mary, we made it."

They crawled out from under the bench and looked about. It was the laboratory that Tom had seen before, lined floor to ceiling with shelves crammed with machines and devices that Tom had no clue about. There was a door at the opposite end of the room, which he assumed would lead to the outside. One side of the room was taken up by a huge metallic screen where he presumed the image from the projector shone. He moved across to this strange looking device and examined it, but could not see how it worked, beyond having a row of switches and dials.

"Now what do we do?" Mary asked.

"We find Charlie and Edward and get home. First though, can you still feel the portal?"

Mary nodded then hesitated and frowned. "Er ... yes, but it is getting faint. The weakness in the air is still there, but I fear it will not be for very much longer. We must make haste to locate our friends before ..." Her eyes widened and she turned to look at Tom, her face ashen.

"What is it?" Tom suddenly had the feeling that bad news was coming.

"I am afraid to say that the portal has closed, Master. I can no longer feel it at all."

"But that means we're stuck!"

Mary nodded. "I fear so."

"It's even worse than that, I'm sorry to say," Tom said and now told Mary that he could neither feel the Flow of Time, nor see the map that allowed him to Walk them to other times and locations in their world.

"So, we are stranded in Redfeld's world: in Fairyland?" Mary grimaced, her eyes wide with fear.

"It looks that way," Tom rubbed his eyes then he shrugged. "We'll work something out. If Redfeld can come and go between this world and ours, so can we. But we can't stay here. We must get away before ..."

"Before what?" snapped a voice.

They both spun round and gasped.

Standing in the doorway was an officer wearing a similar uniform to Captain Redfeld's, although this man was younger with fair hair. Behind him lurked three guards: all armed with rifles. The officer whipped out a Luger pistol from a holster at his waist and pointed it at Tom.

"We shoot any spies we find in this garrison. You will come with me," he ordered, gesturing with a flick of his Luger that they should come out of the room. Then he snapped his heels

260

together, turned and spat an order to the guards. "Bring them for questioning!"

The guards filed into the projection room and using their rifles prodded Tom and Mary out of the door and along a dimly lit corridor. It had many doors on each side and seemed to twist this way and that for a very long way through some sort of building. Tom tried to keep track of the direction in which they were heading, but after the first few turns it was hopeless. Unless he could find a plan of the building he did not stand a chance of finding the projection room again. In any case, how could they hope to get home without the portal?

One more turn and they were walking along a gallery with large windows looking outwards from the building. Tom realised they were high up in a tower block and through the windows he could see a city spread out below them. The most obvious feature was a forest of tall chimneys belching fumes into the sky from hundreds of factories. The buildings in the immediate vicinity were also tower blocks, much smaller than the one they were in, which seemed to loom over all the rest, but they were made of the same dark granite, stained with smoke and very grim looking. On top of each one was a flagpole flying a red flag, which Tom recognised as being the Nazi-like flag bearing the thunderbolt symbol of the Twisted Reality. It was the only decoration or adornment he could see in the whole city. There were no neon lights nor any brightly lit advertising hoardings as Tom would expect to see in his own world; no statues to this nation's past heroes, no parks and most certainly no tourists. Nothing, in fact, to break the bleak, monotonous view, with one exception: on one of the buildings there was a vast portrait of a man. He wore the Twisted Reality's Nazi uniform and his eyes, whilst intelligent, showed no compassion, no mercy. They looked coldly out over the city with an imperious, almost contemptuous air.

In the street below, Tom caught a glimpse of a column of marching soldiers: the army to which Redfeld belonged, he assumed. He looked back over the skyline. In the distance there was a domed cathedral, which looked oddly familiar, as did the tall tower with a clock on it in the other direction. Suddenly, Tom's stomach lurched as he realised what he was looking at.

"Oh my God: it's London!" he blurted out, swallowing hard.

The officer snapped his head round and glared at him. "Trying to pretend you don't know what city you are in, now, are we? That will do you no good, boy," he sneered.

Tom did not reply. He had worked out exactly where they were. They were still in Trafalgar Square, but it was not as he knew it. In the Twisted Reality, the victorious Germans had built their London garrison in the Square right over the top of Nelson's column. More than that, as he became aware of his location, he realised that he now felt a link once again to the map. Yes, he could feel it and yes ... he could now also feel the Flow of Time. It did feel odd, though; and the map was different! It was that same weird feeling he'd had before, like driving on the wrong side of the road. The seconds passing here were those of another world where history had played out differently and where another sun lit the skies. But odd as it might be, he felt just a little more at ease. They might be stuck in this Twisted Reality, but within it he could Walk if he needed to. He tried to wink at Mary to put her at ease, but she was looking out at the city, her face stark with horror and did not see his signal.

Turning yet another corner, they emerged onto a further gallery, but unlike the others, this one was open to the interior of the building. They were now moving along a high balcony lined with pillars, looking down onto a central courtyard. High above them natural light filtered down through a glass ceiling. Below them the courtyard was dotted with statues of what were, presumably, heroes of the German conquest of Britain: officers, admirals and generals, who had achieved what the Germans in Tom's own reality had failed to do.

Amongst them Tom could see two figures that were not statues. One was sickeningly familiar and no surprise – it was Captain Redfeld. He was talking animatedly to another man, partially hidden behind a statue of a fat general. Ah, that statue Tom did recognise, for it was Herman Goering the Commander in Chief of the *Luftwaffe*, Germany's air force in the war, and a close friend of Adolf Hitler. Earlier in the term, Tom's history class had been shown a picture of him almost bursting out of his renowned pale blue uniform. Tom remembered thinking that he looked quite jovial, his fat face wreathed in smiles; not at all as he would have imagined.

A few moments later their movement along the gallery shifted his point of view and he could see who Redfeld was talking to. His heart jumped and beside him, he heard Mary gasp.

The new figure was wearing a German uniform of the type Redfeld wore, although with more braid and decorations – so presumably a senior officer. But of the face there could be no mistake: without a doubt it was the Professor.

"Neoptolemas!" Tom gasped involuntarily.

"Halt!" The officer walking behind him snapped an order. The guards stopped at once and Tom struggled to avoid colliding with the one in front. Mary did collide with her guard, but bounced off, wincing.

The officer marched past Tom and opened a door. He stuck his head inside and then re-emerged. Grabbing Tom by an elbow he pulled him into the room. Then, with a shout of, "Keep her there!" to his men he slammed the door shut behind them both.

Tom looked round. They were now in a room lit by a flickering bulb and full of filing cabinets. From the layer of dust on the tops of the cabinets Tom surmised the room was rarely used. It was unoccupied.

The officer studied Tom for a moment before he spoke. "Tell me quickly what you know of Professor Neoptolemas. It is your one chance to stay alive."

Tom stared at him. Was this some kind of trick? What did this man know of the Professor - unless, of course, Neoptolemas was working with Redfeld after all and was well known to the rest of his army?

"I thought we were to be shot as spies," he mumbled to gain time, thinking furiously.

"You might still be if I don't get some answers I like. Answer me. How do you know the Professor?"

Tom was silent. Was this man working for Captain Redfeld? Was it a trick to find out all he knew? But why drag him into a room full of filing cabinets to question him? That seemed very odd. The man must know that Tom had seen Redfeld and the Professor just moments ago. That and his reaction on the balcony, blurting out the Prof's name, seemed to be the reason he'd been dragged in here. What was this man's game?

"What makes you think I will tell you anything? You are one of Redfeld's officers. I won't work for him, so why should I work for you? How can I trust you?" Tom answered in a defiant voice that he hoped did not reveal the fact that his heart was pounding like a sledgehammer and he was terrified.

"Do you know Captain Redfeld?" the officer asked.

Tom said nothing.

The officer studied him again for a few seconds and then Tom heard a pop as the holster of his pistol was undone and the Luger reappeared. The officer clicked off the safety catch and then pointed it at Tom.

"Don't shoot ...." Tom said feebly, raising his hands and feeling his throat tighten.

The other man's expression did not change, but he suddenly reached up and placed the pistol into Tom's right hand, then stepped back.

"What ...?" Tom's mouth fell open. This situation was surreal. Slowly he lowered his arms and looked down at the Luger nestling in his palm.

"You asked how you can trust me. Well now you can shoot me, if you want to."

Tom hefted the pistol and for a moment considered doing just that and then bursting out of the room to rescue Mary. Instead, he moved over to a filing cabinet and placed the Luger on top of it. He would probably only have shot himself in the foot, anyway.

"Who are you?" he asked the officer. "And what's all this about?"

"Lieutenant Manfred Teuber, UK Special Security Detachment," he said. The way he said Lieutenant sounded like 'loytnant'.

"I am also an associate, perhaps even a friend, of Professor Neoptolemas of the Hourglass Institute in your world!"

Tom felt his heart give a jump and looked over at the pistol. Was this good news or bad?

"My world? I don't know what you are talking about," Tom bluffed. The officer snorted.

"Oh I think you do. You are not from this place are you? What you call 'The Twisted Reality'. You are from *Die Andere Welt* – 'The Other World'. You must be, because you mentioned the Professor by name and no one in this world apart from me, Captain Redfeld and a very few senior officers, know of the existence of *Die Andere Welt* or of the Professor. So you are from that world; either that, or you are working for the good Captain Redfeld ... and I'm a dead man!"

"Then you are *not* working for Captain Redfeld?" Tom asked. The officer shook his head.

"But you are working for Neoptolemas?"

"Not exactly working for him; let us just say our aims often coincide."

"In that case, perhaps you can tell me exactly what his aims are in being here today, dressed in that uniform?"

Teuber blinked and then actually laughed. "If you mean the man you saw just now, that was not Professor Neoptolemas. It was Colonel Heinrich Theilmann, also of UK Special Security Detachment, my superior and a very dangerous man."

"But he looks ..."

"Identical to the Professor? Yes he does and no, I cannot tell you why, that is something you will have to ask Neoptolemas."

Tom nodded and thought of the three men who looked almost identical: the Professor, the Custodian and now this Heinrich Theilmann. How could that be and what did it mean? But there were other questions to ask, so he put that to one side.

"So, you still haven't told me, what aims do you and the Professor have in common?"

Teuber sighed and took off his hat to rub a hand through his hair. Before answering, he replaced the hat and adjusted the peak carefully.

"The Professor wants to protect your world – its past and its future from Redfeld, Theilmann and others who would change it to an image of this world. I too want change, but I want to change this world to an image of yours. I aim to undo much that went wrong here and make it a good world to live in again. The Professor and I have agreed that Redfeld must be kept away from your world and then one day maybe the Professor can help me here, in mine."

Tom nodded. That at least made sense. If, of course, the Professor was genuine and not in a conspiracy with the Custodian: to what end Tom had no idea. Teuber now waited expectantly and Tom realised that it was time for him to reveal some facts of his own; but what, exactly? He knew nothing about this Teuber bloke, did he? He decided to keep it brief.

"My name is Thomas Oakley and yes, I am from 'The Other World'. I did some work for the Professor rescuing two men and a woman. The woman is with me here, but the two men were captured earlier by Redfeld and brought here ..."

"Edward Dyson and Charles Hawker?" Teuber asked.

Tom nodded.

"I know where they are."

Tom opened his mouth to ask more, but at that moment the door swung open and in strode Colonel Theilmann. Teuber jumped to attention, whilst Tom shivered. To be this close to the man who was the spitting image of the Professor was very unnerving: doubly so because he was wearing full military uniform and regalia. Theilmann glanced coldly at Tom and then turned to the officer.

"What goes on here, Lieutenant?"

"I captured these intruders in the guard room near the cells, sir. I was taking them for interrogation."

"Spies or saboteurs?"

"I think neither, sir. It seems their father was arrested this morning for taking part in the strike in the docklands and the children here were trying to see him."

Theilmann turned his gaze on Tom and he felt as if the temperature in the room had fallen ten degrees. The intense gaze from those steely grey eyes was chilling, but worse than that, somehow penetrating. He felt as if the Colonel was peeling away any disguise and deception to seek out the truth.

"Boy, if your father is a dissident and a trouble maker he will be punished and your family informed of his fate. As for you and your sister – you have broken into a secure base of high sensitivity. That will not go unpunished. You and your father ... and sister will learn obedience."

He looked back at Teuber.

"Transfer them to the detention camp at Newbury immediately, Lieutenant."

"Yes sir!"

Colonel Thielmann spun on his heel and marched out of the room. The door swung shut behind him.

"Thanks," Tom exhaled in relief as Thielmann's footsteps receded. "But what will you do now?"

CHAPTER TWENTY-SIX - PRISONERS AGAIN

T euber reached over and retrieved his Luger from the top of the cabinet and put it away in its holster. Then he answered. "I don't have much choice, Thomas Oakley. You will have to come with me."

"To this detention camp?" Tom asked, suddenly alarmed.

Teuber nodded and then it appeared that a thought came to him. "Actually, this might work quite well for us," he said. "Those friends of yours – Dyson and Hawker?"

"Edward and Charlie: what about them?"

"When I last heard, they were due to be transferred to the detention camp to await questioning by Captain Redfeld."

"Well, I suppose that is something. Hopefully, we can find them perhaps. But then what?"

"We must get you home," Tueber said.

Tom nodded. "Can you do that? Open a portal?"

"A portal? Ah you mean the door to your world. Well ... no I can't. Redfeld calls it Projection – that's how he visits your reality. I think perhaps Neoptolemas can – he must have some way of getting here because it has always been in my world that we have met. I assumed you could, for if not, how then did you get here?"

Deciding not to disclose his ability to Walk, Tom explained about Mary re-opening the portal that Redfeld had made during the attack in Trafalgar Square.

Teuber looked thoughtful. "I have been wondering about all this since I learned what Redfeld has been doing. Evidently he has trained a special squad of men in Projection. Yesterday I heard that he had used them to capture spies, as he put it, from your reality. Even in a high security facility like this one, rumours do fly. Until recently I knew he was able to visit your world, but I did not know he could take anyone with him.

"So, you have never heard of him doing that before yesterday?"

"No." The officer shook his head. "So then, this Mary – could she not open the portal for you?"

"No, I really don't think she can just open one up herself, it has to be there to be opened, if you know what I mean."

"Erm ... I think so." There was a knock at the door and one of Teuber's men opened it.

"Is everything all right, sir? The Colonel said we were to transfer the prisoners to Newbury."

"Everything is fine, *Unteroffizier*. I was just interrogating the prisoner. Right you," he now barked at Tom, "outside. You have a transport to catch."

They were marched briskly to an elevator and hustled inside. With a lurch, it descended down through many levels until abruptly coming to a halt. When the doors opened, Tom could see they were in an underground parking bay or garage. To one side, mechanics had a car's engine stripped down and were working on it. Nearby, other vehicles stood ready for refuelling and there was a strong smell of diesel in the air.

Beyond the fuel pumps, a couple of dozen trucks were parked. Tom and Mary were led to one of them and made to clamber up inside. Long, low benches ran down both sides of the truck's interior and they were ordered to sit on one and then a manacle was fastened to their ankles and secured to a chain running the length of the bench. After that the guards jumped back down and for a moment the two prisoners were alone.

Tom glanced over at his companion and saw that she was shaking a little and staring about her with a frightened expression on her pale little face. He tried to reassure her. "Mary, I can sense the Flow of Time and see the map again. I can Walk us away whenever we want."

At this news, the girl visibly relaxed. "Then, why not do it now?"

"Well, firstly, we need to find Edward and Charlie and secondly, that officer who arrested us – Lieutenant Teuber – it turns out he is working for Neoptolemas ..." and Tom told Mary about the conversation with Teuber. He left aside his doubts about the Professor. She had enough to worry about without adding that fear to the pot.

"So you see that if we go along in this truck, we should find Edward and Charlie. If we run now, we may never find them. Moreover, if we did leave, questions would be asked. Sooner or later Redfeld would hear and he is not stupid. When he found out that Teuber had us in his hands and we escaped, the Lieutenant would get into trouble. Even if Redfeld did not discover Teuber was an ally of the Prof ..."

"God forbid!" whispered Mary.

"Exactly; either way he would be blamed and held accountable for our escape. In this world I don't suppose that would be good, do you?"

Mary shook her head. "You're thinking that Teuber has risked himself to keep your presence here a secret, so it seems only fair not to betray him. It is a noble thought and surely God will protect and prosper those who hold such sentiments. I will so pray that he will."

"If you believe that praying will prevent us getting killed for me following my stupid conscience, then by all means pray. But do it in a while; let us make our plans first, eh?"

"So then, what do we do?" Mary asked.

"Well, as the place we are going is where Edward and Charlie are then we go there and we find them. Then we escape and go home."

For the first time in a long while Mary laughed. "That took a lot of planning!"

"Yeah, well," Tom shrugged, "now I came to think about it, we don't know anything, so we can't make much of a plan, can we?"

The noise of marching boots coming closer made them both look towards the rear of the truck.

"So, maybe you had better start with the praying after all," Tom whispered.

The rear doors swung open again and a dozen anxious looking prisoners were pushed in and made to sit next to or opposite Tom and Mary before being secured with manacles and chains. Tom glanced at them. Most were men, but there were some women and also two terrified little girls. They held tightly to a frightened young woman whom Tom surmised was their mother. Then the doors were slammed shut and Tom felt a vibration as the engine started up and they were away.

For the next hour or more the truck droned along, stopping and starting and heaving this way and that. Tom began to feel a bit car sick and to take his mind off it, reached out for the map. They were going west along the main roads towards Newbury. It might have been the M4 – it certainly was following its route – but Tom knew that the motorways were built after the war. So, here, in the Britain of The Twisted Reality, they would have been built by the German occupying forces. Perhaps they were called *autobahns*, like the German ones were, Tom mused idly.

Suddenly, the truck slowed down and gave a lurch to the left before stopping. Tom could hear other vehicles pulling over and the crank of handbrakes being tugged on. Outside, he could hear the roar of other vehicles still hurtling past them. A moment later, the rear doors opened and a guard leaned in, inspected them and unlocked the long chain at one end. Then he waved at the prisoners to shuffle out. This was difficult as their ankles were still manacled together, so Tom had to help Mary. In a few minutes they were standing with their fellow prisoners by the side of the motorway. Woods lined the edge of the road on both sides, but in the distance Tom could see the lights of a large town – Newbury perhaps. Back the way they had come, Tom noticed the glow of a larger city. Was it London? That did not seem possible: they were at least fifty miles from the capital. Then again, a vast swathe of the eastern night sky was stained a darker black by a huge pall of polluted smoke and fumes. It seemed that in this world the factories of a monstrously swollen London had spread out like a cancer across the entire south east of England.

It was getting quite dark now, but Tom could see that there were indeed scores of cars and trucks pulled over to one side, mostly civilian vehicles, but some army vehicles like theirs. Meanwhile, a large convoy of transports was surging by. There were, it seemed, hundreds of them. They were military trucks, painted a greyish green colour, each one adorned with the lightning bolt flag, fluttering from a small pole upon each bonnet.

In front of their truck, Tom could see Teuber talking to another officer who was dressed in a black uniform with a red armband. Other soldiers in the same uniform seemed to be waving batons and directing the traffic. These were Military Police, Tom assumed. He heard a few words in German flow across to him.

"*Sie müssen hier warten. Der Konvoi fährt nach* Exeter ..."

Tom was starting to learn German at school. The military policeman had said something about the convoy heading for Exeter. That sounded odd. Why would a large army be going to Exeter? Dartmoor was near Exeter. He had heard that Dartmoor was sometimes used for army manoeuvres in his own world, so perhaps that was true here too. But, it did seem an excessively large force just for an exercise.

Eventually, the convoy had passed by and soon afterwards the prisoners were all loaded up again into the trucks, the chains locked and they were off. The rocking of the truck was vaguely soporific and Tom saw that Mary had dozed off to sleep. He, though, wanted to know where they were going so he fought against the drowsiness and, leaning back against the side of the transport, connected again with the map in order to follow the route they were taking. This time the journey was not long, for the truck soon left the motorway and then followed a minor road for quarter of an hour before turning off it down a track. Braking suddenly, the transport came to a halt, throwing Tom forwards against Mary, waking her up with a start.

"Sorry!" he whispered. "But, I think we are there, here ... wherever we are."

The rear door swung open and a torch light shone into Tom's face, flickered across to Mary; ran along the one row of scared prisoners and back up the other. The chain was again removed and someone barked an order. "Out you lot!" Tom recognised the voice as belonging to Lieutenant Teuber.

They scrambled out and assembled in an open space lit by floodlights and surrounded by long, low huts. Tom blinked: the place looked just like the prisoner of war camp in the old World War Two movie, *The Great Escape*. These structures, however, were more permanent being made of concrete and steel rather than wood.

Mary and the other female prisoners were directed to one side of the ground and the men and boys to the other; then the women were led off. Mary looked back fearfully at Tom, who tried to go after her to tell her not to worry, but one of the guards stepped forward and shoved him back into line.

The men and boys were now marched off towards a hut, herded inside and the door shut and padlocked behind them. The interior, which was dimly lit by only two light bulbs, was filled with a hundred or so bunk beds. The hut was already occupied by some thirty other prisoners, who studied the new inmates as they dispersed to find beds around the room.

Tom was just about to select a quiet corner and attempt to Walk outside and find Mary, when he felt a tap on his shoulder. Spinning round he found himself face to face with Edward. Charlie was a few feet behind him.

"What took you so long?" Charlie asked smiling at him.

"Thank God I've found you," Tom said, his spirits lifting at the sight of them.

"You should not have tried," chided Edward. "It was far too risky you following us here to Redfeld's world. You know Redfeld is here, don't you? If he finds you ..."

Tom nodded. "I saw him, but I wasn't about to leave you two in the lurch, not after going to all that effort to rescue you in the first place! Anyway, Redfeld does not know I am here yet and we have an ally who might help us. His name is Lieutenant Teuber ..."

"Who the hell is Loytnant Tueber?" demanded Charlie.

"It's how the Prussians pronounce Lieutenant, Charlie," Edward replied. "Well the Germans, to you: but in my day it was Prussia. When I was a wet behind the ears officer cadet, I was sent to Prussia as an observer and picked up a bit of German then."

"Same question, whatever the language," said Charlie in a bored voice. "Who is he?"

So Tom explained how Teuber had helped them and would probably be a friend; or at least not an enemy, anyway. When he had finished, Charlie glanced at Edward with a sceptical look on his face.

"You believe this Teuber then, do you? Did it occur to you that he might have been lying to find out what you know?" Charlie asked.

Tom thought about that and then he thought about the business with the pistol. Would Teuber really have given him a gun if he was working for Redfeld? Well, possibly, if his belief in Redfeld's cause was strong enough. But somehow he felt that he could trust the man. Something about him just felt right. In this horrible dark world there was something good – if that was that the right word – or at least honourable about the officer, which felt very different to how he felt about Redfeld. Charlie was right, though: Tom had only just met him. He shrugged. "Well, alright, I am not sure, but there's not a lot I can do about it. Anyway, I am here now. Septimus and I agreed we need you to help defeat Redfeld's plans."

Edward nodded and then rather stiffly put a hand on Tom's shoulder. "Jolly kind of you to come, all the same."

Tom realised that this was the Victorian's way of saying thank you and smiled. "No problem. We must get out of here and find Mary – she is in the women's hut - and then get away if we can. I have no idea where we will find a portal to get home to our world."

Edward looked up sharply at that. "It is odd that you mention portals. Redfeld has already questioned us once, before transferring us here. He was very keen to know how you were able to Walk a group of us, all in one go. It seems he transports his men by creating portals or what he called 'Gateways in Reality'. He also mentioned 'projecting' or something like that. Anyway he really questioned us on what you knew about them, how you opened them and how often."

"That's crazy!" Tom shook his head, "I don't know how to open them. Mary reopened the one in Trafalgar Square, but only because it was not fully shut – rather like reopening a scar or something."

"Or popping a seam on trousers?" Edward mused.

"I just had a thought," Tom pointed at Edward. "Redfeld cannot Walk other people, but he is able somehow to create these portals and use them to transport his men. Maybe there is some problem with doing it that way and if he could Walk them, as I can, it would solve the problem."

The other two looked confused now. "Oh I don't know... maybe it's dangerous or something ..." Tom trailed off, but he noticed that Edward was nodding.

"Well, wrenching a hole in reality seems dangerous to me. Perhaps that is why he needs you."

"Only now he might not," Charlie put in. "When we were being questioned, that Colonel Thiemann came in and the two of them talked as if we were not there: probably assumed we would not be for much longer, once they had finished with us." Charlie ran a finger across his throat. Tom grimaced.

"Anyway, that Colonel told Redfeld that he had just got a message from the Professor inviting Redfeld to a meeting at the British Museum."

"What!"

"Yes, that's what I thought at the time," said Charlie. "It seems our Professor is talking to the enemy."

Tom nodded and now he told the others about his dreams of the Office; of Septimus and his deal with Redfeld, and of the Custodian's meeting with the Professor.

Edward and Charlie looked very glum by the time his tale had come to an end.

"Who can we trust now?" Charlie asked.

"Each other," Tom said. "We have to rely on each other, Mary too; and I believe we can now trust Septimus. The Professor ...? I'm not sure; I want to trust him, but this news is worrying."

"Yes, very worrying, if he is talking to Redfeld," Edward commented.

"It means more than that. Don't you see? If he could get a message to Colonel Theilmann it means Teuber is telling the truth – about this point at least– that the Professor can travel to this world: to the Twisted Reality."

Edward's mouth dropped open. "Ah ... now I understand why Redfeld got so excited with that message. Perhaps our nasty little Captain saw a chance to get out of the Professor what he has not been able to get out of you, at least not yet."

278

Tom nodded, "That makes sense if he is seeking an alternative way to travel between the two worlds." Tom paced about the room, but stopped when a few other prisoners looked at him suspiciously. He lowered his voice. "We must get back to our world and speak to Septimus. But Walking won't help me here. Leastways, I can see the map of *this* world so I can get us out of this hut; get Mary and escape, but then what? We will still be in the Twisted Reality; we're stuck here."

"Can't you still see the map for *our* world, Thomas? I can," Edward said, looking puzzled. "Maybe it is because I have been here a few hours longer than you, but I can feel two maps now – one clear and in focus, but very confusing because much of it is different to what I expect to see: the places where the Twisted Reality is at variance from our world, I suppose. Then, I think I can feel another map behind it: but the other one is fainter and I can't really focus on it. But it's definitely there."

That stunned Tom. He had not tried to link to the map of his own world since he had attempted it in the projector room and failed. Closing his mind to his surroundings, he did so now and there, behind the map to the Twisted Reality he saw it: dim but still visible − rather like the ghostly shadow you can get on an old portable telly as you try to get it in focus – there was his own world.

He reached out to it, felt a connection and with a pop was gone from the hut and its prisoners and was standing next to a very surprised cow, who for a moment, stopped chewing grass and looked at him. Surprise in the life of a cow does not last long and being a cow who likes to get on with the day, it soon went back to chewing the grass and ignored him.

It was as dark here as in the Twisted Reality, but he was in a field just outside Newbury, with no prison in sight. With a

279

whoop of delight, Tom startled the cow, who took to her heels. He reached out again in his mind and could see the Twisted Reality map, there behind his own world's map and out of focus, just as his own had been moments ago. It was with great reluctance – and a not a little fear – that he returned to the prison hut. When he reappeared, Charlie and Edward had moved and were talking to two of the prisoners.

"What do you mean he just vanished? That's impossible!" Charlie was saying.

"I tell you what I saw with my own eyes. That boy was standing there and just vanished!" insisted a thick set, red-headed man with tattoos on his arms.

"Oh come on, really, does that seem likely?"

"You calling me a liar, mate?" The redhead said, his face reddening and muscles bulging.

Charlie turned and winked at Edward and Tom sensed he was about to start a fight.

"What's all this about?" Tom said and pushed forward between his friends. "I just slipped that's all! We don't want to start any trouble, do we," he added with an emphasis in his voice that was directed at Edward and Charlie.

"Eh? You playing games, pal?" the grunt continued.

"No – look, I am sorry mate, really I am. Just slipped that's all."

"Right – well watch it – no more trouble or you're all for it, understand?" Then muttering under his breath and followed by his cronies, the grunt bustled off towards his bunk.

Edward, Charlie and Tom huddled back together. "Careful, Tom, you almost got rumbled then," Charlie muttered.

"Sorry – but we're ok. I *can* Walk to our world. We just need to rescue Mary and get out."

"Well then let us depart immediately!" Edward said.

Tom did not move.

"What's the problem now?" Edward asked, his voice rising in exasperation.

"Teuber is the problem," Tom replied.

Edward nodded and summarised the situation. "If we accomplish an escape then the fact that Charlie and I, plus a boy and girl, have escaped will reach Redfeld. Redfeld will put two and two together with the extreme likelihood of getting four. Teuber would get questioned and life could get very hard for him."

"You know, lads, in Septimus' absence someone should be the one to say, 'So what – is that our problem?' So it had better be me," Charlie said.

Tom and Edward both stared at him flatly.

"Oh, all right!" Charlie surrendered. "You are right – it wouldn't be on. But, can I just ask, where is Mr Mason when you need him?"

"Nursing a serious wound under the eagle eyes of Doctor Makepeace," said Tom with a rueful grin.

"Well then, we must decide what to do without him," Edward stated.

Tom looked over at the red-haired grunt, who was still watching them from his bunk.

"I have an idea," he said.

CHAPTER TWENTY-SEVEN - PRISON BREAKOUT

Tom wandered across the hut towards the redhead, with Charlie and Edward following close behind. He stopped in front of the huge man, who stared down at him from where he was sitting on the top bunk, rather like a tiger about to pounce.

"What you want, kid?" he growled.

"I just wanted to apologise for causing trouble with my little trick that's all. We are circus acts, you see, and make our living with magic tricks."

The man's face showed something approaching stunned surprise at that. "No wonder the Jerries have you locked away. They don't like gypsies and circuses. But I thought they had rounded you lot all up years ago, in the forties. Thought they sent you all to work camps to 'learn how to become productive members of society' or whatever the propaganda says. How come you are still about? Your grandparents escape, is that it?"

Tom's mind raced. He had forgotten about that. He knew about concentration camps – they had been taught a bit about it at school – but had forgotten that the Nazis in his world had locked up many 'undesirables' as they saw them, including tramps, vagabonds and gypsies.

Edward came to the rescue. Such things were well after his time, but he had been reading a lot of history in the Prof's library. "Yes, that's right. My grandparents took my father into Switzerland when the war started and hid there. But you can't hide forever and so we have been travelling about entertaining folk and avoiding the authorities. Life is grim and folk need fun. We get fed, put up for the night and move on. Alas, our luck ran out and we were caught."

The grunt shrugged. "Ok then, show us a trick," he said and folded his arms.

"Eh?" Tom panicked.

"If you guys are circus acts, show us a trick."

Charlie stepped in, "We don't have any props or kit. Sorry but ..."

"Aw come on; let's see what you can do."

"You want to see a trick?" Charlie asked.

"Yup."

"Right now?"

"Yup," the grunt said, smiling and crunching his fists together. The men nearby sniggered and looked on with interest.

Charlie looked round at his friends and winked. "Ok then. In my act I am called 'Flash Lightning'. Faster than a speeding bullet: speedier than a rocket. Watch me and be amazed," he said dramatically, lifting his arms up high.

"Go on then, amaze me," the redhead said, with an edge of steel to his voice that implied that unless the act to come was staggering, Charlie would be the one to provide the entertainment for his men.

In one movement Charlie left the spot in front of the red-headed giant and like a blur sped down the room to the door, turned right along a row of bunks and looped back round the entire hut to stop in front of the grunt and then wink at him.

There was an awestruck silence. The grunt suddenly smiled. "Now *that's* impressive," he said and held out his hand. "The name is Phil."

There were handshakes all round and some laughter. Phil sat back heavily on the bench, looking glum.

"Maybe you can give us a last performance tonight," Phil said at length.

"*Last* performance?" Tom asked. "You going somewhere then?"

"Lad, you don't leave this place. They bring prisoners here either to send them to work camps in the Welsh mountains, digging for them, or more often to execute them."

"Execute?" Edward asked.

"Well in your case 'cause you are gypsies and the like. In our case – well I guess it don't matter now to tell you, in our case because we are underground – the Resistance. When the Nazis won the war, some of our dads and granddads banded together to carry on fighting the best they could - too few to do much good, though and they are all now too old or else dead. So, when we grew up, we carried on their fight," he shrugged. "Had to try ... didn't we? Now that we are caught, as soon as they've finished interrogating us, we'll be shot."

Tom looked at his friends. Maybe this man could be of use.

"How'd you get caught?" Charlie asked.

"We blew up a munitions train."

"You did what!"

"The whole of Wales is a big arms factory and most of England too. Massive slag heaps, munitions factories and uranium refining plants. We make the guns for their wars, don't we? And the ammunition ...uranium-tipped shells and the like, nukes too and worse. Not that there are many nations left fighting them. But if we blow up a train, that is fewer guns for the wars and fewer guns for the occupation forces. So, last night we tried to destroy a train taking some tanks southwards.

285

Got careless and a patrol caught us holding the explosives and standing by the track. Bit hard to explain that was." He laughed his grim laugh again.

"The train was going south?" Tom asked.

"Yes, that's right," then he looked thoughtful, "actually, to the West Country. Odd that. Usually the trains go to Portsmouth or Liverpool for loading on the big transports bound for Africa or South America or wherever the war is."

"Any idea exactly where the train was going?"

Phil shook his head but one of the other men spoke up.

"Exeter or something like that," said a thin beanstalk of a man with a hook nose.

Exeter, thought Tom, just like that convoy on the road. "So how long have these trains been going to Exeter?" he asked.

Phil shrugged and thought for a moment. "Not more than a couple of days or we would have heard more about it."

Tom took a deep breath. "What if I told you I might be able to get you all out of here?"

The redhead gave a booming laugh.

"I'm not joking, Phil."

"Kid, you've got nerve and I like your style, but you are just a lad. What makes you think you can do the impossible?" The other men sniggered, but one or two studied Tom, their eyes sparking with hope.

Tom shrugged and Walked back to his world for an instant and then back again to stand in front of Phil. He and his mates were staring open-mouthed.

"How the hell did you do that?"

"Ah, but that would be telling," Charlie grinned, "and an artiste never gives away a secret."

"Talent is what he have," said Edward, "a few tricks: the art of misdirection and illusion. With our wits and your brawn we can do this and we can escape."

Phil stared at Tom and nodded to himself, as if he was thinking it over.

"But you have to be willing to free the women, including our friend," Tom explained, "and you will need to fight and take down a few guards."

Looking at the others around him, Phil raised a questioning eyebrow. They shrugged; a few nodded. Phil turned back to Tom.

"The way I see it pal, we are all dead anyway – us from a bullet tomorrow and you most likely from radiation sickness after a few weeks of handling uranium rounds. Might as well go down fighting, right lads?" he asked his companions. They all nodded and one or two smiled.

"So, what's the plan?" he asked.

Tom looked at Edward and indicated that he should speak. He was the soldier: this was his department.

The Lieutenant gestured at them all to gather round and spoke in a whisper.

"Well, this is what I think ..."

It was an hour later and still dark outside, the camp lights having been switched off for the night, but that darkness was lifting slightly and a lighter tone heralded dawn's arrival in maybe an hour. Twenty yards from the door to the men's hut two guards were lazing about beside a small brazier, which was burning with a low flame. They huddled close to it for warmth and spoke in inaudible mutters. Each had a rifle that was laid within reach on the ground. Although on guard duty, they were sleepy and inattentive and did not see the three shadows now hiding near the door to the hut.

Like a blur, Charlie attacked one guard with a whirlwind of fists, while Edward Walked to just behind the other and picking up the man's rifle, clubbed him hard over the head. They both slumped to the ground with barely a whimper. Charlie and Edward dragged the guards to the door where Tom was still standing. He felt around in the unconscious men's pockets and came up with a bunch of keys. One of them fitted the padlock on the hut door.

The door was quickly opened and the bodies heaved inside. Phil and one of his men stripped the guards and donned their uniforms then bustled back outside. Tom, hiding just inside the door, saw them both freeze.

A guard officer had arrived by the brazier and picked up the two abandoned rifles. He looked angry and spat out some words in German at the pair or them. He then peered closer and his mouth opened.

"*Hilfe!*" was all he managed to say before Phil's right fist took out three teeth and his left winded him. A final clout to the back of the head and he was out cold. They dragged him into the hut where Edward now put on his uniform. He adjusted the peaked cap, grinned at Tom and said, "How do I look?"

"Frankly; sinister!"

Edward laughed, "Right then; ready to be a hero, Phil?"

"Or die horribly, I assume? Yes. I'm ready."

"Then we march everyone else over to the women's hut as if we are escorting them," Edward suggested. He seemed at ease and Tom realised he was relishing being back in command and leading men in a fight.

"What if we get stopped?" Charlie asked.

Tom looked at Edward, "Can you speak German?"

"*Nur ein Bißchen.*"

"What?" said Charlie.

"Only a little is what he said," Tom replied, thinking he would pay more attention to his German lessons in future. That was, of course, if he had a school to go back to and a future. It came home to him in a sickening lurch that he had momentarily forgotten he did not exist.

Edward shrugged. "It will have to do. Right everyone, line up. I suggest Phil, you and I go at the front and your man follows at the rear. Walk quietly everyone."

They marched in silence across to the hut in which Mary was held. There were no guards outside; evidently the two guards Edward and Charlie had jumped were also supposed to keep this one under their gaze.

The door was padlocked, but once again, the guard's keys unlocked it.

They opened the door and gazed inside. Peering back at them and huddling together as far away from the door as they could get, were about twenty or so terrified women and girls.

Fear turned to confusion as Tom walked in and looked about him.

"Master!" shouted Mary from the huddle and got up.

Tom was followed in by the others and soon men found wives or daughters amongst the women. A murmur of whispered greetings and some crying broke out, along with much hugging.

Phil hushed everyone and reminded them they were still inside a prison camp; then told them of the plan to escape. Immediately, they all fell silent, listening fearfully for sounds that they had been discovered while Edward went outside to scout out the main gate.

"If we get away, what will you do? Go back to the resistance fight?" Tom asked Phil.

Phil looked thoughtful and then shrugged. "I guess so. It often seems pointless. This army has been here for sixty years now and we have been an occupied state ruled by a military dictatorship since before most of us - and most of them - were born. Yet you have to hope, don't you, that one day it can change. Just needs the right moment I reckon: the right opportunity."

Tom nodded, not sure what to say. He was thinking of his world. Not perfect at all, but it seemed paradise compared to this.

"I don't suppose you could teach me how to vanish like you and your friends do? I'm thinking it is a bit more than just an illusion. How do you really do it, lad? I'm not a superstitious bloke, but it looks like some kind of magic to me."

Fortunately, at that moment Edward returned, saving Tom the tricky problem of how to answer.

"Ok, there are only two guards at the gate. They are up in the little watch tower above it. It's still very quiet all around and there is no sign of any movement in the barrack huts, so I think we risk it. We march to the gates and try and bluff our way out."

The short walk to the gate was uninterrupted by any guards, but moving slowly and in silence, it seemed to take forever. Tom kept glancing east where he could see, off behind the women's hut, a slight glimmer of daylight. It was the glow that preceded the sun: the glow indicating that dawn was only minutes away. He nudged Edward and tilted his head in that direction. The Lieutenant grunted.

"Yes I see it," he whispered. "If this was a British camp, there would be cooks and orderlies all over the place soon, preparing breakfast. I imagine these Germans are the same. Let's pick up the pace a bit and hope they don't switch on the floodlights!"

Now they were approaching the gates. Two tired-looking sentries stood watch, rifles cradled in their arms. They were observing the approaching column with suspicion.

"Halt!" shouted Edward and the prisoners and escort stopped.

He marched smartly to the front of the column and shouted out an order up to the guard post.

"*Schnell, schnell! Lassen Sie uns vorbei!*"

The guards exchanged puzzled glances and then one shrugged to the other and they stumbled down the steps to stand in front of Edward.

"*Entschuldigen, Herr Leutnant, aber ich muss Ihren Befehle sehen!*"

"*Was gibt*...oh stuff it! I said would you mind awfully opening the gates, old man?" Edward replied giving up the attempt at German. The guard's jaw dropped open in astonishment and a moment later he took a deep breath and yelled.

"*Alarm!*"

As the guards fumbled for their guns, Edward surprised them by Walking to stand behind them. Charlie was ready to move as well and the fight was over in a moment.

"It almost seems unfair, don't it?" said Charlie chuckling.

291

"Not quite cricket, you mean?" Edward said. "Do you think we should fight fair, then?"

They looked at each other for a moment then, at the same instant, they both laughed.

"No, I didn't think you did." Edward chortled, searching the guards and locating the keys to the gate.

Behind Charlie and Edward there was a hushed silence. The prisoners had seen Edward Walk and looked at him with a mixture of fear and suspicion.

Phil came to the rescue. "It's ok, everyone, calm down; they are circus acts – magic and all that. It's all an illusion: done with mirrors: trick of the shadows and that kind of thing."

The prisoners did not look convinced, but then Phil hissed in a loud whisper, "Come on, move it: does it really matter how it was done? We don't want to hang around here or we'll all be caught again."

The woman with the two young girls scooped one up in each arm and was first through the gates. That got everyone moving. Soon, hobbling, walking or running, all the prisoners were through and separating out to flee in all directions.

Tom watched them run across the fields and away into the night. What was their fate, he wondered. Would many still be free by sunset? Would any survive the week? He blinked, to bring himself back to the present. Edward, Mary and Charlie were standing beside him and were also watching the last prisoners disappear. The last except one: Phil, the red-haired grunt, was still with them.

"You should go, Phil," Tom said, pointing towards the woods.

"I will, mate. But where are you guys going? I have a place nearby, if it helps."

"We will be just dandy," Edward said, "We have our own place to go to."

"Are you guys Resistance as well then ...?" Phil asked.

"In a way we are. We certainly are not friends with the occupying army, put it that way," Tom answered.

"You all fight well, you know. You could be useful in the struggle."

Tom was about to reply when he heard a pistol being cocked behind him. He swore under his breath; the guard's shout of alarm had been heard then.

"Halt! Do not move! Turn about slowly, with your hands in the air."

They did. Standing about twenty feet away was Lieutenant Teuber accompanied by a guard. Teuber held the pistol and the guard had a rifle pointed at them.

Teuber stared into Tom's eyes for a moment and then turned to the soldier. "Private, go and call out the guard. Tell them there has been an attempted escape."

The guard hesitated, but Teuber glared at him and he ran off.

"Why the prisoner breakout? I imagine that with your, ah 'talents', you could just leave once you had found these two." Teuber waved the pistol at Charlie and Edward.

"We could, but we thought if it was just us who'd gone, it would look bad for you," Tom said. "We didn't want your own, ah 'activities' brought under scrutiny," he grinned.

Teuber considered that for a moment and then nodded, returning the grin, "Yes it possibly would. I am grateful for that. Hopefully Redfeld will not suspect anything."

"Who is this guy? Why does he know you? Are you collaborators?" Phil said, backing off.

"Stay where you are!" Teuber ordered, the pistol now whipping round like a snake to point at the redhead. "The truth is that these four and this boy in particular are no traitors and *if* you want a better world – a free Britain - then these may help bring that about one day. You are Resistance aren't you? Don't bother denying it – I overheard just now."

"So are you going to shoot me?" Phil said.

Far away the noise of alarm whistles and raised voices came across the night. Teuber reversed the pistol and held out the grip to Phil.

"No, I am going to give you a reason to trust me. Take it. When they get here," the officer nodded towards the noise, which was getting closer, "I must be unconscious and you all gone."

Phil looked confused. "Eh?" was all he could say. Teuber put the Luger in Phil's hand.

"Knock me out with the pistol butt. Then, in a week, be in those woods – a week today at midnight. If you are Resistance, you and I need to talk," he said and then turned his back on Phil and closed his eyes. For a moment he opened one and added a few words.

"Go back to your world, Thomas Oakley. Do what you need to do there. Maybe one day, I and others like this man can sow the seeds to change *our* world and maybe one day you can return to help."

Phil still looked dumbstruck and all he managed to say was, "I er ..."

"Do it now, idiot Englishman!" Teuber ordered in full German officer voice and Phil thumped him hard with the pistol. Teuber collapsed like a boxer after a solid right hook.

Phil looked down at him and then at the pistol. "What just happened?" he asked.

The guards were visible now and getting closer.

"No time to explain. Keep that appointment with the man. Trust him. You two need to talk. I think he might be just that opportunity you spoke about needing," Tom shouted. "Now run, man! Make for the woods. We will go this way."

Edward led them off at right angles to the woods while Phil sprinted across the field, diverting attention from Tom and the others by firing the Luger back at the guards as he ran for cover. Returning his fire, they chased after him whilst the four Walkers raced for a clump of bushes and ducked down behind them into the shadows. "Ok, that's far enough," panted Tom, "let's go."

He reached out to touch Mary and Charlie, and Edward put a hand on Charlie's shoulder. When they were all linked, Tom brought the dim, out of focus map of his own reality into clear view in his mind and suddenly, the prison camp, woods and guards, along with the entire Twisted Reality, were gone. For the second time that night a cow got a nasty shock as this time not one, but four humans appeared out of nowhere.

Tom looked about him. They were in the same field in Newbury he had visited before, but maybe at the other end of it. "What's so funny?" he asked Charlie, who was smiling to himself.

"Oh, it's probably nothing, but just before we left I thought I saw Phil glancing back at us as he reached the woods. I think he saw us Walk away. It was only for an instant, but you should have seen the look on his face!" he added, with a laugh.

CHAPTER TWENTY-EIGHT - NEOPTOLEMAS AND REDFELD

On returning to the Institute, Tom ran straight up the stairs from the Professor's office to the small ward that Doctor Makepeace patrolled. The only patient was Septimus, but he was getting dressed and nodding to the Doctor, who it appeared, was lecturing him.

"That wound is healing well, but it won't if you gallivant around history the way you normally do. Try and keep out of trouble. If that is possible, of course," he finished wearily and nodding at Tom, he swept out of the room.

Septimus winked at Tom, but then his face grew serious.

"Edward, Charlie, Mary − are they ..."

"All fine, I left the boys eating a double-sized fried breakfast each with Mary nibbling on a bread roll and telling them they'll get fat."

Septimus chuckled, "She seems to be slipping with ease into the twenty-first century I reckon. She'll be nagging them to eat their five a day next! So, tell me, what did I miss?"

Tom told his friend all about the Twisted Reality and their visit, along with the existence of some resistance groups and those like Teuber, who were trying to make that other world better. Finally he told the Welshman about the Professor contacting Redfeld. "I did not see much of Redfeld there. I think he might have come back here and be trying to meet the Professor. We must find them both and try to work out what is going on."

"I agree. Edward Dyson then: he is the answer. We can use him to find the Professor. Let's go," Septimus said.

Edward was reading history books again in the library. This was becoming his favourite pastime. They found him with a wall of books piled up all around him, like a barricade. Tom saw titles about the Zulu war; both the World Wars, cricket, an *Idiot's Guide to Computers*, and a *History of Pop Music*. He looked up as they came in.

"So, who on earth were the Beatles and what is this rock and roll?" he said, looking puzzled at a picture of Paul McCartney and John Lennon and the album cover from *Sergeant Pepper's Lonely Hearts Club Band*.

"I'll take you to one of their concerts if you like. I think I can get tickets for the Eddy Sullivan show in 1964. Only, not right now. Right now, we need your help," said Septimus sitting down on the corner of the table. Tom threw himself into a chair opposite the Lieutenant and explained that they needed to find the Professor.

Edward nodded. Then, his eyes took on a faraway look as if he was daydreaming. The expression on his face stayed like that for a few minutes and then he frowned and his eyes focused back onto Tom again. He shook his head.

"I'm afraid to say that I cannot sense him, Thomas," he said.

"But I thought you could sense all Walkers wherever they are and whenever in time they are?" Septimus observed.

Edward pursed his lips. "Well, I have to have seen them, I think, or know them. Then, it's like hunting fox. The dogs can follow the scent and it's Tally Ho and away we go. In my case, if the scent is live, I can follow a Walker even if they jump a long way in space or time."

"So, why can't you sense the Professor?" Tom asked.

"I don't know," Edward confessed.

There followed a few moments' frustrated silence, before Septimus spoke. "I think it must mean he is still in the Office." Edward shook his head and opened his mouth to speak, but Septimus held up his hand to stop him.

"I don't mean the Professor's office, Edward. Let's say the Professor was outside this world – say in the Twisted Reality, or the Custodian's Office. Could you sense him then? Perhaps you can only sense Walkers if they are in this world – this reality?" Septimus speculated for a moment.

Edward looked puzzled, but nodded. "In which case ...," he began then suddenly stopped and beamed at them. "Ah, gentlemen, you will be glad to know that the Professor has returned. I can sense him again. He is close, he is..." Edward's hand shot out to point back down the house knocking the *Idiot's Guide to Computers* flying, "... in his office!"

Tom leapt to his feet, followed by Septimus who jumped up too fast and then groaned in pain and held his side. Both of them started off towards the door. Tom sprinted past Septimus and pulled the door open.

"Would one of you like to tell me just what exactly is going on?" asked Edward.

"Tell you later ... must see him!" yelled Tom over his shoulder and he turned around and barged through the door, almost knocking Mary over who was just entering. She screamed and jumped to one side. Tom shouted a brief, "Sorry!" and carried on past, but this time did collide with Charlie, who was standing in the corridor just outside the door, munching on a sandwich. Unfortunately, the sailor did not have time to take evasive action, so they both went down in a tangle of legs and arms.

"Oi! What the heck are you doing?" Charlie demanded as he picked himself up and brushed cheese and pickle off his shirt.

"Sorry! Must catch the Professor," Tom blurted out. "You surely can't still be hungry, Charlie!" he said, stumbling to his feet and running off down the corridor, past the startled Mr Phelps, who had no time to raise his usual objections before Tom burst into the Professor's office. What he then saw sent a chill through him, despite the heat of the July day.

The Professor was indeed in his room standing in front of his desk. But he was not alone. For, standing there, his gaze drawn by the noise of the door opening, was Captain Redfeld. That was bad enough, but what really shocked Tom was the sight of the Professor shaking Captain Redfeld's hand!

Redfeld smiled nastily at Tom and nodded his head in mock salute at the boy.

"Professor, shall we?" the Captain said and with their hands still clasped together, the pair vanished, just as Septimus and the others caught up with Tom. Mimicking Tom's earlier response, they stopped dead in their tracks and stared into the room.

Mary spoke first. "Master Thomas, unless my eyes deceived me, that was Professor Neoptolemas and that evil man Captain Redfeld. Are they in league together?"

"It is as we feared, Tom," Septimus said. "They are, as Mary suggests, in league: the Professor, the Captain and the Custodian as well."

Tom said nothing, but took a few steps into the room and then bent down to pick something off the floor that was just where the Professor had been standing a few moments before. He stood back up and opened his hand. In it was an acorn. An acorn? What was it the Professor had said?

"... yes, you are brave. You will need all that in the time to come. Before this business with Redfeld is finished. Before we try and rescue your family, you will also need belief that what I - what we must do - will come right in the end. It's all to do with acorns really."

All to do with acorns ...

Was it a message? Was the Professor trying to tell him something? Or had it just fallen out of his pocket by accident?

"Is it true, Tom?" asked Charlie, disturbing Tom's train of thought. "Do you think the Professor is helping Redfeld with his plans as the Captain hoped he would?"

Tom was staring down at the acorn. Suddenly he made a choice. He looked around at each of his friends' faces in turn then said emphatically, "NO! It's a dangerous game he is playing, whatever it is, but I think he has not betrayed us."

Charlie exchanged a glance with the others. "He seemed pretty chummy just now, if you ask me, so how can you be sure?"

Tom shrugged and shook his head - it was a gut feeling no more. "I can't be: that's the problem, but for the time being I am prepared to give him the benefit of the doubt. If he has not betrayed us, then he is up to something and could be in dreadful danger when Redfeld finds out that it is *he* who has been betrayed. Or, say I am wrong and the Prof is in league with Redfeld; then we must try and stop them, don't you think?"

"So, what do we do now?" Septimus said. "Go after them?"

Tom nodded at the Welshman, but he was still not sure about involving the other three. "It might be very dangerous. Redfeld on his own is a killer and I have no idea what the Professor or the Custodian are up to - or capable of."

301

Charlie laughed a hollow laugh at that. "Funny how I believed the Nazis were winning and we were just struggling to survive. Then you rescued me and I learned that in the end they were defeated and we had won. Now this man Redfeld comes from a world where *they* won, with the Nazis ruling over everywhere and life there pretty grim," Charlie said. "It just seems such a weird turnaround."

Tom nodded.

"And it seems that Redfeld wants this world to be like his?"

Tom nodded again.

"Well then, I was fighting men like him sixty years ago and there's nothing you can tell me about danger! I am not about to stop now," the young sailor said with determination.

They all looked at Edward Dyson, who grunted. "Firstly, over a hundred years ago I took an oath to fight for Queen and country against her enemies. As far as I can see, it might be a different Queen, but she and the country still have enemies. Whether it is Redfeld, the Professor or anyone else, the job must be done. Secondly, that Redfeld is a nasty piece of work. The bloke captured Charlie and me and tortured us ..."

"Tortured you? You didn't mention that!" Tom gasped.

"We didn't want to worry you. Like I said, he's a nasty piece of work and he needs a lesson and I intend to give it to him. I am with you."

"As am I, Master Thomas ... Tom," Mary said. "And don't look like that; just because I am a girl doesn't mean I can't help. Who else is going to open portals and break down invisible walls for you?"

Septimus stepped forward then to look into Tom's eyes. "I let you down in the past. I won't again. I am in as well!" He smiled and hummed a few bars of a hymn then burst into song,

"... *the strife will not last long. This day the noise of battle the next the victors' song!*" He sang in a rich, melodious voice, like someone from a male voice choir in the Welsh valleys. As his voice died away, he winked at Tom.

Tom swallowed back the lump in his throat as he looked around at his friends; he could think of nothing to say, except, "Thank you."

"Time to gird our loins, whatever that means, roll our sleeves up and get stuck in," said Septimus. Then he hesitated and added, "As I said earlier, what do we do now?"

CHAPTER TWENTY-NINE - TINTAGEL

Now Tom turned to Edward and asked him, "Can you still sense the Professor and Redfeld?"

"Yes, I can – although it's dim. He has some sort of barrier blocking me. But he is still in the present day, although some little distance away: Wales perhaps? No ... south of that; Exeter. No, wait a moment ... ah, I have it now. Gosh, I wonder why there. It's Tintagel. He is at Tintagel. Well, Tintagel Island to be precise, towards the southern end."

There was a long moment's silence as the others stared at him in admiration.

"Now's *that's* impressive!" Septimus said at last.

"Tintagel? Where is that place I have no knowledge of it?" Mary asked.

Tom answered her. "I went there on holiday once. It's in Cornwall: a ruined castle on a headland, with more ruins on an island beyond, reached by a bridge. It has some story about it, but I can't quite recall ..." he hesitated.

"Camelot!" Septimus interrupted. "Or at least one of the locations that claim to be Camelot," he added.

"What, King Arthur and all that?" Charlie asked.

"Indeed – all that," Septimus confirmed.

"I think it's where he was supposed to have been born, before Merlin took him away and raised him. All nonsense, of course," Edward said.

Tom thought idly about Arthur and the Knights of the Round Table. He recalled many stirring tales of ancient battles between knights and monsters; quests to be completed; evil to be fought and good made victorious. But they were just stories. Fables – as his English teacher had put it – mainly invented in the Middle Ages by a Welsh monk, Geoffrey of Monmouth, and later embellished by the Victorians, but having little or no basis in fact or, at least, so she had said.

"So then, I wonder why there," mused Tom.

"It's possible that it is where he first came through from his reality," Septimus answered. "Indeed, it kind of makes sense. Various locations around the world have almost mystic significance as if touched by some other worldly power or influence. In ancient times the Welsh, who first told stories about Arthur, believed in these points and places where spirits could pass from one reality to another. Perhaps there is more to those stories than they first realised. Maybe there really are locations where the barriers between the worlds are thinner than elsewhere."

"Like Stonehenge and Glastonbury?" Tom said.

"Exactly like that."

Tom had a thought. "Hang on a minute, what did Redfeld say he wanted me for, I mean back when he ambushed us in Trafalgar Square?"

Septimus screwed up his face to cast his mind back, and Tom was struck just for a moment by how much he looked liked his father when Dad was doing a Suduko puzzle. A twist of sadness caught in his throat.

"It was ... aha! I have it now," Septimus said, "it was that you would give him time."

Tom shook his head. "No something else. It was that, yes, but also that he needed someone who would give him the key to open certain doors and give him access to the present, the past and the future. Then there is that entire obsession he has with these 'portals' between his reality and ours. Mind you, he can open them himself because he has done so already. We all saw him do it."

"So why did he want you to help him if he can bring his men across?" Edward asked.

Tom was about to shake his head, but suddenly some words from a dream in the Office came back to him: Redfeld discussing with the Custodian what to do about the troublesome boy, Thomas Oakley.

"...We must make alternative plans. I will get the job done but you must grant me and my guards presence in Die Andere Weld *to achieve it. We must be able to interact."*

He repeated Redfeld's words out loud.

"Presence – he means being able to touch things. Septimus, I think that before, when he was coming across to our world, he was just projecting himself and he was not even here. Charlie and Edward: you said he mentioned projection. That is why he was wearing a coat on a hot summer's day once. He could talk to us, create his illusions and alternative histories, but not touch us. *He wasn't really here!"* Tom concluded, his voice rising in excitement.

"Hang on a minute, Thomas, you must be wrong there. He certainly could touch us in Trafalgar Square. He shot Septimus for a start. Then his guards beat me and Charlie up and dragged us away," Edward pointed out.

"Yes, but only *after* he had seen the Custodian. He made a deal of some sort with the Custodian. He must have promised to kill my parents if he and his men were allowed to travel to our world and have physical form and not just be projections or illusions. Teuber was wrong. Redfeld could *not* create portals but just project himself. The Custodian granted him the ability that allowed him and his men to come here and interact with us because the Custodian wanted to obliterate *me*! Teuber did say that it was only in the last day or so that he had heard Redfeld had started taking his men across to our world. Redfeld just took it all further than his promise to the Custodian and tried to capture us all. Indeed, in my case, it was all about trying to force me to help him. It suits his purposes that in fact I somehow continue to exist. He might almost have engineered it, killing my parents at a time when he knew I was in an alternative reality." Tom was talking fast sure he was on the right track. The others stared at him, hanging on his words.

Tom recalled the convoy on the road past Newbury, heading for Exeter. And all those trains that Phil, the resistance fighter, had said were heading that way too. Suddenly, over the last two days a large part of the German army in the alternative Britain was heading, seemingly against all logic, to Exeter. But Exeter was in Devon, just a relatively short distance from ....

"Yes, but that isn't good enough for Redfeld," Tom burst out, speaking his thoughts aloud. "He needs to be able to open portals at will and not just bring a few men, but many. To open a door – that is what he said he needed me for! He meant to open a permanent door to his world. Just imagine if they could do that. Not just a dozen soldiers but a thousand; tens of thousands; along with tanks and guns and maybe even planes."

"Planes?" Edward and Mary chorused.

"Flying machines," Charlie explained, "er ... like huge metal birds that can drop bombs, Mary."

Everyone looked grim as all the implications sunk in.

"Hang on a moment, though, Tom. He can bring a dozen men across already, why not more?" Charlie asked.

"Like I said, only after the Custodian had allowed him to. And he was only permitted a few men. The Custodian would not give him more. I know this: I was the Custodian in my dream and I have seen his mind. He does not want the realities thrown out of balance. He would certainly not permit an army to cross. Unless Redfeld can open this portal his army will be mere illusions and projections, not flesh and blood."

"Master – forgive me, I mean, Tom - I think that Redfeld's portals don't last," Mary said quietly, a look of concentration on her face as she tried to absorb and express concepts well beyond her time.

"Eh?" said Charlie.

"I was in contact with Redfeld's magic door ... er, this portal," said Mary. "It did not last long. From what I felt, I believe it would be limited to lasting for only a certain length of time and also, I think it would collapse after a certain number of men had passed through it."

"Just like what happened to us in the projection room?" Tom asked and Mary nodded.

"So Redfeld's portals don't last long. The Custodian was not too generous with his powers," Septimus mused.

"Maybe he suspected Redfeld planned to double cross him so was limiting the damage he could do?" Edward suggested.

"That's possible," Tom agreed.

"But *you* can Walk many of us across, Tom," Mary said. "He has seen you walk a group of us at ease. If you can drag us with you then who knows what limits you have, how many you could bring?"

Tom shrugged. He did not know, but he suspected that the answer was a great many.

"So, if he wanted to solve his transportation problem, then taking someone like you with your talents to a thin point between the realities, like Tintagel, could be the way to do it," Septimus concluded.

"Fine then, so that was his plan: to use Tom to bring his army here. Is that what we all think?" Edward asked.

Everyone nodded. Tom was sure of it: Redfeld needed help to complete his plans. He shivered as it occurred to him that he could have been the means to his world being conquered. Had he been tempted by Redfeld after all and done what was asked of him, he truly could have changed the world. It did not bear thinking about.

Edward stared at Tom, his face taut with anxiety, "If Redfeld had succeeded, he could have brought across a whole army. Why, in that case he could swarm across England in days. Conquer this country and then, the world!" Edward said, alarm rising in his voice.

"From what Tom is suggesting it could be worse even than that. He could look to invade the past. Imagine ten thousand enemy troops appearing in London in 1940!" Charlie suggested.

"Or in 1879," put in Edward, then looking at Mary he added, "or 1666."

"But Tom, he doesn't have you, does he? So does that not mean all is well and there is no danger?" Mary suggested.

Tom thought for a moment then shook his head. "He wanted me, but now he has the Professor. The Professor founded the Hourglass Institute. I think he probably knows as much about Walking as the rest of us put together - and the rest. He knows a lot about The Event and the Twisted Reality. I think Redfeld doesn't need me anymore. If the Professor has betrayed us, then I think the Professor and he have just gone off to open Redfeld's doors!"

There was a stunned silence.

Tom became aware of the acorn clenched tightly in his palm. Or maybe, he thought, the Professor was up to something else – but what? He looked around at the others. "I'm going to Tintagel. I must stop him. I don't know how I'm going to do it, but I have to try.

"Shouldn't that be 'we'?" Charlie retorted.

Edward and Mary both nodded.

Septimus said, "Definitely 'we', boyo!"

"Look, it is even more dangerous than I imagined; I am prepared to take the risk, but I am not sure that you all should. This is your last chance to change your mind everyone."

They all remained stubbornly silent.

"Ok then; you're all daft," Tom grinned. "So what are we waiting for? Let's go."

They gathered around him and reached out to touch him on the shoulder. In his mind Tom saw the map and he moved it until he could see England. Then he browsed across it: first West and then South West, across Hampshire and Dorset, Somerset, Devon and finally into Cornwall. Then he zoomed in until he could see individual towns and villages, focusing even closer in, to that corner of England and its rugged, sea-tossed coastline until he could see the modern town of Tintagel. For a moment he was distracted as the image and the taste of Cornish pasties and 'knickerbocker glories' came to his mind and hung in his mouth. Tom felt his stomach growling. He moved quickly on, west out of the town and then down the path to the coast.

There was the castle on its rocky island, almost separated from the mainland. Up the cliff face he went until, at last, he was focused on a spot within the ruins inside a slight enclosure, which he could remember from his family's visit. Holding the place in his mind, he Walked to it.

It was dark and very quiet, aside from the endless swell of the ocean. The hustle and bustle of the hundreds of tourists who daily visited the ancient and evocative site had gone and the doors and gates leading to the crossing were secured. The moon was up tonight and casting its silvery glow on the short, dry grass, as well as on the aged and cracked stones that had seen eight hundred summers and whose glory lay long in the past. Tom and his companions stepped back and looked about them. For a while no one spoke and all they could hear was the crashing of the sea against the cliffs and the occasional boom as a surge of water blasted into caves at the water's edge. Then, Charlie whispered.

"Well, what do we do now?"

Tom shrugged and hissed back. "They're not just here, so let's try up on top."

The path wound its way upwards in stages past more ruins and terraces filled with what was left of stone houses or larger structures. Still there was no sign of Redfeld or Neoptolemas, and still the only sounds were the distant noise of the waves far below them and the gentle whistle of the warm wind coming in over the island from the sea. Eventually, the path levelled off on the highest plateau.

There at last they found Redfeld.

CHAPTER THIRTY - BATTLE

From where they were, the pathway slanted across the top of the plateau upon which the ruins of Tintagel castle stood, located high above the sea. The path turned and went on towards a small peninsula of the island. It jutted out and was roughly triangular in shape, barely two hundred feet long and a hundred feet wide at the base, but eventually narrowing to a point. On both sides was a sheer drop to the sharp, jagged rocks far below, wet with spray and shining in the moonlight. At the base of the little peninsula, Redfeld and the Professor stood talking. All around were the Captain's guards – a dozen of them, armed with sub-machine guns, rifles or pistols – and all looking outwards, on watch for any interruption.

Tom and the others hunkered down in a hollow in the ground, from where they were able to observe Redfeld's party at a distance. Eventually Septimus spoke in a whisper, "Tricky them guards. Outnumbered over two to one we are, boyo," he observed.

"Come on, we can take them." Charlie blustered.

Edward looked doubtful, "Leaving aside for the moment that we have no weapons while they are all armed to the teeth, they hold an easily defensible position with only one way in. The ground narrows and we have to cross it in the open. We would get cut down before we got fifty yards.

Charlie was now forced to agree. Even with his speed he would struggle to avoid a hail of bullets as he crossed the gap.

"Hang on, I remember something," said Tom. "Near here there is a canyon – well more a narrow thin cave with the roof gone. It runs towards that direction," he pointed now to a spot about twenty yards from Redfeld. "Come on! Stay in the shadows."

He led the way, crouching and half crawling across the ground and keeping to dips in the terrain. They came to a point where the ground dropped sharply into a rocky culvert or canyon only six feet wide, eight feet deep and twenty feet long. He slid down one end and the others followed him. They could now stand up and were hidden completely. He led the group down the culvert to where some steps ran back up the southern end. He crept lightly up a few steps and found that they were now much closer to Redfeld. In fact, they had come right round the side; the nearest guard was about twenty feet away with his back to them.

Redfeld and Neoptolemas were about fifty feet away in the middle of the rocky peninsular. They were standing side by side and had their arms stretched out in front of them with their hands held upwards. Both faces were turned away, but Tom could see part of Neoptolemas', and he was concentrating intently, his eyes tightly closed and his lips moving slowly as if in prayer.

Tom pointed out Redfeld and the Professor to Septimus, who had moved up next to him. "It's not looking good, boyo," the Welshman breathed in his ear.

Suddenly, they all heard a high-pitched whining sound, which got louder and louder, and in the air in front of the Professor a disturbance occurred. It reminded Tom of the waving in the air when heat seems to ripple off the road on a hot summer's day. It got more and more pronounced and striking.

Tom and Septimus slid back down the steps and told the others what they had seen. "So, this confirms it then," Edward said grimly, "Neoptolemas is a traitor and the two of them are making this doorway. No sign of the Custodian, mind you, but that changes nothing: we have to stop them."

"Those guards though, they are still a problem," Septimus pointed out again.

Tom nodded then turned to Mary and said, "I've been thinking about that. Do you think that you can you make a barrier in time around Redfeld and the Professor and all of us?"

Mary thought for a moment and her face screwed up with concentration. "You mean one of my walls? Yes, I can make walls to surround them, so no one can walk through them."

"Good! Make one when I say. I want it so most of the guards are outside the wall. Can you do that?"

"Yes, Master, I can do that," Mary replied. Tom sighed. She had forgotten again.

"Mary, *please* call me Tom! But thanks." Tom now turned to the others.

"Charlie and Edward, can you take care of any guards that are left; Septimus, you and I will rush Redfeld and the Professor. I won't be much use in a fight but if we can break their concentration, we ought to be able to stop this door business."

"Ok, it's a plan." Septimus said. "Let's get on with it. It won't be long before that door is open."

They all crept up the stairs. Mary peered over the top step for a few minutes. Then she popped her head back down to report to them.

315

"I think I can bend a wall around to cut off those eight guards on the far side. I dare not make it too close to us or we might get confined by it. That will mean that these two guards and maybe those two will remain." She pointed out two groups.

There was a grunt from Charlie. "I will take the furthest, I'm faster than you," the sailor said to Edward, "you deal with these two."

Edward nodded, his eyes already studying his targets.

Just then, the shimmering grew more intense and the sound coming from it grew so loud that Tom could feel the rock vibrating under him. Then, in an instant, the sound was gone and a moment later the shimmering vanished as well and a dark hole in the air appeared. Through it, fuzzy and indistinct like an out of focus picture, Tom could see shapes. The picture sharpened a little and Tom realised he was seeing men: soldiers lined up ready to come through. Not just a few either: many men in fact, all armed and looking fierce: an army ready for invasion.

Redfeld laughed and then said, almost to himself, "At last!"

Septimus gasped and then a moment later whispered. "Time's up. Got to go!"

Tom nodded to Mary and she closed her eyes and concentrated. But, at that moment, the Professor suddenly moved his arms violently and gave a huge shout. The air in front of him vibrated and there was a loud boom like a crack of thunder.

"What are you doing, old man?" Redfeld said in an angry voice, his head snapping round.

The Professor said nothing but kept on gesturing with his arms.

"Stop it!" Redfeld said and fumbled for his pistol.

"I mean it, old man, what are you doing?"

"I am closing the gateway to your world, Captain – forever. Did you really believe I would help you? I set up my Institute to protect my world from men such as you," Professor Neoptolemas said quietly, his voice calm but determined. As he spoke, the black hole in the air grew smaller.

Tom looked round at the others. So his instincts had been right; the Professor was not a traitor after all. In his breast pocket Tom could still feel the acorn and he smiled to himself.

"We had an agreement, old man. I would leave the boy alone and you would open the gateway," Redfeld's voice was almost a growl now.

"I lied, Captain. My mother told me it was a sin to lie, but I am sure she would not mind me lying to a power-crazed lunatic!"

"Why you ... wait. You are keeping me talking so you can close the void. It won't work!"

Then he pulled the trigger. There was a huge bang perhaps magnified by the gateway.

The Professor groaned and slumped to the ground, apparently dead.

Tom shouted out at that and Redfeld spun round.

"Now, Mary!" shouted Septimus and Mary nodding, stretched out her arm and closed her eyes again.

"Stop now," she whispered. A moment later a shimmering silvery wall appeared curving across the headland. Eights guards were trapped the other side of it.

"Now!" bellowed Edward, and he and Charlie charged the two pairs of guards within the wall. The guards turned and fumbled at their sub-machine guns, but the two Walkers were

317

upon them like tidal waves. Charlie simply barrelled into his pair, both arms outstretched and the three went down in a heap. Edward kicked one guard hard on the knee and his leg collapsed under him, the guard screamed in agony and dropped his gun. Edward caught it and struggled to bring it to bear. The other guard fired his sub-machine gun wildly. One bullet grazed Edward's cheek and he cursed before he finally fired his own gun, hitting the guard in the arm and forcing him to drop his own weapon. Edward pulled the trigger again, but the gun jammed and he swung it round like a club, catching the guard on the chin. The first guard reached over and caught his ankle and now Edward went down.

Tom and Septimus charged forward towards Redfeld, who was, for the moment, taken aback by what had suddenly erupted around him. Tom crouched down over Neoptolemas and saw blood oozing from his chest. Pulling the handkerchief out of the Professor's pocket, he pushed it inside the old man's shirt over the wound to try and stem the bleeding.

Septimus was moving towards Redfeld. "Well then, Captain, have you got the courage to fight fair and put down the gun? I mean, it's hardly sporting, is it?" All the while, he was closing in and suddenly made a lunge for the pistol.

Redfeld simply laughed, shook his head and fired. Septimus spun round and landed face down, not moving. Was he dead? Redfeld looked down at the body for a few moments and then turned towards Tom.

Tom backed away down the rocky headland towards the cliff edge. He looked around for a weapon, but there was none. He reached out for the Time Flow to Walk away, but Redfeld shook his head.

"You can't get away that way, boy. I just put up a barrier of my own. No escape! Two of your side are dead and my guards outnumber the rest, even with your lady's little barrier, which won't last long," he said, nodding towards the struggle between Edward and Charlie, and then to the tiny Mary, who was slumped down, looking worn out and exhausted.

"Just one bullet will bring your wall down – shame to kill the young lady, but I am afraid you brought this on her, on all of them in fact. I did warn them, you will recall. You thought to oppose us, you stupid little boy, we who have conquered an entire world. You think a few of you undisciplined louts can defeat us? If so you really are more of a fool than I thought." His face contorted and he spat out the words, "Tell your friends to surrender. NOW!"

Redfeld then moved towards Tom, the pistol at the ready, his finger curling round the trigger.

CHAPTER THIRTY-ONE - WHATEVER THE COST

T om could see that Septimus was out cold – perhaps dead, maybe just wounded, but bleeding heavily from the bullet wound. Edward and Charlie were struggling with four of the Captain's guards. Mary was panting, slumped down on a rock, but was somehow managing to keep her grip on the barrier that was preventing any more guards from joining the fight. Within the barrier itself, time flowed slowly like treacle: each second took hours. So anyone trying to move across it would take an eternity to do so.

So it came down at last to Tom and Redfeld. And the Captain, standing in front of him on the rocky path, was the one with the gun.

Redfeld moved closer. Tom backed away but then realised the path was running out. He glanced behind him; saw a sheer drop to the rocks below. There was nowhere further to retreat. Redfeld gave a shout of evil laughter.

"Give in, boy. The only way this can end is with me winning – one way or another. If you somehow defeat me, the secret of what really happened to your parents will die with me. Think about that for a moment, boy. Your father, your mother," he paused as Tom looked even more uncertain, "...your little sister. Where are they now – wiped from existence? If I die, they will never live again. If you die, their last hope will have gone. Don't be the foolish hero. Give in and do as I say and I promise you will see them again within moments."

Tom thought about this. He truly wanted to see his family – so much so that it actually ached inside him. Yet Redfeld was not to be trusted. He would betray Tom in an instant given the chance. But he was also right. If Tom somehow beat this man, how would he ever get his parents back? The dilemma was anguish and it brought tears welling to his eyes.

"What ... what do you need me to do?" he said quietly.

A look of triumph blazed from Redfeld's eyes. "At last you have made the sensible choice, boy. Firstly, you will repair for me the portal between this reality and my reality. I need it wide and tall; big enough for fifty men to walk abreast. Then later, I need you to take me, and many others as well, to dates in your world's past. We are going to alter time, you and I."

"But why do you need me? Why not go yourself? You went back and killed my parents didn't you?"

"I did, but not alone; I was helped by the Custodian. Your power worries him. You can visit any time and place in this reality. You can take companions with you. You have massive potential to change time and that scares him. He and I did a deal. He gave me power to travel *once* to your parents' past and effect the changes that should have, in his mind, removed you from existence. I helped him and he granted me physical presence in this reality."

"So, I was right, you didn't have the ability to touch things. That's what you lacked. You needed me to make your plans happen. Then, when I refused to, you made this deal with the Custodian and wiped out my parents, but I lived because I was out of time at the instant you also moved back in time, and so I was protected from the murder of my parents."

Redfeld looked surprised for a moment but then he smiled a nasty smile.

Suddenly Tom realised there was more. It was as he had suspected. "No," he said. "That's not the total truth is it? You *planned* it so I would live, didn't you. So you timed your journey to occur at the same moment, but that means you must have been watching me."

"Well it is true that I did see you asleep on that park bench on your sports day," Redfield shrugged. "I was touched when you gave money to that veteran. Very nice, I felt," he smirked.

"But why go to that trouble? Your deal with the Custodian was for me to die, I assume?" Tom glanced at the fight going on behind Redfeld. Charlie was bleeding now. Tom knew he had to come up with something fast or he and his friends were lost. He looked back at Redfeld, who was nodding.

"Simple really; I needed you alive, boy. After you rejected my demands that you use your powers as I suggested, I realised you would never willingly betray your world. I had to find leverage."

"But what leverage? My parents are dead, so why should I help you?"

Redfeld shook his head. "You are forgetting my talents – to create alternative realities. I can create an alternative past in which your parents do not die," he said.

"But that's not real. It's just a mirage!" Tom shouted.

"Not anymore. Don't you see, Thomas," Redfeld wheedled, "with your power I can alter events – any events. Between us we will forge this world of yours into an image of my world: a glorious Reich over two realities!"

So, he had been right, thought Tom, that was Redfeld's ultimate goal. "You are mad, Redfeld," he spat out the words.

Redfeld's face went red at that. "Careful boy – don't forget that we can also use that power to save your parents and sister."

So there it was at last: the choice; to serve this evil man and help him change this world into an image of his home reality for Redfeld's Führer to rule over unchallenged. A world of slaves and oppression and jack boots kicking in doors in the cold light of dawn. Of millions killed; of genocide. But, in such a world, Tom's parents would live and so would his sister. Would they want to? Would he?

Or say he refused to help. This world would be safe, but his parents would stay in oblivion and Tom himself would probably perish. How to choose? What would his parents have said? As tears began to spill from his eyes, he recalled his father's words all those years ago, the time when he and Andy broke the windows in 'orrible old 'enry's house and they had to go and apologise: *"Sometimes doing the right thing is not pleasant and nice. Indeed sometimes it is horrible and painful. But deep down you know in your heart that it's the right thing and you do it anyway, whatever the cost."*

Whatever the cost ... whatever the cost ...

"So boy, what is your decision? Do we have an understanding?" Redfeld said lowering his gun slightly, "do you wish me to alter the past and restore your parents? Will you serve me?"

Alter the past. Tom suddenly had a thought. He remembered that moment when his teacher seemed to recognise him for an instant. He remembered Andy, after they collided near his house, also seeming to know him before shrugging it off. He thought of the difficulty of finding many solid facts about the fire at his house at the records office, apart from one newspaper article. He thought of the fact that his house was still a burnt out wreck years after the fire. Then, there was that strange sensation when he walked back to his house in 1999. Now he remembered when he had felt it before: when Redfeld took them to that alternative Islandwana and to the U-boat. Why did Redfeld need him? Could it be that ... suddenly, Tom knew that his parents were not really dead; that Redfeld's power lay not in bending time, but in bending minds, so effectively that people believed what they saw. Himself included. But what if he was wrong ...? Tom suppressed a shudder.

"Tell me, Redfeld, why you need me. Could it be that you still cannot change time? Could it be that despite your little deal with the Custodian you still have little power apart from lies and illusions? Could it be, in fact, that there was no fire and my parents are still alive?"

Redfeld's gun was back pointing at Tom again, his face split in a horrifying grin, his teeth glinting in the moonlight. "Careful, Thomas, you are close to losing your parents forever."

"No ... I don't think so. Because, all this is an illusion," Tom said with a wide sweep of his arms. "It's impressive, I'll give you that, Redfeld, but it's still an illusion."

"I'm warning you boy!" Redfeld shouted, his face going red.

"The whole thing is a lie. A massive illusion, but that size of illusion – altering time to that degree, must be hard and details slipped by you. I spotted those mistakes, but I only realised it just now. In other words you did a shoddy job ... Captain!" Tom shouted.

Redfeld now looked fit to shoot Tom, but he controlled his temper. He paced round Tom waving the gun back and forth. Finally he stopped pacing.

"It may have been a shoddy job, Thomas Oakley, but you do not know how I did it and you have no idea how to undo it," he sneered. Only I can do that, young sir. This is your final chance. OBEY ME ... or die!"

Tom felt his heart pumping; he tried to swallow, his throat suddenly dry and tight. Yet, from far away, he heard those words again. "... *deep down you know in your heart that it's the right thing and you do it anyway, whatever the cost,*" and taking a deep breath he pulled himself up to his full height and looked Redfeld in the eye.

"You know, for the longest time I wanted rid of these powers. I thought they had ruined my life and perhaps they still have. But in the end, I realise - at least right now – that I want them. I want them to protect my world from you and folk like you. So NO, Captain Redfeld, I will not. I will not obey you. I will not change my world into yours to save myself and my family ... whatever the cost."

Redfeld stared at him in silence for a long time, his eyes wide, his mouth fixed in a snarl. Eventually he spat out, "Foolish boy! You are not worthy of my world, or yours!" and he raised the gun and pulled the trigger.

There was a loud eruption of sound, the crack of a bullet firing.

Tom heard Mary scream. He shut his eyes; waited for the searing pain.

CHAPTER THIRTY-TWO - THE CUSTODIAN

T he shot did not come: instead there was silence. Tom opened his eyes and saw Redfeld frozen in the act of pulling the trigger, his face poised in a visage of rage. Just in front of the gun, hanging motionless in the air, was a bullet emerging from the barrel that was pointing at Tom's head.

He glanced around. Nothing was moving; nothing at all. Even the sound of the sea had stopped. Indeed, the very air seemed frozen. Stretching out his hand, Tom felt it almost cold and snow-like on his fingers. Up the path beyond Redfeld, Mary, the guards, Edward, Charlie and Septimus were also motionless. Tom walked round Redfeld and reaching out, tapped him on his head. Hard and solid like a wax doll.

"What just happened?" he said to himself, "I don't understand ..."

"Ah, but *I* do. It is my job to understand. To observe – to analyse."

The voice came from behind Tom and in this silent unmoving world, the shock made him jump. Turning slowly, he saw an old man in a grey suit. For a moment he thought it was Neoptolemas. But it was not. Now he knew who it was: it was the man in the suit; the man in the Office: the Custodian.

"Well now, we finally meet. We seem to have been dancing around each other these last few weeks and even inside each other's minds. Do you not find it strange to meet face to face? I must confess, I do," the Custodian said.

Tom nodded, not sure how to react. This man had arranged for him to be kidnapped by doing a deal with Septimus and later with Redfeld in planning his death and that of his parents.

"Er ... how did you do that?" Tom said, indicating the frozen Redfeld and everyone else.

The Custodian looked about intently as if studying every detail. "It is not easy. For me to stop time, to cause an unbalance between the realities I have been charged to preserve, is most disagreeable and irregular. Indeed, I can feel right now the pressure building. Temporal energy: the power of the moments − of time itself. It is gradually increasing here compared to *his* reality," the Custodian pointed at Redfeld. "With each second passing there that does not pass here, tension increases. But," he looked back at Tom and shrugged, "the situation warranted my direct intervention."

"I still don't understand. You wanted me dead, did you not? Redfeld was about to kill me. Why not let him do that?"

The Custodian nodded. "True, I did want you dead - or at least powerless, as *he* suggested," he said, this time pointing at the wounded and unconscious Septimus. "This is because you have vast powers to Walk, as you people call it, and change history, and I do not want history to alter except when I need it to. My job is to preserve balance between the realities. Redfeld convinced me that in order to preserve that balance you had to die. He misled me; told me that he had come to your reality because he believed that one day you would destroy *his* reality. He said it had been predicted by his superior officer who had some powers of his own. Given your unique talents, I could see the logic in that..."

The Custodian looked at Tom's face and must have seen surprise or disbelief showing because he shrugged almost with embarrassment. "Well, that is what he told me and I believed him. He rather tricked me with his clever words. I believed him and so I agreed to give him the power he lacked in your reality – to travel back in time and to interact with your world rather than just be a projection. Oh, he could create those brief illusions you saw of hypothetical alternatives to your world's history, but it was only after I let him that he was able to change your world, your family's past, on a larger scale. He promised to destroy you and then go home. He did neither. Instead he used his new powers to create a very convincing illusion you could touch and feel. You had to be convinced your parents were dead so he could force you to do his bidding."

"He wanted me to help him in his plots ..." Tom started to say.

"Yes, to change this world into an image of his own. I heard you and him discussing it just now. I had suspected something was not right when I could still see you alive after all the signs were that your parents had died before you were born. Your Professor Neoptolemas confirmed it when he came to my office. I agreed to help him find Redfeld. And then I watched and waited until you came."

"Intending to do what?" Tom asked anxiously.

"Ah, now then, that depended on you and him. Possibly to kill you after all, or him - or both of you ...," the Custodian said, pointing his finger rather like a gun at Tom, who tensed as if awaiting a blow, although the Custodian had no weapon that he could see.

The old man paused and studied him for a while ... a long while. Then he lowered his hand and looked from Tom to the frozen figure of Redfeld. "You would have allowed him to kill you? You would *really* have allowed him to do that rather than to save yourself and your family, and not used your powers to change your world as he wanted? You would have given up the opportunity of immense power and wealth for yourself, at whatever the cost?" the Custodian asked.

"*Whatever the cost*," Tom's father's voice echoed in his mind. Tom nodded, "Yes, all those things."

"Then perhaps Neoptolemas was right, you are not so dangerous. No, I correct myself. You are dangerous. But perhaps, you are responsible. Again, I am not sure if even that is the right word. But perhaps for now I will let you live. But I will be watching you, Thomas Oakley. That is my job to watch and to guard the future."

Tom let out a long breath that became a whistle.

The Custodian watched him without reaction. "Do not think I do this out of compassion, nor," he looked pointedly at Redfeld, "for evil purposes. No, I feel neither the warmth of compassion, nor the passions of evil. What drives me is order and balance. For now, you offer the better chance of achieving that."

Tom nodded, only half understanding.

"For *now*...," the Custodian repeated with the ghost of a smile.

"So what happens now?" Tom asked with an anxious glance at his friends, at least one of whom might be dead.

"What happens now is we get Captain Redfeld and his men back to his reality."

"Hang on a mo. What about my family?" Tom objected.

The Custodian held his hand up, "Do not interrupt me when I am explaining, boy."

"I'm sorry. I was just trying to say that Redfeld was the man who created this illusion in which my family are dead, and he is the only one who can remove it."

"Redfeld is maintaining this illusion by much effort on his part. When he sleeps or is tired or distracted it is harder for him to maintain it all. Imperfections in his illusion emerge – some I believe you spotted yourself?" the Custodian asked, his grey eyebrows rising in a question.

"Oh – like Andy sort of recognising me – that kind of thing?"

"That is correct. That kind of thing, as you put it. Once Redfeld returns to his world, the illusion will shatter and reality – your reality, will be restored. Your family will still be alive. It will be as it was before."

Tom smiled, a sense of hope rising. In that case he could defeat Redfeld and not lose everything. "So then, how do I send him back?" he asked eagerly.

At that question the Custodian smiled at last, even if ever so slightly, as if his only pleasures were concerned with the complex physics of alternative realities.

"It is all a question of temporal energy and tension. As I said, the tension is increasing between the realities like water building up behind a dam. Shatter that barrier and all the excess temporal energy will surge across to his reality, taking him and his men with it. They belong there. Their presence has created some tension and like an elastic band snapping back from full stretch, that tension will pull them back to their own world in their parallel universe."

Tom nodded, thinking how easily all this made sense to him now, when a few weeks ago it would have seemed unbelievable and quite beyond him; the stuff of science fiction.

"That all sounds simple enough; how do you do it?" he asked after a moment. The old man gasped. Looking up at him, Tom was surprised to see he looked aghast.

"I?" Pursing his lips, the Custodian looked down his nose at Tom, "*I* do not do it! Custodians do not break barriers between realities," he said primly. "But you might," he added, pointing at Tom.

"Eh? I have no idea how," Tom said, suddenly anxious again. Did the Custodian expect something of him he could not do?

"No? What do you use to travel through time, boy? What mechanism or device?"

"Do you mean the clock?" Tom said, puzzled.

"Yes, the clock. You imagine the clock and see its hands turning in your mind, yes?"

"That's right," Tom said after a moment's thought.

"Very well, then you must shatter the clock!"

"Do *what?*"

"Shatter − destroy, eradicate it. The clock is part of the barrier between realities. Mentally destroy it and the barriers will burst and this will all be over."

"But, if I do that will I lose the power to Walk through time?" Tom asked. He was still not sure that he wanted this power. That said; did he want to lose it? Did he have a choice?

"There are other clocks, Thomas Oakley," replied the Custodian, who had now walked over to Redfeld and was inspecting the discharging Luger pistol.

"You didn't answer my question, sir. How do I know this is not some type of trick to solve all your problems in one go? Get rid of Redfeld and remove my powers," Tom demanded.

"Do you want Redfeld to stay here and destroy your world?" the Custodian asked tersely, stamping his foot.

"No, I don't," Tom answered straight away.

"Whatever the cost?"

Tom sighed. Why those words? But he nodded. "Whatever the cost," he replied.

"Then shatter it. And you will just have to trust me after that," the Custodian said and walked towards the edge of the cliff.

Just as he reached the edge he turned back. "And remember, I will be watching you," and with that, he stepped over the edge and vanished. Not down into the sea, which was frozen as if it was part of a museum model made from resin, but just into the air.

And in that instant, so time started moving again.

Bang! The gun blast echoed.

"Wo ... ist ... er?" Tom heard Redfeld say. Tom was now standing off to one side towards the cliff edge where the Custodian had gone. Redfeld spun round, saw Tom and turned his gun towards him. Tom panicked. He had not had time to do anything and was not prepared.

"I am impressed, Master Oakley," Redfeld sneered, "somehow you managed to Walk. But it will not avail you now."

Then, laughing, he levelled the pistol again and pointed it at Tom's chest.

CHAPTER THIRTY-THREE - CLOCK

Redfeld's finger squeezed the trigger. Tom shut his eyes again, knowing that the Custodian would not help him – not this time. It was all over.

"Click!" the Luger's chamber was empty.

Tom opened one eye and squinted at Redfeld, to find that the officer was ejecting the spent magazine and reaching into a pocket, pulling out another. In a few brief moments, he would have reloaded. It was now or never.

Both eyes now open, Tom reached out for the Flow of Time and as before he felt a barrier: Redfeld's barrier, cutting him off from the timeline. At first glance it was as strong as diamond and unyielding as steel. But now Tom knew it was all an illusion. The clock – his grandparent's clock – and Tom's link to the Flow of Time were out there. He just had to push past Redfeld's barrier, the barrier that was keeping Tom from his parents, from his sister and from his friends.

Suddenly, Tom felt angry at being duped by this evil man's trickery. He stared at Redfeld with contempt, his anger rising alongside the hope that all would be fine soon. The anger and the hope were so intense that it gave Tom belief – and belief was all he needed. There in his mind he could see the clock and feel it ticking and counting the moments that lay beyond Redfeld's illusion: moments of Tom's life that Redfeld had tried to deny him. And now, the anger and the hope swelled into an outburst of emotion.

"Redfeld – you are a complete psycho, you know that, don't you?" Tom said, as he heard the click of the magazine sliding into the stock of the pistol. "And what is more, you really are a total loser!"

"We shall see who the loser is," Redfeld said and with a clunk-click he cocked the weapon and levelled the pistol again.

And Tom shattered the clock.

He pushed through the barriers that Redfeld had created, powerful barriers – but still an illusion – and in his mind he made the clock burst asunder, showering metal cogs, wooden splinters and springs, everywhere. A moment later he envisaged a hole and through the hole, another Tintagel.

Then the hole became real and visible and he and Redfeld could see through it to the sun burning high in the sky above another sea. Here, in Tom's reality, the ruins of a castle were preserved, but there, in that other reality, stood a guard tower. Flying above the guardhouse was a flag bearing that strange thunderbolt symbol so like the Nazi's Swastika of the war years in Tom's world. They were looking at the Twisted Reality. Another world: the same but different, for in Redfeld's world, history had taken another path. Tom had been there and knew its horrors and now he felt a chill just looking at it. Dark, terrifying and so very real: Tom's world as it might have been; as Redfeld would make it.

Tom flinched as he felt a tension building around him as though something was about to explode. He glanced at Redfeld; the man's expression was one of stark horror. Then, with a great whoosh, the tension released like a coiled snake lunging forward in its fury, or an elastic band snapping back into place. Like water gushing through a hole in a dam or air rushing out of a balloon, the forces of time rushed to equalise once more and Redfeld felt it.

"What have you done, boy!" he shouted, panic rising in his voice. He swung his gun round to fire at Tom, but the pull from the other reality yanked it out of his hand and it spiralled away through the tear in the sky and was gone. It belonged to the other reality and that is where it went.

The massive drag of temporal energies shattered Mary's barrier and knocked her, Charlie and Edward to the ground. Redfeld's guards screamed in terror as they were lifted high into the air and went spinning like circus performers, head over heels, through the rift.

Tom watched them go and then felt Redfeld's hand close, vice-like, on his wrist. Redfeld was being dragged toward the rift, but he did not intend to go alone. He was pulling Tom with him towards the Twisted Reality! Tom struggled, but Redfeld was holding firm and the officer had a nasty smile on his face.

"You will come with me, boy. We know how to treat enemies like you!"

"Let me go, Redfeld. I won't come with you!" Tom yelled, but now he was the one to panic: he could not get free. Redfeld was defeated, but Tom was going with him. Tom had saved his world – but it was going to cost him.

Whatever the cost ... again he heard his father's voice and sighing, he realised that the cost of saving his family and his world was going to be his life.

Then, suddenly, a swift movement came out of the corner of Tom's vision. It was Septimus, staggering along and swinging his fist. With a crunch that sent one of Redfeld's teeth flying through the rift, he hit Redfeld's jaw and the officer let go of Tom. For an instant Redfeld hung in the air – suspended in the

337

void between realities– and his eyes met Tom's. Tom saw in them not hate, arrogance or evil but, finally and for the first time, true fear.

"Noooooooooooooo!" screamed Captain Redfeld, and then he was spinning, dragged by an unstoppable force as he spiralled through the rift and disappeared.

The rift was still open and now Tom and Septimus could feel the pull dragging them toward it. They clawed at the ground. Then with panic Tom felt himself being lifted up.

"CLOSE!" boomed a commanding voice. Tom turned his head and saw Professor Neoptolemas leaning on a boulder looking pale and weak, but still mustering enough strength to yell a second time, "CLOSE!"

Tom felt the pull from the rift reduce and he was able to grab hold of a rock and hold on to it. With the other hand he reached out and held onto Septimus. A moment later the force lessened further and he could stand with barely any effort.

"CLOSE!" came the command a final time and with a boom the rift closed.

"It is over," Neoptolemas said, crumpling to sit on the boulder, exhausted. Tom staggered over and collapsed nearby, as did Septimus, blood still tricking between his fingers from a wound in his chest that he was holding. "Thanks, boyo," he gasped.

Weakly, Tom grinned, "No, thank *you*! I thought I was a goner."

The others came and joined them. For a long time there was a relieved silence as they each took stock of their wounds. Charlie and Edward were both cut and severely bruised; Mary, deathly pale from the effort of holding the barrier, was otherwise unhurt. Only Septimus' and the Professor' wounds looked serious.

"What just happened?" asked Charlie.

Tom explained what had happened in the last fight – about the Custodian's visit, shattering the clock and sending Redfeld back to his reality.

"But then, I felt that Septimus and I would be dragged in as well. I didn't know how to close it. The Professor did that," Tom said, looking over at Neoptolemas and asking, "How did you do it, sir? You just yelled, 'close' and it closed."

The old man smiled and Tom thought he actually winked.

"There *are* some reasons I am a professor, as I've told you before, young man. But that is a tale for another day perhaps, Thomas. At this moment, I am really quite tired. Let us just say for now that I have experience of such things and protecting *this* reality is my job," the Professor said weakly.

Tom nodded whilst at the same time thinking that it was a bit like what the Custodian had said. So, were they brothers? Tom guessed so: brothers who seemed to feel that saving the world was their job. What then of Colonel Thielmann in the Twisted Reality? Did he feel the same way and could it really be a coincidence that three men so motivated and talented, who looked identical, existed in the three realities? Tom wanted to ask the Professor, but guessed this was also a question for yet another day.

For a long while no one spoke then Septimus said, "I knew we would win!"

That was followed by silence for a moment as they all resisted the urge to ask the question that eventually Lieutenant Dyson asked.

"How did you know, Septimus?"

Forgetting his wound, Septimus swept his arm dramatically around and winced, grinning through his pain. "This place was Camelot: Arthur's castle. The Welsh were bound to win."

"But the rest of us are English, Septimus; you're the only Welshman," Tom pointed out.

"That doesn't matter. One Welshman is a match for half a dozen Redfelds. Because, you do realise don't you, boyo, that the big loon has absolutely no idea how to play rugby!" They all stared at him, then, out of relief to be alive, they all laughed.

"Well, thanks to everyone for helping," said Tom as the laughter died away. "If my family are ok – and I think they are – I have you all to thank for it." He dragged himself to his feet meaning to add something more, but then he looked at everyone. They all needed Doctor Makepeace: Mary, Edward and Charlie looked all done in; Neoptolemas was almost asleep and Septimus was still bleeding. So much for the speech, Tom thought. Save it for later.

"Right then, back to the Institute I reckon," Tom finally said. Septimus nodded and the others all grunted their agreement. Automatically, Tom reached out for the Flow of Time. Suddenly he realised that it was not there and he could not feel it anywhere! In his mind, following the Custodian's instructions, he had shattered the image of the clock that his grandfather owned; the clock that controlled his link to the Flow of Time and the means he used to travel in time.

With horror he realised that now, no matter how much he tried, he was just not able to visualise it anymore.

CHAPTER THIRTY-FOUR - *CUSTOS CRASTINOS*

The Clock was gone! Perhaps the Custodian had indeed tricked him and got him to lose his powers whilst defeating Redfeld – killing two birds with one stone, as it were. He could ask the Professor or Septimus: but the Professor was weak, and Septimus was injured and neither looked in a state to answer. Later perhaps – but not now.

But how to get them all back to the Institute? He looked around at them; each one was staring at him in consternation as he stood there, his mind working overtime. The sea crashed on the rocks below; way over on the horizon came the glimmer of approaching dawn and with it a sharp drop in temperature. Tom was just about to shake his head and admit his loss of power when he realised he did not need the Clock if he still had the Map. He did not need to move them in time, just in space - and only across England, from Cornwall to London. He searched for the globe and laughed with relief to find it was still there. So, he could still Walk, even if just in space not time.

"Right, hold on to each other everyone – here we go." He reached out and held Septimus' shoulder; the Welshman did the same to the Professor. Edward, Charlie and Mary linked arms and Mary also touched the Professor's other shoulder. When everyone was in the chain, Tom Walked them back to the Professor's office, where they all landed in an untidy heap in front of the desk – apart from Septimus who ended up sitting on it and knocking off a paperweight in the process. Both paperweight and papers went flying.

Hearing the commotion, Mr Phelps was in the room in an instant, still in his pyjamas and dressing gown. His usual irritation vanished when he saw the state they were in, and in a bustle of activity he whisked everyone off to the rooms upstairs and was soon on the phone to Doctor Makepeace.

Septimus and Neoptolemas were the most hurt and in need of medical attention, but almost everyone had cuts, bruises and scratches, so it was a good two hours before Tom was able to go upstairs and into the room occupied by Septimus, to see how he was.

Septimus smiled at him and added a weary wink. "You did well, Tom. That was impressive with the clock and all, boyo."

Returning his smile, Tom shrugged. "You know, I just remembered something," he said.

"What was that?"

"Back in my house, before we were attacked and went off to Ancient Persia, you were about to say something to me about my parents."

"I was?" Septimus said vaguely then, his eyes lighting up, added, "That's right, so I was."

Tom waited a moment as Septimus nodded but said nothing.

"So ... would you like to share it with me, or am I keeping you up?"

"Sorry, boyo, was miles away. Ok, this is the deal: I remembered your parents."

"What!"

"I could remember hearing your dad shouting at us on New Year's Day and seeing you and him in the car in that car park."

Tom was confused now.

"So?"

"So, Tom, if they really had died in that house fire, I don't think I should have remembered that. You were the one away from the present day when Redfeld supposedly went back and murdered your parents. You were insulated from the effect. But no one else was. So, *if* your parents had died, I don't think I should have remembered them. So I think the penny dropped that day and I worked out they were still alive."

Tom's mouth fell open. "And you didn't think it might have been a good idea to tell me that, you daft Welshman?"

"Sorry. If you remember, it all got a bit busy after that!"

Tom stared at him for a moment and then relaxed. "It did that, it certainly did that!" he said softly.

They sat together for a few minutes, before Septimus' eyes became heavy and he drifted off to sleep. Tom left him to rest and quietly left the room.

The Professor was next door and was wide awake sitting up in bed reading. The book's title was *A History of Tintagel*. There was a chair beside the bed. Tom perched on the edge of it and tried to frame a few questions, but the Professor spoke first.

"I guess I owe you some explanation. I kept you in the dark a lot and I apologise for that. You are young and I was trying to protect you. In the end it did not quite work out that way and it was you who protected me."

"I might not have done had it not been for this," Tom grinned and pulled the acorn from his breast pocket. They both looked at it and Neoptolemas laughed.

"Ah yes, the acorn; I hoped you would find it and realise its significance. You keep it, Tom, as a memento – and a reminder that from little acorns great oaks do grow."

"So, Professor, you were trying to do a deal with Redfeld to get him to leave me alone?"

343

"Well yes, but far more than that. I am very fond of you and can appreciate your talents *but* there was a lot more going on here than just the fate of one schoolboy."

"And so you went along with Redfeld, pretending to help him to open his portal, but then planned to close it?"

"Yes."

"What was the point of that? Wouldn't he have just opened another one?"

"Ah well. That's the thing. Redfeld used his projection device to come across to our world at Tintagel. He couldn't just open these portals at will, you see. He only managed to do it at random weak points between the realities. He had to move his equipment around to these weak points when they were suitable to use, but they were unstable. Trafalgar's portal was closed down and could not be used again, but he had found a particularly viable one at Tintagel. What he wanted was to stabilise the portal there and make a permanent connection for his invasion."

Tom nodded – he had been right about that then.

"But," the Professor went on, "he could only pass back and forth to his equipment; he could not move through space and time as we Walkers can. I knew that if I could collapse the Tintagel portal he would be cut off and stranded here in our world. It would have taken him many years to build another projection device, if indeed he ever could. Yes, he might have caused some trouble here in our world, but far less than if he had been allowed to reach his own reality and organise his invasion force." The old man sighed, "That was the reasoning behind my plan."

"You must have known he would kill you?"

The Professor shrugged. "It was a possibility, but it seemed a risk worth taking."

"So then, when I shattered the clock ..."

"Well in a way you did muck up my plan, yes, but I think the catastrophic surge of energy created by that calamity will have destroyed any electrical equipment close by..."

"Like his projector?"

"Indeed. And on top of that, from what you say Redfeld and his men were likely to have been badly injured, if not killed, by the speed at which they were sucked through the portal. You did well, Tom. You stopped his invasion. His equipment is almost certainly wiped out and with any luck we will not see Captain Redfeld again."

Tom nodded thoughtfully, "He *could* still be alive, though, Professor."

The old man nodded. "He could; but one day at a time, Thomas, eh? Let's savour the victory we have for the moment. So, do you have any more questions?"

"Well, there is the little matter of how you look so much like the Custodian and Colonel Theilmann. You are even similar in personality − at least to the Custodian if not the Colonel."

The Professor said nothing for a long time. Finally, with a shrug, he spoke. "You know what they say, Thomas: you can't choose your relatives, just your friends!"

"So you *are* brothers?"

"A little more than that, in fact."

"Well triplets then. That is what I meant."

"Thomas, I was an only child."

"Eh?" Tom frowned, "Well then what ... I mean, how ...?"

"I was an only child who happened to be present at The Event, the cataclysm that split The Twisted Reality from our

345

reality. I do not recall most of it, so it's no good asking me about it right now. But just at the moment the realities split I must have been positioned at exactly the right co-ordinates; in the right spot you might say – or the wrong one, depending on your point of view - for I was also split: divided into three in fact. Theilmann and the Custodian look like me and are similar to me because we are – or rather, were once – the same person."

Tom's mouth dropped open and he could feel his heart pounding in his ears, "My God! I never guessed," he said, rather inadequately. "That's awesome!"

The Professor shrugged. "Well, it is ancient history now. We all have a job to do," he added, yawning. Tom could see he was tired and got up to leave. The Professor flicked through a page or two of his book and ended up gazing at a photo of the castle.

"Anything they got wrong?" Tom asked gesturing towards the book.

"They certainly make no mention of a portal to another world, but some of the legends make a little more sense, I would say."

Tom laughed at that and turned away.

"Before you go, Thomas, one more thing: have you decided what you will you do? Now that Redfeld is gone, your family is safe and the Custodian seems content to leave you alone, you could be plain old Tom again. Schoolboy Thomas Oakley as you once said you wanted to be. We can take this talent away and make it not bother you ever again."

Tom turned back and looked down at the Professor for a long moment, not sure how to answer.

"So, is that what you want, Thomas," the old man prompted, "or do you want to keep your powers and use them? You might be young and it might just have been circumstance that made Charlie, Mary and Edward – all a few years older than you – follow your lead, but follow you they did and I believe they would again. You make a good team and Redfeld is not the only threat to our world. There will always be unscrupulous men and women with the ability to Walk, who dream of amassing wealth and power for themselves. What do you say, Tom? Will you join us in the fight for good against evil?"

"I did almost die more than once, Professor. I did almost lose my family. What you suggest does put me at risk of that again in the future."

The Professor nodded, "That is certainly true and I have no right to ask it of you. Forgive me."

Tom sighed and shook his head wondering if now was the right time to tell the old man that he had lost the ability to move through time. Or had he? He clung to a small hope that the Custodian had spoken the truth and all would be as it had been before. "To be honest, Professor," he said, "I don't yet know myself what I want to do. I need to have a think. I need to get home and see if everyone is all right and if I have my life back."

The old man looked a little disappointed, but nodded without further comment. Tom leaned forward and held out his hand. With a brief smile, Neoptolemas clasped it and they shook hands. "See you Professor; I will talk to you later."

'Now we shall see if the Custodian lied,' thought Tom. He turned away from the bed and Walked the ninety miles home to his house. He actually planned his arrival to be at the corner of his street as he dared not appear outside his own house; not until he was sure it was there.

347

He peeked slowly round the corner, almost afraid to look. The door was there. So too was the rest of the building. Tom felt a lump rise in his throat as he walked along the street. Just walked: using his own two feet. Never before had the simple terrace house seemed so wonderful. Tentatively he approached his home. It suddenly occurred to him that his parents might have missed him. How long had he been gone? What day was it now, Friday? When had he last seen them - was it Thursday morning? Had they been worried and called the police. If so how would he explain where he had been? In the end though, he realised none of that mattered if they were still alive. He would explain it away somehow.

At last he stood in front of his house, in his road, lined with his neighbours' houses. It was with a vast sense of relief that he heard the noise from the telly in the living room. Out of the corner of his eye he caught a movement and turned to see Kyle Rogers and his gang coming towards him.

"Oi, Oakley, you nutter, come here and give me yer money!"

Tom drew a deep breath all of a sudden aware that he was no longer afraid of this pathetic bully. He had been in a battle against Zulus, survived a raging inferno and a flooding submarine, escaped from Alexander the Great and from another reality, and finally he had defeated an evil enemy. This stupid boy was nothing compared to that. Tom gave a bored yawn, "Push off, Rogers, and take your gang with you!"

There was silence.

"What did you say, you little rat?"

"You heard me. Get out of here!"

Kyle stepped forward and swung a club-like fist, but Tom was ready for him. He Walked just a tiny fraction to his left, but enough to move like a blur. The other boy lost his balance, swung round and then fell over, landing heavily on an elbow. Tom heard a crack and Kyle gave a scream and grasped his arm. He took one terrified look at Tom and then scampered to his feet and backed away, his face alternating between agony and a new look of surprised respect. Kyle's gang melted away like butter on a hot day and Tom was left alone feeling suddenly liberated. He punched the air in triumph.

Then he chuckled softly to himself and, taking out his own front door key, opened the door and went in. His dad looked up as he passed the living room.

"Hello, Tom – I didn't know you were out," he said. Then a slightly puzzled expression came on his face as if he was trying to remember something. "I could have sworn you were in your room. Not seen much of you this weekend. What you been up to? Saving the world, eh?" he asked, with a grin.

For a moment Tom stopped in his tracks and his mouth dropped open, but he could see his dad was teasing him. "Something like that, Dad, something like that!"

His dad studied him for a moment. "You ok, boy? You look ... I don't know, different: older somehow," he asked, with an anxious voice. You haven't had another of those funny turns, have you?"

"I'm ok, Dad – just a bit tired. Think I will go and rest. Where's Mum by the way? "

"Oh, Tom, that is really weird. She is out at Gran and Granddad's. You won't believe this, but about two hours ago their grandfather clock – that one in the hall you like a lot – it just cracked. The whole face of the clock. Must be some type of metal fatigue or something. Can you believe it?"

"Oh, I can believe it, Dad!" Tom said, then seeing surprise on his dad's face, added, "I mean, blimey Dad, how weird is that!"

"Right, off to your room and study – your mum said don't forget you have that French test again tomorrow. After flunking the last one your teacher will *not* be pleased, nor will your mum if you fail again. Better go and learn it!"

"French test?"

"Tom, you came home on Monday night with a two out of ten in the last test and a note from your French teacher threatening serious penalties if you did not perform better."

"Er, ok Dad ... it's Friday today though. I have the weekend to learn it, I ... " but his Dad was staring at him.

"It's Sunday afternoon, Tom, what are you talking about! The French test is tomorrow. Get upstairs and get learning. Friday indeed!!" His dad said incredulously.

French test! Tom thought. What French test? This was the problem with Walking back and forth in time you tended to lose track of what you were doing before you left. From Tom's point of view he had left his house to help rescue Charlie on a Thursday. But soon after that, Redfeld changed the past so it seemed as if Tom's parents and his house had perished. Tom's own body clock told him that he had only spent about thirty-six hours since that moment, but somehow in all his travels back and forth it was now Sunday evening and the correct timeline and history had been reinstated.

To his dad, his sister and everyone else it seemed as if the days were just following each other as they always did. Presumably then, when the Custodian had said, *'Your reality will be restored...'* he had meant that he would tidy up the timelines and history so that no one would notice what had happened; so did that mean he had reinstated their memories as well? Tom thought for a minute; there was a way he could check. He ran upstairs to his room, switched on his PC and got into his online messenger program. He nudged Andy, whose messenger name with the tag line, *"Great and powerful god of doom"* was showing up as online. Would Andy remember him too?

'*Andy – it's Tom, hi.*'

'*Wotcha Tom wot's new?*'

'*Not a lot. Er, do we have a French test tomorrow?*'

'*Er, yes of course we do. Don't say you forgot! You'll be dead 2morro if you only get 2 out of 10. You better go learn it m8,*' Andy typed his reply.

'*Yer right, ok I will. One thing tho. Do you remember when we swore to be loyal desparados no matter wot happened?*'

'*Course I do. Not like I'd ever forget that idiot! Pals to the end, that's us.*'

'*Ok – that's all.*' Tom rattled off on his keyboard.

'*Wots wrong?*' Andy typed.

'*Nothing m8. It's ok now. Everything is ok.*'

'*Well push off and learn that boring French ;–)*'

'*Oui mon ami!*' Tom jokingly replied.

'*Eh?* Andy asked.

'*LOL. Maybe you better learn some as well pal. CU*'

'*CU,* typed Andy.

Tom closed down the box sat back and sighed. His family were alive. His house was still standing. Andy knew him and it sounded like he had a school to go to in the morning. He had his life back and Redfeld was gone, back to his world and its horrors. Tom's own world was safe, at least for now.

351

So this left only one thing he had to do: one thing to decide. Did he want his powers? With them he had saved his world and also rescued his new friends Charlie, Edward and Mary from various horrible deaths to water, steel or fire in the past. And yet, he had almost lost his own life and his family forever.

He knew he had to choose and soon. But without the Clock, did he still have the power to Walk through time? *'There are other clocks, Thomas Oakley,'* the Custodian had said.

Tom looked across his room at his brass alarm clock – once his father's before him – it was on his bedside table ticking away the seconds. He watched it for a while, remembering how he had seen it shattered and looking like screwed up sweet paper in the flame-blackened ruins of his home. The tiny second hand sped round its circuit. The minute hand plodded ponderously in pursuit, whilst the hour hand appeared to ignore them both, moving so slowly that you could hardly notice.

Then, as he had once done with the antique grandfather clock when Septimus first taught him how to Walk, he closed his eyes and visualised it in his mind, ticking gently. He watched himself reach out with his fingers, touch the hands and turn them. As he did this, he became aware of the Flow of Time; it was exactly the same as it had been with the old grandfather clock. He was in contact again. The Custodian had been right after all ... there *were* other clocks.

The Clock and the Map were there, within reach. If he wanted them he could use them to protect his world ... or he could use them for himself ... or he could go to the Professor and ask to have the powers taken away. He could be normal again. Safe and anonymous: just an 'ordinary' schoolboy. He let his mind wander over that possibility. These powers had cost him a lot: ridicule, fear and pain. Had they been worth it? *'Whatever the cost,'* his dad had said. *'To a very few these powers are granted,'* Redfeld had said. What had the Custodian said? *'But I will be watching you. Thomas Oakley. That is my job to watch and to guard the future.'*

Tom knew he was not 'ordinary' and his life would never be normal in the future. He had made his choice. He stared at the clock for a moment, then at last, aware that he had made his decision, he spoke out loud.

"No, it's not your job, Custodian, to watch and guard the future. It's mine. Mine and the Professor's: *Custos Crastinos*; that's what I am. I am Tomorrow's Guardian!"

For a moment longer he gazed at the clock then he opened the French text book and began studying for the test the following day.

Read on for a sneak peek at the sequel to Tomorrow's Guardian:

Yesterday's Treasures

CHAPTER ONE - THE FORT

The bronze gun barrel loomed over the narrow strip of water, keeping a silent watch upon the straits it had once, long ago, been positioned here to guard. Thomas Oakley peered down its length imagining for a moment that he was a gunner aiming at a distant target. Then he turned and gazed along the fort's battlements, which stood like a silent sentinel upon the coast. 'Fort Belan' - that was the name of the place. His dad had fancied coming here when he saw it in a holiday brochure.

"It's an old fort built back in Napoleonic times to keep an eye out for a French invasion," he had explained to the rest of the family. *"Been turned into a holiday camp now with cottages and apartments. Fancy going there this summer?"*

The suggestion had not been enthusiastically received. Tom's sister, Emma, wanted to stay at Centre Parks and Tom and his mother both preferred the idea of an 'all inclusive' vacation in Corfu, but his dad, having lost his job that spring and only just got a new one, had said that money was tight; so a cottage in North Wales was where they went.

In the end, it was not as bad as it had first sounded. The weather was a bit mixed, but when it was dry there were beaches not far away, a number of towns with amusement arcades, interesting shops and castles to visit. Nearby, the mountains of Snowdonia loomed over the skyline; it was great scenery and there was plenty to do.

Thinking back, Tom had to admit that he had certainly needed a break. The year so far had involved some unpleasant, dangerous adventures; he had been quite ready for - and had enjoyed - the two weeks they had spent at the fort: two weeks of peace and quiet with no complications. He sighed with satisfaction, feeling relaxed and happy.

Tomorrow they were going home and in a couple of days the new school term would start, so, after lunch, his mum, dad and sister had gone to nearby Caernarfon to buy some souvenirs and presents. Tom had turned down the offer, fancying instead a few hours alone in the cottage and a final look around the fort.

Bringing his camera with him he strolled along the battlements stopping every so often to take a photo of a cannon; the fort; Anglesey across the bay in one direction and the distant mountains in the other. On the top of the fort a Union Flag fluttered in the breeze and he snapped that. Then he checked the image in the small screen on the back, staring at it in amazement as it came into view.

"Uh?" he muttered as he studied the picture. It clearly showed the flagpole and on the top of it a flag. However, this was not the familiar red and blue crosses on a white background that he expected to see, but an altogether different flag: one with three broad stripes of red, white and blue. It was the tricolour of France!

Shading his eyes, he peered up at the flagpole and the standard that flapped about in the gentle breeze coming in off the Irish Sea. It was, without a doubt, the Union Flag. Baffled, Tom turned his head to glance around the fort, but he could not see a second flagpole anywhere nearby.

"That's stupid!" he muttered. Then he slapped his forehead and smiled. This image was obviously an earlier photo left on the memory card from another day. He checked the image date and time then frowned: the date it recorded was today and the time a couple of minutes ago. 'No complications', he had thought to himself only moments before – he should have known better! His pulse beginning to race, he murmured, "So what is this all about?"

Shaking his head, he looked again at the flagpole and gaped as he now saw the French flag hanging there. He was certain it had been the British one. Behind him he heard footsteps coming closer. He looked around; there was no one in sight. His skin prickled. As he stood there and stared at the empty battlements he felt something brush past his right arm and heard the footsteps pass on by.

"Oh flip!" he muttered to himself. The guide book to the place had mentioned a ghost that was supposed to haunt the battlements but, like all visitors, Tom had dismissed the story. Was whatever it was that had just passed him a ghost? A chill passed down his spine and he felt goose pimples creep along his arms.

"Come on Tom!" he chided himself. "There are no such things as ghosts." Not convinced that he actually believed this, he decided to go back to the cottage. He walked a few paces towards the stone steps that ran down inside the fort to ground level.

"*Garçon, arrêtes-toi!*" bellowed a voice behind him.

Tom's heart seemed to leap in his chest and he spun around. He gulped as he saw that he was gazing right down the end of a gun barrel. Not a modern gun, like a shotgun or rifle, but an old fashioned one: a musket. That was frightening enough, but even more terrifying was the man holding the musket. His face was scarred on the right cheek as well as above the left eye, and he leered at Tom with a dangerous expression that threatened violence. He was in uniform: a blue jacket and white trousers. On his head he wore an odd hat - tall, round and black with a brass plate bearing the number 31 and a green pompom on the front.

Tom stared at him for a moment, then slowly he relaxed. This was no ghost. He knew who this was - or rather what kind of man it was. Almost he laughed.

"You're a re-enactor aren't you? Here to re-fight a battle or something? I've seen that kind of thing before. You had me going there for a minute," he smiled.

"*Comment t'appelles-tu?*" The man demanded.

"Oh, I get it, you like to play the role. Ok then, *Je m'appelle* Tom Oakley. *J'ai douze ans...*"

"*Es-tu un espion?*"

"What ... I mean, *Je ne vous comprend pas,*" Tom said, forehead wrinkling under the effort of remembering his French lessons. It was no good though: he had no idea what '*espion*' meant.

"He said, are you a spy?" another very heavily accented voice replied, but this time in English and coming from behind Tom. He turned around and saw another man in similar uniform, although smarter looking and adorned with some gold braid - an officer perhaps. This man was brandishing a long curving sabre in one hand and a pistol in the other.

"Well, are you?" he asked pointing the sword at Tom.

"Say, you guys really take the part seriously, I'll give you that. So then, when is the battle? I would love to see it. Only we go home tonight and I think ..." he trailed off as he noticed the officer shaking his head.

"I am afraid you will not be going anywhere *mon ami* unless it is the cells. Now, speak: what is all this about a battle? Is the English army finally coming to face us? Or are the mountain rebels planning an attack on this fort? *Mon Dieu* but I dearly hope so ... we will teach them a lesson for that raid on Conwy last month. I will have half a dozen strung up by nightfall if they come here."

"I ... what?" Tom asked, now utterly confused.

"Come with me!" The man ordered and turned to walk towards the steps.

"Wait ... this is fun and all but joking aside, I'll just go back to my cottage. If we are still about, we will come and see the battle if you tell me what time."

The officer glared back at Tom.

"*Vite, maintenant!*" he shouted and Tom was suddenly and violently thrust along the battlements by the other man - the one with the musket.

"Wait ... wait ..." Tom stuttered, then a terrible thought dawned upon him. That French flag above this Welsh fort, these men dressed as French soldiers from the Napoleonic wars of two hundred years ago and what the officer said offhand about rebels in the mountains and a raid on Conwy: all these facts fell in to place and he suddenly realised where he was.

"Oh God, this is the Twisted Reality isn't it? How did that happen?"

The only answer was a puzzled glance from the officer and another painful shove from behind, but Tom knew he was right. The Twisted Reality: a world parallel to his own, but where history had taken different paths. Tom had been there before earlier in the year and visited Britain in the twentieth century: but it had been a Britain where the Nazis had won World War Two. Now, he seemed to be in that other world again, but at an earlier date, when the French under Napoleon had invaded Britain. In Tom's world, Napoleon had been defeated by Wellington at the Battle of Waterloo, but clearly, in the Twisted Reality the outcome had been different and the French had occupied at least part of the country. Tom frowned, so how did he get here? A third shove from the musket butt told him that it did not matter, at least not for the moment: what mattered was to get away.

He needed to find a place to get his bearings and then he could transport himself back to his world. He stumbled along a few feet until he was just behind the officer and then took off and barging past him, landed on the top step and careered down them, two at a time.

There was a loud bang from behind. Glancing over his shoulder Tom saw a cloud of smoke around the soldier's musket. Having discharged his weapon and missed, the Frenchman was quickly fastening a bayonet to the end of the musket as he scuttled after his quarry.

Tom carried on down the steps and landed with a crunch on the packed earth of the fort interior. Thirty yards away were the fort gates - both open and apparently unguarded. Tom made for them, but after ten strides stopped in his tracks. The gates were open because a horseman was coming through them. The man wore a green jacket and a shiny brass helmet and he sat on a huge, dark brown horse. His eyes narrowed as he took in the sight of the officer and soldier chasing after Tom. He drew his sword with a metallic swish and dug in his heels. The horse leapt forward at the gallop - heading straight for Tom.

Behind, the soldiers had almost caught up with him. Desperately, Tom reached out in his mind for the Map - the connection he had with the world about him and the tool by which he could transport himself anywhere. But in his panic he could not focus on it. The thundering beast charged down upon him and the cavalryman's sword arm went back ready to strike down and cut him to pieces.

Tom closed his eyes and waited for the blow!

To find out what happens next read
Yesterday's Treasures
ISBN 978-0-9564835-8-4
Published by Mercia Books
Find out more at:
www.richarddenning.co.uk

Follow the series via Facebook:
www.facebook.com/TomorrowsGuardian